𝒯HE RELUCTANT BRIDE

"I SHALL NEVER MARRY," Avalon said in a perfectly normal voice, as if she were saying a wheel was round.

"That might be difficult," Marcus said. "Since I have over a thousand people and a family prophecy that say you will."

"I don't see how you're going to do it, my lord." Her look was amused. "You cannot force a bride if she does not wish it."

He leaned over on his hands and came up close to her face in one quick movement. Her eyes widened; she pulled back.

"I think you wish it," he said.

A hot blush was stealing up her cheeks. "I do not!"

"I think so." He let his gaze linger on her lips, deep pink, erotic curves. "I know what you feel, Avalon. I know what happened to you today, when you kissed me back. I know"—he came even closer, not touching her—"what you want. Because I want it too."

Her breath was quickening, her eyes tinged to match her amethysts in the afternoon light. He bent down even lower, letting his lips hover over hers, so close they took in t

"It is inevitable.'

Bantam Books by Shana Abé

A ROSE IN WINTER

THE PROMISE OF RAIN

THE TRUELOVE BRIDE

THE
TRUELOVE
BRIDE

Shana Abé

BANTAM BOOKS

New York Toronto London Sydney Auckland

THE TRUELOVE BRIDE
A Bantam Book / June 1999

All rights reserved.
Copyright © 1999 by Shana Abé.
Cover art copyright © 1999 by John Ennis.

ISBN 0-553-58054-X
Published simultaneously in the United States and Canada

Bantam Books are published by Bantam Books, a division of Random House,
Inc. Its trademark, consisting of the words "Bantam Books" and the portrayal
of a rooster, is Registered in U.S. Patent and Trademark Office and in other
countries. Marca Registrada. Bantam Books, 1540 Broadway, New York,
New York 10036.

PRINTED IN THE UNITED STATES OF AMERICA
OPM   10   9   8   7   6   5   4   3   2   1

DEDICATION

For the lovely and talented Gwen, who very generously took me with her on her tour of Great Britain and Ireland, and who insisted that I have the window seat the whole time. It is thanks to her that this story was written. I love you, Mom.

Also my deepest gratitude to my father, Ted, who gave up his ticket so that I could go; to Adriann for the names; and to Darren for his devotion.

This book never would have been finished without the unending patience and help of Ruth Kagle and Stephanie Kip. A thousand thank-yous to you all.

Prologue

"MADNESS."

The courtier standing in the royal great room said the word with relish, drawing out the syllables. "It's from her mother's side, I heard. Some Scottish thing."

Lady Avalon d'Farouche brushed by the hushed conversation, which ceased altogether as she approached. She threw a languid smile at the trio of young men who bowed in return to her, not meeting her eyes. Deliberately she paused by them, pretending to flick a speck of something from her gown. The faces of all three grew heated as she stayed, looking to each other and then finally at her.

Again she granted them a slow smile, letting them see the coldness of it, the gathering ice in her eyes. She hardly ever did this—it would only serve to feed the rumors—but the temptation was impossible to resist.

Though the third man was unfamiliar, two of this trio had been stalking her since her debut at court a year and a half ago. They had publicly hounded her in spite of the well-known fact of her betrothal, had at first tried to woo her, and then, when she continued to politely rebuff them, they had lashed out against her, banding together to nurse the seed of gossip until it was in full flower. . . .

Avalon d'Farouche of Trayleigh was cold, she was inhuman. She thought herself better than everyone else. She was tainted with dark Scottish blood and barbaric rituals. Her heart was nothing but black shards of ice.

How little they knew her at all.

But the rumors had not needed very much prodding to blossom. They were hurtful and ridiculous, but people had listened, as people always did when scandal was the topic. And beneath it all lay the real root of her problem: Avalon did not fit in here at King Henry's court, and she knew it full well. So did everyone else.

Now she looked directly into the eyes of the man who had spoken, watching him redden even further under her scrutiny.

"Nicholas Latimer. How do you fare, good lord?"

"Very well, my lady," he replied. A small, thin line of sweat was beading up over his upper lip. Avalon let her gaze drift down to it, considering.

Fear. Nightmare, whispered a voice in her head, a thing only she could hear.

"How relieved I am to hear it." Her words were sweet and smooth, giving no hint of her objective. "I had heard such unhappy stories, my lord, about your rest."

"My rest?"

"Oh, yes. Some of the ladies are quite concerned." She took in the other two men, both of them staring at her avidly, then gave Latimer a gentle smile. "We have heard that you . . . dream, my lord."

Now Latimer blanched. "What?" he asked, a whisper.

Nightmare slave, suggested the sly voice.

"Do you not dream, my lord?"

"How did . . ."

He seemed unable to complete the sentence, over-come with the loss of blood from his face, the flicker of something unmentionable in his eyes.

Avalon examined the man who was almost trembling before her—*darkness, lips, taste, want, afraid*—and de-cided abruptly to take pity on him. "It is nothing, I am sure," she said now. "I wish you well, all of you."

They watched her walk away, a lone figure in the middle of a crowded room. An invisible barrier seemed to surround her.

"How could she *know?*" she heard Nicholas ask be-hind her.

"A witch," said his friend.

The third man spoke in hushed tones, almost reverent.

"She is the most beautiful woman I've ever seen."

Avalon nodded thoughtfully to those who greeted her, reflecting.

A witch.

Surely not. Surely not, though she knew that most people at this polished, useless court were secretly con-vinced otherwise. But it wouldn't take a witch to notice the constant circles under Nicholas Latimer's beady eyes. It wouldn't take a witch to catch the haunted look he wore, the rabid visions that danced in his pupils even while he was awake. He had nightmares, it was so plain. Anyone could see that. Not just a witch.

She was not a witch. In fact, she didn't even believe in them. Witches were a convenient evil thought up by fearful men to describe the unknown. Witches did not really exist. They were just poor, lonely women with no protectors, and certainly Avalon was not one of them.

Because witches were publicly killed. It happened all the time.

Avalon was not poor, not lonely, and she had the most reliable of protectors with her at all times: herself.

It was not the normal way of a noblewoman, and she felt her difference sharply here in the royal court of King Henry. When she first arrived in London, she had thought the separateness she sensed was because of her rather unusual history, which was very much on the tongues of the gossips.

Well, there was nothing she could do about that. Her history was what it was.

That the peculiarity in her—this difference—had been with her all her life, Avalon tried not to consider. It had taken the rude shock of her seventh year to understand that not everyone was like her. Not everyone could see the things she saw, could hear the things she heard. Not everyone could tap into the moods of animals, could be dragged into the groundswell of any strong emotion around them.

Only her. Only Avalon.

It wasn't all the time; there were long stretches of days, weeks, even a few glorious months when it seemed this *awareness* in her, this awful beast, would just go to sleep, and she was able to slip completely into the role of a normal girl. Avalon had treasured those times, yearned for them. But eventually it always woke up again, opened the ruthless eye in her that let her see all that she didn't want to see.

As soon as she realized this, she had worked hard to change it, both in body and mind. Over time she'd almost convinced herself that these incidents were mostly her imagination, fueled by the constant and relentless superstition that had saturated her childhood.

In her darkest moments, in her waking dreams, the voice took on a vaporous form in her mind, that of a fabulous monster, a legendary thing her nursemaid once told her about that had stuck in her memory. It coalesced into a hybrid of shapes: the head of a lion, the body of a goat, a serpent's tail.

A chimera. It breathed misty fire only through her, it had eyes and a voice that lived only in her. It was her terrible secret, and when the darkness would turn to daylight again, Avalon would banish the image with all her might.

Chimeras, like witches, were not real. These things that happened to her were curious, yes, even inexplicable at times. But they were *anything* but supernatural. To succumb to that would be to admit belief in all she disdained: the irrational folklore that had sustained Hanoch Kincardine and his kin in Scotland, their abiding faith in an arcane fairy tale of which they thought she was an intrinsic part.

Avalon was not just the manifestation of the Kincardines' bizarre family legend. She would not believe in that.

But for all her rationalization, nothing ever fully stopped the strange moments that took her, nothing ever totally succeeded in killing the chimera. And so, for most of her life, Avalon had simply acted as if it wasn't there.

Hanoch had laughed at her efforts.

"Ye belong to the curse," he had so often told her. "Don't think different, lass. Don't hide it. It's the only strength ye have."

But she had denied it, had fought him bitterly to prove that she had many strengths, that she was not weak or frail, that his jeers did not hurt her. She had fought him almost every day in large and small ways. She'd refused to submit to his clan's foolish fable, she'd refused to believe the nonsense they told her—that she would be the one, that she would break the curse that had been laid upon them.

Deep inside her, coiled around her heart, the chimera would echo Hanoch's laughter, mocking.

Now, at King Henry's crowded court party, the madrigalists began a slow song, strumming softly on their lutes as the tenor sang something about lost love. Avalon accepted a goblet of mead from a servant and sipped it pensively. To her left was a group of young women about her age, close and closed in a circle. They tossed her haughty looks.

Hatred, sighed the chimera, that whispering voice. *Envy.*

The walls of this royal room were covered in splendid colors, elaborate frescos of fantasy and fact mixed together: dragons and griffins soared above knights, kings, and saints. Avalon walked to an empty corner and made a pretense of studying one of the painted saints, crowned and robed, tied to a stake. Burning.

"Look at her. . . ."

The saint had a curiously blank expression, no reflection of the flames or the smoke at his feet.

"Look at her there, flirting with any man who will pass by. She shouldn't be allowed at court."

"She shouldn't be allowed in the kingdom!"

The yellow flames were pointed and sharp, unbending, thrusting forward like painful swords of light from the sticks of wood. A starburst of redemption for the saint, no doubt, who at least had never had to endure the agony of being the most notorious guest at a king's formal affair.

A glance over her shoulder showed her that the circle of young women was growing bolder; they said her name in tones that were not quite docile, and they seemed to shift as one, moving to see her more clearly.

"I heard she's mad, you know!"

"Hardly surprising, raised by animals—worse than animals, those Scots. . . ."

Avalon stared back at them for an endless moment, then glided off again in search of peace. Yet their stream of dislike followed her, directed straight at her, and for one disconcerting instant as she walked away the chimera blinked and let her see what that circle did: a young lady of no realm, tall and pale in a bliaut of pink lined with pearls; shining hair that glowed silver in the candlelight, bound by a coronet but no veil; strange eyes that had no focus. . . .

In a dusky mirror by the madrigalists a quick look confirmed the view. True, the mirror burnished her hair to phantom gray, hid the odd color of her eyes with murky darkness. But certainly that was her own face in that sideways reflection, the unusual blending of colors and features that, Avalon was sure, had doomed her debut from the start.

"Can you believe she would shun a veil at a royal gathering? No doubt she thinks her hair her only glory, showing it off as she does. Perhaps that's how the heathens do it in Scotland!"

"So unfashionable to have such pale blonde hair. . . ."

Silvery blonde, like moonlight, Avalon's nursemaid used to say.

"And so coarse that the rest of her does not match even the peculiar hair, that her brows and lashes are as black as pitch. . . ."

A delightful contrast, insisted Ona, the nursemaid.

"I don't know why she thinks she's fetching at all. The style au courant is dark hair, of course. And look at her complexion! White as a ghost!"

Ona used to proclaim: Alabaster, a sign of superior breeding.

"And her eyes!"

"Indeed!"

"What color are they, my dears? No one can say!"

Not sky blue, not deep purple, but something caught between, a blend of mist and light before dawn. Violet, had claimed the devoted Ona.

Nothing normal and ordinary, like plain blue or green or brown, Avalon reflected wryly. Violet.

She kept walking, sipping the king's mead and wondering when she would be allowed to leave. Her feet were growing cold in the paper-thin slippers that went with her bliaut.

Her chaperone, Lady Maribel, was talking to three women and a man, laughing, and Avalon hated to spoil her moment. London was her glory, not Avalon's, and she liked Maribel enough to allow her to make the most of the hopefully short time they would be spending here.

It certainly wasn't Maribel's fault that Avalon had not taken to court life. Maribel had done all she could, schooled her at her own small estate at Gatting since Avalon was fourteen, taught her manners, history, French, Latin. She had ordered all of the most fashionable gowns for her, procured one of the most skilled handmaids to style her properly for every hour of the day.

Lady Maribel herself had labored almost an entire half year to rid Avalon's speech of the "ye."

It was a sorry thanks that Avalon had proven to be so unpopular in London, and for that Avalon felt remorse. Lady Maribel—an aunt so many marriages removed Avalon could not count them—had been kind if distant, and deserved to have her young charge set the town aglow, reigning in wit and beauty and popularity, a tribute to all the good woman's work.

But no one, not even Avalon, had expected the reaction she actually received.

Most men seemed afraid of her, the rest had attempted to seduce her. Women scorned her. It was all baffling to Avalon. The first few months here she had endured bewildered anger and hurt each night.

"They will come around," Lady Maribel had comforted her. "You'll see."

But they had not. Perhaps her difference truly was visible to all, despite her efforts. No matter how she tried to make friends at court, she had been rejected, over and over again, until she had learned to stop trying and began merely to wade through the sucking waves of gossip and spite.

She would always be a stranger here.

The madrigalists jumped into a new tune, something livelier, prompting many of the guests in the crowded hall to speak louder, laugh longer. The servants were having problems keeping goblets filled. Avalon waved away another cup of mead and tried to find a place to stand where she would not be trampled by the swirling mass of elegant nobles. In a corner she found a candelabra of black iron and white candles, soft beeswax melting in droplets. She ducked behind it and tried not to appear as though she was using it as a shield.

The girls across the room were not yet done with her. They nodded and swayed together, a sea of gilded gaiety.

"I heard her cousin didn't even want her! I heard he refused to allow her back to Trayleigh, he was so embarrassed at her manners. . . ."

"Oh, aye! And goodness knows they are already embarrassed enough that she managed to survive the raid on Trayleigh Castle and live seven years in Scotland while everyone here assumed she was dead. . . ."

"Shocking!"

"Well, I heard that even that Scottish brute she is betrothed to does not want her! That Marcus Kincardine will not come back from his crusade to wed her!"

"I heard she's gone mad from the raid! That she cannot even recall what happened that day, when those savages came and killed everyone! That all she knows are the common ways of the Kincardines who raised her—"

"No, no, I heard that she went mad from seeing the murders of her father and her serf maid by those Picts!"

"Aye, isn't it delicious? And I heard that Lady Maribel seeks to wed her off to someone here rather than to that Kincar-

dine! That she honestly thinks one of our good lords would have the harlot, when anyone could see she is a mockery of all that is respectable!"

"Aye. . . ."

"Aye, a mockery. . . ."

Avalon lowered her head and pretended not to hear. How many others caught the malice in the room? Only her, she hoped, please let it have been only the chimera listening in, and not that their voices were so loud her shame was to be shared by all.

Someone bumped into her, a woman who laughed shrilly and apologized as she moved off with her escort. A cloud of oversweet scent clung to the air from either the man or the lady, or both. It aggravated the beginnings of a headache wrapped around her temples.

The ring of young women were still staring at her, their gazes openly hostile. They had been joined by a few of the men in the room, who were bowing their heads to listen to the whispers. It was not her imagination that she was the topic, not when some of them dissolved into laughter as they looked over at her.

"Even that savage Kincardine won't have her. . . ."

That savage Kincardine, indeed. Avalon took another sip of the mead and smiled determinedly at no one in particular.

That damned betrothal had taken her life and twisted it to suit the needs of a few power-hungry men, kings and barons and lairds. As long as she had lived Avalon had been betrothed; it had haunted her and protected her and sealed her destiny as surely as only the stamp of fate could. So naturally she had to do all that she could to break it.

Avalon had told no one of her own plans for her future, nor would she. Like a magic secret, she half feared that even to say the words out loud would spoil the dream. She kept these thoughts to herself.

The room was rapidly growing hot, too many people now, some of them dancing, even singing as the wine and mead made tongues looser. Another couple came by too close, shoving her unexpectedly, making her nearly spill her drink. They did not apologize.

Enough. Avalon handed off her goblet to a serf, found the main door, and slipped past the guards to the antechamber, which retained the coolness of the night. It was much less crowded out here, most of the benches and chairs were empty.

She found a cushioned bench by a bower window, close enough to allow a curling breeze to wind around her face and hair, her shoulders, cooling off the anger until it was nothing more than her usual faint resignation. She looked around, seeing only shadows and dark corners, then leaned her head back against the wall, closing her eyes.

"How did you know?"

Nicholas Latimer loomed over her, then quickly sat beside her on the bench. He took her arms and held them tightly, his breath heavy on her startled face.

"Tell me how you knew about the dreams," he demanded.

Avalon looked around but this section of the room was deserted, offering no help. She backed as far away from him on the bench as she could, striking his hands off of her.

"It is obvious," she said bitingly. "Leave me alone."

He moved to hold her again, and she stood and whirled away. A couple across the room saw the abrupt movement; they stared over at her. Latimer leapt up to follow, then boldly blocked her way. She could not side-step him now without causing a scene. For Maribel's sake she stood where she was.

"You are a witch, aren't you?" he asked, his voice filled with derision and fear. "You are. You came here and you cast a spell on me, didn't you? You came with your hair and your eyes, you looked so fair. You tempt honest men with your face, you torture me, you make me feel these things, hot nights—"

"Don't be a fool," she snapped.

The couple was still watching, joined by two more.

"You would lie with the devil before you lie with me, wouldn't you? And you think you will! You think you will lie with Marcus Kincardine, that he's going to come back from that crusade of his and claim you. But he's been gone so long, hasn't he, witch? Why wait for a bar-barian Scot when you could lie with me?" Latimer stepped closer, too close, and there was danger in his look, a sense of crossing some line. "Lie with me," he said again slowly, hoarse and lost in himself.

Look, invited the chimera, a second danger, *see.* . . .

Against her will she was caught for a moment in La timer's mind. His intensity drew her in in that old fa-miliar way she dreaded; the feelings sweeping over her, the dizzying contact. The cursed chimera in her taking over, opening the gate—

Look. . . .

And what she felt from him was a deep longing, fear and more longing. Shame. She tried to block the shifting images that filled him, a woman dressed only in sheets, a man on top of her, doing things to her, and Avalon saw that the woman was herself, and he was the man . . . and these images became blended with something else, something darker, smoke and flesh and food, a bitter taste, he was ashamed of this, that it consumed him. . . .

Lips, darkness, taste-touch-want-witchfearlipsbedtaste—

Latimer came back from that dangerous place and she with him, light-headed. He reached for her, heedless of their audience, but before he could grab her again instinct and training took over.

Avalon whisked her hand up and captured his, centering her thumb on the back of his palm, turning his wrist over and bending it backward as she took a step forward. She pulled his hand down between them to the folds of her skirts, hidden now, and put her other hand on his elbow, locking it into place. It all happened in a fraction of a heartbeat.

She then gave him a dazzling smile, as if he had just told her some romantic nonsense that brought them close together.

Latimer's eyes grew wide with the unexpected pain. Avalon held him there, immobile, applying just enough pressure to let him know she could really hurt him if she wished.

Across the room she could hear the murmurs begin, her name spoken in rising whispers.

"Listen to me very carefully," she said, keeping her voice as low as possible. "It is not witchcraft that lets me see that your nights are sleepless. If I ever hear you say that word in connection with my name again, you may be sure you will be very sorry, my lord. It isn't witchcraft that holds your hand right now, it is simple flesh and blood. Are my words clear to you, my lord?"

He looked around, then back at her, gritting his teeth. "Yes," he said.

"Excellent. In exchange for your reason, I offer you a favor, Lord Latimer. I have heard, you see, that you enjoy eating the flesh of a most unusual mushroom, that you have fallen into the habit of it with a few of your friends. I may not be your friend, Nicholas, but neither are they. And I wish you no ill. But those mushrooms you crave are bringing your dreams. Let them go and the dreams will go, as well."

She released his hand. He yanked it back, rubbing his wrist.

"I truly wish you no ill," she said again.

He turned around and walked away from her, straight into the crowd of people who had gathered to watch them, everyone rapt with heated speculation. They broke apart and swarmed around him, eager to keep him in their center and soak up the beginnings of a new scandal.

Avalon knew with pure certainty that all hell was about to break loose.

Chapter One

TRAYLEIGH, ENGLAND SEPTEMBER 1159

*T*HE RIDING PARTY that approached the castle was notable for many things: the blazing heraldry of the d'Farouche family, splashes of red and green and white, bold and unmistakable; the number of men in the entourage, forty at least, soldiers with shining swords and proud steeds. They moved as one, an imaginary beast of glittering metal stretching across the landscape, weapons and armor and polished steel—the menace of war, proudly displayed.

But perhaps the most notable thing of all in this party, as they made their way across the gentle hills on the path to Trayleigh Castle, was the object they guarded.

Near the lead and yet surrounded by men rode one woman on a sorrel mare.

Lady Avalon had shunned not only the covered litter which was supposed to carry her, but also the hood of her cloak, which meant that the sun played on the brilliance of her hair, a mix of blonde so fair more than a few of the men had privately compared it to an angel's halo.

Those that had argued with her about riding in the litter, however, muttered that no angel would be so stubborn. And some had even heard the other rumors, the whispers traded behind hands, the dangerous word few dared say aloud—especially not when confronted with the uncommon stare of this particular lady.

"Look there, milady." The lead soldier turned in his saddle and pointed off into the distance, prompting the young woman to follow his direction.

Unfolding around the long corner of a low-slung hill was the sight of Trayleigh Castle, revealed in bits and pieces through the autumn trees surrounding it. Home of Bryce, Baron d'Farouche—her cousin and guardian.

Twelve years ago Lady Avalon d'Farouche had watched that very castle, her family seat, burn as she clung to the top of a birch tree she had climbed after an afternoon of playing alone in the forest.

From her view at the edge of the nearby woods she had seen most of the details of the raid, and contrary to what the Londoners said, she remembered every second of it.

Fat clouds of black smoke erupting from all over the castle.

People everywhere, running, crying, chaos. Some of the people unmoving on the ground, spilling rivers of blood.

Her nursemaid, Ona, running for the tree where she was perched, calling her name in a panic.

A group of men following the woman.

The men pursuing Ona were bloodied like everyone else, but oddly colored with paint and carrying weapons. They were coming to the birch, and there was a menacing intent in their steps. Even though Avalon had scrambled out of the tree to warn Ona of the danger behind her, it had been too late.

Also contrary to what the gossips said, Avalon had not seen her father die. Only her nursemaid, slaughtered beneath the birch beside her.

The painted men were insurgent Picts, men without homes or honor. But to seven-year-old Avalon, they were creatures straight from a nightmare: goblins, streaked blue and red with screaming eyes.

She would have died with Ona in that moment at the base of the birch, her throat slit just as ruthlessly. But Uncle Hanoch had come. Hanoch had been visiting her father, and Hanoch had fought his way to her past the arrows and the axes and the blood, and he had killed the goblins instead. He had saved his son's future bride and carried her away, away, to the coldest place in all the lands, Scotland.

Yes, the last time Avalon had seen Trayleigh she had been in the arms of Hanoch Kincardine, being dragged away from it while she shrieked at the top of her lungs, while she cried and kicked until they had stuffed a wad of cloth in her mouth that had tasted of smoke and death.

But today was fair and warm, a lifetime away from that moment. It was a day of rolling green hills and long meadows, with no sign of trouble anywhere. Lady Avalon d'Farouche, the young woman, now saw that Trayleigh Castle was much recovered from that terrible day twelve years ago.

Throughout her time away she retained not so much the memory of the splendid castle she was born in but rather the ravaged mess that she had glimpsed from the woods that day. In her mind, Trayleigh lingered in that distressing state, burning, bloodied, and brought to its knees.

The Picts had never been caught. They had plundered and raided and then melted away, back into the wilderness. The best that anyone had ever been able to explain to Avalon was that they were the holdouts of a remote northern clan, resisting the rule of any king, resisting civilized order. Whether it was bad luck or fate that made them pick Trayleigh to show their wrath, no one knew.

So when Avalon shifted in her saddle to take in the first glimpse of her old home, a corner of her still expected to see the same smoke she remembered eating up the skies.

But the castle that greeted her now was not burning. Nor was it quite what she recalled from happier times.

It was smaller, for one thing, not nearly as imposing to the eyes of an adult as it had been to a child. The straight, plain lines of it stretched up to the blue heavens but didn't seem to reach all the way to the angels, as she used to imagine. The lawns were better kept, the hedges more neatly trimmed. Or perhaps she had simply never noticed these things as a girl.

The old birch tree that had been her shelter during the raid was taller, the branches thicker. It had not, apparently, burned with the castle.

But the air smelled just as she remembered, and Avalon felt a burst of gladness at this, that something was familiar after all this time: the scent of honeysuckle and grass.

Her cousin's armsman saw her smile, pushed back his visor, and stared at her appreciatively.

"Right lovely," he said, and she nodded, still looking at the castle.

The watchmen had sighted them and the gate was rising.

Avalon tried to remember if her father had kept the gate closed all the time. She had no idea. Probably not.

Geoffrey d'Farouche, for all his fame as a knight to his king, had been an older man by the time she was born, and ill equipped to raise his toddler daughter after his young wife had died of a fever. Avalon had been handed off to her nurse and nearly forgotten, as far as she recalled. Her memories of her father summoned up merely his eyes, his beard, the timbre of his voice. She could not say if he was kind or harsh, pragmatic or sentimental. There were really just two things she would always remember him for: that he had arranged both her betrothal and the fateful timing that had brought Hanoch Kincardine down from Scotland right before the raid.

The procession took on a solemn air as the group filed through the giant portals and on inside to the cobblestone courtyard. They pulled up in the middle; a serf came over and helped her off her horse, then took the reins and led the steed away.

"Cousin!" came a hearty cry, and Avalon turned to face a large, richly dressed man around what would have been her father's age, coming toward her with open arms and a wide smile. She took a few steps forward but he was faster, pulling her into his embrace. The heavy onyx studs decorating his tunic dug into her skin.

She allowed this and then pulled back, straightening the train of her gown.

"Never say you rode all this way on your mount?" The man—her cousin Bryce, she assumed—gave her an incredulous look, opening his gray eyes wide, almost an act. He turned to the armsman.

"And you allowed this, Cadwell?"

"I'm afraid I insisted, my lord," Avalon broke in quickly. "I do so dislike being confined, you see."

"Ah." Bryce looked back to her, and though his smile was still there, slightly puzzled, Avalon had a glimpse of something behind it. Irritation.

"You must not be so formal with me, dear Avalon," he said, still sounding perfectly jovial. "You may call me Bryce, of course."

"How kind," she replied. "You may call me Avalon. But of course, you already do."

He paused and then laughed, taking it for a joke, which was probably for the best. She had no idea what had come over her. She didn't want to make an enemy of this man any sooner than she had to.

"Welcome home!" he said. "I do hope we did not inconvenience you too much by sending for you, cousin?"

"Not at all," Avalon replied, most sincerely.

"Your companion—what was her name?"

"Lady Maribel." She had only been Avalon's constant chaperone for the past five years. Too short a time, Avalon supposed, for her guardian to bother to remember her name, even though it was he himself who had instructed his ward live with her.

"Yes, of course. Lady Maribel was not too put out by having you leave her in London, I hope?"

"I do not believe she was at all bothered, my lord."

Lady Maribel had practically thrown together Avalon's trunks herself in an effort to help her flee the coming scandal. Maribel's reputation was much too sterling to consider besmirching, however remotely compassionate she had been to Avalon over the years.

"It was my dear wife who suggested you come to Trayleigh, but the haste was my idea!" Bryce laughed, spreading his big hands on his belly. "I am not a man of patience, I fear!"

"Your haste was not unwelcome," Avalon murmured.

The summons had come the very night of the party, delivered with some urgency by a man in her family's colors. She had not seen the d'Farouche heraldry in so long that it took more than a minute to recognize it, to approach the man, and accept the missive from her guardian.

She was wanted at Trayleigh. She was wanted at home, by order of Lord d'Farouche, etc., etc., and it had taken all her restraint not to dance around in joy in the middle of that crowded room. It didn't matter why he wanted her, not really. All that mattered was that she would escape London.

How ironic that her rescue came at the hands of this man who had taken over her father's title after the raid. The gilded young ladies had been correct in at least one thing: Five years ago Bryce had not wanted her. Had not even wanted to see her once she emerged from Scotland, the unexpected survivor of that long-ago raid on her family castle, even though he had never met her. It was a very public humiliation. At the uncomfortable age of fourteen, Avalon had been sent to Lady Maribel's estate in Gatting and—as far as Avalon knew—had been completely ignored by her family ever since.

But Bryce had finally sent for her. At long, long last she was home.

And now, as she watched this cousin, this stranger who thought to control her fate, Avalon was struck for the first time with a tiny prick of unease. She could not say what it was that caused it—the width of his hands, the florid stain of color on his cheeks. Something was not quite right. . . .

It was perfectly natural to invite her home, she had told herself. After all, she was still family, her father had been Lord d'Farouche before him. Perhaps her guardian had finally decided it was time to acknowledge her, that she had spent enough time in Gatting and London with Maribel.

Bryce laughed again. "Come and meet my wife. She has been so eager for the day of your arrival! I daresay she has spoken of nothing but your coming for almost this past sennight!"

Waiting in the shadows of the doorway leading to the great hall stood an auburn-haired woman in a gown of scarlet, surrounded by a line of other women, most likely servants. Bryce took Avalon to this group with her arm firmly held in his, almost causing her to trip over her skirts to keep up with him.

He pulled her up beside him and presented her to his wife as if she were a prized trophy.

"Look who is here, Claudia. Our fair cousin Avalon."

The woman named Claudia stayed in the shadows. She leaned her head back, as if trying to focus on something too close, and then looked away over Avalon's shoulder.

"Welcome to Trayleigh Castle." Her voice was husky and blurred. "Or welcome back, rather."

"Thank you," Avalon replied, almost at a loss, fighting

the crush of disappointment at the woman's words. No one could possibly call Claudia eager, and perhaps to cover for her lack of enthusiasm Bryce became even louder.

"You must be fatigued, dear cousin. Come inside. Rest. How happy you must be to be home again."

Avalon walked with him past the long line of women, all of them but Claudia watching her closely.

The great hall had also changed from her girlhood view, seeming smaller again, with different tapestries hanging, different tables. Even the light seemed changed, sharper and harder. There was a strangeness in the air, a sense of *wrongness* that Avalon could not define. The tiny prick of unease she felt before grew stronger, harder to ignore.

She felt the chimera in her roll over in its sleep, disturbed.

Bryce waved his hand and a servant appeared, a woman little older than Avalon.

"You will be taken to your chambers, where you will rest until tonight. We look forward to your company then."

Avalon looked up at her cousin—fair-haired and imposing in his stone-studded tunic—and noted the understated command in his words. The *wrongness* around them uncurled further—long, grasping tendrils.

"Good day to you, cousin Bryce," she said, curtsying.

His smile was brilliant.

"Good day, Avalon."

The rooms they assigned her were not the same as those she had had as a girl. It seemed to her these rooms used to be the quarters of some noblewoman, a gentle lady who had always had a kind word for her, who was it? Ah, Lady Luedella. Avalon wondered what had happened to her, then blocked the thought from her mind. If the Picts had found her, Avalon didn't want to know.

The rooms were fine. The pallet was clean and covered with ample furs. The rushes on the floor were fresh and fragrant; there was a small fire going in the fireplace. She even had a rug, a fanciful Persian thing that had so many intertwining lines and flowers in it that it gave her a headache to look at it.

Everything was perfectly satisfactory—even better than that, practically luxurious, a clear reflection of the wealth of the estate. So why was Avalon unable to rid herself of the feeling of entrapment?

She wandered over to the window and peered out, searching for that old birch. The farthest-reaching branches were in her sights, but that was all. The birch faced the other side of the castle, really. She was glad that there was green on what little of the tree she could see.

No one ever talked of the raid to her. Not Hanoch, not Maribel, not even the servants. It was as if everyone wanted it wiped clean from the very memory of God. Was there anyone left from that time, back when Avalon had thought her life whole and happy? Perhaps. Perhaps there was someone. . . .

A maid entered, small and deferential. She bobbed a curtsy, then opened the door wide for the series of men who came in carrying Avalon's trunks. There were a lot of them.

Avalon and the maid watched the men enter, set the trunks down against a wall, then go back out only to return with more.

"Tell me," Avalon began, and provoked a startled jump from the girl. She smothered her smile. "I beg your pardon."

Embarrassed, the maid blushed, not meeting her eyes.

"Could you perchance tell me what became of the woman who used to have these rooms?"

The maid looked tortured, as if the simple question was beyond her, then shook her head down at the floor.

"Well, then. Could you tell me of someone who would know?"

At this the girl looked up into Avalon's eyes, almost fearful, then glanced over at the men still coming and going. Avalon followed the look and saw something she doubted the maid did: the *wrongness* creeping into the room through the open door, its sliding tendrils winding around the ankles of the girl. Avalon blinked a few times and the vision was gone.

The maid had not moved, and Avalon addressed her again.

"Perhaps you could simply tell me your name?"

"Elfrieda, milady," the girl whispered.

"Elfrieda." A man entered with the last trunk on his shoulders, heaved it next to the others, and bowed as he left. Avalon considered the maid. "How old are you?"

"Fourteen, milady."

"Fourteen! So old! You look as if you could be my daughter."

Elfrieda looked up, swallowed the silly lie with a

lighter heart. "Indeed not, milady! You look younger than my sister, milady, and she being older than you!"

Avalon gave a little laugh. "Do you think so? Then I feel better." She walked over to one of the trunks and perched on its lid.

"Elfrieda, tell me, is there no one you can think of who would know of the Lady Luedella? She is the one who had these rooms when I was a child. I would be grateful for any help."

Avalon couldn't say why she was suddenly so determined to discover the fate of the woman. It just seemed important, immensely so.

She reached into the folds of her skirt and withdrew the small jeweled pouch she carried on a chain on her belt. Loosening the drawstring, she shook two golden coins onto her palm.

Elfrieda watched, disbelieving, as Avalon held them out to her.

"Any help at all," she said quietly.

The maid inched forward, threw an agonized glance at Avalon's face and then back to the coins. Avalon grasped a fragment of her thoughts.

Food, enough for weeks! New seed for the crops. Mayhap even a cow for Mama, milk for the baby. . . .

"Take it," said Avalon flatly. She stood up and slapped the coins into the girl's hand then turned away, disgusted with herself. What had come over her, toying with a child like that?

Elfrieda was leaving, bobbing more curtsies at the door, mumbling something incoherent and thankful before she was gone.

Avalon went back to the window and stared, unseeing, at the view.

⌒ᴄᴍᴍᴏ

$\mathcal{C}$OUSIN BRYCE WAS laughing loud and long at something Avalon had said which was not particularly humorous.

Avalon found that the evening meal was punctuated with such laughter from him, accompanied by exclamations of her wit and charm. It was both unnerving and tiresome. Perhaps he actually thought her completely lacking in wit, Avalon considered, to think he was fooling her—that she would believe his show was natural, that he really cared enough about what she thought of his presentation of the leek pie to bring it up three times.

But she smiled cordially and nodded and made the appropriate comments to her host as they ate at his table on the dais in the hall that used to be her father's.

Soldiers and nobles alike sat alongside each other in the large room, dining almost in silence as her cousin plowed on with his anecdotes and solicitations of her opinion. He offered her the choicest portions of each serving, fawned over her as she tried to eat, admired her manners repeatedly, and constantly refilled her goblet until it remained brimming with wine, untouched.

It was almost as if he were courting her, Avalon thought, disbelieving, but then shook her head at the idea. No matter how overly friendly he might be, Bryce d'Farouche was still her cousin, albeit once or twice removed. And he was already quite married.

Lady Claudia ate almost nothing, Avalon noted. She merely sat back in her chair and sipped her wine, watching her husband, watching Avalon. She had not joined in at Avalon's tentative attempt to include her in the conversation, but had instead stared at her, silent, letting Avalon's polite observation of some insignificant fact drift off, unanswered. Then she turned her head away and took another drink from her goblet. Bryce had talked over the moment, distracting Avalon by offering her another serving of venison. Avalon had declined.

She had never had such a strange meal, not even in Scotland, where the men remained boisterous while they ate, nor at Gatting, where all attempts to show her the world of the well bred had included dinner conversations not monopolized by one person.

Her father's hall had always been loud and cheerful, or so it had seemed to the little girl who watched enviously from the top of the main stairs, still too young to join them.

This was a different time and place, obviously. This was not the home she remembered. There was a tension here, no doubt about it, the *wrongness* around them all fed by the nervous looks of the nobles, the grim chewing of the soldiers.

Lady Claudia, watchful and filled with wine, now sat with a slightly curling smile on her lips.

Avalon had to stop herself from leaping to her feet when the last course was finished.

"I thank you for your hospitality, cousin," she said, pushing back her chair in what she hoped was a slow enough fashion.

Bryce stood up much more quickly. "What? Are you thinking of retiring so soon, dear Avalon?"

The hall fell silent.

She paused, still sitting, then replied, "Why, yes, I am. It has been a very long day."

Bryce maneuvered himself until he was standing behind Claudia's chair as Avalon watched from hers, wary. He placed one meaty hand on his wife's shoulder.

"But the hour is yet early, Avalon! Do not say you will leave us so soon. Why, Claudia has been telling me how much she looked forward to hearing you play for us after the meal, is it not so, my wife?"

Lady Claudia's teeth were stained with red wine, making her mouth ruby bright. She licked her lips and gave a lazy smile. "It is so."

Avalon stood up and spoke firmly.

"Indeed, I am sorry to disappoint you both, but I'm afraid I have no talent for music. I cannot play."

Bryce put his other hand on Claudia's shoulder. "Of course you can't. How clumsy of me to suggest such a thing. Growing up as you did, there would be no opportunity for you—"

"They have music in Scotland, my lord," she interrupted, more amused than irritated. "All I am saying is that I have no skill for it."

"Then Claudia will play for you, won't you, my dear?"

Claudia bowed her head, seemed about to burst into laughter. "Of course I will," she gasped, after a moment.

There seemed to be nothing to do but to follow Claudia, who walked over to the fireplace, holding on to her peculiar smile.

She played the psaltery, and fairly well, Avalon judged. She would have thought that the wine would make nimble fingers ungainly on the strings, but Claudia kept the pace of her song steady, tapping her foot against the floor as she sang a lively tune in her husky voice.

The women were clustered around the fireplace, the remains of the meal had been cleared by the serfs, the men were off doing Avalon had no idea what. Even Bryce, after making certain that his cousin was firmly entrenched by the fire, had left the group, entreating his wife in his loud and happy voice to keep playing.

And play Claudia did. After Bryce left she switched songs, moving now to a French ballad, slower, more melancholy. The mood seemed to permeate the group of women. Claudia stopped only to take swallows of wine between songs.

Avalon rested her cheek on her hand, staring into the fire, wishing she could be in the solitude of her rooms right now instead of here listening to this sad plinking of notes and tragic themes. The flames were beginning to slowly die, settling down to embers, molten centers, scraps of smoke.

Claudia finished another piece and Avalon quickly stood, intending to take her leave.

"You play delightfully," she said, edging away from the group. "How sorry I am I must retire now. I simply cannot keep my eyes open anymore."

Claudia, to her surprise, made no attempt to stop her, only strummed a few strings as she watched Avalon back away. The dying flames were clearly reflected in her eyes.

"Thank you so much," Avalon said, impatient to

leave but still seeking a thread of normalcy in the moment. "Good eve to you."

"Cousin," came a voice behind her.

Avalon turned around to see Bryce, returned from the darkness, standing quiet for once in the doorway. She wondered how long he had been there.

There was a man beside him, further back in the shadows. Both of them began to walk into the room.

Claudia continued to pluck at the strings of the psaltery, pursing her lips and looking down.

"Lady Avalon, I present to you your cousin Warner, my brother. Please do forgive his appearance, he has only just this moment arrived from the Continent."

Warner came forward and took her hand, bowing over it. He was large and fair, like Bryce, with gray eyes and sandy hair, at least two decades older than Avalon. There was a fine layer of dust over all of him, marking the creases around his eyes and mouth in pale spider lines.

"Cousin," he murmured against the back of her hand.

The chill came immediately, snaking up her arm, and she thought: *Of course, of course, Bryce wasn't courting me, good heavens, he doesn't want me for himself—*

He wanted her for this man. For his brother.

The air left her lungs at her discovery, her fingers grew cold even as Warner squeezed them. Bryce was watching her closely, monitoring her reaction.

For an instant she had to admire his audacity. He actually planned to break the betrothal. He would brave the wrath of two kings and the Clan Kincardine to keep her in the family, and that wrath would not be inconsiderable.

And thus he would also keep all her lands and her wealth. Which were also not inconsiderable.

She stifled the laugh that rose in her throat, made herself take back her hand from Warner and nod to him coolly.

"A pleasure," he said, inspecting her face, moving boldly down to her shoulders, her breasts.

Avalon took a step away. "I regret I cannot tarry further, my lords. I have traveled far today. Though not as far as you, I am sure, cousin Warner." She gave the smallest smile to Warner, watched his gaze linger on her lips.

Claudia at last hit a sour note on her instrument.

"I find I am fatigued as well," she said, rising and handing the psaltery to one of her attendants. "I will escort Lady Avalon to her chambers, my lord."

Bryce examined his wife, then looked at Avalon, who strived to appear impatient.

"Good eve, then, my dears," he said to them both, and bowed.

"I look forward to seeing you in the morn," said Warner to Avalon, and she nodded again, taking Claudia's arm and ignoring his stare on her back as they left.

Avalon remembered the way to Luedella's chambers but walked back in silence with Claudia, matching her slow, measured pace, perhaps a result of all the wine.

Marry Warner! Again Avalon smothered an amazed laugh at the thought, then threw a glance at Claudia, who kept moving forward in her haze, unperturbed.

Obviously the notion was completely mad, but Bryce's plans threw her own into disarray, and the damage could be anything from inconvenient to disastrous, depending upon how soon he thought to push her into the engagement.

"Tomorrow night we are having a celebration," said Lady Claudia evenly to the walls as they walked.

"Oh?"

Perhaps Claudia had her own chimera; she seemed to know what Avalon was thinking. Her face was serene as she met Avalon's gaze. "Can you guess why, my lady?"

Disaster.

"I believe so."

"I thought as much."

Claudia let that hang in the air for a moment until they passed a sentry guarding a doorway, then she continued.

"Men do strange things, do they not?"

"Aye," Avalon agreed, wholeheartedly.

"Take any man. Take my husband, for instance. Your own cousin. He may have a castle of his own. He may have lands reaching out forever. He may have power, serfs, knights. He may have all this, but will it quench his thirst for more?"

Avalon didn't reply.

"A man is an unfathomable thing," Claudia said, thoughtful. "We women cannot comprehend the desires he keeps in his head and in his heart. Perhaps it is better this way. Perhaps it is better not to know why a man would do something rash, for example. Something certain to bring trouble onto his house."

They had reached Luedella's door. Claudia released her arm. "Perhaps it is better not to understand why a man would turn his life into a dare against two kingdoms and a mighty group of families, just to gain more of what he already holds."

The torchlight softened Claudia's features, was captured by the darkness of her eyes and sunk down into them, absorbed.

"Perhaps," Avalon said.

"I have heard that your fiancé has returned from his crusade, Lady Avalon. I have heard that Marcus Kincardine has come home again."

Avalon took in this new shock, tried not to let it show on her face, but Claudia gave a bitter smile.

"It's true. I have heard that even now he rides to claim his bride. Which is why, I think, Warner has hurried over from France so quickly, and why my husband has brought you here so suddenly. I believe now you have a very clear idea what will happen at the celebration tomorrow night. Warner will not have the luxury of asking you nicely to wed. He is a man after my husband's mind, I think. Not opposed to—" she seemed to consider her thoughts, raising a finger to her lips, "—to force, I would think."

There were no words on Avalon's tongue, surprise had taken them away and left her with a pounding heart and the whining tinge of panic in her mind.

"Are you aware of what the Kincardine has been doing in his absence, cousin Avalon? Are you aware of what they call him, your betrothed, this man my husband thinks to cross?"

Avalon, mute, shook her head.

"He is called Slayer of the Unholy," Claudia said, the words falling flat around them. "A slayer. He has been off these years killing and killing and killing. What a small thing it would be, I suppose, to kill the family who would dare to steal his bride."

Claudia turned aside, appearing overcome with her own statement, but soon looked back again and studied Avalon. Her face was impartial once more in the shifting shadows.

"You are most fair, cousin. Indeed, you are as fair as I had imagined you would be. You have the look of your mother's family. Marcus Kincardine will appreciate that. Good night. Dream well."

And she faded off down the hall, walking her slow, measured step.

Avalon ducked into her room, walking blindly over to the pallet. She had to think. No—She had to act.

Her plans were disintegrating in front of her. She still had her money, the gold that she had carefully sewn into the lining of her capes, the jewels which were small and hidden away easily. At least there was that!

But for the rest of it . . . tomorrow was too soon. How could she locate a suitable nunnery in the course of a day? Where would she go?

Avalon had long considered the notion of how best to escape from her life. Her childhood in Scotland had convinced her soundly that she never wanted to go back there. Hanoch had seen to that, ironically enough. And yet he was so determined to wed her to his son, his only child. That determination had seemed more like an obsession to Avalon, even as a girl. After the Picts came he had kept her closely guarded and cloistered in a remote Highland village. It had taken the combined proclamations of the kings of England and Scotland to return her to her legal guardian's custody, and even then, only on the sworn promise she would come back to the clan as the bride of Marcus.

Avalon had never met Hanoch's son. He had already been a squire to a zealot knight by the time she was seven years old, and he had remained away in the Holy Land during her entire stay in Scotland. That suited her well.

She didn't care about him or any bridal contract made in her name. In her mind Marcus was just another version of his father, fierce and redheaded and cruel, and there was no force on earth that was going to convince her to marry him. He could go to hell with the betrothal *and* Warner, for all she cared.

She needed a convent, a powerful one; one strong enough to resist the outrage that would result on all sides from her defection. The closer to Rome the better, Avalon imagined, but she knew she would not get so far as that. She had heard of an order in Luxembourg that seemed ideal, and as second choice she thought perhaps France, at least something out of England. But now, dear God, she could not even hope to get there. Not in one day.

She should never have come to Trayleigh. She should have left for that convent months ago. But Gatting had been so comfortable, Lady Maribel so gentle. And in all honesty, convent life had never seemed ideal to Avalon—even though it always remained the best solution she could conjure up from her dismal choices.

But forever lingering in the back of her mind had been the thought of Trayleigh, her old home, how wonderful it would be to see it again, to be invited back.

Over time, it had taken on the image of a haven to her. This last opportunity to come here before locking herself away with nuns for the rest of her life had been a lure too sweet to resist.

A terrible weakness in her legs made her sink down on the pallet, sitting, almost winded, fighting the sense of disbelief that all her dreams were about to be destroyed at the whim of yet another man.

For years she had drifted along in the strange currents of her life, privately planning, yearning for a measure of control over all the forces that had been vying to bend her—yet never quite managing to grasp that control herself.

Years she had wasted, as it turned out, on a false hope: the hope of finding a home again at Trayleigh. And now she would pay for that wasted time.

There was a faint scratching at the door, so small she almost didn't hear it. It persisted, quiet and mouse-like.

Avalon took a deep, shuddering breath, then crossed to the door and opened it.

It was Elfrieda, hooded and timid, peering up at her.

Avalon stepped back and the girl darted in, still cloaked, then curtsied.

"Milady, I thought you should know. The lady you asked about, I have news of her."

It took Avalon a long moment to understand her, that she was responding to a conversation that seemed like years ago, instead of only hours.

"I see," she said. Even in her agitation over Warner and Marcus, the mention of Luedella brought back that peculiar sense of import, that overwhelming feeling that there was more here she needed to discover.

Find her, whispered the chimera, opening its terrible eye, suddenly awake and strong in her head.

Avalon recoiled mentally. Of course she wouldn't find her. Merciful heavens, she had no time to go chasing cobwebs of memories now!

Find her, persisted the chimera.

No, no, I don't have time for this, Avalon argued back silently, desperate.

Find her.

Warner! Bryce! Tomorrow was but a few hours away!

Find her.

She surrendered to it with a combination of anger and despair, knowing that she would be unable to ignore the incessant feeling. It would consume her, blocking everything else, pounding louder and louder in her head, her body, even if it meant her doom, even if it meant falling helplessly into Bryce's trap tomorrow.

It made no sense! But then, her chimera had never bothered with anything sane like sense before. It infuriated her.

Find her.

"Where is she?" Avalon asked, hating herself.

Elfrieda twisted her hands together. "That lady is dead, milady."

Ha! Avalon wanted to jeer at the voice in her head. *So there!* Lady Luedella was dead. She felt a spiteful gladness at the news, followed by a spurt of shame.

Poor Luedella was dead. She had been so old even when Avalon was a child, there was no reason to think that she might have—

Elfrieda, who had been watching her intently, interrupted her thoughts.

"But you may speak to Missus Herndon, if you wish."

"Mistress Herndon? Who is that?"

"The one who took care of the lady, after they made her leave. I mean"—Elfrieda gave a frightened glance around the room—"after she left."

The sensation of her own doom grew stronger, tightening in her stomach.

Find her.

"Where is she?" Avalon asked again.

"In the village, milady," answered the girl. "She's the grandmother of the innkeeper in the village."

Chapter Two

———— ᗒᗊᗕ ————

*T*RAYLEIGH'S GUARDS nodded to the two maids as they passed through the main gate along with a group of other serfs, all of them heading down the road to the village for the night.

Elfrieda, cloakless, shivered in the night air, though Avalon suspected it might be more from fear than cold.

The young woman had bravely offered to take Avalon down to find Mistress Herndon, and that was before Avalon had given her three more gold coins. It seemed she had earned a sort of dogged loyalty from Elfrieda with her initial offering, an experience so out of the ordinary for Avalon that she didn't quite know what to make of it.

The girl's cloak was mud brown and coarsely spun. It chafed the bare skin of her cheeks and hands, but still Avalon kept the hood low over her face, her head down and her walk meek, like the other serfs.

Just beneath the cloak was her own clothing, the plainest she could find but, nevertheless, obviously a noblewoman's finery. A dark blue veil covered the telling brightness of her hair from her brow to her shoulders, secured with a simple band of linen around her crown. It was a belt, actually, and Avalon fully credited

Elfrieda for thinking of making it into a circlet, since all of Avalon's coronets were made of gold or silver or both.

They both had high hopes that from a distance Avalon looked just like the other women walking home.

The guards went back to ignoring them after they'd passed, complaining to each other about the sudden influx of gentried guests to the castle.

"Won't sleep in the stables, I heard," said one, spitting on the ground. "Too good for that, these lords. Want the great hall for themselves."

"Aye, we're to the stables," said the other guard morosely.

Elfrieda tripped in the dirt path, righting herself by clutching at Avalon's shoulder. The cloak jerked perilously to the left, exposing the veil and part of her face. Avalon reached up and immediately pulled it back down, not daring to look over at the guards or the other people.

The girl gave her a distressed look.

"I'm sorry, milady, sorry, I—"

Avalon threw her a warning glance and Elfrieda quieted at once, though she continued to look upset. Avalon attempted a smile, then took the girl's hand in her own.

The guards had noticed nothing, were now talking aggrievedly about the pungent smell of horses and how remarkably similar it was to that of these unwelcome lords.

It was all bad news to Avalon. It seemed that Bryce wanted as many highborn witnesses as possible for whatever he had planned for tomorrow night.

Later today, she mentally corrected herself. It was well past midnight by now.

The village was close to Trayleigh Castle, a sizable cluster of huts made of sod and wood, even two taverns, plus the inn. The crowd of serfs began to split apart in the narrow streets, lost in the black doorways.

The inn had only four rooms to let. Avalon remembered it from her childhood; Ona would linger here whenever they were down in the village. It was a resting stop with sweet ale and meat pies.

All the rooms would be taken now, Avalon guessed, and then some. When they entered the main room it was bursting with people, mostly men, drinking, eating, and laughing loudly. Elfrieda seemed daunted by the unusual sight but kept her grip tight on Avalon's hand and began to weave through the crowd. Only the white lines around her lips betrayed the maid's emotions as she pulled Avalon past the long tables and benches of men.

They received not a few hoots and calls, and once a tall man with a red beard reached out and swatted Elfrieda on her bottom, prompting appreciative shouts all around. Nothing stopped the girl's course, however, and within moments they were at the narrow, twisting stairs leading to the rooms above.

Elfrieda led the way, both of them pausing and bowing their heads at a lord going down, pressing to the walls to let him by, then moving on again. The noise from below came up easily through the wooden floor; the air was rich with the smell of ale and sweat.

At last they came to the top, and then down to the end of the corridor to a stout door.

Elfrieda knocked twice and entered, still pulling Avalon behind her.

The room was only a dim, crowded space that had

been sectioned off with wood and thatch, probably bring-ing the four previous rooms to five, Avalon thought.

There was a man by the door, and Elfrieda turned to him, moved quickly into his embrace with a muffled sound that Avalon read as complete happiness. The man held her tight, brought his head down to hers and whis-pered something in her ear.

Avalon had to look away. Elfrieda had been nothing but brave and kind in bringing her here, and did not de-serve the spark of envy that bloomed in Avalon's heart at the sight of the lovers.

There was a wisp of a woman in a chair by the meager fire. She was old and fragile, draped in shawls with a ratted fur across her legs, peering up at Avalon now with expectant curiosity, her hands fluttering on her lap. Mis-tress Herndon, no doubt.

Avalon waited for the chimera to come alive again, to tell her what to do next, but it remained perversely silent, apparently having led her here only to go back to its slumber. She let out a sigh of frustration, then moved closer to the woman, pushing back the hood of the cloak without thought.

Mistress Herndon's eyes widened, milky white and brown, and then she gave Avalon a quivering smile.

"Why, 'tis Lady Gwynth," she said, surprised. "I had almost forgotten about you, and yet here you are. Lady Gwynth."

Avalon knelt at the foot of the chair, close to the old woman, and spoke gently.

"I am Lady Avalon, mistress. Gwynth was my mother's name."

"Avalon?" The gaze turned confused, the smile faded. "Avalon? But little Avalon is dead."

"No." Avalon placed one of her hands carefully on the woman's, feeling the slight trembles that would never stop.

"Aye," insisted the woman. "She died in the raid. And Gwynth is dead too, my sweet lady, both of them dead, and who are you, then, looking just like them?"

"Gram, this is Lady Avalon." The man released Elfrieda and came to stand by them both. He was young and not very handsome, but had earnest brown eyes and a temperate look. "Remember I told you, Gram, about Lady Avalon, that she would come to see you tonight."

"Did you, now?" Mistress Herndon leaned back in her chair, squinting at Avalon.

Elfrieda moved behind her lover. "Lady Avalon seeks to know something of your friend, missus. Remember Lady Luedella? Remember how she came to live with you? Lady Avalon would like to hear of it."

"Oh, Luedella." Mistress Herndon clicked her tongue in dismissal. "She's dead, as well."

"Aye, Gram," said the young man, helpless. He looked at Avalon and shrugged.

Avalon turned back to the woman. "Can you tell me what you remember of Luedella?" She felt her own aggravation at not knowing what she sought, struggling to put a half-formed idea into words. "Tell me why she left the castle, for instance?"

Mistress Herndon looked away, then down at her lap. "Oh, aye," she said, soft. "I remember how she left, my Luedella. And my lord, dear Geoffrey . . ."

The fire spat and sizzled; a surly coil of smoke wafted out into the room. The old woman spoke again.

"She lost everything, so many did. But they did not kill her. I don't know why. I don't think she knew, either. Yet she lived. He hated her, I think. He used to mock her to her face. He used to hit her. I saw it."

"Who?" asked Avalon.

"The lord. The baron. I don't know why. Mayhap she just reminded him of what he had done."

Avalon was astonished. "Do you mean Geoffrey used to hit her? My father?"

Mistress Herndon gave her a startled look, then scowled. "Of course not. The baron would never do such a thing."

"Then it was Bryce." As Avalon said it she found herself nodding, matching the agreement in the woman's expression.

"Aye, Bryce."

Elfrieda made a tiny sound, almost a whimper, and quickly walked over to the door. The man followed her, took her back into his arms.

"And—" Avalon stopped, then made herself say the words. "What was it he had done? What did Luedella remind him of?"

Mistress Herndon sucked in her cheeks, then lifted up her head and stared down at Avalon.

"Why, he bought the Picts, girl."

The floor was hard and cold beneath her. Avalon found herself braced with her hands behind her, fighting for the balance that had vanished in an instant. Then Elfrieda was there with an arm around her shoulders, slight but strong.

The room fell silent again, only the dim clamor of the barroom below them leaking up through the wood.

Avalon found her voice.

"Are you certain?"

"Aye." Mistress Herndon shifted in the chair. "And Luedella knew it, too. I suppose it came down to the fact that he could not kill her so openly after the raid. Others might have realized what he'd done. She was the grand-daughter of a baron. She was highborn, my lady was. So Bryce vanquished her. I was her maid," the woman said proudly. "And so she came here, with me."

There was no proof. Avalon understood this without bothering to ask; she had gleaned it already from the nervousness of Elfrieda, the grim face of her young man, both of them now helping her to her feet.

Bryce had bought the Picts. Bryce, who had every-thing to gain from the death of Geoffrey and his daughter, and who had not invited that daughter back to her home once it was discovered she still lived. After all, Avalon had inherited a great deal of Geoffrey's wealth; Bryce had the title and the castle, but Avalon got all three of the manored estates, direct endowments from her mother's side, plus a good portion of the wealth of Trayleigh.

Bryce had had to give it all back to her when she resurfaced from the dead, a fourteen-year-old heiress. And he had never complained about it at all.

Mistress Herndon was lost in her memories again and didn't look up as Avalon bent over and brushed her lips against one of the withered cheeks.

"Thank you for taking care of Luedella," she said, and saw the shining path of a tear that slipped down the old woman's face.

"She was a fine lady," Avalon heard her whisper.

Elfrieda opened the door, taking a cautious look out, then let Avalon precede her.

Avalon turned her back as the lovers said good night, pretended to study the blackened walls of the hallway as the two exchanged kisses and murmurs. At last they finished, the man going back into the room, Elfrieda beside her again, reaching up and pulling the hood close over Avalon's face.

Avalon couldn't help it; she stared down at the girl, her swollen lips.

Elfrieda caught the stare, looked away, and then back at Avalon.

"We're to be married this harvest," she said, defensive.

"I wish you all the best," replied Avalon gravely.

The noise was much louder than before as they approached the top of the stairs. Elfrieda took the lead again with determination.

The uproar grew and grew as they crept down the spiral, much too loud to Avalon's ears, almost deafening. It left her dizzy, it slammed into her head and wouldn't leave, making her put one hand on the wall to find what was up and what was down again. And still the noise flourished, rebounding inside of her, an insanity of sound that made her falter and start again, until she was lost and blind.

She wanted to call out to Elfrieda but couldn't focus enough to do so. How could she go on? How could she even make it down into that room itself, the source of her confusion? She must conquer this; it was a reflex of the chimera, alive and now gone mad with its own power, keeping her feet numb and her eyes from seeing where she stepped on the slippery stairs until she crashed into something.

Into some*one*.

The world came into focus again.

There was a man in front of her, between her and Elfrieda. Even though he was two steps below her his head was still above hers, darkened in the obscure light of the passageway. Elfrieda was attempting to turn back to her, under his arm, her face the picture of fear. The man noted the disturbance behind him almost casually, and then he faced Avalon again.

She belatedly dropped her chin almost to her chest, hunched her shoulders.

"I beg your pardon, milord," she said, changing her inflection to match how she thought Elfrieda would say it.

The man didn't move aside, but remained solidly in the middle of the stairs, blocking her path. Avalon waited, staring at the tremendous sword strapped to his waist, then took a small step to the right, as if to allow him to go on. Still, he didn't move.

Behind him Elfrieda was paralyzed, peering up at the two of them in agony.

Avalon shifted again, this time to the left. The man stopped her with his arm, then placed one finger under her chin to tilt her head up. The contact of his skin against hers seemed to sear her, almost causing her to jump.

She took in his face and had only the impression of strength, power, before looking away hastily.

"Who are you, child?"

His voice was deep and sure, the purity of his accent clearly marking him as one of Bryce's visiting nobility.

She bit her lip with the urge to yank her head away from his light touch. She felt so odd, like nothing she had ever experienced before. He seemed to set off a kind of nervous hum throughout her entire body, a sensation of heightened awareness. . . .

This was insanity, she had no idea why she was reacting so strangely to this man, but they could not be discovered here. If Bryce found out he would kill them all, he would have to, and desperation made her words that much more convincing.

"I am no one, milord."

"No one?" He flicked back her hood with dismaying ease. Avalon heard Elfrieda give a little cry.

The stranger ignored it, silent and musing. Avalon felt for the veil, praying it still covered her hair, and found it in place. She remembered to lower her face again.

Imprinted in her mind was all that she could see of him with the light behind him: black hair tied back, unsmiling lips, pale eyes that reminded her of frost.

"No one," he repeated softly, almost to himself, and she heard something new in his cultured voice, something wild and alarming. "I think not."

She tried to brush past him but he stalled her once more.

"What is your name?"

Astonishingly, amazingly, nothing came to mind. She blinked down at his chest, unable to say a single word.

"Rosalind!" squeaked Elfrieda. "We must leave! We will be late!"

The stranger again spared a glance for the girl behind him, then looked back at Avalon. She had abandoned the idea of looking down and met his gaze steadily. His winter eyes were narrowed; there was a tautness around his mouth, as if what he saw didn't please him.

"Rosalind." He seemed almost to taste the word, saying it with cool speculation.

She dipped a little curtsy on the stairs, wondering how to escape this man and this moment, the strangeness surrounding him, that heated sting still lingering on her chin where he had touched her.

"Please, milord," pleaded Elfrieda now. "Let my sister be. We must return to our father's house or be punished."

The man shook his head, just once. The light behind him reflected off the ebony of his hair.

"Rosalind." Even in the way he repeated it he implied disbelief, as if he could easily see through their thin plot. It unnerved her so much that at last she found the will to move, ducking quickly under his arm and hopping over two stairs to regain her footing. Elfrieda started moving again just as fast, both of them almost running down the remainder of the stairs.

He didn't follow. Something told Avalon he wouldn't. And as the two women made their way out of the inn and back into the night, Avalon thought about that delicate moment in time, when she had acted and he had not, though it would have been simple to block her escape and keep her there with him perhaps forever, there with his thick black hair and frost pale eyes, his muscular body almost engulfing her own.

But he had let her leave. Avalon tried to be glad about it.

*T*HE NIGHT HAD HELD no peace for her. When morning arrived Avalon shrank from it, burying her head under the blankets of the pallet, wanting to sleep on and on, slumber a shield between her and the looming problems of her life.

The sun was insistent, however, and eventually she sat up and faced the brightness surrounding her.

Directly across the room in front of her was the long row of her trunks, each filled with fine clothing—Maribel's delight—and Avalon couldn't help but feel a little sorry that she was going to have to abandon the handiwork of all those seamstresses.

Perhaps she could pay one of the servants to send the trunks back to Maribel in Gatting after everything died down. Perhaps Elfrieda or her lover would do it.

The door opened quietly, and Avalon watched the little maid appear and creep softly into the room, carrying a tray with bowls and a cup on it.

She tried to smile when she saw Avalon sitting up.

"A fine day," Elfrieda said, and then burst into tears.

Avalon crossed over to her, still standing in the middle of the room with the tray, tears rolling down her face. Taking the tray from her, Avalon led her over to the pallet, then went back and closed the door completely.

The tray held her breakfast, porridge and honey and bread. She sat down beside Elfrieda and settled it carefully on her lap, then tore off a chunk of bread, offering it to the girl. Elfrieda took it, still crying.

Avalon poured a dollop of honey on the porridge, touched the bread to it and took a bite. Very good. She realized she was famished and began to eat in earnest.

Elfrieda was nervous, that was all. She thought Avalon had no idea of Bryce's plan and didn't know how to tell her. Avalon let the girl's tears come to a stop, then took the cup of ale and made her take a sip.

"Milady," she hiccuped, "I must tell you something."

"I know it already," Avalon said, tearing off the bread. "Drink more."

Elfrieda did, rolling her eyes at Avalon over the rim.

"You are good and kind and brave," Avalon said around bites. "And there is something I have for you, to remember me by."

As soon as the porridge was gone she set the tray aside and went over to one of the trunks. Inside she found her best cloak, dark green wool lined with satin. It was extremely heavy.

"See if you can leave before the party tonight. When you do, wear this under your other cloak."

Elfrieda only gaped up at her, so Avalon laid the material across the maid's lap, letting it shift and slide over her legs until it covered her.

"I could *not*," the girl exclaimed, aghast.

"Yes, you could. You will. I shall be offended if you do not."

"Nay, milady—" She moved to stand up, and the cloak began to slither to the floor. Avalon pushed her back into place with one hand, then sat beside her again.

"Look," she said, and lifted up the weighted hem of it.

Elfrieda looked but did not see.

Impatient, Avalon took the girl's hand and placed it on the cloth itself, making her feel the hard, circular outlines of the coins sewn within.

"Sweet Jesu," Elfrieda breathed, staring up at Avalon.

"My wedding gift to you. Buy a cow," Avalon said. "Buy many of them. Buy your way out of this place."

❦

*H*ER PLANS HAD NOW boiled down to one perfectly simple essence: flight.

For years she had plotted, had charted her own path to her future, outwardly agreeing to all the edicts and proclamations about her that bustled back and forth from Scotland to England. She had acted as everyone thought she should. She had voiced no opinion whatsoever on her kidnapping, her betrothal, or her return to England.

Hanoch had not been completely fooled. Perhaps he had not been fooled even a little, and that was why he had held on to her so tightly, hiding her, shaping her, making her into the thing that he wanted for his family.

At first she used to cry, Avalon recalled. She would cry over the loss of Ona, Trayleigh, even her father. She would cry when she was told to be quiet, she would cry when she was confined to the tiny pantry they kept bad girls in.

The first time they struck her, however, the tears had stopped.

It had been instructional, of course. Hanoch's slaps always were. He was trying to teach her something in his own severe way. He was teaching her how to fight back.

She used to hate him. She used to envision horrible things happening to him, that the goblin men would return and hurt him as they did Ona, they would burn his cottage down to ashes. . . .

She no longer hated Hanoch. He was mean and savage but he had kept her alive, after all, even if he was a victim of his own ignorant beliefs. Hanoch was just another strand in the intricate web that made up her life, he and her father and Bryce and Marcus Kincardine, as well. Avalon was about to set all those strands on fire and watch them vanish in a puff of smoke.

It seemed only fitting. Bryce had ensured that her own years of planning were now nothing more than worthless memories. The least she could do was destroy his.

The celebration was at hand. Avalon had spent most of the afternoon in Luedella's room, avoiding her cousins and gathering up what she thought she would need for her final hour here. The small bits of jewelry had been easy to hide in the seams of her bliauts. She had three gowns with precious stones—some set, some loose—hidden away in the linings of their sleeves and hems, her mother's inheritance that Bryce had been unable to withhold from her once she was at Gatting. She had another cape with coins.

She would endure the celebration tonight. She would again smother her true emotions and follow the lead of Bryce and Warner. They would engage her to Warner, they would drink to it, all those fine nobles would see her agree. And by the morning she would be gone.

Most likely she would not get far, but it didn't seem to matter anymore. She would retain her integrity until they had to kill her. Perhaps she might even be granted a stroke of luck. All she needed was one convent, just one. She would hand over all the jewels and money and then fall into a religious ecstasy if need be, claiming divine inspiration to devote her life to God. Warner would be unable to marry a bride of the church.

And then someday, someday far ahead of her, she would leave that convent and come back to Trayleigh to avenge the deaths of her father and Ona and Luedella.

She dismissed Elfrieda when she arrived to dress her, forcing her to take the green cloak and telling her that she should leave the castle now. It seemed important that she not witness what Avalon was about to do, the bald lie she was about to enact.

"God be with you," she had told the girl, and Elfrieda had looked back at her, speechless, then gathered the cloak and left.

Avalon chose the finest bliaut she owned for tonight's charade, a splendid brocade and velvet thing, deep blues and greens and purples in shifting colors, a low bodice, amethysts ringing her shoulders and dripping down in looping swirls over the skirts.

Warner certainly appreciated it. As she came down the main stairs to the great hall he pushed through the gathered crowd to greet her at the bottom. He bowed only low enough to keep his eyes in the vicinity of her breasts, though she could not say if it was her bosom or the jewels that he admired most.

"Glorious," beamed Bryce, taking her hand. "Doesn't she look glorious, my dear?" he said to Claudia.

"Oh, yes," that lady agreed, once again offering her curling smile.

All the people in the hall were staring at her, examin-

ing the heiress, evaluating the gown, the gems, her smile.
Thank goodness London had prepared her for this.

Someone handed her a golden goblet of spiced wine
that smelled too sharply of cloves. Bryce had melted
away into the crowd, laughing loudly, keeping up an almost frantic pace as he moved from person to person, a
line of servants trailing him.

Warner seemed fixed to her shoulder. She could not
move without him moving with her. He introduced her
to the avid flocks of people; she felt the blazing curiosity
among them, the brazen looks, the buzz of speculation
that was getting more audible as the sun sank lower over
the horizon.

Lady Claudia made no effort to play hostess. She sat
in a corner with two other women and a flask of wine.
Every now and again Avalon could feel her eyes on her,
the barely suppressed simmer of anger and fear that filled
the woman.

Avalon took a sip of the pungent wine and tried not
to let pity for Claudia cloud her judgment. True, it
could not be easy being married to a murderer, but
she had suffered through that well enough. The anger
Avalon felt from her now came from that place in
Claudia that was furious with Avalon, actually, for appearing to comply with her husband's scheme.

Merciful heavens, what had she expected Avalon to
do? It was hard enough having to conceal the things she
had discovered already. Had Claudia really expected her
to stand up and deny the baron and his brother in front
of their cronies and peers? Hardly likely.

She would be imprisoned in Luedella's room, no
doubt, until she came around. Or worse, locked away

with Warner somewhere, allowing him to force her into the marriage in his own way. . . .

He had the effrontery now to keep his hand on her waist—lightly, true, but still there, a clear proclamation of his ownership.

Avalon gritted her teeth and endured it for as long as she could stand.

"You are the most beautiful woman here," he said once, bending down too close to her ear.

"How kind you are," she replied, and turned quickly to greet some approaching lord, knocking Warner's hand away.

He had it back in place in a second, taking over the conversation.

She couldn't help but look for the man from the inn, half-dreading his arrival for fear he would recognize her, but half-anticipating it . . . for no good reason at all. If she concentrated, she could almost feel again the strange awareness he had provoked in her, that unique, buzzing hum just beneath her skin that had come to life at his touch.

He might denounce her. He might accuse her in front of everyone of masquerading as a tavern wench. He was an incalculable danger to her.

But still Avalon looked for him, and still she felt a grain of disappointment that he did not appear in the seething crowd.

It seemed endless, the swirling rumors that chased themselves from mouth to mouth, the living storm of conversation, the knowing looks directed at her and Warner. The gossip rose and echoed off the stone walls and ceiling, coming back and bringing with it a throbbing pain in her temples.

Her goblet was empty, the spiced wine finally gone. It burned a hole in her stomach; the food was not yet served.

"More wine?" asked Warner, hovering.

She gave him a faint smile. "Only if you fetch it for me yourself, my lord."

His eyes widened, then grew hooded. She met his look without withdrawing her offer, but then pretended to be overcome with modesty, lowering her gaze. If only she had mastered the art of blushing on demand.

"It would be my honor," he said at last, and kissed her hand before leaving to search out a serf.

It would not take him long. As soon as his back was to her she took the few short steps necessary to reach the side doorway that led out into a hall. She walked through it without looking around, maintaining an air of purpose.

No one stopped her, though she was sure many had seen her go. It didn't matter. She would return soon, but she had to take in some air, had to get out of that stifling room. She had to feel a breeze on her face for just a moment, and she knew the perfect spot to do it in.

Her father had kept a garden, of all things, inside the bailey, a small plot of trees and plants and whimsy. Her mother had started it, Ona had told her, and it had been one of Avalon's favorite places, a garden of surprises, pure luxury.

". . . has arrived. He is in the chapel now, my lord, awaiting your pleasure."

Avalon stopped at the muffled words coming past a closed door she had just walked by, and glanced around her. The hall was deserted.

"Good, good." Unmistakably Bryce, not even bothering to lower his voice. "Tell him we will be there within the hour. Make certain he is ready."

There was a moment of silence; Avalon imagined the serf bowing before leaving and looked around frantically for a place to hide. But then Bryce's voice came again, the tone of having forgotten some trifling thing.

"Oh, and tell the priest the bride may be somewhat . . . unwilling. Tell him to expect it."

"We have already done so, my lord."

"Fine. For what I'm paying him, he can overlook a maidenly scene or two."

"Yes, my lord."

Avalon fled down the hall, mindful now only of getting away from the door. Her skirts were heavy in her hands, the amethysts winked in sparkling bursts from the torchlight as she ran.

Idiot! she cursed herself, turning corners, following a path she only partly remembered. Bryce was much more desperate than she had thought, and just as ruthless as she had feared.

He would wed her off tonight—tonight! In front of all these people, he would drag her willy-nilly to the altar and force her hand and ruin what was left of her life for his own private profit.

Wed her off to Warner, large and menacing, his thick lips wet against her skin, sending shudders through her whole being.

The garden was still there, slightly overgrown, all the trees larger, the bushes reaching out into the path now. Avalon slowed down to a walk as she entered it, letting the twilight envelop and surround her with its tricky light. She pressed her hands up to the sides of her head and wondered desperately what to do.

She could go to her rooms, pleading a headache, which was very real. She could gather her things and sneak down to the stables, steal her own horse, ride away—

She could pretend to fall ill suddenly, faint and not rouse out of it until the priest grew tired of waiting—

She could stand up as Claudia wanted her to do, refuse to wed Warner, publicly accuse Bryce of plotting her father's death—

Madness, all of it. Avalon gave a despairing laugh to a bayberry bush. Perhaps Nicholas Latimer had been right all along. Perhaps she really was insane.

Up ahead came a rustling sound, limbs shaking and falling still, so insignificant she might have imagined it.

Her steps slowed on the white stone path, then stopped. In one of the old trees a lark began and finished a song, short and trilling.

The sky was drenched in purple and blue, matching her gown, fading quickly to the inky blackness of the night.

The lark sang again.

A curious sense of calm fell over Avalon. She moved forward into the garden. There used to be a marble bench somewhere here. There used to be a succulent vine of honeysuckle draping over it, creating a cave of leaves and flowers. She would like to see that again, the emerald leaves and yellow-throated flowers. She would like to smell the dewy perfume until it took away her troubles, let her understand clearly what she must do.

The rustling came once more as she neared the end of

the little path, and this time it was directly to her left, behind the smooth leaves of a winter cherry tree.

Or rather, not really behind the leaves. Next to them, actually, where the stranger she had met last night at the inn now crouched.

She stared down at him, unsurprised, as if it were completely natural to find a man hiding in a garden at dusk.

He looked different in the lingering eventide light. His hair was loose and fell to his shoulders; the fine tunic he wore last night had transformed into a plainer one, covered with a tartan of black and gold and red and purple.

That tartan. She knew it well, had worn it herself for seven years of her life.

The man's eyes met her own. They were both frozen, caught up in the odd instant of one monumental second turning over to the next, where nothing would ever be quite as it had been.

His look turned feral, then triumphant.

"Rosalind," he said, and God help her, she still didn't hear the Scottish accent.

Of course not, because Marcus Kincardine had been away from his homeland for most of his life. He would speak as his knight had done.

There was nothing she could do. She took a step back anyway, holding out one hand in front of her as if to ward him off.

Marcus stood up, towering over her, matched the step she had taken away with a forward one of his own. His teeth flashed white in the darkness.

"Or Lady Avalon, I should say."

And then they took her.

Chapter Three

⟨⟨⟨⟩⟩⟩

*T*HEY SMUGGLED HER OUT wrapped in a burlap sack, trussed and gagged and buried underneath a damp mound of hay on a cart.

There were eight of them at least, including the son of Hanoch, who had personally tied her hands and bound her mouth, but not before she got in one powerful jab to his chin. She had fought as well as she could, but eight were too many, and they had her pinned down with barely a sound.

Marcus had stood over her, dabbed the blood from his lips and given her that feral smile again as he leaned down to tighten her bonds.

"Hanoch got to you, I see," he said, sounding nothing like his father.

The sack was a thousand times rougher than Elfrieda's cape had been, smelling of sour apples and dust, making her eyes water. Someone lay almost on top of her in the hay cart, kept her from moving about.

She didn't need to hear his voice again to know it was him.

"You're doing very well," Marcus whispered next to her ear. "Rosalind."

Beyond the hay she could hear others talking in the

bailey, men discussing the day, the party, the weather. It would be the serfs, leaving again for the village. Bryce's guards were still disgusted with their lord's guests, waving the hay cart and its occupants on with no pause in their conversation about last night's lack of sleep in the stables.

The wheels creaked and thunked their way over the road, down to the village and then beyond it, only the crickets accompanying them now.

Avalon shifted in the hay, testing the rope that tied her wrists together. Marcus inched closer, taking her hands in his through the sack and holding them immobile.

"Not yet," he said softly.

Hay poked through the loosely woven sack, pricking her all over. The gag was clean but her mouth was becoming unbearably dry, making her long for something to drink.

She had a sudden vision of Warner, standing bewildered in the middle of the great hall, a filled goblet in each hand. A laugh rose in her chest and caught there, delirious.

She had wanted to escape.

Well, by heavens, she certainly had pulled it off.

It seemed like an eternity that the cart rolled and creaked along. Except for the sharp bits, the hay was somewhat comfortable, cushioning her from the worst of the pits in the road, but the air was musty and scarce. Marcus kept his hands firm on her own, letting her know without a doubt he had control over her.

At last they halted, and for the first time she heard the others speak, clipped tones and hushed commands. Marcus moved; she felt the hay lift and lighten, then he was pulling her upright, yanking her down off the cart to stand on the path.

"Are they here?" she heard him ask, still holding on to her as she balanced in place with her ankles tied together, blinded in the damnable sack.

"Aye," said a new voice. "Over here, my lord."

As soon as the words came she was swept up in his arms, sack and all, handed off to someone else and then handed up, presumably to Marcus, now mounted on a horse.

"Ye got the lass so quickly, then?" asked someone else.

"We had a change in plan," Marcus replied. He put one solid arm around her waist and pulled her back to lean against him. When she resisted, he pulled her harder, holding her there.

"The lass obliged us by coming out to the garden alone. We didn't even have to go in."

"Are ye sure it's the right one?" asked the same man, doubtful.

"Oh, aye," drawled Marcus, low and certain. "It's her. She had her hair covered last night, but it's her. She has the mark."

They spoke in English, certainly not for her benefit, Avalon thought. Perhaps this man was as unused to his native tongue as she was. She could probably muddle through the Gaelic in her head, but this made things simpler.

Hanoch's son had tied her hands in front of her, a serious miscalculation on his part. The rope around her left wrist had loosened slightly, just enough for her to slowly, slowly begin to ease her hand out of it.

The horse leapt forward and she bounced back into

his chest, unable to stop herself. Marcus held her tighter, then pushed the horse to a gallop.

She could breathe better, but the wind brought the dust from the sack back into her face. Avalon turned her head to the side and squeezed her eyes shut. Her wrists were aching, her skin had a hot, slippery feel that had to be blood. But her hand was almost free.

There were more than eight of them now, no doubt, but how many she could not guess from the pounding of the hooves. If they had planned to steal her away from the party, they could not be an inconsiderable number. If they had planned an all-out attack, there might be hundreds.

It seemed so implausible that she let out a muffled laugh past the gag. A hundred men would never, ever reach the border in time.

Marcus was silent behind her, moving to the rhythm of his horse's steps, faceless to her, and, Avalon thought, brutal but not stupid.

So there wouldn't be hundreds of them. There would be just a core group, perhaps no more than thirty, his best warriors who would know how to move swiftly and stealthily on their mission.

Thirty Highlanders. She would not be able to escape them. But she might outwit them.

Her hand came free. She kept it down with the other, waiting now for her moment.

They rode for hours, faster and slower in turns, until the stifling blackness around Avalon's head gave way to faint, gray light, and if she wanted to, she could make out the texture of the burlap weave next to her face.

Her body was aching, her lungs were scalded from

the dust and wind, and her backside was beyond pain, sitting sideways in the saddle. She would have slept if she could, but the constant turns and jolts kept her miserably awake.

The horses were exhausted; she felt it clearly. The Highlanders had to stop soon. Their mounts would not hold out.

Within minutes of this thought she felt the group begin to slow. They all came to a stop. From somewhere far away Avalon heard the crystal splashings of a creek.

No one spoke. But there again sang a lark, exactly the same pattern of notes she had heard before in the garden, and then an answering warble in the distance.

"Over there," said someone, and the horses walked on.

They dismounted in a place that crunched with fallen leaves, Marcus handing her down to someone before leaping down himself with a grunt.

She was placed feet first on the ground, felt the cold smoothness of a blade between her ankles. The ropes were cut free. The sack was being pulled off at last.

She blinked to get the dust out of her eyes, remembered to keep her hands together. Marcus was standing right in front of her. He began to work at the knot behind her head that kept the gag in place, his features totally impartial.

The gag fell around her neck and then to the ground. Avalon tried to swallow past the dryness in her mouth, touching her tongue to her bruised lips. She saw something in Marcus flare to life at this, his eyes following the movement almost unwillingly before the blankness in his face returned. For the first time she felt a jagged streak of genuine alarm.

She was in the middle of a circle of men, most in tartans. There were less than thirty, after all, and they stared at her—the crumpled gown with its amethysts, her hair fallen from its coif—and she stared back, trying not to wince at the rush of feeling to her feet.

There was a herd of fresh horses nearby in the trees, she saw with dismay. Fresh horses. It meant they could ride all day.

"My Lady Avalon," said Marcus at last, looking away from her and over to his men. "Meet your new family."

She gathered herself, raising her brows as if she were only marginally interested in what he had to say. "I think you must be mistaken."

This got her some laughter, a few of the men elbowing each other. Marcus didn't join them. His eyes roamed over her, held on to their frost.

"Not at all," he said. "Avalon d'Farouche has the Kincardine curse." He indicated her hair and her face in a short gesture. "You are unmistakably Lady Avalon. And I am your husband."

"I know who I am, sir, and I know who you are. But you are mistaken in our relationship. I am the bride of Christ."

The group of men fell silent. After a long moment Marcus began to laugh.

It was a deep, chilling sound that brought goosebumps to her skin.

"Oh, I don't think so," he said, piercing her with that feral smile.

She clenched her fingers into the palms of her hands.

The light was growing stronger, allowing her to take in his face in full measure for the first time.

Dear heavens, he was nothing like his father. He was handsome and elegant, tall where Hanoch had only been burly; sinewy and strong where Hanoch had only been bullish. An Adonis to a Minotaur.

In daylight his eyes became the palest blue, icy and rimmed with black lashes. His lips were sensual, his chin firm, his nose straight and unbroken. Of course she hadn't recognized him. Not once in all her years in Scotland had anyone told her she was to marry a god.

He was examining her too, the trace of that smile still shading his lips. There was no warmth to him at all, only cold, hard will. Perhaps he was not so different from his father, after all.

"It is true," she lied, fighting the sensation that she might be drowning. "I am a nun. I took my vows in Gatting."

"Really?" His tone implied nothing. She didn't know what to make of it.

So he took her by surprise when he pulled her into him and secured her there, using one hand to tangle in the mess of her hair and hold her still for his kiss.

His body was massive and hard but his lips were skilled, covering hers before she could even draw breath. He slanted his mouth over hers, punishing her. The blood from the cut she had given him mingled between them, warm and salty.

The sting from his touch swarmed back over her, so much stronger than it had been at the inn, leaving her frightened and yet darkly thrilled. The hum tingled through her again, sparking a prickling heat at his touch, taking her breath and making it short, letting her skin feel every unique sensation of this moment: his kiss, his breath, his scent, the roughness of his cheek against hers. . . .

His hand in her hair loosened, became less a hold and more a guide, now gently tilting her head back further.

The pressure of his lips lightened; the kiss grew slower and even more disturbing. There was a new tightness unfurling in her chest, it stretched and filled her whole body, making her acutely aware of him against her, her chest to his, her legs to his, her hands pinned between them. Everything else—the men, the forest, her abduction—faded away.

Marcus tasted her lips with his tongue, plunging and invading. She gasped as the heat turned to melting honey, making her want to lean into him more, relying on his support.

He brought his other hand up and cupped her face, no longer holding her prisoner, stroked her cheek, moved his lips over to the side of her mouth and savored her again by gently sucking her lower lip. She felt him smile against her, slow and victorious.

"No nun ever kissed like that," he said.

She pulled back and pressed the point of the dirk she had stolen from him to his neck.

"Take the lands," she said, struggling to keep her breath even. At least her hand was steady and sure. The sight of her own blood, now dried and smudged against her wrist, took away the last of that stinging honey he had given her.

Marcus didn't move; none of the men did. She was

afraid to look away from him, however, to confirm it. He had a challenge in the angle of his head, and she could not afford to lose.

"Be reasonable, my lord," Avalon said now. "I offer you everything you desire. I will freely give you all my lands, all my money. It's yours. Only let me go."

The winter look grew colder. "Everything I desire?"

"Come, come," she said, impatient. "You must agree. You may have all the d'Farouche fortune with none of the trouble of me. How can you resist?"

He was not afraid, she realized suddenly. Not at all. His manner at best could be said to contain a mild annoyance, as if he were dealing with a troublesome horse on the journey.

"But what of the curse?" he asked, still mild.

"Oh, the curse." Avalon dismissed it with her tone. "Surely you don't believe in such fantasy, my lord."

"It doesn't matter whether I believe it or not. Everyone else does."

"No," she said.

"Aye," he replied, with the beginnings of that chilling smile. "You have the look, Avalon. You meet the requirements. My people will not be content until they have you in the family again."

"It is naught but superstition!" she cried, forgetting herself. "You cannot be guided by the fears of a hundred-year-old story! There is no curse!"

He moved like the wind, knocking her hand away, making the dirk fall to the leaves.

"It is just a story," she said to the circle, wanting to convince all of them, including herself.

Marcus took her arm, turned to his men. "Let's go."

*O*NE HUNDRED YEARS AGO . . .

The tale always began that way, and Marcus wondered how it could always be that same number of years when he himself had been hearing the story for at least the past thirty.

One hundred years ago there lived a laird and his lady, and she was the fairest lady to ever grace the lands. Her hair was light as moonlight, her eyes were the color of the rarest heather flowers, her brows black as jet.

Lady Avalon sat quietly now in the saddle before him, only her hands had been bound again with a soft strap of cloth torn from a blanket. Whether or not her eyes were really the color of heather flowers Marcus couldn't say, because she kept them cast away from him, kept them fixed on the horizon, searching for something he could not see.

The laird loved his lady fair and she him, both of them ruling just and right over their clan. It was the days of riches for them, of long summers and gentle winters, when the mountains still sang their songs at night and the deer were plump and plentiful. Each day was a jewel in the mind of God, and the Clan Kincardine was the most blessed of all people.

Into this peace came an evil faerie, who had watched the laird's lady for such a time until he fell into envy. He wanted her for himself, her moonlight and heather and jet, and set about to win her, using magic and gold and gossamer promises.

But she would not be won. Her heart was true to her laird.

Marcus found himself focusing on every part of Avalon that touched his body, the softness of her lines pressed to him in the confines of the saddle, the heat of her stomach against the arm he had wrapped around her waist. She smelled of apples and flowers. She had tasted of spice.

He wondered briefly if she was naive enough to be in love with her oafish cousin. She had seemed to accept his hasty plan to wed her without protest, even knowing the disgrace it would bring upon her, the war that might ensue.

But she was a woman. He had no idea why women did anything.

One day our lady went off wool gathering to the glen. She was so gentle that the thorns would bend back from the branches of the brambles, allowing her to harvest their treasured wool without harm.

But the faerie came upon her, and he had lost patience with his wooing. He took her honor there in the glen and broke her true heart until she died on the spot, weeping for her love.

The laird found her in the grass and knew what had happened.

Understand how much he loved her. Understand how great was his loss, for then and there he abandoned his faith and called on the devil to avenge the wrong done his lady.

The day had favored them by turning cloudy and dark, making their movement through the woods more obscure, turning them all into mere extensions of the shadows.

Lady Avalon was trying to resist falling asleep, Marcus noted. Her head would sink lower and lower, then jerk back up, only to repeat the process.

He thought about the offer she had made back in the circle of his men. She had told him she would give him everything he desired if he let her go. But if he let her go, he would never get the one thing that it turned out he desired most. And he was not a man to take his inclinations lightly.

Her chin dropped down and stayed there. With a subtle shifting of his arm he leaned her back against him until her head rested against his shoulder. Her hair was the only brightness around them.

The devil came with smoke and sulphur to the glen, and he brought forth the wicked faerie and held him in chains of fire in front of the laird.

"What would you have me do?" the devil asked.

"Revenge!" called out the laird, holding his poor lass in his arms.

So the devil took the faerie with fiery hands and twisted and turned him, shouting shrieks and spells until it wasn't a faerie any longer, but something else, black and burnt. And the devil tossed him onto the side of the mountain where he burned deep into the rock and melted there, gone forever.

"Now," said the devil. "My payment."

And it was only then that the laird realized what he had done.

When she was asleep it was easy to forget the fire in her eyes, a fire he provoked. It was easy to think about how she might have been if they had met under different circumstances, his own version of a fairy tale. She would have been trusting but strong, clever but kind beneath all that beauty. And he would have never, ever left on any crusade for any man or god.

"I find I have too many souls right now," said the crafty devil. "Yours will only crowd my halls. I will take something else from you. I will take your children away from you, and your children's children, and their children and their children, as

well. They will be banished from you and with them all your
golden days, and your clan will languish without them, and
your lands will be barren, and your animals will drop."

The laird cried out but what could he do? He had called on
the devil and now his people would pay the price.

She wasn't that heavy against him. Marcus thought it
would be no problem to ride the rest of the day with the
sleeping Avalon in his arms, to ride off into eternity
with her relaxed before him, the sweet softness of her
hair flowing down over her hips to brush and curl
against his leg.

The laird wept and begged for mercy but the devil would
have none of it. Only when an eye opened in the sky did the
devil stop laughing, and from the eye came a ray of sunlight,
falling down only on our dead lady.

Perhaps she was up in heaven right then, entreating the
Lord to have pity on her true love. For this was the Eye of God
in the sky, and He had taken an interest in the laird's fate.

Now, the devil knew what this meant, that God was lis-
tening and noticing, and the devil knew what he had to say. But
it filled him with spite that he had to soften his curse, and he
spat the final words to the kneeling laird.

"This curse will last one hundred full years, until there
comes from these children a lass with the mark of your lady, a
daughter of your clan to wed the laird. Until she returns you
will not prosper, not you or any of yours."

And because he was the devil, he added one more thing be-
fore being swallowed up whole by the ground:

"And she will be a warrior maiden who will know your
deepest hearts and thoughts. And she will hate your very name."

$\mathcal{T}$HEY ENDED UP CAMPING in a woods so tight with trees that they had to scatter the campsite. Even this was to their advantage, however. The plentiful trunks and branches offered ideal protection. Marcus had a watch set up to scout the perimeter of the camp and put Lady Avalon squarely in the middle, where she could be seen from all sides.

There was a stream nearby, cold black water, and he had taken her there himself after untying her hands, watching her slake what had to be a tremendous thirst, watching the water dissolve and sweep away the dried blood around her wrists.

It pained him somehow, the sight of that blood against her white skin, and he didn't want it to. She wasn't really harmed. The ropes had merely scraped her. He had endured far worse almost every day for the past twelve years.

She caught him staring at her with her enchanted eyes and almost shamed him into looking away. But he didn't.

He had no recollection of a heather flower of that particular shade of purple. It would have to be a magic flower, clearer and sharper and more pristine than life to match those eyes.

That night on the stairs at the squalid inn he had thought them more blue, but it must have been a trick of the light, because it was plain to see now that blue was not their tint.

What a surprise it had been, Marcus thought to himself as he walked her back to the camp. What a complete and total surprise it had been to find that the distant voice in his head had awakened that night on the stairs, had called out to him with absolute command to stop this particular girl before she could pass.

She had dressed like a peasant girl. She had spoken like a peasant girl. But one look at her face—the creamy skin, the pure line of her brow, and of course, those eyes—and he knew something was wrong.

He couldn't prove it. She had faced him boldly at the end, and though her beauty was staggering, he had to let her go.

All he had seen was a lass with midnight lashes and eyes that reached his soul. Sweet cherry lips.

All that he had felt was pure lust.

It coursed through him, stronger than the ocean tide, stronger than opium or pain. Just lust, just want, just the desire to claim this woman, whoever she was, and bind her to him until the lust was spent and he could be free again. It had never happened like this before, not in Jerusalem or Cairo or Spain. This was the first time.

She had felt the power between them then, he knew she did. But he had thought his mission involved a different woman, one that was about to destroy his clan with her ill-advised marriage to another, and Marcus had too many people relying solely on him to dally with the mystery of a woman in an inn, lust or no.

Rosalind, her sister had called her.

It hadn't sounded quite right. But he had no cause to go asking discreet questions among the villagers about a dark-haired girl named Rosalind. He had plans to make and obligations to fulfill before the baron's party. He'd had no time for inquiries.

But he had asked them anyway.

And naturally no one knew of such a girl; there was

one Rosalind, but she was too old, a mother of five, and her hair was red.

Because Rosalind had never been her name after all. Her name was Avalon, and she was the end of the curse, one way or another. Thank God he had her now.

Balthazar walked over to Marcus where he leaned against one of the trees, openly watching the woman he would soon wed.

Lady Avalon had accepted someone's cape and curled up in it on a bed of leaves the color of autumn, no longer fighting them, it seemed. Her eyes were closed. Her hair shielded half of her face.

"It is done," Balthazar said. The fading light made the tattoos on his face almost slip away against his dark skin, disguising their exotic lines.

Marcus didn't reply. He knew it wasn't done at all, that his friend actually meant just the opposite. It was Balthazar's habit to speak in short ironies, one of many of his unique ways that most of the Scots had yet to comprehend. They had accepted the Moor because he came home with their laird, and they would always obey the laird, even if he had been away for so long. But Balthazar, with his tattoos and long robes and gold earrings, was something the Highlanders had never before seen, even though to Marcus his friend's appearance was as common as the sand in the desert. Which was another thing impossible to explain to the Scots.

Marcus had lived in both worlds, that of the wild mountain Highlands and that of the unforgiving deserts, and how could he ever bring the two together for his clan when he couldn't even do it for himself?

He was caught, precarious, on the line that separated

these two opposing poles, trying to find a peace somehow between them.

"She is quiet," said Balthazar now, nodding his head to the lone woman in the leaves and ferns.

A very bad sign, Balthazar was saying, and Marcus could not help but agree.

"We'll make the next marker by tomorrow noon." It was Hew, his lieutenant, approaching the two men with bread for each of them. All three then turned back to look at Avalon.

"Did she eat?" Hew asked.

"Aye," said Marcus. "Not much."

"Ye should make her eat more," observed Hew.

"Aye." Marcus took a deep breath, clearing the aggravation from his head. Making Avalon eat the little she did had been trial enough.

She didn't want the bread. She wouldn't touch the cheese. She turned up her nose at the oatcake and clamped her lips shut, turning her back to him.

It had taken Balthazar to get her to eat even an apple, both of them sitting together in the woods as if they were all alone.

Marcus had watched the scene while bent over his saddle, adjusting a loose seam in the leather. He had to walk away from her after she refused the oatcake. He didn't want to but she was trampling his reputation beneath her pretty feet without having to utter a word, just the straight line of her back and the unequivocal rejection of him tearing him to shreds. Everyone had been watching; Marcus was sharply aware that he was still relatively new to most of these men, and they would be judging him by his actions.

It was either walk away or force her. And he would not force her. That had been his father's way, not his own.

He thought now that it was fortunate for both of them that the legend had it she would be predisposed to hate him. Her behavior now, in fact, served only to seal the idea in the clansmen's minds that she would be their salvation.

But she had to eat, and it frustrated him that she would not.

Then came Balthazar, graceful and dignified, a blaze of indigo and saffron robes amid the muted colors of the woods. He had squatted near Avalon but not too near. Just enough to get her attention, Marcus supposed.

Marcus had no idea what his friend had said to get her to eat, if they had spoken at all. He had not heard any words exchanged, but after a few minutes she had reached for the apple Bal handed her.

She had even changed her mind about the bread, consuming it in tiny, slow bites as she stole glances at Bal.

"She has pride," said Balthazar now, and Marcus thought this was meant to be an understatement. "It will not let her eat from your hand."

Hew frowned. "Not eat from the laird's hand? She'll be changing her mind soon enough on that, no doubt."

"No doubt, as you say," agreed Bal serenely.

Marcus knew then he had more than a battle on his hands. More, in fact, than he had ever anticipated. It was going to be war.

Chapter Four

⎯⎯⎯⎯⎯◠₥₥◠⎯⎯⎯⎯⎯

*F*OR SEVENTEEN YEARS of his life Marcus had dreamed of his family tartan. It was black with thin, even stripes of gold and red and purple, and to the young man he was, it had represented everything of meaning in his existence.

He had worn it with pride all the way to Jerusalem with Sir Trygve, had mended the tears it gathered on the journey, washed out the blood—his and the enemy's—when he could. It had lasted a powerful long time, that thick woolen tartan, and even though the Holy Land had days so hot it seemed the skin would melt from his bones, he had not taken it off. It was the symbol of his clan, his home, his hope.

Aye, he had worn it thin, until the pleats were stiff with grime and blood and desert dust, and every night he had dreamed of the day he could go back to Scotland.

Until Damascus. Until that one night when it had been torn off his body and burned, his boyhood dreams burned with it.

When it was over he had taken up Sir Trygve's hauberk and shield, and that had been his uniform ever since. But every now and again the dreams had crept back, slipped through the cracks of his defenses and made him think impossible thoughts: snow, woodsmoke and crisp air, green valleys. Innocence.

It had taken an act of will greater than he knew existed to don the tartan again when he finally returned. Only Balthazar might have understood how hard it had been. Only Balthazar had been there in Damascus and watched Marcus abandon his hope.

Still, he would not give in to the seduction of the comfort the plaid offered. Not so easily. He kept his own Spanish sword at his waist, a clear outward sign of his inward difference. That the people of his clan had admired it, thought it a cunning and lethal thing was fine. It would not have prevented him from carrying it even if they had loathed it. He needed something, some visible thing to keep him in check amid the rough paradise of Scotland, to keep him from forgetting the trials he had endured in foreign lands.

Nevertheless, the tartan he wore now was new and sturdy, and Marcus could not help but think it a miracle of sorts, the straight threads of gold and red and purple, the solid black around them. It was the inviolable tie to his heritage he needed as much as that Spanish blade.

So here was Lady Avalon in front of him this morning, and the sun had decided to rise and shine through the trees, catching in the ivory silk of her hair, caressing the curve of her cheek.

She was so lovely, even in her fancy ruined gown. She was so lovely as she took the tartan Marcus held out to her and threw it to the ground at his feet.

"I have made a vow never to wear it again," she said, defiant and delicate all at once. He was not fooled by that delicacy. She was the product of Hanoch as surely as he was.

"Alas for you," Marcus told her, picking it up. "For you are going to wear it anyway."

She didn't back down, not one bit, but stood ready, fists at her sides, leaves clinging to her. The amethysts on her bliaut were undimmed, glinting in the sunlight.

"You will have to make me," she said, soft and deadly.

In his mind's eye she was undressed suddenly, fully undressed and delightfully available, beckoning him with a smile. By heavens, he was more than ready for that, to have that unbelievable hair wrapped around him, to taste her again. It would be sweeter and hotter this time, it would not be a lesson but a pleasure—

Marcus blocked the vision, shocked at his loss of control.

Her eyes had become very wide, her whole body grew still as she stared up at him.

She knew. She knew what he had thought. *He* knew that she knew.

It was unexpected, that they would be able to touch thoughts like this, the curse had never mentioned it. But Marcus didn't doubt the power was real. He had grown up on the legend, it had been ingrained in him from babyhood, his mother crooning his destiny to him in her soft voice as he went to sleep. After she died, when he was ten, it was the women of the clan who took her place, who told and retold the legend to him so that he might understand his role in it when he became a man.

Marcus believed in the curse, and strange as it was, he believed that the bride could know the thoughts and hearts of others. He knew such a power was real, because a tiny fragment of that gift lived in him, as well. And it was a gift. He would not believe it could be anything else.

Avalon snatched the bundle of cloth from his fingers, walking briskly away. She pushed aside the flap of blanket he had hung between a pair of bushes for her privacy and disappeared behind it.

He could see the outline of her shadow, blending in and out of those of the branches and leaves. A perfect profile, a perfect arm reaching out, a perfect teasing glimpse of a shadow thigh. Perfect everything.

When she emerged again, she wore the tartan.

Praise the clanswoman who had thought to include the silver brooch to secure it and the black gown that went beneath it. Marcus would have never remembered such things.

Lady Avalon threw him a glance as she walked over to her unfinished breakfast. A glance that meant . . . what? Anger, yes. But something else less easily defined. Wariness, perhaps. Fear—he hoped not. No, it wouldn't be fear, not in her. More likely caution.

Well, that would be a good thing. She was already almost more than he could handle; a little respect tossed in his direction would not be amiss.

His men watched her eat in silence, noted the neat pleats in the tartan she had managed by herself, all of them exactly right. They exchanged satisfied looks over her bowed head. No one else knew what Marcus did, that she had only capitulated so that she could walk away from him and not have him follow.

Avalon sat on a flat stone in the ground and morosely chewed an oatcake.

Here it was again, that horribly familiar plaid enclosing her body. She really had sworn not to wear it again. She had been fourteen, and the night she had crossed the border from Scotland back into England she had taken it off for what she had thought would be the very last time. She had burned it herself in the hearth of the inn where they stayed, had watched the flames eat into it, and no one had said a word to her, not the king's emissary nor the soldiers nor the innkeeper. They had all witnessed it turn to ash with her.

And now like a bad dream it had returned, the Kincardine tartan draping over her shoulder and wrapping around her waist, just as it did the shoulders and waists of all the other women of the clan. She had remembered how to handle the giant square of material without thinking twice; her fingers had readily managed the tricky tucks and folds that had taken her untold time to master as a girl. She knew she looked no different from any of them now. It filled her with gloom to realize how easy it was for the Kincardines to absorb her into themselves again.

And was this moment of relative freedom worth the loss of that vow she had made? Was it worth it just to stem the torrent of feeling she had sensed from Hanoch's son when he faced her over the rejected bundle of cloth?

There could be no denial of what had happened. She had said something—already she couldn't remember what—and he had latched on to her words and transmuted them into churning desire. He had taken her with him.

It had been too abrupt, too stunning. It had been too much like that moment on the stairs in the village of

Trayleigh, when he had touched just her chin and she
had felt her entire body go aflame, awake in a way she
had never known before.

What to make of it? She had no idea. She had seen
looks like his aplenty from men in London, had even
begun to notice them all the way back in Gatting, and
none of those others had involved her as completely as
his did. None of them had invoked the chimera so
strongly.

None of them made her feel so . . . *alive*.

The oatcake was flaky and dry, the bland flavor of it
coming back to her in slow degrees. Another thing she
thought she had seen the last of.

Marcus Kincardine, all in all, had proven to be
nothing like what she had expected. He was talking
to a cluster of his men now, all with serious demeanors,
each of them as acutely aware of her as she was of them.
Marcus had his back to her; he was saying something
to a brown-haired man who looked vaguely familiar.
Probably one of Hanoch's minions.

The wizard Balthazar stood slightly apart from the
others, holding on to the magnificently tooled silver
bridle of his stallion. He gave her a stately nod.

Avalon had noticed right away that this man had a different aspect; it had not been his foreign clothing or his
earrings that set him apart, but rather his bearing. The
chimera had whispered the right word for him as soon as
he came close: wizard.

It was a laughable thought, one fantasy being identi-
fying another. Yet even if such a creature were only fantasy, surely this man embodied it in full. His *wholeness*

seemed so right, it shone from his eyes. Avalon knew that he alone had accepted her as she was, without judgment, without forethought. Just her. She almost wanted to talk to him, to discover his secrets, but he was the friend of her enemy. So she could not afford it.

They rode on, for two long days.

No one spoke on the ride. The only sounds were from the horses, snorting and whickering, and the steady push of their hooves in the leaves and peat. Birds stilled as they passed, a few flying up in a mad rush to the sky, living shapes that soared and scattered.

Avalon knew the moment they crossed back into Scotland. She knew it even before they did. The air changed, the light changed, everything changed.

Marcus, behind her, might have felt it at almost the same time. He straightened in the saddle. From him emanated a single word:

Home.

No, she thought, not my home.

But if not here, then where? Not Scotland, not Gatting, not London. Not even Trayleigh, not anymore. Her life had been broken down into so many fragments that she no longer felt any allegiance to anyone or anything.

Only the chimera seemed glad to be back in Scotland. Avalon felt it shift within her, benign now, but so much stronger than it had been before. . . .

It had been born here in this country, the product of fierce Highland tempers and her own will to survive. Before she was brought here, as a young girl, the beast had been nothing but a voice to her, a guide, a different eye. It had taken Hanoch to strike the beast into existence from the sparks of her mind. It had taken Hanoch to show her how black black could be.

That night the party camped under a relentlessly starfilled sky. Here the wind had already embraced the coming winter, growing harder and sharper, heavy with the promise of a bitter, cold rain. Beneath the gown and tartan, a blanket, and a pitiful excuse for a tent, Avalon shivered alone on the ground, arms tucked in and curled close to her body. Her dreams became a tangled confusion of memory and imagination, until at last she could sort out the scene being played.

Uncle Hanoch had been so angry. Yes, how could she have forgotten it, that moment in the circle of dirt. . . .

"She's naught but a weak female," said Uncle in disgust. "Look at her."

She sat up slowly, pushing herself up from the ground, and resisted the urge to place a hand over her eyes to stop the world from reeling.

"Ye let yer concentration drop." The other man—the instructor—scowled down at her. "I told ye to concentrate!"

She climbed to her feet in front of both men in the ring of dirt, not bothering to brush the dust from the fall off her tartan.

"Do it again!" barked Uncle.

The instructor didn't wait for her to regain her balance. He moved in with a rapid feint to her right, prompting her to skitter in the other direction, hands out, trying to ward off the attack she knew was coming.

Her eyes were teary from the rising dust around them; the blur impeded her vision. So, although she knew her instructor was about to cut her off with a sweep of his foot to her knees, she could not see it at all. Her breathing was ragged, almost weepy.

She made the mistake of moving one hand up to brush across her eyes, trying to clear the tears.

Down! screamed the monster-beast in her head. *Roll!*

She did as it told her to, instinctive, ducking the blow coming from the man, hitting the dirt with her body curled, using her meager weight to carry her over and up, a full tumble before she sprang back to her feet and whirled around to face the man, now behind her.

The beast let her feel the grudging approval of Uncle, who stood watching with his lips pressed to a thin line, saying nothing.

She hated the line of his mouth, it was all he ever showed her: a sign of constant dissatisfaction from this man whom everyone but she was allowed to call "laird."

Her instructor had not relented at her surprising move. He came toward her again in half steps, both hands held out an equal distance in front of him, giving her no hint of which one would be the one to fell her again.

A fall of hair, locks of silver brilliance, had escaped from the tight knot on the back of her head, and the strands teased her now, blowing up in front of her with a slight puff of wind. She shook her head to clear her vision.

Left! shouted the beast, but this time it was too late, and the instructor's hand caught her across the face, an open slap, sending her spinning down to the dirt again.

"Ach," said the laird in disgust. "A warrior maiden, indeed."

Avalon, eyes closed, head bowed, listened to him rant at the instructor.

"She's never going to be the one. She's a disgrace!"

"Give her some time, Hanoch. She's young yet."

"Time!" The laird's voice was booming, incredibly loud in the silence of the courtyard in front of the cottage. "Time! She's had three years already! How much more time does she need?"

"Battle skills are not simple, Hanoch. Ye know this. And she's only a child."

She raised her head at this and watched the men argue from her vantage point on the ground. The escaped locks of hair had drifted down past her shoulder to lay coiled in the dirt, a ring of brightness against the dun.

"She won't be a child forever, MacLochlan," said Uncle Hanoch. "Soon enough she'll be of an age to marry my son, and ye know she must meet the standards of the curse! I entrusted ye to bring me the legend come to life, and ye give me *this*?"

The instructor threw her a look and Avalon met it with defiance, the first trace of it she had dared show in a long while.

"She'll get better," the instructor stated, and she didn't need the keen ears of the beast to pick up the doubt in his voice.

The laird walked over to where she was, still on her hands and knees, and glared down at her, his lips pressed even thinner in distaste.

"Avalon d'Farouche. Ye are a disgrace to yer clan."

She pushed back on her hands and spat out the words that had been swelling up in her for the past three years:

"I am not of your clan!"

Uncle Hanoch's eyebrows climbed almost to his hairline; his red beard bristled.

"What did ye say?" he asked in a ghastly voice.

Avalon came fully to her feet, and the monster-beast in her now was cowering, cringing, running around in circles inside her head.

Fury! wailed the chimera, *Oh, horrible fury, mistake, mistake, take it back—*

Quiet! Avalon shouted at it soundlessly. She had waited so long for this moment, and it was too late to take it back. She knew that.

"I am not of your clan." She spoke with as much dignity as she could muster. She said it as she thought her father might have, back when he was alive.

Uncle Hanoch's skin grew very pale beneath his beard, making his wild red hair seem suddenly garish in the afternoon sunlight.

The beast let out a howl of fear that only she could hear, rolled over to expose its stomach, total submission, and she knew that perhaps even this would not satisfy Uncle now.

He loomed above her, blocking out the whole sun.

"Your curse is stupid!" Avalon cried, and couldn't believe that it was her own voice coming out, her own words that would surely prompt him to kill her. His eyes bulged, his hands clenched into tight fists. One blow would finish her, but maybe it wouldn't even be so bad, maybe it wouldn't hurt so much, and then she could leave this place, see her mother and father and Ona. . . .

"Stupid!" she yelled again, resigning herself to death. "It isn't real! Only little babies believe in curses!"

Ona had told her that, long, long ago, back when

Avalon had had a nursemaid, and a castle as her home, and people all around her who cared for her. Not like now. Not like this, living in a tiny cottage, no nursemaids, no playmates, no companions of any kind, save the instructor.

"Lass, hold yer tongue." It was the instructor, shouldering between her and the laird, a new threat, and a diversion.

"No, I won't!"

It was as if she had been waiting three years for this moment—ever since she'd been brought here—to be in the circle of dirt with these two men, both of them giants against the sky, huge and terrifying. What they wanted of her, what they expected of her, was incomprehensible.

"It's just a story!" she taunted, reckless with the power of saying at last what she thought. "It never really happened! And I *won't* pretend it's true, and I *won't* ever get married, not for you or for anyone but *especially* not for a made-up story!"

The words she had been biting back for so long now tasted wonderfully wicked on her lips, dangerous and utterly unstoppable: "I will never marry him! I vow it now—I will never marry your son!"

Avalon took a breath and felt the world go hushed around her, the final echo of her true thoughts at last fading away into the trees. She felt defeated suddenly, her outburst having drained what spirit she had left. She didn't belong here, she hated it here, she wanted—more than anything!—to be able to leave, and the pain in her was so acute that even the beast was quelled by it.

"I want to go home," she said now, quieter, pleading. "Please . . . let me go home."

There was a long moment of silence, as if even the birds and the streams had frozen in fear for her, of what wrath would surely follow her words. At last the stillness was broken by the indrawn hiss of air from Hanoch.

"Well, this is the thanks I get." He shoved the instructor easily out of the way, and the instructor let him do it, folding back into the background of the woods and the mountains, leaving Avalon alone with her nemesis.

Hanoch was white with rage.

"After I save ye from the raid that killed yer father and bring ye here to my home, my people—after I take ye in, Avalon d'Farouche, for the sake of yer father, and my son. After all this, and ye whine and snivel at me, and ye mock the very thing that spared yer life!"

"Curses aren't real," she whispered, and was too terrified even to wipe her eyes anymore. Her hair was entangled with her lashes, stinging, a curtain of blonde between him and her.

"Real?" he roared, stepping toward her. She flinched as his hands came down on her shoulders but didn't try to run away. She knew that would not get her anywhere. Uncle had posted his guards all over.

"Real?" he shouted again, picking her up easily, lifting her as he would a cloth doll, her feet dangling in the air. "I'll show ye real, my lass! I'll show ye the realness of a day and a night in the pantry, how's that?"

Her lips moved but no sounds came out. He wouldn't have heard her anyway, because he was taking her back into the little cottage. He was taking her to that dreaded place.

She began to struggle as he entered the kitchen and passed the pinched face of the cook, who hurried out of the room. Uncle controlled her easily, holding her up with only one hand, using the other to pry open the pantry door.

"Ye think about what's real now in there, ungrateful child!"

She was tossed in, came up hard against the back wall of the cramped space and slid down to the floor, a hand pressed over her mouth.

Uncle stood still in the doorway, looked down on her with that familiar thin line again creasing his face. "Ye *will* marry my son. Whatever else ye want or think is *nothing* compared to that, selfish lass, and don't forget it again!"

He took a step back, began to shut the door, inviting the thick blackness to creep closer.

"Ye'll stay in there until tomorrow morning, when ye are ready to apologize for insulting the clan. Ye'll not come out before."

The door slammed shut, immersing her in darkness.

Avalon hunched in the corner, closing her eyes, keeping her hand in place to press back the sobs that wanted to come out.

I will never marry him! I will never marry him! I will never marry him. . . .

In her mind, the all-seeing chimera, bitter legacy of Uncle's *not real* curse, laid its head down on its feet and began to weep for her.

$\mathcal{S}$HE WAS HAVING A NIGHTMARE.

Marcus heard the first, tiny hitches in her breathing, the sound of her hands moving restlessly against her blanket.

He was closest to her, so when he raised his head to check on her, he had a clear view even past the makeshift shelter they had set up for her of a spare tartan and sticks. From here he could just see her face past the edge of the cloth.

Lady Avalon was fitful in her sleep, turning her head to the side, breathing in that terrible, uneven way that somehow brought a hard lump to his throat. It was surprisingly awful, listening to her, hearing the verge of tears brought on by whatever it was she saw in her dreams.

He got up slowly, pushing his own blanket back, unsure of what to do. If he woke her, chances were better than good he would get no thanks for his trouble. But if he left her alone, how could he sleep with the poignancy of her unshed tears taunting him?

So instead he just looked at her. The starlit shadow of the half-tent threw a soft netherworld glow on her, a fragile soul astray. Her smooth brow was marred by a frown, her lips were downturned, then parted.

Marcus thought somewhat helplessly about how beautiful she was, this promised bride of his, and how damned hard it was going to be to get her to accept him. Perhaps she never would.

The thought filled him with a curious despair. She was a fey creature, strong but delicate, warrior but woman, a faerie herself snared in the contradictions of her life. She was almost beyond his understanding. Yet she tossed and turned in her sleeping torment, and right then Marcus felt more kinship with her than he would have thought possible.

He knew about nightmares. Aye, he knew all about them. Her dream would pass, and the unshed tears would pass, and she would face tomorrow with the same stubborn defiance she had been showing him so far. He had to admire that, he supposed.

But right now, how much closer he felt to her, lost in her netherworld. Even the lovely Lady Avalon, it seemed, was human, and had demons of her own to face.

How much he would give to fight those demons for her.

In time she relaxed, releasing her struggles, her face clearing, her breathing becoming even and uninterrupted again. But Marcus found that he could not regain his own sleep.

———————— ⟨⟩ ————————

THE NEXT MORNING they both mounted up and began the ride as if the night had been just another like the rest. Avalon sat in front of him on his stallion in stoic silence, watching the landscape change, the mountains growing taller, the trees growing thicker and more piney.

Marcus would periodically take his arm from around her waist, switching hands on the reins. He would then settle the other one around her with complete familiarity, as if it were something he had done all his life. And wasn't it odd how it felt that way to her, as well.

They would reach Sauveur Castle within days, Avalon guessed. She wasn't quite certain, since she had never been to the castle that belong to the laird of the clan. Hanoch had not trusted the circumstances enough to take her there. He had known the Picts were bought, Avalon realized. He must have known all along. It would explain so much.

It would explain why, for example, he had lived half his time in that forsaken little village with her and a few of his most trusted people, taking a cottage when he could have had a castle all the time. The village had always belonged to the Kincardines, but it was an outskirt town, and the neighboring lands had belonged to their sworn ally. In case of attack, there had been a place to run.

Hanoch had never been unaware of danger. He would go back and forth to Sauveur, maintaining the facade of his regular life, but she had always remained in that village. How she had dreaded his visits.

Yet his scheme had served to hide her well, she supposed. It had taken six years before news of her survival leaked south to England, and another year for the English king to get her away from Hanoch. She had been presumed dead in the raid that killed her father and so many others. Her body was thought to have been burned in the castle, and Avalon had not known any of this until after she came back to England.

She had always assumed that everyone knew she lived in the little village in the Highlands, and that it was fine with them. Hanoch had let her believe this. But all along it had been only the Kincardines who knew she was still alive.

How furious Hanoch had been when the English demanded her return. He had not planned to release her, not until after she was wed to his son. And by then, of course, she would be bound to both of them forever.

"Your father must be gratified to have you home," Avalon said into the silence of the forest, wondering what it would be like to see him again.

"I have no idea," Marcus replied after a while. "He died eleven months ago."

"Eleven months?" No one had told her. She couldn't believe no one would have told her.

"Aye." He let the thought settle between them before adding, "I'm told his last words were of you."

She let out a caustic laugh. "Something to the effect of, 'Don't forget to abduct the heiress,' I suppose."

"Something like that," he said.

It had been nothing at all like that, from what Marcus had heard. Hanoch had taken to bed and died quickly, a fever or the ague or who knew what. There had been no time for a doctor. One of Hanoch's elderly cronies had sent Marcus a letter stating that his father had died, and bade him to come home from the holy wars, to abandon the pilgrimage he had been on and come back to lead the clan.

And when Marcus had, the same old man told him the rest over a late night of whiskey and haggis. Told him that right before he died Hanoch had spoken of Lady Avalon and called her his lass as if she had been in the room with him, had told her that she was going to be fine, that she had learned well what she needed to know. Hanoch hadn't quite said he was sorry for all that had happened to her, the man reported. But he thought that the old laird might have been, anyway.

"I think he was quite fond of you," Marcus said to his future wife, and felt her stiffen against him.

"A strange fondness," she said, scathing. "To hit and demean and mock that which you like."

If Hanoch had not been sorry, then Marcus was, sharply so. He could not imagine anyone striking this lovely girl, even though he knew for a fact she could hit back. It left him mute, this image of her abuse, mute and filled with a pointless anger at his father. But it was too late to despise Hanoch. The old man would have laughed in his face, anyway. He had been forged of some material Marcus could never fully grasp, sword and steel and not an ounce of tenderness. As a boy he had feared him, as a man he had tried to forget him. But this girl had not been given such a choice.

He remembered the first—and until now, the last— time he had seen the Lady Avalon. He had been twelve and she had been two. Just two, a chubby toddler with an angel's face already, a crop of white-blonde hair and a happy smile. His father had taken him down to Tray-leigh to see the bride. Hanoch had wanted to confirm her appearance personally, not trusting the stories he was hearing.

But she had been all that he expected, Marcus sup-posed, and the agreement that had already tentatively existed between the old allies and kinsmen, Hanoch and Geoffrey, was retoasted that night and irrevocably sealed.

They had sat her on Marcus's knee for a while, that baby girl, and the awkward youth he had been didn't know what to do with her, her incoherent burbles, her constant squirming. After a brief, uncomfortable moment he had given her back to her nurse and everyone went on toasting.

That was all he remembered of Avalon, the girl who was to be the bride. Just another baby, albeit a cheerful one.

"He would knock me down and yell until I got back up." The woman she was now kept her voice low. Marcus had to bend his head to catch the words, spoken down to the hands clenched in her lap. "He would go at me until I could not fight anymore, and then he would tell me I was unworthy of the clan."

"Interesting," Marcus said. "He would do the same to me."

"He was a monster," she said.

Marcus couldn't deny it. When he turned thirteen it had been the greatest day of his life, because that was the day he was to be sent off to the household of Sir Trygve to become a squire. He had escaped his father. But Avalon, younger and far less skilled than Marcus at dealing with him, had taken his place.

Lost in Trygve's crusade, Marcus had had no real idea of what happened at Trayleigh. There had been only one short mention of Lady Avalon in a letter from home, and her name had never actually been written. It had been his father's code, something about how the sire had perished in a raid but the girl was well taken care of. In time he forgot about even this; Marcus had plenty of other things to think about in Jerusalem, and later Damascus.

In all the years he was away he received only five letters from Scotland, the fifth one just that simple note telling him to come back. And that had been the second greatest day of his life, when he read that letter and knew at last he could go home.

"I'm not going to marry you," Avalon said tersely, interrupting his thoughts. "I will not deceive you. You may try to beat me or starve me, but I will not do it."

"I would not beat you," he said quickly, appalled.

Her silence was skeptical.

"Nor will I starve you, my lady. I would not treat a woman such."

Still she said nothing.

"I would not," he repeated. "I will not."

He took the hand he'd kept around her waist and brought it up to her face, hesitant, giving in to the ache of wanting to touch her. He stroked her cheek, rubbed his thumb over the smoothness of it. She sat perfectly still as he did it, and he couldn't gauge her reaction. His own was a mix of things, mostly wonder and bewilderment at himself. It was imperative that she believe him incapable of his father's barbarism. He had to convince her, but that urgency was becoming intertwined with something else, the desire for her welling up once more, filling him.

"I would not," he said again, breathing it into her hair.

He wanted to bury his head in her neck and kiss her there, he wanted to hold her to him not as a prisoner but as a man would hold a woman, he wanted to taste her again so badly. . . .

Her lips had parted slightly as these sensations raced through him. He thought maybe her heartbeat had quickened, coming closer to the pace of his own. He

moved his fingers slightly lower and traced the outline of
her lips, mesmerized as he looked down at her, following the rose color, the lush lines. Her eyelids drifted
closed, displaying the sweeping curves of sable lashes
against pearly skin.

"You will wed me," he said, husky, and then knew
immediately that he had blundered.

Avalon pulled his hand away, turned her head
from him.

"Nay, I will not."

Marcus let her have her denial, focusing now on
calming himself. She was as wine to him, making him
think of things that hindered his focus, delightful as they
were. But it would be as he said. No matter what she
thought now, she would be his bride. He had a legend
on his side.

———————— ⟨ఌఌ⟩ ————————

*T*WO DAYS LATER they reached Kincardine lands.
One day more and they were at Sauveur Castle itself.

It had been a difficult end to the trip, with the early
autumn rain promised before now finally beginning to
lash at them, and winds so strong they could tear a man
from his mount were he not careful. But Marcus would
not stop for shelter, nor did any of his men want him to.
Everyone was eager to return home and be done with
this task.

Avalon's mood grew to match the weather. He sheltered her as best he could but she was as rain-soaked as
the rest of them. The tip of her nose turned pink with
cold, her hair clung in long tangles to them both.

In the early dawn hours before they reached the castle they had to wallow through a ferocious storm, much worse than even the rain before. After a meeting with his men Marcus decided to press on in spite of the tempest, because to camp this close to Sauveur seemed bitter to them all.

Avalon had not quite felt the same way.

"You are a fool," she cursed at him, disbelieving when he ordered them to mount up in the midst of the squall. The wind was taking her hair and making it dance behind her in drenched tendrils. Rain dripped off her chin. "It is madness to travel tonight! They will not be chasing you this far into Scotland. You know it. I know it. Yet you push us on."

His only response was a shrug, knowing it would infuriate her but unable to help himself.

He did know d'Farouche would not dare follow this far. They had already passed through the territories of four other clans, all of them on mostly friendly terms with his own. But they would not be so generous with trespassing Englishmen. Not unless they brought an army with them.

And neither the baron nor his brother would be able to muster an army so quickly. That would come later. By then it would be too late to take her back.

Moving on in the face of the storm was not about avoiding d'Farouche. It was about returning to Sauveur.

Avalon wrapped her arms around herself, shivering as everyone got ready. Even the tartan was not much help in this weather. Marcus wanted to go to her and hold her. He wanted to spark a heat between them that would burn away the rain and the wind, burn away her rancor.

But he had noticed whenever these thoughts took him that she retreated further into herself, brooding, no longer responding to anything he said. So instead he put her atop his stallion as before and then climbed up behind her.

The storm grew fiercer; he only vaguely remembered weather like this from his boyhood. Men and beasts alike kept their heads down, water sheeting off them all, the wind bruising them.

Thunder began to rumble over the howling, making the horses toss their heads nervously. Now and again lightning arced across the sky, distant at first, but slowly growing closer.

Avalon didn't want to but she kept her head behind the wall of tartan Marcus held over her. Any pride she had felt at shunning his aid had disappeared hours ago. Now she was just sore and wet and completely wretched. The tartan over her face was as drenched as everything else, but at least it kept the stinging lash of the storm off her head. She imagined it was not easy for him to keep his arm up like that to shield her, and she wanted to be glad that he was taking the brunt of the weather, in retaliation for his foolhardy order to make them go on. But it wasn't true. She was too tired to entertain spite right now. All she wanted was for this insufferable journey to be finished.

Then the world split apart in front of her. Like the arm of God, a bolt of lightning exploded the mighty oak next to them, an encompassing wave of violence and sound and light that seemed to Avalon to be the end of everything.

She felt herself flung through the air, weightless, and

then landed on her side in the mud. There were no sounds left in the world. Everything was black and silent.

It was a relief.

But it turned out she couldn't breathe in the mud, and her body made her rise to her elbows, gulping in the singed air around her. Still she couldn't hear, but she could see, and what she saw was terrifying.

It was a dim glow to her at first, but her vision cleared until she could see a series of pictures, flashes of blue light against the darkness, intermittent lightning crackling though the thunderheads. Chaos everywhere, men mounted and on foot running together, horses rearing and circling. The glow was the fragmented remains of the oak, laid open and on fire despite the rain.

Right in front of it Marcus lay in the mud, motionless. A horse screamed over him, bounding up on two legs, boxing the air with his forelegs in a panic. The reins were caught on a smoldering log that would not let him run. The stallion went up and down again and again over the fallen body of her captor, missing the man by inches each time he landed.

She was up before she knew she was moving, still stranded in her silence and slipping through the mire with no thought except getting to that horse.

It was Marcus's stallion, the one they had both ridden, and the whites of his eyes made a visible circle around his pupils. His lips were pulled back as he screamed, and though she could not hear the sound, she felt his overwhelming terror.

Calm. Avalon sent the thought with all her might, struggling to get closer. *Calm, peace, calm . . .*

The stallion turned his head to her, still kicking. Marcus was a blurred outline beneath him in the rain.

Peace!

The corners of her vision held diversions she could not afford to think about, men coming toward her. Someone tried to take her arm. She blocked the move without pausing, but then he grabbed her shoulder. Avalon twisted to the side and kicked her foot out, tripping whoever it was.

The stallion suffered during her momentary distraction. She felt him scream again, coming down to the ground, barely missing Marcus before rearing again. Mud splashed up in angry spurts beneath the sharp hooves.

No harm, no harm, peace, she thought, capturing his attention again. Almost there.

Two more men were to her left. She felt their intent to restrain her and it infuriated her, that they would dare to stop her now when their laird was about to be trampled to death. She began to run, risking a fall in the slick mud.

The men came close but then fell back. The wizard had materialized from the rain, and he had stopped them. The wizard was allowing her to go on.

Ho, called Avalon with her mind to the horse. *Here, here, over here!*

The stallion threw her his terrified look but did as she commanded, turning his body to her before landing on his forelegs again. Marcus was now exactly between the powerful legs. Before the horse could rise once more she was there. Only one of her hands seemed to work but it was enough; she used her fingers to pinch the flesh of his upper lip and deaden the pain in him until the whites around his eyes receded to normal.

Thank you, she thought, and didn't know if she was addressing the horse or God or both.

The wizard and some of the other men were pulling Marcus away from where he had fallen, taking him to the side of the path. Someone came up to her and the beast where they stood eye to eye. It was all right now. The stallion was quieted.

She didn't know the man talking to her, red haired and bearded, freeing the reins from the log. He was insistent about something, talking to her, and at last she let go of the horse and shook her head at him, tapping one of her ears to indicate she couldn't hear.

The man paused, comprehending. He turned away from her and addressed the others. The wizard approached Avalon, gave her a look more subtle than a smile. She followed him back to the side of the road, beneath the shelter of a pine.

Marcus was awake, sitting up. He tried to stand as she drew near, and she threw him a disgusted look.

Her ribs were in agony. She had just now noticed it. The shoulder she had landed on felt as if it had been torn from its socket, and that arm was useless. She was covered from head to toe in leaves and filth; the tartan was a cold, slopping mess on her; and all of this was his fault. If he had not ordered them out in this storm, she might be warm and dry and free of pain now.

For that matter, if he had not stolen her at all, she might have been living the fulfillment of her dreams, tucked away in an obscure little nun's cell right now, clean and happy and counting her blessings and making her plans for the future. In fact, if he had not come home from his crusade—

Everything, *everything* was his fault. She had no idea why she had bothered to save him.

Marcus winced as he hobbled over to her, both of them slightly hunched over beneath the branches. He tried to take her hand and she jerked away from him, but she must have made a sound from the pain that shot through her. Marcus scowled and Balthazar was at her shoulder, exploring it with light fingers.

She let him, but then he said something to Marcus and the other men who had trickled in and clustered tightly near. She heard his words from very far away, as if he were at one end of an enormous tunnel and she at the other.

". . . dislocated. It should be set."

Something shifted in the crowd, pity and intent and determination. They thought she was going to fight this, and they were correct. The wizard touched her again but she shook him off, biting back the wave of nausea that rose at the movement. She took a step away but they were behind her, too, and she had only one good arm.

Marcus put himself directly in front of her, shaping his words very clearly so that she could read them.

"It must be done. I'm sorry."

"Don't touch me," she said, and heard her own words in that tunnel.

His glance moved to someone behind her, and she felt herself taken firmly on both sides. The pain shrieked from her shoulder to her ribs, making her weak.

Marcus had one hand around her injured shoulder,

the other on her arm, and—after one quick, cold look at her face—began to pull.

Black dots exploded in her vision, her knees gave out, and still he didn't stop, keeping up the pressure, harder now. Avalon bit her lip to stop from screaming until she felt the blood running from her mouth, and then there was a sickening pop and she didn't know what happened next.

She was on her knees in the pine needles and mud. They were supporting her and pressing something to her lips, something that burned. Whiskey.

It inflamed the cut she had given herself on her lower lip, and she spat the mix of alcohol and blood on the ground.

"I hate you," she said, knowing it was Marcus in front of her.

He stood up and walked away from her, taking most of the men out into the chilly rain again, gathering the horses. She was left with Balthazar.

When Marcus came to fetch her she had nothing more to say to him. The wizard had produced a long sash of fine, diaphanous material from somewhere within his robes, bright orange with a yellow sun embroidered on it, and he had fashioned it into a support for her injured arm. Marcus noted the sash, but all he did was gesture for her to walk with him to his stallion. Two men helped her up into the saddle.

The worst of the storm had passed; by the time they rode up to Sauveur Castle three hours later, the rain had lightened to a drizzle and the sky had turned dull gray. The road was nothing but thick slime, the horses skidding and fighting the muck with each step. Avalon held on to the mane of the stallion with her good hand to keep her balance. She would not look up at the castle.

The scouts had alerted the inhabitants already and a crowd greeted them, people pouring out in spite of the rain and cold to see at long last the arrival of the laird and the bride.

There were so many of them, Marcus thought, filled with pride and secret awe. There were so many, here and scattered like stones over the mountains, all of them loyal and brave and fierce and hungry. They were his responsibility. They looked to him with shining faces and all Marcus ever saw there was hope, and a faith so deep it scared him to his bones.

He could not fail them.

The group of warriors came up to the edge of the castle wall, the horses at last on even ground, and his men spread out behind him. All of them faced the expectant throng of people.

Marcus carefully pushed Avalon forward a bit so he had room, then stood up in his saddle, keeping her in place.

"Clan Kincardine," he called out to them, his words frosting in the air, "I bring you your lass. I bring you the bride!"

Avalon looked up at last, cold and wet, still covered in golden leaves and streaks of dirt. "Go to the devil," she said to him, loud and clear.

The entire crowd erupted into cheers.

Chapter Five

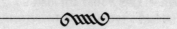

$\mathcal{S}$HE HAD REFUSED to undress in front of the women sent to attend her.

There were six of them. They had set up a tub of steaming water for her; they had placed sprigs of lavender and mint in it. They had clucked over her and brought her barley broth with gentle, blurring words.

Avalon wanted none of it. She wanted to be alone in this small room. She didn't want to succumb to the kindness of these women, because they were still her enemy, no matter how much lavender they had to offer.

But it seemed that even after everything she had been through last night and this morning, when her body was trembling with exhaustion and her mind kept fizzing to blankness, she could not be cruel to them.

She thanked them for the broth and the bath. She used the most normal voice she could muster when she told them she wanted to wash in privacy. When they had given each other bewildered frowns and tried to dismiss her words, she sharpened her tone, backing up and away until they had no choice but to leave.

As she was exiting, one of them picked up the tartan Avalon had discarded on the floor.

"I'll just rinse this for ye and set it to dry, mistress," the woman said, carrying it over her arm.

Oh well. It had been too wet to burn anyway.

The black gown was tight. It took a good while and several spells of sitting to clear her head before she had it off completely. Her shoulder throbbed from her efforts. But worse than that, she now saw, were her ribs. This was the real reason she had wanted the women to leave.

One look at the bruised, vivid mess of her side and they would have gone screeching to the laird, Avalon was sure. And she did not want the laird to know about this. God knew what he would want to do about it, and she still had some pride left.

She settled into the short tub of water slowly, allowing the heat to sink into her skin as she went, until her knees were up by her chin and the water to her neck. Fragrant steam reached up and tickled her nose, helping the blankness in her head to expand. Avalon's eyes slowly closed. Her head leaned back against the tin edge. Everything faded away.

When she woke up the water was considerably cooler, so she found the cake of scented soap they had left her and began to scrub, starting with her hair and working down, until all the dirt was gone. She stood up, took the pitcher of clean water that had been placed beside the tub, and poured it over her head.

There was a white woolen nightgown on the pallet, sturdy and warm, a tiny embroidered collar rimming the neck. She got it on just as the women returned with beaming smiles and a mug of something hot and delicious for her to drink.

Avalon took it from them, and only after she had finished the buttered ale did they tell her it was from the Moor, and that he had wished her a pleasant sleep.

Dammit. The room began to lose its shape. The women led her to the pallet and laid her down as carefully as they could manage, touching her side only twice. But the pain seemed distant now, Balthazar's drug smothering it.

There was nothing she could do but give in to it. As the sun began to break free of the clouds and saturate the room with gradual light, Avalon surrendered to sleep, letting out only the smallest of sighs at the end of her long journey.

⟞⟝

WHEN SHE OPENED HER EYES again the light in the room looked exactly the same, and for a moment Avalon was confused. She knew where she was, she remembered all of the past few days, but had she slept at all? Hadn't the wizard given her some potion?

She sat up and stretched her good side, taking care with her sore shoulder.

"How do you feel?"

The deep voice came from a corner of the room, a place where the sun had not yet touched. Marcus stepped forward into the light.

He had changed in small ways. He wore a tartan that was clean and crisp, a black tunic beneath it. His dark hair was tied back neatly. That tremendous sword he carried caught a sunbeam and let it slide down its polished sheath, sharp blindness.

She rubbed her eyes against the metallic light, turned her head away.

Marcus looked down at her, then glanced at something in his palm she could not see. He frowned down at it, then back to her, considering. She knew then what he held.

It had not helped to quell the legend that there existed a miniature painting of the comely wife of the hundred-year-old laird, and that she had resembled Avalon to an uncanny degree. The wife was said to have been the daughter of nobility, and in the painting, as Avalon recalled, she looked it: her gown was rich with elaborate embroidery, she wore a necklace of hammered gold.

"Impressive," said Marcus, holding his frost-blue eyes on Avalon again.

"Coincidence," she replied.

Marcus handed her the framed oval without comment, letting her see for herself. She took it reluctantly, not wanting to give him the satisfaction of agreeing with him. But she knew the woman in the painting did favor her, even when she was a young girl the similarity had been remarkable. Avalon had not forgotten.

If she had not been shown the miniature back then, she would have now thought it was painted as a trick, to convince her of the Kincardine fable. The laird's wife had Avalon's face, her very own. Those were her eyes, their strange shade of purple quite clear. Her own silver-blonde hair—in the painting loose, with a delicate band of gold across her forehead—her own black lashes. Even her own lips, with their distinctive cupid's bow.

And this was the face of her ancestress, her grandmother she didn't know how many times back.

To solidify the curse, there had come a plague a few years after the death of the wife, or so the story had been told to Avalon. This plague killed only the children, left the heartbroken parents untouched and frantic. Many scrambled away from the area, taking what few youngsters remained to safer grounds, trying to save the future of the clan. Eventually most came back, after the threat was seen as gone. But some never did, blending in to other places, and among these people had been the line that eventually led down to Avalon's mother, and to Avalon herself.

Marcus read her thoughts, or guessed them. "You are the daughter of the clan, after all. I believe it was—who again?—our great, great, great grandmothers who were sisters. That would make you and me . . ."

"Cousins," she finished for him flatly. "I find I have too many cousins for my taste."

She stood up and handed the portrait back to him. He gave her a cold smile.

"I think it's fate," he said. "But you never answered me. How do you feel?"

She walked away across the stone floor in her bare feet, only now remembering that she had on just a nightgown, and not really caring. There was a narrow window set back in the wall, and she crossed over to it and looked out onto a cloudless day.

"I feel as if I could sleep a thousand years," she said to the sky.

"I think two days will have to be enough," Marcus said behind her.

"Two days?"

"Aye. You would not rouse. We let you be. I suppose you needed the rest."

A hawk soared by, hovering and then dipping down to the bottom of the window frame, gone from sight.

"I saved your life," Avalon said, still looking out. "Honor dictates you owe me a boon."

"What boon?" he asked.

"Release me, my lord."

His voice was impartial. "Your boon is impossible, my lady."

"I saved your life!" Her hands clenched on the window frame. The sky was a bowl of sapphire blue; it stretched out to forever before her, just beyond her reach.

"Your mistake, then, for I'm not releasing you. That's the way of war."

Avalon uncurled her fingers. "I see how it is," she said at last. "Very well. I have three manored estates and most of the income from Trayleigh. I have lands that reach almost to the border of your country."

She heard him stir, come closer to her, though he made no move to touch her.

"There is enough of everything to keep your sense of war satisfied, I would think. Lands and wealth. I offer it all to you. I will petition the king myself to hand it to you. I will sign whatever notes you want. Make it a ransom, if you wish." She turned around now, sunlight behind her. "Only let me go."

He was closer than she had thought, not even an arm's length away. She couldn't read what he was thinking. There was a barrier up, there was nothing but cool deliberation in his look.

"Not enough," he said.

"Crops, herds, rent. Fine manors. All of it yours, your people's."

"Not enough."

"It's all I have," she said faintly.

"No."

Now he did reach out to touch her, just her hair, picking up a strand and holding it in the sunlight, letting it wrap around his fingers. He studied it, the halo the sun made bouncing off of it, as if it were worthy of his undivided attention.

"It's not all you have," he said slowly, looking up and capturing her gaze.

She was drowning again, instantly, hopelessly, and his lips were on hers, tender and hot, his hands were stroking her back, feather touches. He was pulling her into him, and she was welcoming it, all of it. All of him.

The nightgown shielded almost no secrets from him, let her feel the doubled folds of his tartan, the tunic, and beneath that, the hard planes of his body. The heat of him bled into her until her whole being was glowing with it, the slow nectar of his kisses, their breath mingling. She was alive again, she was awake and alive and *he* did this, this man, her enemy. . . .

Marcus handled her carefully, mindful of her shoulder, now smoothing his hand down her back to cup her bottom, lifting her, making that intimate part of her press into him to feel how ready he was for her.

"This is what I want," he said against her lips. "This." He pushed her hair aside and brought his lips to the delicate spot beneath her ear. "Can't you tell, Avalon?"

She couldn't say yes, or no, or anything. He had taken

her body and turned it into molten glass. All that she was flowed around him, into him, his arms and chest and thighs, that hardness between them. She wanted more of him. She had to satisfy this craving in her that was new and totally controlling.

It didn't matter who he was. It didn't matter who she was. All that mattered was that he kept touching her.

"You want it too, don't you?" He took his hand and placed it on her breast, something no man had ever done, and she loved it, she arched into it.

"Don't you." It wasn't a question, he knew the answer already. His fingers found her nipple, he rubbed the gown over it in circles.

She couldn't stop the moan that came. Pleasure shot from where he touched all the way through her, like another bolt of lightning.

He kissed her again, harder now, a different intent to it, shifting his hands down and then sweeping her up suddenly into his arms.

And now she couldn't stop the tiny cry that came, and it was not from pleasure. Her ribs were crushed amid their bruises.

Marcus heard the difference and paused uncertainly.

"What is it?" he asked, frowning down at her.

"Put me down," she managed to say around clenched teeth.

He eased her to her feet, careful again. "That wasn't your shoulder. You're injured, aren't you?"

"No," she said, trying to stand up straight without much success. He gave her a keen look, his gaze going right to where she had inadvertently put her hand on her side.

"Let me see," he said, reaching for her.

"No!" Avalon backed up quickly.

All traces of softness in him had vanished. The man who walked toward her now was purely the laird again, a mantle of winter around him.

"You have a choice," the laird said to her. "Take off the gown and show me your pain, or I will do it for you."

Avalon knew she could not win. "Turn your back," she snapped.

He did, folding his arms across his chest as he waited. At least it was only one side of her that was useless, Avalon thought, pulling off the gown with the hand that worked. She picked up a blanket from the pallet, wrapped it around her so that only her ribs would show, and sat down.

"Fine," she said sullenly.

Marcus knelt and examined the spreading bruise, his face revealing nothing. It looked awful, she knew, growing more colorful with the passing of time.

"It looks worse than it is," she said.

He leaned back on his heels, not replying. His face was perfectly empty.

The chimera sounded a warning, alert,

"I cannot believe you rode the rest of the way to Sauveur like this," he finally said. There was a frigid undertone to his voice that went much deeper than his outer calm; it struck a previously unknown chord of fear in her.

She stared over at him, suddenly, horribly aware that she was nearly nude with the man who had kidnapped her, who had almost managed to seduce her—and that he was utterly furious. God in heaven, what had she been thinking?

"It doesn't hurt," she whispered.

"No?" He reached out to touch the bruise and without meaning to she flinched. His hand stopped, not touching her. His voice was ice. "Doesn't hurt? Don't lie to me, Avalon. I will not abide it."

I will not abide it.

Hanoch's words to her, countless times. *Don't be disrespectful, don't complain, don't cower, don't snivel, don't cry. I will not abide it.*

"Won't you," she sneered, scrambling up and away despite the pain. "You have no right to tell me what to do! I don't care who you are! You don't own me!"

Marcus made no move to go after her. She was panting and clutching the blanket to her as she balanced on the mess of the pallet. Her hair had tumbled down everywhere; even as she stood she had to keep one hand on her side, as if to hold in the sharp ache.

"Nay, I don't own you," he agreed, watching her hand, then moving his gaze up to her face. "Not yet, Avalon. But I will very soon."

He left the room. She heard the lock turn and catch. She was a prisoner, after all.

Fifteen minutes later came the same women as before, this time bearing a load of bandages and a salve that they insisted upon applying themselves.

She could not refuse them. She was tired, for one thing. Still so tired. And also they were genuinely concerned for her. They patted her with compassionate hands and persuaded her to sit, exclaimed over her bruises and rubbed in the greasy salve.

Also from the Moor, Avalon was told. It had done great things for other members of the clan, they assured her. Betsy had been kicked by a sick ewe, and this very salve healed her within days! Ronald had his skull half cracked open from that fall of his in the gorge, and now he was better than ever!

And don't forget the mare, added one of the women happily. That old mare had been colicky for days, and she was fine after the Moor put his salve on her belly.

"Oh, well, the mare, then," Avalon said, trying not to shrink from their touch. "I'm sure it must be a fine salve."

"Aye," chorused the women, delighted she understood.

The bandages made the black gown too tight to fit around her now, and half her nursemaids fled to secure something a little more befitting for the bride. The other three picked up their bowl of salve and the rest of the bandages, folding them up between them.

Marcus had left the miniature of the laird's wife. He had probably forgotten it in his anger, Avalon thought, and tried not to feel woeful. She cradled it between her palms, studying the painted face that was her own.

One of the women noticed, sidled over to her, and made the inevitable comparison.

"A miracle," she breathed, looking at the painted lady.

The other two came close, solemn.

"Our miracle," said one.

"Our bride," finished the other.

"Please," Avalon began, and they looked at her, hushed, expectant of spectacular pearls of wisdom, no doubt. She took a breath, wanting to dispel this fantasy, but unwilling to crush their fragile hopes.

"She was my ancestress," she said at last, a pathetic attempt to concede to the conflicts within her.

The woman with the bandages picked up the miniature, handling it like treasure. "We know, lassie. We know."

⚬᷈ᨓᨓᦰᦰ⚬

Ⓗᴇ OWED HER A BOON. Marcus knew he did, and it hurt him in some way that he could not give her what she wanted.

He had no memory of what happened after the lightning split the oak. In the seconds before it struck he had felt a clap of humming air hit him, burning his lungs and making the hair on his arms stand up. But that was it. After that, he was beneath the pine tree, and Bal had been examining his head.

Hew filled in the gaps, how he had lain beneath the wild beast and the bride had tamed it, had run right up to it and calmed it with her touch. Hew looked to Bal for confirmation and Bal had agreed, wiping his hands free of mud.

"We tried to stop her," Hew said. His eyes shone with admiration. "But she wouldna stop. She took down Tarroth, tripped him as easy as ye would a child."

"Ach," said Nathan, standing beside them. "It was a glorious sight."

Marcus wished he had been awake to see it, the warrior maiden felling his mightiest man. With a dislocated shoulder and broken ribs, no less.

And Avalon had ridden without complaint three

more hours like that, hiding her pain, keeping her thoughts mute.

Marcus sighed, rubbed his chin, and looked out over the view of the green and gold horizon from the turret at the top of his castle. Patches of scarlet already embellished some of the trees.

It had made him sick to set her shoulder. Physically sick. He knew that he had to do it, he knew there were no options. But the sight of her face, pale and resolute beneath that pine, and then with the line of blood coursing down the side of her mouth from where she had bitten her lip, because she wouldn't scream, he knew Hanoch had trained her never to scream. . . .

Marcus had hated himself then, that he had to hurt her and hurt her to save himself and his people. When it was over he had to leave before he embarrassed himself, before he fell to his knees and begged her forgiveness.

It was a cowardice in him, and how those monks and priests in Damascus would have loved to learn of it. Thank God he hadn't known Avalon then. It would have broken him. It would have been the thing they had been seeking all along.

"She will recover," said Balthazar, coming up behind him, the wind catching his robes and turning them into moving flags of color. Balthazar had seemed almost unconcerned when Marcus told him of Avalon's ribs. Bal had produced the salve and said there was no great cause for alarm, broken ribs mended easily enough. Marcus knew it. His own ribs had not gone without almost half a dozen breaks in the past seventeen years, but on Avalon how devastating it had looked.

"She has great strength with her pride," Bal said now, beside him in the turret, allowing himself the smallest smile.

Marcus gave a short laugh. "She is her own worst enemy. She could have died from it. She could have had bleeding inside her."

"It is true," Bal conceded. "But even if that had been so, then knowing of it would not have changed the outcome. If she had been bleeding inside, she would have died anyway." He let out a whistle, a perfect sparrow's song, and then nodded to himself. "She is a woman unlike any other."

"She is going to kill me," Marcus replied.

Balthazar laughed, truly laughed, one of the few times Marcus had ever heard him do it. "Oh, not quite, Kincardine. She will not kill you. But she will temper you, I think. Yes, as a strong fire does to iron." He shrugged. "It is a good thing."

"Not for the one in the fire," Marcus muttered.

Bal clapped him on the shoulder. "You will survive."

There was a flock of sheep decorating the side of the hill immediately west of Sauveur. There were three dogs barking in the distance around them, running, circling, moving the herd.

There were fields of stubble as far as he could see, shorn crops already brought in for the coming winter. There was even a cluster of cows in a meadow, a precious few, supplying milk and cheese and finally beef only when they died on their own. They could not afford to slaughter the cows.

Avalon had offered him all her possessions, not once but twice now. Just a fraction of her wealth would be like a magic wish granted here. The clan would rise from an impoverished existence to a state approaching lavishness. Sauveur could afford some long-needed repairs. The stables could be improved, expanded. They could offer barter at all the fairs, they could buy the extra looms needed to make their woolen trade profitable. They could keep herds and herds of cows. Beef every night. They would surpass all the neighboring clans in riches.

But he had told her it wasn't enough.

Under the pine tree, rain-soaked and on her knees, she had said that she hated him.

Marcus hoped it had been the pain in her saying it. He hoped it wasn't true. Because what he felt for her was nothing like hate, nothing at all. It was admiration. Respect. Desire.

Ah, yes, desire. That was what had been talking in him when he rejected her offer. He could claim it was practicality. He could tell himself that he had been considering the welfare of the clan, how broken they would be with the loss of the bride, after waiting a century for her. But that wasn't truly it. Marcus had turned away her plea because he—just him—was unable to let go of her. Not without bedding her first. And he would not bed her without wedding her. It was the least he could do.

To hell with the legend. He wanted Lady Avalon the woman, not the myth. He would have her, or die trying.

"I sense a storm brewing," said Balthazar, scanning the mountain peaks and valleys.

"What, are ye daft?" It was Ronald, passing by and overhearing the remark. "The sky is empty, man."

"A different sort of storm, my friend," replied Bal,

with a significant look to Marcus, who nodded in acknowledgment before walking away.

He found his way back to the room he had assigned her, greeted the guard he had chosen to watch her door.

"Terrible quiet in there, it is," said the guard, indicating the door. "Mayhap she's asleep."

"Mayhap," Marcus said, and took the brass key from the ring at his waist and opened the lock.

She was sitting cross-legged on the hearth in front of the fire, which gave off an indolent heat in the stone room. Her back was stiff and straight, her hands rested on her knees. She stared into the fire, not looking up as he entered.

Marcus closed the door carefully, then just stood there. He didn't know why he had come back. There were other things to do right now, the endless details of running the castle and the lands; he had been away too long, he needed to familiarize himself with the routine. And there was the wedding to plan. He must consider that, how soon he could manage it, how soon until she would not be protesting their union in front of everyone there. . . .

He found himself observing the rise and fall of her sides, the rhythm of her breathing. It was slow, almost sleepy. She was dressed in the tartan again, and it masked much of the movement. Her hair had been braided into a single thick plait that fell down her back and coiled onto the hearth. A slash of bright orange across her back told him she wore the sling Bal had fashioned for her arm.

"Ask of me a different boon, my lady," he said into the silent room.

"A different boon?" she echoed, her voice thin and far away, as if the words were an enigma to her.

"I will grant it if I can." He crossed to the hearth, stood awkwardly for a moment, then gave it up and squatted in the eastern way, which was much more comfortable to him. She lifted her eyes and threw him one violet glance, then lowered her head.

"I know not what," she said.

Neither did he.

"A gem," he suggested. "A pearl. A favored serf to join you here."

Her laugh was muffled, as if it had hurt her too much to do it. "I do not need gems or pearls. I have no favored serf."

"Who was that girl with you at the inn? That night at Trayleigh? What of her?"

Her hands were clasped together in front of her. She turned her whole head this time, gave him a level look. "That girl is content where she is, my lord. I would not bring her here."

"She named you Rosalind." Marcus smiled at the memory. "It did not suit you."

"She was afraid. I do not blame her. She took a great risk for me that night."

"What risk?"

Avalon pressed her lips together. She seemed about to tell him something, then changed her mind. "She took me to see a woman who had cared for a friend of mine."

"What was the risk?"

"Come, my lord," she said. "It was risk enough to steal out of that castle for even a moment. My cousin would have risen to a rage had he heard of it. He had other plans for me, as you well know."

"Aye, I do know." Marcus watched her face closely. He had to ask the question that had been haunting him. "And tell me this, Avalon. Would you have wed Warner d'Farouche willingly?"

She let out another of those little laughs. "It would never have come to that, I assure you."

"But would you?"

"Nay, of course not," she scoffed, and Marcus felt the power of her conviction. "He was naught but a bumbling fool, a servant of his brother. I had never even met him before that night."

Satisfaction coursed through him; he couldn't help it, he couldn't stop it, and he didn't try to understand what it meant. She had not been a part of that plan. She didn't want Warner over him.

"I shall never marry," she said now in a perfectly normal voice, as if she were saying a wheel was round.

"That might be difficult," he said. "Since I have over a thousand people and a family prophecy that say you will."

"I don't see how you're going to do it, my lord." Her look was amused. "You cannot force a bride if she does not wish it."

He unfolded out of his posture, leaned over on his hands and came up close to her face in one quick movement. Her eyes widened; she pulled back.

"I think you wish it," he said.

A hot blush was stealing up her cheeks. "I do not!"

"I think so." He let his gaze linger on her lips, deep

pink, erotic curves. "I know what you feel, Avalon. I know what happened to you today, when you kissed me back. I know"—he came even closer, not touching her—"what you want. Because I want it too."

Her breath was quickening, her eyes tinged to match her amethysts in the afternoon light. He bent down even lower, letting his lips hover over hers, so close they took in the same air.

"It is inevitable."

She scooted back, putting room between them.

"Marriage has nothing to do with this," she said.

He raised his brows.

"It is an aberration," she said very quickly. "It means naught. It is not grounds for marriage."

"Ah." He came to his feet smoothly and walked over to a small table. "I will not argue with my lady. Let us say, for the moment, that you are correct. It has nothing to do with marriage."

She watched him warily, unmoving.

"But I think even you will agree that something that *does* have to do with marriage is a betrothal contract, such as the one between our fathers."

Avalon looked away.

"Legal," Marcus said, leaning against the table. "Established. Binding. Recognized by not merely one king but two."

There was nothing she could say to this besides the fact that she did not care, but he already knew that.

"In this instance, I believe, I do not need your consent to wed you, Lady Avalon. Your fate has already been decided for you. Our betrothal has been granted royal approval. I'm certain I would have no difficulties finding a man of the church who would be willing to marry us over any objections you may have."

Her blush drained away. "You would not."

"I don't see why not." He gave a careless shrug. "If you will not act sensibly, you leave me no choice. You will have no one but yourself to thank for your situation. Rethink your stubbornness, Avalon."

He was bluffing. He had no desire to force her into a wedding. In fact, he was fairly certain there was no way she *could* be wed against her will. He needed her cooperation to have a legal ceremony. And besides, when the challenge from Warner came—and Marcus was sure it would—his own claim would be much stronger if he had a compliant bride.

"I will let you consider my words, my lady. You must rest now. I pray you feel better very soon."

He pushed off the table and went to the door, knocking twice for the guard to unlock it. He bowed to her before he left. She had not moved from her perch on the hearth. But there would be fire in her eyes, he knew that.

"I should have let the horse have you," he heard her say as he shut the door.

He had gone in to grant her a boon, and come out handing her an ultimatum. Marcus shook his head at his own impulsiveness. Bal had been right about that looming storm.

Chapter Six

⌒⌒⌒⌒⌒

SHE STAYED IN THE ROOM another two whole days, not quite pacing in the confining space, not even going mad with boredom—for she had visitors aplenty.

There were her caring women, as Avalon had begun to think of them, the six who fussed over her and sighed and petted her. But behind them were a legion more, men and women both, all of them coming to the room on some pretense or another, or none at all, just to watch her, to study her as if she were a fabulous ancient mystery.

She had not known any of them when she lived in the cottage in the remote village. Her contact with others had been strictly controlled. But apparently they had all known of her, and each made certain to tell her—each in their own way—how delighted they were that she was here at last.

Tegan, the castle cook, wanted to know what the bride might like for her meals.

Hew, Sean, Nathan, and David—all in Marcus's guard—loitered their way around the room before gathering enough courage to ask her how she had escaped the giant Tarroth that terrible night in the storm, and then spent the next hour practicing her elemental combination of moves in front of her until each of them had it right.

Tarroth himself, come to ask the same question without the companionship of his peers, frowning down at her, repeating her moves until she relented and showed him a way to counter it.

Ilka, chatelaine of Sauveur, and her three daughters—who stayed in a row and stared up at Avalon with identical pansy eyes—making certain she had enough furs on her pallet, that the hearth was well swept, that the black gown beneath the tartan was not uncomfortable.

And many more, all of them deferring to her as if she were a queen and not the injured captive of their laird. The one overwhelming emotion Avalon caught from them, the one common link that each shared, was excitement bordering on joy. It bubbled up around them as they spoke to her in respectful tones. It glimmered in the room after they left. Even Tarroth had bowed to her with respect, feeling no resentment toward the woman who had defeated him with seeming simplicity. He was proud, in fact, that he had been the one chosen for the display of her battle skills.

They all believed in this story of the laird and the wife and the devil, Avalon realized. They believed it with every ounce of their being, just as much as Hanoch had, this silly superstition, this impossible fable.

The women became more forward over the course of the days. They sat beside her and asked her opinion on hundreds of things, why a husband would do this, how to best punish a child about that. Did my lady think the pigs would breed again this season? There was one sow with a gleam in her eye. . . .

Someone's husband had strained his back before the harvest. He had been unable to do his share of the work.

Would my lady grant the family an extra measure of oats for pity?

Half the grain in the northern fields had spoiled due to some mysterious black growth on the stems. Did my lady think it the work of the devil? Would my lady be able to change the crop for them? Would she bring them new grain from her bounty?

The salmon this year had been scarcer than ever. Would my lady bring up her own sheep from England, to last them through this winter?

She was terrified, she was appalled. What to say to them? Avalon tried to tell them she was not qualified to give them answers, but it was as if her apologetic denial was an expected reply; so they would wait for it to subside and then begin the tale again, this time hoping for a different response.

Avalon wavered between laughter and tears, unable to reconcile the image of herself she saw in the eyes of these fine people to the person she knew she was.

She was no icon. She was no queen, no living symbol to end their curse. It petrified her even to think about what they might expect of her. All she could do for them was offer a very material solution—her wealth—and Marcus had rejected even that.

When Balthazar arrived there were about twenty women in the little room, all clustered around the pallet Avalon had moved directly beneath the window. They had formed their own order of rank, from most important to least, and they took their turns seeking an audience with her ladyship, who sat on the furs and kept her hands together in a clasp not coincidentally resembling the supplication of prayer.

As the Moor stood in the doorway each face turned to him, each quickly looked to the others, then the women gathered their skirts and their entreaties and curtsied their way out.

"Already see how they love you," he said, coming forward and granting her a graceful bow.

"It's not me they love," Avalon said, rising from the pallet. "It's an idea. It has almost nothing to do with me."

Behind Bal appeared another man, taller, broader of shoulder. She knew who it was before he stepped into the room. She felt his presence with a delicious shudder, a secret pleasure followed by quick denial.

"Is she well enough to leave the room?" Marcus asked of Balthazar.

Bal raised his eyebrows at Avalon. "Is she?" he asked her, wry.

She didn't know what to say. She wanted to go out so badly that the need was a painful knot in her throat, and yet if she seemed too eager, would they back away? Avalon gazed at the Moor in torment, unable to reply.

Marcus walked over to her, looked down at her with eyes that reminded her abruptly of a caged wolf she had seen long ago: intense and glowing and untamed.

"Come," he said, and offered his arm.

She took it because the knot insisted that she did. The walls of the room had been steadily growing closer over the course of the last two days, the narrow window had not been enough to spare her from the old feelings of spiraling suffocation. She would have done almost anything to escape it.

They walked down the hallway and out to the great hall of Sauveur, enormous and cold, with black and gray pillars of stone holding up the mighty arches above, a fire roaring in each of the four fireplaces set back in the walls. There were tables and benches of smooth, dark wood. There were colorful tapestries and heraldry hanging from high above.

Scattered autumn leaves clung to the floor by the main entrance. A crisp breeze blew in, pushed back the wisps of hair by her face.

Beside her, Avalon felt something in Marcus pause, lost in a memory, though he kept their pace steady.

People who saw them stopped whatever they were doing and stared at the couple, most of them breaking into broad smiles, a few of the women dabbing tears away.

Terrifying, what they were thinking. Infeasible. Avalon couldn't believe it, the reckless hope the mere sight of her engendered.

Our bride, they all thought, and with it came a crushing realization. She was everything bright to them now. She was one half of the magic ending of the bitterness of their lives, and the other half was the new laird, home at last. Against her will she began to understand some of what Marcus must be feeling, why he took the risk of abducting her.

Outside, the sky had that particular hue that came only with the precious few weeks between summer and winter. Deepest blue, pure and infinite, with occasional hints of snow-white clouds gliding over the horizon. The air was cool and lively, smelling of leaves and smoke and faraway waters.

It felt refreshing and welcome, like an old friend who had been away too long. It was so familiar to her. It felt like . . . home.

Of course it was familiar, Avalon chided herself. It was the same as every other autumn she had spent up in the Highlands. She had not needed to be at Sauveur itself to experience a Scottish turn of seasons. That was all it was.

She had tried to rest her hand lightly on Marcus's arm, but it was so much easier just to relax and let him take her meager weight, to release the stiffness of her shoulder to him, allowing their movements to flow together. She had nothing to lose with this small concession, Avalon thought.

The land around Sauveur was wild at the edges, the pastures and fields that had been cleared of trees and boulders were hemmed on all sides with heavy forest, mountain grass, and chunks of white quartz.

Marcus led her down a well-trod path, gathering people behind him on the way. The wizard was keeping a respectful distance, followed by a growing tail of others, mostly children, drawn to the spectacle.

He had to hear the whispers, Avalon thought, looking up at Marcus only once. He had to hear the voices behind them, saying their names. But he kept his face even, his steps firm and unbroken. He seemed a man with a purpose. Avalon knew this was more than just a leisurely stroll for her benefit.

He was showing her off—as sure as a man would display a prized new steed, he was offering her to his people.

Avalon tried to summon anger. But what came instead was a reluctant kind of approval. If she had been him, she would have done this as well. She would have taken whatever steps were necessary to encourage those depending upon her. She would have taken the figment of a legend and made it real herself, if she could have. And even this admission to herself made her afraid, for approving of the laird's actions was only a step away from willfully participating in them. And then Hanoch would have won.

They went to a glen, a sheltered place with a rolling pasture of wild grass and even a few white and yellow flowers, still clinging to life through the coming cold. The green grass waved with the illusion of silver outlines; it seemed to flow from a place of blue mist and dappled lands down a great mountainside, to spill into the circle of the small valley below. There were artfully tangled clusters of brambles in the valley. There were young girls with long hair and woven baskets collecting wool from the thorns of the bushes.

And on the side of the mountain, though Avalon had never seen it before, was the end of that wicked faerie of the legend, an incredibly humanlike formation of black rock amid the green and silver.

Avalon's steps slowed to a halt. She stared up at the figure.

It was easy to see why a legend might shape itself around these rocks. It would have been a giant faerie, thrice as big as a person if it were a fleshly form instead of stone. But otherwise, it indeed resembled a twisted, broken man, albeit one with the black wings of a crow spreading up and out from behind him. The shape of the head was clear, two arms—outflung—two legs. The wings. The green and silver grass not growing over any of the black stone body.

Avalon was clenching her jaw but was unaware of it

until she looked away and saw Marcus doing the same thing. The glen was silent. No birds, no insects. Even the breeze had settled to nothing. All the people around them were still.

Suddenly it seemed like truth to her. There really had been an evil faerie. The laird's wife was no myth but an actual woman, dishonored in this field. There was a vengeful laird. There was a devil. The curse was genuine.

The world took on a sickening curve. Outlines became distorted, blurred. A noise filled her ears, the sound of a man weeping. A terrible smell surrounded her, a stench so foul it made her want to retch. The air was unbearably hot and humid.

The man would not stop weeping, and he was saying words now, too: *Treuluf, my life, don't leave me. . . .*

Avalon sucked in her breath and the glen came spinning back to normal. The man was gone, his tragic voice—the smell that lingered was only the mountain air. Nothing seemed to have changed in that moment, everyone stood as before, looking at either the mark on the mountain or at the laird and his bride.

She was astonished. It had been so real! Yet no one else looked odd, no one else glanced around and back up to the black stone. Only Marcus gave her a hint that she might not have imagined it all. He took a deep breath and frowned, as if he too had caught the foul stench of something not right.

His look met hers.

"Sulphur," he said.

Her refusal was strong and immediate. It could not have been real.

"No."

His voice was low, meant only for her. "Another lie, Avalon?"

"It was an illusion." She matched his pitch. "Not real."

Now she got his chilly smile. "We have our ghosts everywhere up here, my lady, whether you believe in them or not."

The young girls in the glen had ventured closer, pale and hollow faced, and Avalon felt their wonder, their admiration, the soreness of their fingers, the wetness of their feet from the holes in their shoes.

She wanted to weep with the ghost laird she had heard. She wanted to weep for these children, who could not remember a night without feeling the pain from work, who had never even conceived of a bliaut with fine jewels scattered on it, much less dreamt of owning one. She wanted to weep for the scarce salmon, the ruined grain in the fields. Dear God, what would become of them?

Marcus released her arm, walked away from her to the collection of people behind them. He blended in right away, one tartan fading into the next, a sea of likeness filled with the unhesitant acceptance of its own.

The wool-gathering girls watched him go, adoration clear on each face.

Avalon was left to stand alone in the silver-green grass, the black faerie overlooking them all.

The wizard approached her, the two outsiders in this scene now standing together. He contemplated the glen, the brambles, the shaped rocks above them.

"A strange country," he finally said.

Avalon crossed her good arm over her stomach.

"Savage lands and brave people," he continued. "Mountaintops that seem to speak to God, should He will it. Magic and legends and strong liquor. It is a heady mix."

The breeze returned, whispering through the grass at their feet, turning the young girls back to their tasks at the brambles, though they did not stop looking from Marcus to Avalon.

Balthazar bent down and plucked a flower with bluish-white petals. "I have a question for you, lady. Will you answer it?"

Avalon watched his fingers amid the petals, dark against the light. "If I can," she said.

The wizard smiled. "A wise answer from an old soul. My question is this: What do you remember of this place?"

His words were already baffling. Avalon looked around, uncertain, then tried to explain. "Nothing. I never came here. Hanoch placed me in a village far to the north. I spent my time there."

"No, no," the wizard said, waving his hand in front of him as if to chase away her words. "Not from this lifetime. From before. What do you remember?"

"Not from this lifetime?" she echoed, confused. "I don't understand."

"Some people believe we come back to these bodies again and again. They say that each lifetime is a lesson to advance the soul to God."

She grasped the thought, considered the heretical content. "No heaven? No hell?"

The wizard smiled again; this time it was smaller, the

ends of his mouth almost tucked down with amusement. "That is a matter of fantastic debate. However, I
would think that the hell would be to continue to return
without learning the lessons."

The ghost had wept. His words had been tearing at
her, an unwilling participant in his anguish. The smell of
sulphur had been choking.

"What would be my lesson?" Avalon asked slowly,
half-believing as she looked down at the flower he held.

"Only you may say," Balthazar replied. "Only you
will ever know. It is in your heart of hearts. Look there
for your answer."

He gave her a small salute, placing his hands to his
forehead as he bowed, and then presented her with the
flower.

She took it, stared down at the symmetrical petals,
the velvet green stem. When she looked up again the
wizard was gone, making great strides down the hill
back to Sauveur. Marcus watched her from his crowd.

She turned from him to see the girls staring at her,
talking to each other without taking their eyes away.

Without warning Avalon found herself desperately
lonely, lonely in such a way as she had not experienced
since she was a child. Loneliness was her enemy, and she
had fought to banish it as fiercely as she had fought all
things that had wanted to quell her, from Hanoch on
down. Having it surround her now was not a welcome
experience.

There was a bramble bush nearby. She meandered
over to it, noting the fluffs of wool caught inside and out,
token remembrances of a careless ewe grazing nearby.

Her hand reached out for the nearest tuft. It came

loose from its thorn with ease, soft and light between her fingers. There was a bigger one just behind where it had been. She reached for it, as well. The thorn snagged her finger.

Avalon yanked her hand back and looked at the droplet of blood the thorn had drawn, irrationally close to tears.

"Oh, milady," said a girlish voice at her shoulder. "Ye must have a care with these. They will bite every time."

The girl clutched her basketful of fleece under her arm, then took Avalon's hand in her own, examining the scratch. The other girls abandoned their jobs, gathered near.

"Not so bad," pronounced one.

"Press out the bane," advised another.

"Aye," agreed the girl with Avalon's hand, and began to squeeze her finger until a full, round drop of scarlet was balanced on the wound.

"If ye leave it be, the nettle will sting awful," said the girl.

Avalon looked at her hand held firm in the smaller ones, noticed each of the other girls had cloth wrapped around their palms and down their fingers. Each of them bore scratches, many of them.

"I suppose I am not so gentle as to make the thorns bend back for me," she said, a feeble jest, and then regretted making light of their legend. But the girls took her seriously, shaking their heads and offering fast reassurances that she was surely as gentle as that first wife, but since the curse the thorns would have changed as well, no longer so pliant and kind.

It was a painful moment, knowing these trusting girls believed her to be a literal truth come to life, knowing that there was nothing she could do for them that would ever be truly worthy of their faith.

"What happened?" It was Marcus, come to see the reason for the crowd of girls.

"Nothing," said Avalon, gently disengaging her hand and placing the wool she had managed to gather in the first girl's basket.

They scattered like a flock of startled starlings, off into the bushes again.

Marcus's form blocked out the mountain, the black rock. He took her hand, solemn, and examined the scratch, the smeared droplet of blood.

"You must get the poison out," he said, lifting her finger to his mouth.

"I know," she began, but then his lips closed over her finger and he began to suckle the scratch gently.

She stood before him, spellbound, feeling the wild beating of her heart, the shocking, strange sensation of this man, his tongue against her finger, his lips soft and warm on her. His eyes were lowered, masking the winter blue with black, deepening their color.

There was no pain, only a heated pressure. The uniqueness of this intimate act quaked through her, stilling all thoughts until the only thing she could feel was his touch, the only thing she could see was his face.

He unmasked his eyes, locking her there in front of him, captivating her as surely as if he held her in chains. Avalon felt something shift inside of her, a reawakening of that liquid pleasure only he knew how to give to her.

It was matched in his eyes, a flame in the blue, masculine and powerful with shades of something she didn't want to think about. Something like possession.

"Better?" He spoke against her finger, still holding it close to his lips. He didn't wait for her to reply, but unfolded the rest of her fingers and opened her palm, bringing it back up to place a kiss there.

Her hand was burning, and a deep, shadowed thrill raced down her arm to the rest of her, making her lean even closer to him, to his magnetic heat.

Marcus watched her do it, holding her hand there, trailing kisses down to her wrist, over, letting go of her hand to cup her neck and bring her all the way to him.

The kiss was sweet and light, only an invitation to greater things, because they were there in the glen, and there were many who watched them, and because Marcus could not do what he really wanted, which was to lay her down on the meadow grass and love her completely. So he contented himself with that one kiss, a promise of what would come, before pulling away from her.

"Truelove," he murmured.

Avalon jolted back. "What?" she asked, stricken.

"Truelove," he repeated, than shook his head. "It is merely an endearment, my lady."

He had no idea where the word had come from. He had never used it before. He had never even heard anyone else use it, that he recalled. But it seemed a word made for her, fitting her just exactly, even if he had made it up. And it had had a definite effect on her—unfortunately, the wrong one. She roused out of that place where he had wanted her, came back to the facts of the glen and her own situation.

"It is *not* real," she said, looking past him to the faerie.

"Why not?" asked Marcus, following her look. "Why not, Lady Avalon? Surely stranger things have happened. It is a tragic tale, but rich in romance, don't you think? That's the redeeming quality of it. The high-born wife, wed for love—"

"Yes, and look where it got her," Avalon said darkly.

He began to escort her back down the meadow. "Aye, well," he conceded. "Mayhap not the happiest of endings, true. At least, not for the clan."

"Nor for her or her laird," Avalon said, thinking of the wizard's concept of returning to these bodies. If it were true, were the laird and his wife among them now? Would they find happiness now in completing their lessons?

Treuluf, the laird had called his dead wife.

"And what of this curse, my lord?" She interrupted her own line of thought. "Your people have not prospered, perhaps, but I would not say you were destitute. Clan Kincardine has power, I know it well. You have the ear of the king. You have connections in royalty. It took your King Malcolm a full year to capitulate to Henry for my return to my homeland. A whole year of defying another king, merely to please your family. I would not call that a curse."

He stopped her abruptly with a look that made her want to take back her words.

"Do you think this is an easy life, Avalon?" he asked, narrowing his eyes. "Would you wish this upon yourself? There is barely enough food for winter. There is barely enough wool to trade out. Even Hanoch could not manage a fortune that did not exist."

"Take my income," she said to him again, ashamed and then angry that she should feel so. She was not heartless. She felt for them all, the wool gatherers, the thin women, the proud men. She hated that they lived so close to want. She hated that he would think so poorly of her, think that she did not notice. "I offer it to you freely."

"I will, when we wed."

Beneath the hulk of the stone faerie Avalon at last lost her temper.

"I cannot marry you!" she shouted. "Don't you understand? I can't! You may have all but that!"

The people in the meadow grew still. A raven circled above them, landed in a tree and watched them all, cocking its head.

Marcus started to laugh.

It was slow at first, a deep chuckle that grew into an unmistakable sound, louder and louder until he was joined by others, a wave of mirth that buffeted her.

Avalon felt the heat rise in her cheeks. He was laughing because he was genuinely amused, she felt it clearly. And the others joined in from relief, that the laird would shrug off the temper of the willful bride, either from the ease of his own temperament or his acceptance of her place in the legend, that she was *supposed* to resist joining the family.

She marched off, heading back to Sauveur because she knew if she went in any other direction she would be forcibly halted, and she had had about enough embarrassment for one day.

He let her go. She felt him watch her all the way down the path, still chuckling.

People goggled at her. She saw a trace of pity in some of them, especially the women. A few of the faces looked too familiar.

Hanoch had kept the cottage household to a very few people. A chatelaine. A cook. Eight men who doubled as servants and guards. And Ian, of course. Even when Hanoch went back to Sauveur, Avalon had been unable to escape Ian.

Ian MacLochlan was not of the family, not really. He was the son of the third cousin of a Kincardine, from an allied clan, but the real reason Hanoch had so readily accepted him—indeed, welcomed him—was that Ian had a way of fighting that no man had been able to defeat. And Ian had become Avalon's tutor.

Where he learned his odd moves he would never say. All that was known was that he had traveled a great deal out of Scotland, had been to distant lands with names no one could pronounce. Many people claimed he made up the tales. That Ian was touched, that he had never been beyond even England. But no one could dispute his skill in hand-to-hand combat.

He was gray and cantankerous by the time the child Avalon had met him. Time had only increased these attributes. He had been a merciless instructor, as hard as Hanoch in his own way, the two of them sharing a pact to make this female into a prodigy of their own, to chisel out from the soft child the warrior maiden that the people needed.

Ian was dead. He had died just before she left Scotland, in fact, so she knew it to be true. Otherwise she might still have cringed at the sound of anything like his voice. Ian and Hanoch had been the ones to watch for. The guards had been constantly rotated, so she never became too close to them. The cook had not stayed in the cottage, having her own hut in the same village and her own family to care for.

The chatelaine had been her only companion, really. Zeva had been her name. Among the rows of faces Avalon saw now—all of them studying her so intently— no one resembled Zeva. Perhaps she was dead as well.

Only Zeva had shown her any compassion at all, secretly unlocking the stifling pantry when the men were not about, passing in food and water for the child trapped within. Only Zeva had shed a tear when Avalon left at fourteen, had bade her well and hoped to see her soon.

And Avalon, seasoned by then, had not responded to that wish. She knew better; indifference was her main defense, and she would not let go of it even for Zeva.

No, Zeva was not here, not in the meadow behind her, nor in the mass of people before her.

She didn't know what to feel about that. Would Zeva have laughed in the glen with the others? Or would she have stayed still, remembering the little girl with the blackened eyes and bruised body who hated the dark? Perhaps only Zeva could have understood her.

As she walked back to her castle prison, Avalon thought about how ironic it was that she had managed to carry her careful impassivity with her into her new life— until now. Until Marcus Kincardine: the one person she most needed her armor of indifference for had turned out to be the only one able to breach it.

A man on horseback was galloping toward her along the road to Sauveur. He was a Kincardine, his tartan waved straight out behind him like a marker.

He carried excitement, and the sight of him generated a new ripple through the crowd. He was one of the scouts, Avalon understood, piecing together the jumbled thoughts around her. If he was riding up to the castle this fast, there would be urgent news.

About her.

The scout was aware of the attention he garnered and part of him gloried in it, but most of him was absorbed in his duty. He had to find the laird. He had to tell him of the party of men approaching.

The chimera blinked and showed her a glimpse of what the scout had seen, about ten riders, three different standards between them, including Malcolm's own, which would protect them. The other two flags were unfamiliar to the watch, but not to Avalon. The royal crest of King Henry. The red cross of the papacy.

She felt the excitement of everyone else combined with her own, soaring up now for different reasons.

She would be saved! The kings and the church meant to save her!

Marcus had come down from the meadow. With a small gesture he had placed a guard around her where she stood, large men forming a tight circle.

The scout dismounted, bowed to Marcus, and began to talk. Around them clustered more people, men and women both. As the watch continued his tale the women gasped and looked at Avalon, and she felt their fear. The men were less demonstrative but equally worried.

Only Marcus seemed composed. He listened without

interrupting, nodding his head at the right times. When the scout had finished he said something to him and walked away, coming over to where Avalon stood in the middle of the circle of men.

"Take her back inside," he ordered, and then moved on.

Chapter Seven

~~~~~ ∾ᗢᘏᗢ∾ ~~~~~

*A*VALON DIDN'T HAVE TO RELY on the power of her chimera to tell the way matters were going just hours later. She gathered from the silence of the walls that all of Sauveur was riveted on the visiting emissaries: a man from each king, two men from the church, six guards between them.

Malcolm's guard had mingled readily with the castle inhabitants. They had accepted food and whiskey and seemed very merry, or so said Nora, one of Avalon's caring women. Nora bustled back and forth at the behest of the bride, soaking up whatever details she could and reporting them.

Her aide was Greer, another of the women, who said the laird had been in with the travelers for over a full hour now, and no one had heard any shouting or cursing.

"Mayhap they want only to see that ye be well treated," she suggested hopefully, gazing at the bride, who stood by the hearth.

"Mayhap," Avalon said, biting her tongue to stem the torrent of words that swelled up. Freedom! Rescue! Farewell to the legend!

Greer put a bowl of stew down on the sole table in the room.

"Have a wee bite," she said. "Ye must eat."

"I will."

But the woman would not be satisfied until Avalon had the bowl in her hands and took a spoonful. It had no taste to her but she complimented it anyway, which contented Greer.

After the woman left, Avalon put the food down again and walked to the window, standing with one foot on the pallet to look out. The thin clouds of before had swollen with rain and turned the color of spent charcoal, portending another shower. The cold air came through the opening and brushed against her, only slightly cooling the flush of her skin.

It would be over soon. The emissaries were demanding her release, and sooner or later Marcus would have to give in.

She would leave here and never return. She would find her convent, retire there and wait for the right time to return to Trayleigh. . . .

An uncomfortable memory intruded upon Avalon's dreams.

The wool-gathering girl in the glen had been truly upset by Avalon's injury on the thorn. She had dismissed her own discomfort to see to the bride. Something that happened to that girl every day would not be endured for Avalon, and the girl had felt the bride's pain almost as her own.

Avalon would send aid to Sauveur. She would send sheep, coin, grain, whatever she could. She would not abandon the clan entirely. She knew now that she could not. They could not be held responsible for the travesty of her childhood, nor for the ways of their old laird. Not even for the myth that had sustained them.

She would help them. But she would do it from England.

The door opened. It was the wizard, bowing low as he always did.

"You are summoned, lady," he said. "Will you come?"

At last.

She had not seen most of the castle, and the halls she was taken down now were new to her, though they kept to the style of the great room. Arched ceilings. Pillars of black and gray. Most of the doors were closed, and at the end of the largest hall they paused outside one of these doors. There were men everywhere, women on the fringes. Avalon spotted Nora near the back, chatting softly with another woman. Mostly, however, the people were silent, straining to catch the sounds behind the door.

They parted into halves as the wizard led her forward. Two sets of guards stood ready at the door, Englishmen from Henry, Scots from Malcolm. Malcolm's men were relaxed against the wall, looking ready for more whiskey. Henry's were staunch and straight, alert and unhappy. They noticed her at once, boldly took in the beauty whose plight had disturbed such crowned and holy heads.

Avalon went to the door and opened it herself, stepping past the startled guards.

Four men were seated at a long table of polished

wood. Behind them were two more guards, from the church this time, heavily armed. Marcus stood in front of them all, and before she could take another step into the room, Avalon was hit with the sensation of danger brewing around her.

Marcus was so furious he was almost in a rage. It was like a writhing, twisting snake around him; it was a wrath so deep, so sunken into him it was on the verge of breaking him in front of her very eyes. He emanated it, he was becoming it.

She froze, realizing there was something here that no one else could see. Not the guards, not the smug-faced men at the table. Not even the wizard.

Marcus was a man on the brink of collapse. He was about to splinter into a thousand slivers and what would be left might not be controllable. And the guards would hack him down before his own men could interfere.

Instinctively Avalon knew Marcus's snake was different from her own burden: the chimera stayed within her but had never overtaken her like this; in fact, the chimera was harmless in comparison. But the snake had completely captured the man. It was about to destroy him.

Avalon didn't know what to do. Thoughts of her own rescue receded, until all she knew was Marcus and the demon snake that was invisible to everyone but her.

He heard her enter and turned his head. The snake stared out at her from Marcus's eyes, uncomprehending, a beast without forethought.

Against her will her feet brought her forward to him. She stared down the snake and then looked to the other

men, the emissaries of Malcolm and Henry and the two
men from the church.

The men from the church. Here was the danger, she
perceived. Here was the cause of the demon.

They wore the heraldry of the righteous, white tunics with red crosses stitched into them, chain mail beneath. They were not too old, not too young, carrying
identical expressions of prim lips, sanctimonious eyes.
They seemed innocuous enough. But they had done
something, all right, to bring out this menace in Marcus.

"Lady Avalon d'Farouche?" one of them asked,
giving her name a nasal cast.

The snake in Marcus rolled over, constricted its coils.

"Yes," Avalon replied. She drew up even with Marcus,
let him see her easily from the corner of his eye. It
seemed important that he be able to see her.

Henry's emissary leaned forward and pointed to the
orange sash that supported her arm. "Have you been injured, my lady?"

Marcus focused on the man, his mounting wrath
redirected.

"It was an accident," she replied. "It was nothing."

"Why then the sling?" asked the pope's man.

She shrugged. "Merely a precaution. I don't really
need it."

All four looked at her, unconvinced. Henry's man
stroked his beard. Avalon felt the snake tighten another
notch.

It would not take very much more to break him. She
didn't have to look at Marcus to see the process begin.
She could feel it as if it were happening to her own

body: the danger bleeding into his muscles, the primal threat growing darker, darker, to blackest rage. It made her heart race and her breath seem cold, stabbing.

She couldn't let him die like this, not for this. Not because of her.

Avalon feigned nonchalance, slipped her arm out of the sling and flexed it in front of her, looking bored. Her shoulder howled in protest. She took the orange sash and dropped it to the ground, proud of the smoothness of her movement.

"I am fine," she said to the men.

"Lady Avalon," said the elder of the pope's men. "We have it that you were abducted by force and brought here against your will. Is this true?"

"Yes," she said, after the barest pause.

"Warner d'Farouche has petitioned the church with an official complaint. He claims to have a prior agreement with you, my lady. Is this true as well?"

"A prior agreement?" She hesitated longer now, searching for the best option.

Marcus turned to her. She looked back at him, drawn in despite her facade of tranquility, and saw that the snake was about to rise.

Perhaps the other men began to sense the peril. The elder man of the church spoke again.

"We would speak with you in private now, my lady."

"Nay," said the snake, swift and menacing.

"We will have a private audience with the lady, my lord!" Henry's man had unwisely chosen to stand, daring Marcus to argue.

It took her only a fraction of a second to put her hand on his arm, and it was almost too late, anyway. She felt

his muscles tensed and ready to spring, lethal n̠...
ating from him.

"My lord," she said, and sent the thought with
her mind.

It broke his concentration for the second she needed.
His pale eyes flew back to her, a moment's uncertainty.

"I would make this my boon, my lord," she said, quiet.

The snake wavered, weakened by her request. Avalon
pushed her advantage, seeking the man she knew was
listening to her. "You said you would grant me it."

The other men said nothing, all of them closely
watching the scene.

"It is not so much to ask." Avalon looked around, behind her, seeking inspiration, and found the figure of the
wizard lingering by the door. "Leave him here with me,
if you do not trust what I may say." She nodded her head
to Balthazar, then turned back to the men. "I am certain
that would be acceptable, would it not, my lords?"

"Aye." Malcolm's man spoke for the first time. His
look down the table challenged the others. "It would."

Still Marcus did not move away, not until Bal came up
beside him and deferentially made his unique bow with
his hands to his head. Marcus stared down at him, fists
clenched.

Bal said something in a strange language, flowing
words that ran together, and Marcus turned back to the
men, inclined his head stiffly, then left.

It would be better now, Avalon thought. The snake
had slipped enough in its hold, and the man would take
over once more. The next time she saw him he would
be whole again. She felt her body slowly begin to
unclench.

"What manner of man are you?" demanded one of the churchmen, taking in Balthazar's tattoos and darkened skin.

"Naught but a servant, your grace, from the Holy Land," the wizard replied, and Avalon wondered that they could not fathom the contradiction in his words.

But they didn't. The man waved a hand at Balthazar, dismissing him to a corner.

"From the Kincardine's crusade," clarified the other churchman, and the kings' men looked comprehending.

The wizard bowed again and retreated, disappearing into the shadows.

"Lady Avalon," said the elder churchman, the one who had not recognized the regal bearing of a wizard. "Your cousins, Lord d'Farouche and his brother Warner d'Farouche, have pleaded a grievance with the majesties of England and Scotland and His Holiness the Pope. They claim you have been wrongfully taken from them. They claim a prior agreement regarding you."

"What is the nature of this agreement?" she asked.

The other church official broke in. "Before we continue, my lady, we must ask you a question. Have you been—" He broke off, beads of sweat forming on his forehead, then cleared his throat. "That is, have you in any way been compromised, Lady Avalon?"

Foolish men. Would she be standing here before them like a statue had she been raped? Would she not have given them some sign already, to indicate her distress?

"I have not been compromised in any manner," she said distinctly.

All the men looked relieved. The elder continued.

"Very well, your ladyship. In this case, I must inform

you that the nature of your betrothal is very much in turmoil. The claim of the Kincardine is well documented, of course. There is no doubt it exists."

"Aye," said Malcolm's man again, scowling.

"But Lord d'Farouche says his brother's claim supersedes that of the Kincardine family. He declares the right of plight-troth. He maintains he had an agreement with your father that was sealed before the one with Hanoch Kincardine, which would betroth you to Warner d'Farouche."

Unbelievable. She could not allow this, despite the fact that she had been abducted.

"I have never heard of such an agreement," she said to the men. "What proof has he?"

"He says he has papers, my lady. He is collecting them now for his case."

The second man leaned forward on his elbows. "Until this matter is clarified, Lady Avalon, you will remain a ward of the church, in our custody. We shall determine who has the right of your hand."

It was the solution she had been praying for not half an hour ago. She could go with these men, safe and chaste as could be, and when they were sufficiently lulled she could leave them behind.

And if she did that, she would never be able to help the people of Sauveur. She would never gain access to the wealth that was in her name. There would be no aid for the Kincardines. There would be no grain or sheep or coin to send to soothe her secret guilt at abandoning these people, who had looked to her with nothing but desperate hope and their own sort of kindness.

Yet even if she stayed with the pope's men as their ward,

there was a chance that Bryce and Warner would convince the church of their lies and gain everything, after all.

And that would be unbearable.

She would do anything rather than hand her fortune and her fate to her murdering cousin. She would rather die! She would rather . . .

. . . remain here.

Yes, remain here at Sauveur, and wait. And watch. And plan for the future—up here, away from Bryce, away from the church, she would be able to take control of her future, at last, and help the Kincardines in whatever way she could before she chose to leave.

"Alas, good lords," Avalon said now, throwing her fate to the winds. "I'm afraid I cannot go with you. I took a fall from a horse not long hence, and as of yet I cannot travel."

"What's this?" said Henry's man. "You said you were fit."

"My shoulder is fit, good sir. My—" She did manage a blush now, amen, and stumbled over her words as if in shyness. "My side is not fit, good sir. You may ask this man if it is not so." She pointed to the wizard. "He is the one who has been healing me."

"Serf," barked Henry's man. "Come forward."

Balthazar walked up, bowing again, and Avalon marveled at his composure.

"Is it true that the lady is injured, serf?"

"It is so, great lord. She fell from a vigorous steed and has cracked her bones apart. If she were to ride, it would be a great misfortune."

"Indeed," sneered the man. "And how would you know a cracked bone from a hole in the sky, serf?"

Balthazar showed no anger, keeping his placid tone.

"I have traveled with my lord from a distant land, great sir. I have studied with healers in Alexandria and Syene. I have studied with them in Jerusalem."

"Pagan spells, no doubt," muttered the elder churchman.

"I have been before the Great Church in the holiest of lands, your grace. I have carried my cross to Bethlehem itself on my pilgrimage."

"But you are marked by heathen signs," said Henry's man. "You have the mark of the devil scrawled across your face!"

"It is the way of my people, sir, to stain our skin such. And this was before my conversion to Christ. I joined the Monastery of Saint Simeon."

"A Coptic?" The elder and the younger churchmen looked to each other, then back to the wizard.

"So you are a Christian monk?" asked the elder.

"I bear the mark of a Christian." Balthazar unhurriedly opened the robes that met at his throat.

A tattooed crucifix spanned the width of his chest, ornate and unmistakable.

"Another mark, but of our Lord," said the younger churchman, almost admiring.

"Coptic ways are inclined to mysticism," said the elder, doubtful.

The younger cut in. "But they are of Christ. A monk would not deceive us, no matter his order."

"We are in a quandary, still," fretted the elder. "We cannot leave the lady here, yet it appears we cannot take her. And we cannot stay. It is an unfortunate situation!"

"If I may be of service, your grace." The wizard folded his robes again, hiding the cross. "I offer to watch your lady for you. I will be her protector."

Clearly the men were taken aback by this suggestion, though Avalon could see they did not find the idea that unpalatable. They leaned in to each other, exchanged whispers.

Avalon looked at Bal from across the room. Once more he gave her a smile that almost wasn't there, then erased it, looking courteously to the men.

"I don't see why not." Malcolm's man stood, stepped back from the table. "It is a proper solution. He is a man of God, of the church. He cannot break his word."

The others stood as well. "He will favor the Kincardine," said Henry's man, not entirely satisfied.

"Indeed he cannot," said the younger churchman. "He is a neutral party, as is the church. Is it not so . . ."

"Balthazar, your grace," said the wizard.

"There you have it. A fine Christian name for you. We cannot do better than this."

The elder churchman approached her. "My lady, I am distressed at this news of your injury. But you say you have not been mistreated, and we cannot tarry here. We were instructed not to spend the night at Sauveur, and are to return immediately."

"I understand," Avalon said.

"I pray you will be guided by your servant, who has vowed to protect you as we would. When we have news for you we will come again."

"I trust the matter will be resolved quickly," she murmured.

"As do I. Before we go, have you any message for your cousins?"

"Only that I pray for their good health, my lord," she replied evenly.

"Very well."

Avalon curtsied, then added, "And would you also kindly send word to Lady Maribel of Gatting that I am well, and wish her good peace?"

"As you say, Lady Avalon."

She curtsied again to all of them, then began to leave. Balthazar came behind her, a rustle of cloth. Just as she put her hand on the door handle she turned back to the others, as if she had only now remembered something else.

"Oh, kind sirs, forgive me. I have but one more request."

They looked at her, waiting.

"Pray send word to my cousin Bryce that I would require my clothing sent to Sauveur until I leave here again. I have but this one gown, and it is a great difficulty for me. There are just a few trunks at Trayleigh. The handmaid I had there will know the ones I mean. If he would send them up, I would be fair grateful."

The men bowed to her, but she was afraid it wasn't enough. Avalon made an effort to block out the thoughts of Malcolm's man as she spoke again.

"Tell my cousin I wish to wear aught but this tartan, my lords. I am sure he will understand me."

She left before the affront of the king of Scotland's emissary grew too big for her to ignore.

Balthazar closed the door neatly behind them.

───────────── ⌘ ─────────────

AVALON WENT BACK to her room because she knew of no other place to go, and besides, she needed some time to think about what she had just done. Balthazar trailed her, a mute witness to the fact that she had abandoned her previous life's plans on an impulse that she would now never outlive.

The little room had not changed since she left. The bowl of stew still sat on the table. The narrow window still showed her fat clouds not yet rid of their rain.

The wizard opened the door for her, allowed her to pass through, and then waited, as if he expected more.

Avalon looked at him over her shoulder. "Have you another sash, I wonder?" she asked.

From some hidden pocket he produced it, this one a luminous pink with silver threading.

She smiled in spite of herself, stood still as he fastened it around her and helped her ease her arm into it.

"A brave show," the wizard commented.

"Mine was not the show," Avalon replied. "What happened to your lord?"

"Why, lady, what do you mean?"

Avalon tried out the strength of her new sling, adjusted it until she was satisfied with the position. She looked up at the wizard, considering, and then decided to test her instincts.

"There is demon in Marcus Kincardine," she said.

The wizard raised one eyebrow, then went to the door and shut it, blocking off their words from the guard nearby.

"You must know of this. You are a holy man. You have traveled with him."

"An unholy demon, does the lady mean?" Balthazar's light words seemed loaded with double meaning.

Into her mind came the image of her chimera, a creature of vapor, her enemy and her ally. But she knew it was not evil, and neither was the snake in Marcus.

"Not unholy," she said. "But something *is* there. I saw it myself as I stood beside him in front of those men."

"What did you see?" asked the wizard.

"A snake," she said at last. "It had him trapped."

Balthazar folded his hands together in front of him. "My lady has great insight."

"What is this thing, then? It had him so that I feared for his life. He would have done I know not what. He was . . . not himself."

"In each of us there is such a thing. In each of us lives the penchant for doing good, and doing ungood. In some, however, the ungood has turned inside out. It tortures only the spirit within."

"Why would that be?" Avalon whispered.

"The result of an unusual event. A sustained battering of the soul. This is my guess."

"You don't know?"

"It is not my story to tell, lady."

The wizard bowed to her, reopened the door.

"Would you inform your lord that I wish to speak with him?" Avalon asked before he could vanish.

"I will, lady."

She was alone again. The stew had grown cold and thick but she ate it anyway out of habit, one small spoonful at a time, watching the clouds outside as they gathered closer together and their darkness spread down to their bellies. Faraway thunder shook the heavens.

She felt him enter the room, but he gave no other indication that he was there. The door was silent on its hinges, and Marcus Kincardine said nothing once he was in the chamber.

Avalon wondered if it would always be like this, with her feeling him before anything else, before the rain or the thunder or the voices of all the other minds around her. She shook her head at the clouds, banishing the thought.

"My lord, I would not be a prisoner in this room," she said, without turning around.

He offered no response. Avalon counted to twenty, then faced him.

He leaned back against the small table as he had before, when he had told her she was being stubborn. His hands were behind his back. His hair was untied and flowing, smooth waves of purest black down to his shoulders, more pure than even the black of the tartan it touched. His head was tilted slightly, frost-blue eyes alight, curious, studying her. She saw no hint of the snake.

"I must not be confined. I cannot bear it," she said, hearing her own words but almost not believing she was handing him such a weapon.

"I see." He remained where he was, a figure of rain shadows and storm light.

Avalon made an effort not to sound pleading. "I have informed the emissaries that I will be remaining here at Sauveur for the time being."

That got her only a sardonic twist of his lips. She continued, ignoring the feeling that she was being subtly mocked.

"And since that is the case, I do not see the need to

keep me imprisoned. I freely offer to stay, at least for the moment."

The wind outside gave her a sudden push from behind, blowing her hair around her shoulders, up into her face. She shook her head, pinning it back again with her good hand.

"I suppose I should thank you for saving my life," Marcus said, watching the wind.

"Oh! Well." For no reason at all she grew flustered at this, and resisted it by looking away from him, at the bare wall beside him, the layered stone.

"That's twice now," he added, moving his gaze from the invisible currents in the room back to her.

"Twice? I don't think so," she said, confused.

"Oh, most certainly twice." Now he came forward, and again he was the wolf, the snake, the untamed thing she had glimpsed before, only slightly subdued. How had she not recognized it until this moment? The demon was still very much alive in him, contained now by a steely will. It must have been the storm, she thought, not afraid but amazed. The storm threw her off, the thunder scrambled her thoughts.

Marcus stopped only a few feet away from her, scanning her face, keeping that sardonic look.

"First from the stallion," he said, barely audible. "Now from the men in my solar, sitting at my table, claiming they would take away my wife."

"I'm not—"

"For do not doubt, Avalon, that I would never have allowed it to happen. They may preach as many edicts as they want, but you belong to me, and you are staying with me and our people. And they would have to kill me to take you away."

The storm broke behind them, around them, filling the room with the boom of rainfall, suddenly loud and fierce.

"But I am staying," she said above the storm, monitoring his eyes.

"Aye, you are," he agreed.

He took her hand without warning, held it in his own and stared down at it, and Avalon followed his gaze. Her skin was ghostly in the rain light, his was darkened and calloused, his palm so much bigger than hers, his fingers lean and strong. He held her delicately, using almost none of the power she knew he possessed, and yet still there came the keen awareness of him, the searing sensation only he could produce in her. It enveloped her hand, moved up her wrist, her arm, spread with burning warmth throughout her whole being.

Marcus brought their joined hands up to his lips and kissed her fingers, watching her as he did it. Avalon tried to disguise what was happening to her but she knew he knew. He had already told her he did, earlier today.

He threw her a sensual smile.

"I'm pleased you have chosen to stay, Avalon. It makes everything so much easier."

When she blinked he was gone, already at the door, departing to someplace where she would not see him again for who knew how long, and this made her almost chase after him, stopping the door from closing completely.

"My lord!" she called, her hand on the latch.

Marcus reappeared from the corridor beyond, surveyed her.

"I would not be a prisoner in this room," she said again, chagrined.

"When the emissaries leave you will be free to roam the castle as you wish. Until then, my lady, grant me the favor of staying where you are. It gives me such peace of mind, you understand."

She released the latch.

"Oh, and one more thing, Lady Avalon. You said you had offered to stay 'for the time being.' When you decide to change your mind and try to leave, I hope you will do me the courtesy of informing me first. It will save a great deal of manpower not to have to go hunting after you."

The guard began to shut the door. Avalon watched as Marcus grew thin in the wedge of her view and then was replaced with solid wood. The snake was alive in him, yes. And it had been smiling at her.

Less than one hour later Avalon spied the three groups of men riding off into the woods, their standards now soaked with water but still raised high.

When she went back to the door of her chamber, she found it unlocked.

Chapter Eight

⟨IIII⟩

*T*HE STORM TURNED his solar into a mystery of soft darkness: cool air, pewter shadows, the fresh smell of rain.

Marcus left all the lamps and torches unlit. He liked it this way, he preferred the natural light of the storm to illuminate his surroundings, to remind him that there truly was more to this vast world than sand and sun and parching thirst. It was the opposite of the Holy Land. It was as heaven was to hell. If it rained every day from here to eternity, Marcus would not be sorry for it.

And for this feeling—the gratitude of rain—Marcus could thank his knight, Trygve.

Sir Trygve had been educated in a series of monasteries, growing more fervently devout as his youth slipped away to middle age. By the time Marcus arrived from Scotland to be his squire, the knight had required prayers of his entire staff no less than four times a day, and Marcus was to spend many an hour kneeling at the cold stone altar of the family chapel in the tiny English shire that made up Trygve's home.

The knight's lifetime ambition had been to make a pilgrimage to the most holy of cities, Jerusalem. But the news that the infidels grew stronger and stronger in the

Holy Land, that they were invading and plundering Christian shrines everywhere, galvanized the knight. The church sent out a war cry. It needed good Christian men to defend it. Trygve had found his cause.

Marcus had been only fifteen when they set out. They had collected their indulgences from the pope, they were guaranteed a place in heaven for their good deeds, Trygve told him. And this, the knight had continued, looking down at his squire with joyful eyes, this was what set men apart from animals. This was a sanctified war, a glorious cause, and how blessed they were to be a small part of it.

Marcus had believed him. He had no reason not to. For all his pious words, Trygve had been a wonderful change from Hanoch. For the first time in his life, Marcus had found praise from a man of the world instead of the constant condemnation of his boyhood.

In every way, he had attempted to match the zeal of his benefactor. He had embraced the church, he had embraced the cry of "Deus vult!"—because Marcus had thought God *had* willed it, and he was but His vassal to be commanded.

For all his brave words, Trygve had proven to be past his prime in battle. It was Marcus who shone best there. It was Marcus, growing older than his years under the burning disk of the desert sun, who fought better than most men twice his size, and who gained his reputation as Slayer of the Unholy.

Trygve seemed to overcome his mounting awe and envy of his pupil. He had seemed truly pleased with Marcus's progress, which indeed reflected directly upon him. He had bathed in that glory to the extent that the knight declined to return home even after the official Crusade had ended and all the Germans and the French filtered away, leaving just a handful of the dedicated to fight the battle.

Sir Trygve and his squire lost not only their battalion but their servants, who had one by one crept away into the starry nights, never to return. They took the horses and the camels with them.

"A true Christian will never abandon the cause," Trygve had rallied. "We will carry on, squire. We serve only God."

His devotion had been real, no doubt of that, Marcus reflected. His pride in Marcus had seemed equally real. The only sign of Trygve's growing discontent was the ever-increasing bouts of prayer, punctuated with louder and louder supplications, screaming fits to God, and, five times in that last year—Marcus had been there for all of them—falling into deliriums on the ground, writhing and spitting in a religious frenzy.

The last one had taken place just outside of Damascus. Lost Damascus, held quite firmly by the Muslims. Trygve had come out of his fit and announced that God had spoken to him through one of his glorious angels, descended from heaven to instruct Trygve on what he must do. God had indicated that Trygve had a holy mission, one no other could fulfill.

Sir Trygve made it his quest to free all of Damascus. Just one crumbling knight and his horrified squire.

A growling rumble of thunder shook the wood of his table, bringing Marcus back to his solar and the blessed rain.

Into the hilt of the Spanish sword he carried, some

long-ago fervent knight had pressed a minuscule chip of amber said to be from the shroud of Saint Cuthbert. It was firmly entrenched in the metal. Long had Marcus sat and looked at the dot of glowing gold and wondered how best to remove it.

In the end he left it as it was, more out of concern for destroying the balance of a fine sword than out of any reverence for a dead saint.

In the dim light now the brilliance of the little chip dwindled to almost nothing, outshone by the polished silver and cabochons of rubies of the hilt.

Marcus sat at his table, right where the elder of the church had sat, and examined the grain of amber once again, marveling that it had never fallen out, no matter how fierce the battles had become.

Avalon had stood so close to the wooden edge of the table, closer than even Marcus had when he faced the pope's emissaries and their self-serving demands. She had seemed fearless. She obviously had no idea what those men of God had been capable of doing to her.

Balthazar entered the solar, walked leisurely over to a chair of dark oak and cracked leather.

"Behold," he said, waving his hand about. "She walks."

Since Bal was the third person to come to the laird and inform him that the bride had chosen to leave her chamber, Marcus only nodded, still staring at the amber.

"She cannot go too far," Marcus said.

"Oh?" Bal leaned back in the chair.

Marcus gave a short laugh. "There is nowhere much to go, in case you had not noticed. Half of Sauveur is a ruin. Outside the rain has not eased."

"It is so," Bal admitted.

The rain crashed against the leaded glass window of the room, running down the panes in smears, rubbing together the brilliant September colors of the trees and grass outside. At least the habitable portions of Sauveur would be dry and solid for the coming winter. That much they had managed to ensure.

"Did you know my father kept horses in what used to be the west gatehouse, after the stables collapsed?" Marcus watched the rain outside. "I remember that. He said the horses were more important than the stones."

"A wise man," said Bal.

"Now, there's an extraordinary thought. That Hanoch might have been wise."

"Horses are valuable. Stone is free."

A woman poked her head in the study, looked at Marcus, and said, "Begging yer pardon, laird, but the bride is out, ye know."

"I know," he replied.

The woman eyed him expectantly, then left when nothing more seemed forthcoming.

Marcus shoved a hand through his hair, finally looking down at the mess of letters and scrolls and bits of paper that littered the table. There was so much to do. It overwhelmed him so easily, he wanted to close his eyes and wish it to oblivion. Or wish himself to oblivion. Whichever.

"Your lady requires some clothing to be delivered," said Bal now. "I believe you may expect it quite soon."

"Clothing?"

"It will be sent up from the castle of your enemy."

"What the hell does she need clothing for?"

Bal looked away. Now a guard entered the chamber, gave a short bow. "The bride is loose," he said, concerned.

"I know," Marcus sighed.

"She is in the buttery," continued the guard.

"Let her be," Marcus said.

The guard bowed his way out.

The papers were stacked up in precarious piles across the desk. There were ledgers and scrawled notes in his father's handwriting, almost illegible. One regarding the payment of an ewe and her lamb for the loss of a hut. One on giving three sheep to the traveling priest, payment for a visit. One on a dispute over eight reams of woolen cloth. One on the formal protest of one farmer regarding another, claiming he had plowed five rows of oats into the other man's land, set aside that year for barley. It was endless.

"So, what do you do now, Kincardine?" Bal watched from his chair, his words easy, affable. "Do you think to wait for your king to grant you leave to wed the woman?"

"I already have his leave," Marcus said, bristling despite the casual tone of his friend. "I'm not waiting for that."

"From the English king, then. The pope."

"I don't give a damn what they say. I'm not waiting for their approval, either."

"But you do wait. For what, I wonder?"

Marcus shrugged, looking over the stacks of paper again. Bal studied him for a moment, then spoke once more.

"Are you not worried these English will come back and take her?"

"No," answered Marcus. "That won't happen."

"You are certain of this?"

"It doesn't matter. They may try, but they will not take her. We will be wed before the pope can make up his mind to be bribed by d'Farouche."

"She is a jewel, a worthy prize for any man," said Bal, testing him, perhaps.

"Not just a prize," Marcus responded. "She is a woman first."

Aye, how well he knew that: flesh and lips and sweet warmth, burning passion, kisses like illumination to his soul. . . .

"A jewel," said Bal again, "craved by powerful men. Men who think to steal her from you, who enlist the aid of the holy and the mighty to do it."

Marcus scowled down at the papers, each word a sharp threat to him, as they were meant to be.

"And yet, you wait for her," Balthazar finished, and the question was still there in his voice.

"I have to . . ." Marcus trailed off, unable to put into words what he felt. He wanted to gain Avalon's trust; he wanted to prove to her that he was worthy of her. He wanted to avoid anything that reeked of his father: force and violence and crushing dominion.

He wanted to *win* her, he realized.

Bal had been watching him, silent, assessing his thoughts with that slightly uncanny way he had.

"To woo such a woman," Balthazar said now, "surely takes the bravest of men."

Marcus brought his hands up to his eyes and rubbed them, letting out another sigh.

The cook came into the room. What was her name again? Tara? Tela? Tegan.

"Laird," said the cook. "The bride has left the buttery. She is off to see the south tower, she said."

"Thank you."

The papers would wait. They had waited this long, some of them years old already—what the devil had Hanoch been doing all that time, anyway?—and they could wait a day more. Or a week. Marcus pushed back his chair.

"Where do you go?" asked Bal, his voice rich with mirth.

"South tower," said Marcus as he left. "I don't believe I have taken in the view there yet."

⟨⟨⟨∞⟩⟩⟩

$\mathcal{S}$HE SOUTH TOWER had needed no major repairs, as Marcus recalled. The stairs had all been fit, the beams still solid. Perhaps Hanoch had concentrated on maintaining it because it faced the Auld Enemy, England. Marcus had continued his father's regimen of keeping a steady change of guard in that tower, a constant eye on the horizon.

But the guard was not looking out at the horizon when Marcus had finished climbing to the top.

He ducked out to the wall-walk to discover the rain had stopped as if on command, and now a field of stars was poking through the remains of the clouds above, sparkling even though the setting sun had left painted bands of teal blue and pink and lavender in the western edge of the world. And surrounded on all sides by these celestial diamonds was Lady Avalon d'Farouche, talking amicably with a group of men and boys on the wet walkway, puddles of the night sky everywhere.

He had to stop to admire her, he couldn't help but do it. If Trygve had ever truly seen an angel in his visions, Marcus doubted it had been more glorious than Avalon right now, with her ivory hair that caught the starlight, almond-shaped eyes framed in black, an easy smile on her face at the question of one of the boys.

He had never seen her like this before, relaxed, unguarded. As she talked she moved the hand that was out of the sling in a graceful arc, slicing the night air in a gesture that was at once feminine and strong. She did it again, slower, a demonstration. Another boy added a comment and she laughed, prompting the same in those around her. Marcus moved closer, fascinated.

"No," she was saying, "no one has ever actually fled from me, not in battle or otherwise, I imagine."

She broke off before she saw him; he could see her head lift from talking to the child, those marvelous eyes turning in his direction.

He could watch her forever. He wanted to stare into her eyes, violet or heather or whatever they were, and stay there, happy at long last, living in her world, the splendor of Avalon.

But when she finally spied him the smile disappeared, her manner grew guarded. The moment withered.

Don't fear me, Marcus thought, half a plea, and could have sworn he saw her falter.

She had heard him. He knew she had.

By now the others had noted his presence, the guards

snapping away from the group, the boys looking up at him with open mouths, then back to her.

"Good evening," he said, because he could not think of anything else.

The boys chorused back his greeting; Avalon offered only a downward glance to her feet.

They all stood like that for a while, until Marcus ventured closer. The youngsters broke apart and allowed him in their circle.

"Can ye hit, laird, as the bride does?" asked one bold fellow.

"Well, I can hit, but not like your lady. She has a special skill."

"Anyone can learn it," Avalon said quickly.

The boys' attention swung immediately back to her, hope and excitement teeming around them.

"Will ye teach us, milady?" asked the same boy.

Avalon hesitated, looked over at Marcus and down again. Faint starlight adorned her cheekbones, her lips, the very tips of her lashes, marking her in utterly feminine lines with cool blue light.

"I will, if I can," she said at last.

Marcus crossed his arms over his chest. "Why couldn't you, Lady Avalon?"

It was another challenge; he didn't seem able to stop himself from issuing them to her.

She lifted her head, gazed at him deliberately. "I will if there is time," she amended, and the boys gave their enthusiastic approval to this.

In their excitement they began the lesson plans without her, discussing between them when would be best to start, who should participate, and where to hold it.

"A moment, lads," broke in Marcus. "Our lady has an injury. We must wait for her to heal."

The boys settled down amid exclamations of disappointment. Avalon listened to them, then shook her head.

"We may begin as soon as tomorrow, if your laird allows it," she said. "I can tell you what to do, and you may practice it before me. It would be a good beginning."

Twelve pairs of young eyes swung back to him, and Marcus gave in with apparent grace. "As you wish," he said to Avalon, and had to bow his head to hide the triumph he felt. One more small step taken to bind Avalon to Sauveur. He silently praised the persistence of the boys.

It seemed, however, that persistence had its drawbacks. The boys would not leave even after Marcus gave them his look of dismissal. They had turned back to Avalon and were again peppering her with questions, talking over each other, hardly waiting for her to respond. Avalon noticed his growing impatience; he saw the corners of her lips tilt up whenever she looked in his direction, each time the smile a little more obvious.

Eventually he had to physically break apart the group and motion them away, telling them it was time to go back down to wherever it was they came from, that the lady would still be here the next day to grant them an audience.

They dispersed at once, running off into the night, excitement undimmed about what great fighting the future would hold for them, armed with the battle skills granted by the warrior maiden of their infamous curse.

Avalon faced the damp stone wall, looking south over

the sea of treetops and sheer mountain faces. Marcus noted her sling looked different, a different color, a different pattern. He only somewhat recalled that moment in his study with those deceiving men, but it seemed to him Avalon had done something rather amazing at the time, something about removing her sore arm from the sling to prove her health. When it happened he had watched it from a distance; it had been one more ingredient in the volatile mixture of words and intentions in that room. But now Marcus wondered why she did it.

The emissaries would have been appalled if they thought she had been mistreated. They would have taken any injury and held it up as an example to suit their claims. Marcus was certain Avalon knew this as well as he did. And yet, she had acted in his favor. She had dismissed their concerns with princessly dignity and spared Marcus the necessity of taking action against them.

He came up beside her on the walk. "New sash."

The top of her head reached just over his shoulder; she inclined it now, looking down at the sling.

"Yes. Your wizard gave it to me."

"My wizard?"

"Your holy man," she corrected herself. "Balthazar."

Marcus grinned. "A wizard. How flattered he would be to hear it."

"Don't you think he's like that?"

"Oh, aye, I agree with you." Marcus leaned his elbows on the battlement, examining the sky. "Wizard is a good word for him. You found him out right away."

"It's his bearing," she replied, serious.

He couldn't help the question. "And what do you call my bearing, my lady?"

She really seemed to consider it. A slight crease formed between her brows. "You . . . you are the laird. You walk with authority, and I think this is natural to you. But there's more. You also walk with open eyes, and I think you have learned this."

"Open eyes," he repeated, captivated.

"Awareness. Even caution. And swiftness. Underneath all that command is the swiftness, like a falcon. A hawk."

In Egypt, as a squire, he had seen a desert hawk once up close, tethered to a vendor's arm but not hooded, with ferocious eyes to match the color of the sand and wings as long as a man's arms. The hawk had been wounded, perhaps from its capture, and kept one taloned foot drawn up close to its body. Marcus had wanted to rescue it but Trygve had not allowed it, calling it a frivolity. Which should have given Marcus a clue to the knight's true nature, now that he thought of it.

Marcus had never forgotten that hawk, its tethered leg, its spirit uncrushed and undaunted despite its pain.

Avalon was nodding to herself. "A hawk," she murmured, then seemed struck by a thought. "A hawk may kill a snake."

Marcus couldn't follow her line of reasoning. "Am I the snake or the hawk?" he asked, not really joking.

"The hawk," she said instantly. "You are the hawk. You must remember that."

Anyone overhearing them would think them absurd, Marcus thought, but at her words he felt a soaring kind of relief, as if she had unlocked a private fear in him that he had never even known existed and blown it away on the wind. Following this was gratitude, great gratitude. He was the hawk.

"Your people have been talking to me," Avalon said now. "I think you should know."

"Know what?" he asked, still feeling bouyant.

"They are troubled, my lord."

"I wish you would call me Marcus," he said, letting slip the thought that had been on his tongue. She looked taken aback.

"It's not that difficult," he teased. "A small name, really."

"You're not paying attention to me, my lord," she admonished. "I speak of your people."

"I am," he countered, surrendering to her mood. "They come to you with their troubles, you say."

"Yes."

"Well, Avalon, what do you expect? You know what they think of you, who they consider you to be. Are you truly surprised that they seek your comfort?"

"But there is nothing I can do for them! I've tried to tell them!"

"For many it's enough simply that you're here."

"It's not enough, you and I know that. Marcus," she said, startling him, "I beg you once more to take the wealth I have. It would help so much."

"Don't you know?" he asked softly. "Haven't you realized it yet? Your wealth is not the legend. It's you. They want you, Avalon."

The crease in her brow became more pronounced. She couldn't seem to manage a reply to this, so she looked away again, shoulders slumping.

He edged closer to her, ventured one hand around

her waist, and to his wonder she allowed him the gesture, unmoving, as a doe might be when confronting a foe.

He didn't want her to feel apprehension with him. He didn't want her antagonism, her anger or dismay. He wanted her to want him as he did her, Marcus realized, and more. He wanted much more than that from her, things he could not even define. It almost made him afraid, the feelings that hovered in the recesses of his heart that all sang of Avalon.

"Will you marry me?" he asked, both of them touching so carefully.

"I cannot," she said. "I'm sorry."

He had expected this answer but it hurt him anyway, a deeper pain than was warranted, considering their circumstances. No matter. Her response changed none of his intentions. They *would* be married.

Far off in the mountains a lone wolf cried as the moon began to rise, heavy and round, the color of bronze.

"It's late," Marcus said, but he did not move his arm.

Avalon didn't reply. Like an enchantment her hair now took on the reflection of the moon, growing warmer and more golden. Her skin picked up this light as well, casting her with a suggestion of the tan of the people he had known in the Holy Land. Her eyes were dark and unfathomable. She leaned her head back to look up at him, exotic angel, and her next words jarred him back to their reality.

"My lord. How did you learn of Bryce's intention to wed me to his brother?"

"A note. We were sent a note."

"May I see it?"

He shrugged, removing his arm. The spell h
away into the night. "I don't see why not."

Marcus took her back to the only place Avalo
she knew in Sauveur besides the little room she had
stayed in. She had spent the late afternoon exploring as
she could, walking aimlessly from place to place until she
grew tired of the crowd that followed her and announced she was going out to look at the rain. The procession of young boys, however, had been undaunted by
the prospect, and even seemed disappointed that the rain
had stopped by the time they found the south tower.

But this room must be Marcus's solar, for she had seen
none like it in her roaming. It had a good feel to it; neither too large nor too tight, a nice-sized fireplace, two
sets of glass windows with excellent views. She had not
noticed it before when she faced the emissaries, but
then, there had been more important things to consider.

The long table they had used was now covered in papers and loose scrolls, even open bound books with
scribbled notes on the leaves.

Avalon watched as Marcus walked over to the mess,
rummaged around in it. His profile was to her, intense
and sober; he was so heart-stoppingly handsome even in
the tartan, enough to make her reason drift loose for a
moment. . . .

If only their lives had been different. If only he was
not the son of Hanoch. If only he did not believe that
nonsense of the devil's curse. If only the horror of her
childhood had not forced her to take that vow never to
marry. . . .

But this man was a part of it, all of it, whether he
willed it or not. Avalon thought that even if he had had a

choice, Marcus would have embraced that wretched curse anyway. And she would not be drawn into that devouring whirlpool of superstition and lies again. It would be a bottomless death to her.

She walked away from him, went to examine an intricate stitched scene on a tapestry by one of the windows. It was a noblewoman bathing in a stream, her long, golden hair cloaking her. Maidservants were nearby, watching their mistress with black sewn eyes and necks bent like swans. The water had been given threads of blue and green and white. There was even a school of little fish around the lady.

"I don't know," she heard Marcus say, frustrated. She looked around and found him seated, staring at the pile of papers with aversion. "It was here before," he said. "It must still be here. All of these papers have been together."

"What is this?" she asked of the mess, coming over to him.

"God knows. I inherited it."

Avalon picked up the tattered paper nearest her.

" 'Four barrels good ale,' " she read to the room, translating the Gaelic to English. " 'In most excellent French oak and iron. Two ploughs with leather. Winter seed for . . . twenty fields. Thirty lamb in payment.' " She looked up. "A statement of account?"

"So it appears. I would suppose Hanoch had no inclination for such mundane things as record keeping."

Five years at Gatting. Five years of Maribel's diligent tutelage, from fashion to Latin to the complete management of the estate.

"You have need of a steward," Avalon observed.

Marcus let out a laugh that had no humor.
has need of many things, my lady, that I do not
give it. A steward is there among them."

Avalon fingered the paper she held, looking down
with misgiving at the faded ink. But she still made her
offer.

"I may help you, if you like."

Marcus looked up, alert. "What?"

"I've done it before. I studied with the steward at
Gatting. I know the way of these things." She put the
paper back on the pile. "He said I had an uncommon
mind for mathematics, for a female," she added derisively.

"You would act as steward?" he asked, disbelieving.

"No," she said, fast. "I will train someone for you.
Pick a man. Pick a woman. I will help as I can."

He seemed lost in thought, staring at a space behind
her, out of the circle of brazier light that flickered
around them.

Avalon picked up a few more of the papers, glancing
at them, moving them aside. Without planning to she
found she was making deliberate groupings: bills for
payment, receipts for bills paid. Miscellaneous and almost laughably disparate notes, some regarding griev-
ances from one man regarding another, some apparently
nothing more than opinions of certain people.

"'Keith MacFarland. A shifty coward. An evildoer,'"
she read, and put it in her miscellaneous group.

"That sounds like something Hanoch would say,"
Marcus said dryly.

"Yes, but he felt it strongly enough to write it down.
Odd." Avalon kept sorting. "He did not strike me as the

kind of man who thought much of writing for any purpose. It was Ian who insisted I learn to read, in fact."

"Ian?"

"Your father's friend, Ian MacLochlan," she said shortly. "The one who taught me to fight. Did you not know him?"

"No," he said.

"You're lucky."

Before he could respond she held out an unfolded note to him. "Is this the missive you received, my lord?"

Marcus only glanced at the familiar lines. "Aye."

She studied it. A swath of ivory hair had escaped from her loose braid and flowed down the line of her neck to curl across her chest. Marcus watched her dissect the words, knowing she was completely unaware of her own beauty.

"It was delivered by some lad from Clan Murry," he said, unable to look away from her. "Who said he got it from another clan, who got it from England. That's all we knew."

Avalon d'Farouche is to wed Warner d'Farouche in the next month, she read, *at Trayleigh Castle on the second night of the waxing moon.*

The handwriting told her nothing. It had the typical flourishes of a hired scribe, untraceable. The paper was vellum, thick and expensive.

The chimera yawned and stretched and took Avalon to a dark room, a single lamp of smoking tallow on a bench. A cloaked figure stood over a scribe, who scratched out the words as the woman recited them. The woman was hurried, frightened, thrilled.

Claudia, Avalon thought. It had to be from Claudia.

No one else had both the inclination and the resources to warn the Kincardines of Bryce's plot, in hopes of spoiling it.

Marcus's deep voice intruded on her thoughts. "What do you see?"

He didn't ask her what she thought but rather what she saw, a deliberate implication that he knew of her vision, that perhaps he could read her thoughts, as well. Avalon kept her face impartial. "Nothing. Merely a note."

"Really? Because I rather thought you might know who sent it."

Avalon handed him back the message. "I do know who sent it. And I know why. It is obvious, when confronted with the facts of the matter."

He waited, steepling his hands in front of him.

"Lady Claudia, wife of my cousin Bryce, had much to gain and nothing to lose by preventing the wedding."

"Is that so?"

"She said she didn't want a war." Avalon let her hand drift over the stack of papers again. "She was the one who warned me of her husband's plan the evening before. She indicated she wished me to stop it somehow."

"She wanted you to stop it? How?"

"Oh, I don't know. Stand up in front of everyone, denounce Bryce and Warner." She shook her head.

"Would you have, Avalon?"

He seemed serious, looking over at her, sitting at his table, and she had to look away from the blue light in his eyes.

"I had a better plan," she said, and wanted to leave it at that but felt compelled to go on, to satisfy that look he had. "I was going to pretend to agree to a betrothal. I was going to leave as soon as the party was done. But I didn't realize Bryce wanted a wedding that night, not just an engagement. I had gone to my father's garden to consider what was best to do."

"And that's when I found you."

"Yes," she said, annoyed for some reason.

"So, in essence, I spared you from your cousin's plan, isn't that so?"

"If you mean to suggest that by forcibly abducting me—"

"I actually rescued you from a situation that you could not have escaped so easily on your own."

"*Rescued* me!" she gasped.

"And it seems to me, in light of these new facts, that indeed, you owe me a boon, my lady."

Avalon opened her mouth but couldn't find the words to express her outrage.

"It turns out I did you a great service, after all," Marcus said mildly.

She stalked away from him, to the door.

"Good night," he called, laughter in his tone. "We can discuss my boon on the morrow."

She slammed the door behind her.

Chapter Nine

ᘯᗢᕫᘰᗢᘰᗢᕫ

*Y*OU MUST REMEMBER to keep your wrist straight." Avalon bent over the brown-haired girl, ran her fingers down the girl's arm and tapped them against her wrist. "Here, you see? If you bend your wrist when you hit, you lose power, and you might hurt yourself."

The girl was named Inez, and she dutifully repositioned her hand, following Avalon's example. She was about thirteen, Avalon would guess, beginning to learn to fight at an age almost as old as Avalon had been at the end of her training.

Inez had soft brown eyes and a sweet, engaging smile. She was one of seven girls in Avalon's rather eclectic group who had volunteered to learn the bride's warrior skills. There were twenty-eight pupils in all, every one of them young. But there were adults lingering on the fringes of the crowd, men and women both.

When Inez and her friends shyly came forward that first morning to join the class, the boys had moaned and hissed them off, until Avalon silenced them by stating that unless all were welcome to learn, she would not teach any of them.

The boys had looked at her, and then back at the girls, who were sullen but still hopeful.

Avalon had walked over to the girls and begun there, showing them the proper stance before a hit. One by one, the boys had come over.

Every now and again she caught a glimpse of Marcus, watching through a window that looked down on the bailey, walking by with a group of men, even standing and just looking at her, the wizard at his side. His face had been dispassionate, his expression mostly matter-of-fact, but underneath that exterior the chimera told her he was pleased, greatly so. She probably should have found that disturbing, but couldn't.

Over two weeks had passed since he told her she owed him a boon. Sixteen days, and he had not mentioned it again. Nor had he talked to her of marriage. In fact, he seemed content to allow her a measure of freedom, to discover Sauveur on her own, apparently taking her at her word when she said she would stay. For now.

The door to her room was never locked now, and this gave her some comfort at night, knowing she could walk out any time she wanted. There was no guard trailing her. People still stared, yes, and they still talked and thought about her; she was still a novelty here. But in these two weeks she had had time to gradually come to know both the castle and its inhabitants, and they her. It was taking some of the shine of mysticism off her arrival. She was a woman. She did normal things that women did. Well, she tried to, at least.

She had gone down to the buttery to visit Tegan and her helpers. She had joined in the making of a meal. She had kneaded dough herself over the protests of the kitchen women, who had ended up standing back, watching her work with a kind of scandalized delight.

She had gone down to the woolen mill, watched the weavers at their looms, watched their hands work in steady rhythm, turning lines of thread into blankets, tunics, tartans. Small children knelt on the floor at their mother's feet, sometimes helping, more often just playing. Avalon had not tried her hand at weaving; she had more sense than that. But she had praised what she saw, words honestly given, and the ladies had begun to open up to her and tell her bits and pieces of their lives as she watched them work.

She had talked to sentries, to the men who had taken her from Trayleigh. She had gone to the stables—what there was of them—and seen for herself the care of the horses, the stable lads who put aside their pitchforks and took her around to introduce her to each animal, including the cats.

And now this. Sixteen days of lessons, and the men were doing more than observing. Some of them were repeating her instructions to themselves under their breath, were moving their hands in a small imitation of her actions.

Soon, she thought, they would step into her circle. Until then she would rather have them watch, grow more comfortable with her at their own speed. Not to mention her own. She had abandoned the sling days ago, but her shoulder was still sore, and she moved it carefully. Her ribs were almost healed.

Inez was getting tired. It was no surprise to Avalon. They had been working for over an hour now in the late afternoon. An hour had been but a small portion of what Ian had demanded of her in training, but Avalon was not going to repeat his unrelenting schedule.

These students of hers had chores on top of this. She would not wear them down any further than she had to. They already seemed to be slips of children to her, too thin, too weary.

Not enough grain, not enough fish, chanted the chimera, as if Avalon didn't already know.

"That's enough for today," she said, curter than she meant to be. She softened her tone. "You've all done extremely well. Tomorrow I'll show you something new."

The children were slow to scatter, a few running to their parents, more walking off in thoughtful steps, discussing what they learned.

Marcus had come out to witness the end of the lesson, leaning against the wall of the keep with his arms crossed. He watched only her now. She felt his look as a singeing awareness, as if he could peer into the heart of her, as if he could see her chimera and was curious about it—he wanted to examine it, know her every thought, her dreams. Her soul.

In the mists of her mind the chimera looked back at her, offered a toothy grin. *Not enough, not enough . . .*

Avalon lifted her face to the sky, letting rays of the distant sun warm her cheeks, her eyelids, for a moment. The smell of burning pine came to her on a breeze, perhaps from one of the fireplaces in the great hall. It was sweet and smoky, blending impeccably with the briskness of the day.

The children had dispersed into pockets of laughter, good natured, warmly clad in their tartans, off to finish their duties in their own world.

Not enough.

Well, why not? Avalon demanded of the chimera.

Why wasn't it enough? What was she supposed to do about it? She could not make grain appear with the wave of her hands! Salmon would not jump from the rivers at her command! What was she supposed to do?

Marcus was still watching her. The sun had come out and wrapped him in slanting rays. It made glossy rainbows in his black hair. It showed her the stubble of a day without shaving, enhancing the square line of his jaw, the contrasting smoothness of his lips. It turned his eyes the color of the sky reflected on snow: not blue, not white, yet both.

Their eyes met across the golden grass and dirt. They turned as one in the next heartbeat, looking out to the road a scant second before the scout appeared, galloping toward them.

More news, Avalon thought, and a feeling of dread flowered in her stomach. What if it was the emissaries, back so soon with news of her betrothal? What if Bryce had won? What if she was to be commanded to marry Warner?

Avalon picked up her skirts and joined the gathering crowd waiting for the scout. They parted and made room for her, surrounded her without thought, kept her in the middle, safe.

Avalon politely pushed her way to the front to stand beside Marcus, who threw her one look before facing the man riding up the road.

The horse was sweating, lathered to a foam. "A caravan," called the scout, before he had even come to a halt.

The crowd began to murmur, a rise and fall of sound. "How many men?" Marcus asked.

The scout swung down easily from his saddle, slapping the horse on the neck. The animal lowered its head and shook it as if to rid itself of the wetness on its coat.

"Not many," said the scout. "No more than half a dozen. They carry Malcolm's flag. And another. I don't know it."

Avalon tried to see what the scout had seen, as she had before, but the chimera turned its back to her, refusing.

"What colors?" she heard herself asking.

The scout looked down at her, then over to Marcus, who nodded.

"Green and white," said the scout to Avalon. "With a beast of red."

"A lion with a poppy?"

"Aye," said the scout. "That's it."

"Bryce," Avalon said to Marcus, and the crowd exploded with comment. They pushed forward, began to pluck at her sleeves, taking her back into themselves. Hide the bride, don't let them take her. . . .

"Wait," said Marcus, freeing her from the hands all around. His voice echoed off the stone of the keep, capturing the attention of them all. "Six men are not an army. Six men are not coming to take the bride. This is something else."

"What could it be?" asked one of the women.

"An edict!" shouted someone.

"They were at the Valley of Kale when I left. They will be here shortly," said the scout.

"Take the bride into the keep," suggested a man, and many voices seconded him.

"I'm not going!" Avalon shouted over them.

Everyone quieted, all eyes fell on her.

"I said I would stay at Sauveur, and I will," she said now, quieter. "But I am remaining here to meet the party."

Marcus stood behind her, at her shoulder, tall and indisputably the laird. "Aye, she stays," he said. "She has a right to hear what is said."

The caravan was visible now down the winding road, just one wagon pulled by a team of four horses, four outriders flanking it. Two held the flags.

The d'Farouche heraldry covered the wagon's load. Avalon marked their progress up the hill with a sinking heart.

It was not possible that all her trunks would fit on that one cart. Not even a third could. Not a fourth.

The horses clambered up to the gate of Sauveur; Malcolm's men were in front.

"Who among ye is the Kincardine?" called out the lead man, a grizzled warrior in a tartan of a clan Avalon did not recognize.

"I am." Marcus stepped forward.

"Laird Kincardine," said the same man, looking down from his mount. "I bring ye greetings from our sovereign. Malcolm instructs me to tell ye that the cause is not lost, and that the woman will yet belong to ye."

A collective sigh swept through the clustered people. The man dismounted, followed by Malcolm's three other men. The two driving the cart, both in Bryce's colors, stayed in place, scowling.

The Scot who had spoken approached. "I am Gawain MacAlister, captain in His Majesty's royal guard. Malcolm sent me to reassure ye that he is doing all he can to press yer claim."

"I am grateful," said Marcus. "And curious. What do you have from Trayleigh?"

Gawain looked surprised. "Why, the lady's clothing, man. As she wanted, or so I heard."

Avalon was walking over to the wagon. She didn't recognize the two men still seated, which was just as well, considering what she was about to do.

"Pray, unload them over here," she said, pointing to a plot of grass in the bailey.

The men looked at each other, then back down at her.

"What are ye waiting for?" growled one of Malcolm's guards. "Unload the wagon for milady."

The men, grumbling, stood up and began to sweep back the cloth of heraldry.

Seven trunks. That was all. Avalon couldn't tell if the one she needed was included; she couldn't quite recall what it looked like. She had remembered it mainly for its position in the lineup along the wall of Luedella's room.

"Take them inside," said Marcus, clipped.

"No." She looked back at him, surrounded by a brace of his kinsmen and Malcolm's guard. "I would open them here, my lord."

"Here?"

"Yes."

It was a standoff of wills, hers clashing against his, their audience rapt. He was cold again, the laird, giving her nothing but a chiseled look, obviously displeased with the situation. The chimera stirred, rattled its tail.

Not enough.

Avalon turned her back on him and the rest of them, to hell with what they thought of her. She was her own mistress in spite of what they said, and she would do as she wanted. Bryce's men shrugged the first trunk down from the wagon, carried it over to where she pointed.

For a long moment it seemed the crowd would not part for them. None of the Scots moved; they only stared at the two men carrying the heavy trunk, a human wall, blocking them.

Avalon moved briskly to face the crowd. She met each gaze with cool authority, and the people were not immune to it. Slowly a rift opened in the wall. Avalon pointed at the ground, near the middle of the bailey.

"There," she said, and Bryce's men almost tossed the trunk to the grass.

"The key." She held out her hand before they could walk back.

One of them fumbled at the heavy belt on his waist, pulling out a small ring with the ornate brass keys she remembered. He gave it to her without comment, then both men returned to the wagon for another trunk. This time the clan left the path open for them. They had all turned to watch Avalon.

A fine fool she would look if the right trunk was not here, she thought to herself as she worked the lock on the first and snapped it free of its catch.

She pushed the lid back and the mass of people inched forward, craning for a look. Marcus and the wizard and Malcolm's soldiers moved to the front, but no one came very close.

Yes, these were her clothes. Her bliauts from Gatting, in all colors imaginable, finely stitched, worth a fortune by themselves, actually, but nothing compared to what she was looking for.

It wasn't this trunk. She had taken care to sew the

coins and the jewelry into only the most sensible of her clothing, not knowing what the weather would be like when she fled, nor what her circumstances might be afterward.

And indeed these were the style that Bryce had sent her, hording the fancier finery for his own purposes, or perhaps for when he thought he would have her again. But still, this was the wrong trunk. Avalon had placed the altered bliauts and the cloak on top, ready to be grabbed when the time was at hand.

To be certain, though, she lifted up the gowns nearest her, tossed them so they draped over the sides of the trunk, and rummaged through the rest down to the bottom.

Bryce's men brought forth another as she was finishing. They looked at her curiously but didn't pause, heading back to the wagon.

She found the key to the second trunk and opened it. Wrong again. These were the wrong gowns. The wrong bliauts, the wrong undergowns.

She opened the next four trunks, none of them the right one. By now she was slightly frantic, tossing the gowns randomly about, causing a growing concern she could feel at least among the women. She wondered why the chimera would not tell her if the right trunk was even here. Had she missed it? Was it possible she was mistaken in which gowns she sought? No, no, because she had spent hours on them herself, she knew exactly which ones she had picked apart and sewn back up again, the simple green wool, the dark blue linen, another wool, this one dove gray—

The men set down the last trunk and then stood back,

watching her as closely as everyone else did. Avalon could feel the expanding doubt around her: What was she doing? Why was she acting so oddly? Was she touched somehow, had she a fever?

Avalon abandoned the trunk she had just gone through and wiped the moisture from her forehead. What a stupid risk she had taken, what an imbecilic thing to do, trusting that Bryce would bow to her carefully hidden agenda, that he would send up the one trunk she had been praying for. . . .

The last one was it. As she opened it the first thing she saw was the dove-gray bliaut, sturdy and plain, finely woven, artfully deceiving.

Avalon let out a cry of delight and whisked it out of the trunk, holding it up in front of her. The people watched, mystified, as she whirled around and approached Marcus, who stood with his arms folded.

"Your dagger, please," she said.

His thoughts were closed to her, his face had that hard, impartial look that meant he was deeply involved in some emotion. But at her request he inclined his head, then took the dagger at his waist and gave it to her, hilt first.

Balthazar, standing next to him, nodded to her approvingly.

Avalon walked back to the trunks and then turned to face the multitude of puzzled men and women.

"Clan Kincardine," she said, raising her voice to be heard all around. "I bring you your true savior!"

Avalon hefted up the hem of the gown, took the dagger and began to split open the stitches. The blade was sharp and exactly the right size, making swift work of it. She held up the gown and shook the contents onto the grass.

A rainfall of gemstones landed with soft thuds, brooches and earrings, rings and pendants. Pearls and sapphires, emeralds, rubies and gold, topaz and citrine and aquamarines and amethysts—all from Gwynth, all purely Avalon's to give.

After one tremendous gasp of air, no one said anything.

"Here!" Avalon bent down and picked up a figured brooch with two large, perfect pearls, one white, one black. She held it up, let everyone see, then found a ring with a rounded green emerald, bright and vibrant, a dragon's eye set in gold. "And here!"

She looked around at their stunned faces, Marcus's stony one, Balthazar and Gawain MacAlister openly smiling at her. Avalon walked over to the wizard and handed him the brooch and the ring, knowing that Marcus would not accept her gift.

Back at the trunks she pulled forth the dark blue gown, opened it up, and more pearls slid out, great strands of them, white and black and cream and pink and even a rare blue. Everyone watched. No one moved.

"Here," she called again, but she was more subdued now. She gestured to the earth at her feet, a treasure fallen to the grass, all the gems gathering up the sunlight, the gold bright and telling, the pearls like tears on the ground.

"It is for you," she said, looking just at Marcus now. "For grain, and salmon. For the stables and the fallen walls and more looms."

A sound was flitting though the crowd, garnering strength until it became a great shout, a cheer, men and women alike throwing up their arms, embracing each other, hailing her and her gifts, another prophecy of the curse fulfilled!

"No—" Avalon said, but she was not heard. This was not prophecy! This was fact, a fortune of real things, not myth.

All around her swam the emotions, almost delirious, the bride had come, aye, and she was bringing her prosperity, she was ending their time of want and all of Sauveur would be whole again!

Some of the people were tumbling up to her, were bowing to her feet, kissing the hem of her skirts. Women were weeping and Avalon was trying to lift them all up, trying to get them to stand.

"No, no," she was saying, attempting to explain it to them. "It's not the curse. It's not!"

And again they did not heed her, but passed around the precious jewelry in trembling hands, taking it all to Marcus, offering it to him. He broke his concentration on Avalon to shake his head at them but then had to give in, because they insisted he take them, the rings, the necklaces of pearls, the brooches. A growing mound of gold and jewels weighted his hands, and still Avalon could see that this was not enough for him.

The chimera nodded, agreed.

This was not what she had wanted. She had not meant to encourage the legend but to silence it, to show these people that what they needed was not flimsy stories but hard fact. And they had taken her intent and wrapped it around their fable, defeating her as quickly and as ruthlessly as Ian used to do, knocking her flat, leaving her winded.

Avalon pressed her hands to her cheeks, then looked back at Marcus. He was smiling now, all right, knowing her thoughts, watching the legend take firmer root around them all in this moment.

She stepped through the people, picked up the third gown and the cloak of coins, draping them over her arms.

Marcus kept his smile as she approached, an amazing sight, the masculine radiance of him heaped in gold, glittering in the jewels he held. He truly looked like a god now, a heavenly creature touching down to earth only for a moment, just long enough to scatter the treasures of paradise to the mortals.

Avalon stopped in front of him and met his look without conceding defeat. "There is more," she said, and tossed the gown and the cloak at his feet, then laid the dagger on top.

Not enough! laughed the chimera.

And Marcus's smile grew, as if he had heard the chimera speak, and knew that she did, too.

"A fine beginning," he said, "from our bride."

❧

THE BUTTERY WAS vacant. Avalon imagined they were still stunned out in the bailey, still singing the praises of their absurd curse, and Marcus standing there, the laird burdened with golden riches under the admiring eyes of all.

Let *him* be their savior, Avalon thought acridly. He believed in their superstition. He was as steeped in it as the rest of them, and no better than they, when it came down to it.

She found a wedge of cheese and the heel to a loaf of bread. It was enough for now. Avalon took the food back into the keep and then made her way to what used to be a gatehouse, but was now long overgrown with thistles and grass, with clutches of little birds nesting in what remained of the roof. They greeted her in warbling trills.

A square-cut stone, long ago fallen from higher up, made a comfortable seat as she sat down and began to eat.

Her shoulder seemed much better. Even after the exercise today the stiffness was barely there, and her ribs no longer needed to be wrapped. Soon she would be perfectly healthy again, and when the emissaries did return, her excuse to stay would be gone.

What to do about that? Avalon sighed. Her life, once so strangely but surely mapped out, now seemed as nebulous as fog. There was no solid right or wrong any longer, and that was troubling enough. But add on top of that her mounting attraction to the laird of the Kincardines and what seemed only nebulous before grew to be impenetrable.

Attraction meant nothing, Avalon scolded herself. Attraction was a tricky diversion, and if she let it, it would trap her here for the rest of her days. And that was not what she wanted. Was it?

Of course not! If she stayed here her freedom would be forever curtailed, and the superstition would eat her whole, and Hanoch would laugh at her from purgatory until the day she joined him there, choked dead from the muck of his damned legend. She would end up being nothing but what he had planned for her to be— a creature with no identity but that given to her by a

ridiculous fable. Her entire existence would turn into a
sick joke.

And if she stayed, she might never have the opportunity to make Bryce pay for what he had done, a very real
crime, no fantasy. If Marcus discovered that Bryce had
bought the Picts, he wouldn't allow her her revenge, he
would assume command of it himself. But it was her
quest, not his.

She had to leave. Yet if she did, she would never see
Marcus Kincardine again. For some dark reason, the
mere idea filled her with despair.

One of the birds came closer, taking short, nervous
hops in her direction, tilting its head, tiny bright black
eyes, a short yellow beak.

Avalon tore off a piece of bread and tossed it to the
bird, watching the creature skip back in fear, then stop
and dart forward again.

"I wouldn't hurt you," she said to it, holding still.
"Go on, it's yours."

The bird hopped forward and picked up the crumb,
then fluttered away.

"So, the people are not enough for you, my lady. You
think to feed even the animals of Sauveur?"

As if just the image of him in her mind had summoned him to her, Marcus was here. He blocked the entrance to the round room, making a huge shadow that
draped over the thistles and stone and grass, edging into
her lap. The birds above grew silent at once, then rushed
around in circles up to the sky.

"Shouldn't you be off counting your blessings?"
Avalon replied, then took a bite of cheese.

"Consider them counted."

He came forward through the thistles, stepping carefully around the hidden barbs in the weeds. "I have discovered an interesting method of locating you, Avalon. I think of the most deserted place, and there you are."

"How convenient for you," she said wiltingly.

"Aye, indeed. It brings me much solace, knowing where I can find you."

He chose a rock much like hers, fallen haphazard into the room from above, embraced by the grass. It set him across from her, with a rectangular window just to his left, a framed picture of colorful hills, a meandering river in a valley that emptied out into a small, rounded loch.

She tried to go on eating, ignoring him, but he made it impossible, even though he stayed silent. He watched her every move with sharp winter eyes, he sat there and brooded before her, and again she felt as if he were trying to understand her, the heart of her, her deepest secrets.

"Is there something you want of me, my lord?" Avalon asked, giving up, putting aside her food.

The change in him was certain and fleet, a darkening of his eyes, a small twist to the curve of his lips.

"Aye, most surely," he said.

There could be no doubt of his implication. She had to look down at the grass to hide her reaction, a flush of heat, a tug that led her back to him.

"What will you be doing with the rest of your clothes now, I wonder, Avalon?" His voice had not lost its sensual undertone. "Do you think to wear them instead of the tartan?"

She had not considered it. When she had told the

emissaries she wanted more than this plaid, it had been merely words to her, another tool to convince them to send the trunks. But now Avalon saw that the arrival of her clothing could be seen as a rejection of the Kincardines. And she didn't want that.

Ridiculous, her mind scolded. Don't let anyone dictate to you how to dress! You are not a serf!

But she heard herself say, "Take the gowns. Sell them. They'll fetch a fine price."

He arched one eyebrow at her words, leaned back on the stone with a hand around his knee. "As much as I like the idea of you being without them, I wouldn't sell your clothing."

Avalon pressed her lips together, resolving to ignore his double meaning. "Why not? I have more."

"For one thing, it doesn't appear that I need to. You have bestowed rubies and pearls aplenty."

She shrugged, looking out at the winding river, the silver-black loch.

"And was this why you sent for the trunks?"

"Of course," she snapped. "I could hardly ask Bryce to fetch me my jewels so that I might give them away."

He was silent, absorbing this, his stare never wavering. It was unnerving to her after a long moment, and so she stood up and brushed the bread crumbs off her lap, then walked around the sitting stones and past him, to the window with the view. Marcus spoke to her back.

"So now I must contemplate what my bride will do next. You think you've saved the clan, isn't that right? You thought to rout out the curse and bypass the legacy. You thought that a bestowal of jewels would end your obligation to Sauveur, and you could leave."

She *had* thought that, more or less, and wondered why it didn't feel as wonderful right now as it should have. And who was he to belittle her efforts? Why should he take her to task with that slightly mocking tone when all she had wanted to do was help him and his people?

"The coming cold will not be so harsh now, you cannot deny it," she said. "Your spring will have new seed, new cattle. I fail to see how you need me any longer."

"You fail to see how I need you? I hardly think so."

She bit her lip at her mistake, but he continued.

"I think you see everything quite clearly, Avalon. You see how the people need you. You see how I need you."

She turned. "What I see is that you now have the means to stave off want. With careful management, your clan will prosper for ages to come. This is my gift to you. I would not scorn it."

He stood, a little too close, a little too fast, surprising her again with his lithe nobility. "I never said I scorned it."

"Excellent. Then we have nothing further to discuss."

The winter cold in his eyes did not lighten. "Do you think to seek your nunnery now?"

She didn't want to. Avalon knew it right away, as soon as he said it, that the idea of leaving to join a convent had become nothing but dreary and bleak. Endless days, endless routines, solitude, lasting reflection, stoic women, only those things for the rest of her life. It had seemed bearable before; at one point it might have even been a welcome respite from the turmoil of London.

But not today. Today, with this man in front of her—

so large and sure of himself, so handsome as to make her even now look away from him before the blush overcame her—the thought of a nunnery was almost worse than anything. And yet it was all she had left herself.

"There is nothing to stop me from leaving," she said, trying to make the words real for both of them. "At a convent I may retire in peace."

"Oh," he replied, low. "I thought we had already covered that."

It took almost nothing to lean down and kiss her, he was so close already, and she had nowhere to go. His touch was light but commanding, an exploration of the shape of her lips, the softness of her. Avalon took a breath against him and he took it back, hands now firm on her, pulling her to him.

The passion flared from nowhere, it swirled through her so that her arms wound up around his shoulders, she fell into the solid form of him, she flowed into him and he into her, holding her tight. His hand cupped the nape of her neck, his fingers caressed the curve of her jaw, brushed down to the delicate shape of her throat, her shoulders.

She was lost, hopelessly lost and didn't care, as long as Marcus held her and kissed her like this, hard and ruthless now, something deeper and wilder than before.

"Avalon," he said against her throat, pressing a kiss there, "I don't want to argue with you."

He was going to win, she realized, because she was unable to stop him, she couldn't make him stop kissing her, she couldn't block out the feel of his body against her, hard muscles and rigid lines. The honey of his lips, his mouth, was back, drugging her. She couldn't help but kiss him back.

"Please," she gasped, one last effort, and the roughness of his cheek stung hers, a painful pleasure. "Go away."

"I can't." He shifted his arms around her. "I can't."

Marcus used his body to take them both down to the ground, cushioning her but not yielding his embrace, until she was flat on the grass and the sky was a dizzying ring of blue above her, framed in jagged stones.

His weight was something unexpected and alarming, not crushing but holding her completely, taut against her, his leg between hers, his thigh pressing up against a place that filled her with hot desire.

She turned her head to the side and he followed her there, relentless, using his mouth to torment her, to whisper her name across her cheekbones, down to her ear, back again. There was a rhythm that was taking her against her will, it blossomed in that place where he touched her, it left her short of breath and he began to match it, moving with her, something fiery and hard against her leg, and he shifted down her, his hands on her breasts, skimming them, causing her to arch into him more.

His hand was farther now, finding her skirts, pulling them up and aside until he caressed her bare skin and she turned toward him, dazed but wanting more of this, craving his touch. His fingers found where his thigh had pressed, the center of her, and Avalon let out a startled sound that he took with his lips and covered as he began to caress her there.

The honey was inside her now, overpowering her, it was molten flame, suffusing every part of her, and he knew it; she felt his fierce smile against her, his kisses more urgent.

"Stay with me," he said, mastering her, and she could only close her eyes and shake her head, the honey made her mute.

"You will stay." He slipped a finger inside of her and she let out a sob, pressing into him.

"You will," he murmured, "truelove."

Everything caught and rose in her, shattered apart in an explosion of clenching pleasure, a storm that left her weak and spent amid the grass.

The circle of the sky above her burned her eyes now, she had to shut them to block out the light, to hide from its openness.

Marcus moved his hand, pulling down her skirts again. "You will stay." He kissed her lips, lightly now. "You belong here, with me."

I love you, came the thought, and Avalon didn't know if it was from her or him or the wind, or just an echo from the chimera.

Marcus pulled her upright, brushed off the grass and leaves that clung to her as he would do for a child, turning her around until she was neat again, only the flush of her skin telling of something beyond the ordinary. He smoothed her hair back; she felt his fingers in her braid, tucking and weaving, slow and careful.

When he was done she looked up at him and he down at her, and there was something almost like pain in his eyes.

"It's time to sup," he said, quiet, and then he took her arm and led her back inside the keep.

Chapter Ten

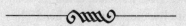

THE LAMP WAS LOW ON OIL, and the flame was beginning to sputter too much for Avalon to decipher the cramped lettering on the ledger she was reviewing.

" 'Seven full-blooded . . . Angles'?" she read aloud.

"I believe that is 'Angus,' milady."

Ellen leaned over Avalon's shoulder, frowning down at the faded writing. "Of course," she added hastily, "I cannot be sure."

"No, you're right." Avalon slumped back in Marcus's chair and closed her eyes, blocking out the dim yellow light.

Ellen was Avalon's personal choice for the role of steward for Sauveur. She was the wife of one of the warriors, and after Avalon's dramatic show in the bailey, no one dared voice opposition to her choosing a woman for the coveted position.

Ellen was bright, willing, and enthusiastic. She had an instinctive way of grasping matters at their root, and she could add and subtract large numbers in her head. No one else had come close to being as good. When Avalon told Marcus her choice, he had merely agreed, saying he was sure she knew what she was doing.

Full-blooded Angles. If only Marcus could see her now, hunched over these papers in his solar in the darkest night with burning eyes and a headache.

"Go to sleep," Avalon said to her pupil, who looked up from the ledger in surprise.

"To sleep? But milady, there is so much to do—"

"And we have come far in two days, I think. Have you not noticed how quiet it is, Ellen? Everyone else has retired."

The other woman looked around at the shadowy room, the guttering lamp. "Nathan!" she exclaimed, standing.

"Go on," said Avalon. "Your husband is waiting for you."

This was a fact. Nathan seemed to be completely devoted to his wife, and proud that Avalon had picked her from the many volunteers for the stewardship. He had even gone so far as to bring both women their dinners as they worked this evening. That was hours ago now.

Ellen curtsied and apologized. Avalon waved her away, smiling as Ellen almost ran for the door.

And Avalon, who had no husband to run to, took a moment of self-indulgence and leaned her forehead on the back of her hand, closing her eyes again.

Five days ago Marcus had met her in the abandoned gatehouse. Five days ago her entire perspective on the world had changed forever, all because of him. Five days ago Avalon had learned that she could be nothing more than a slave to her own senses, and that the laird of the Kincardines knew it, and knew how to control her with it.

Humbling, embarrassing, intoxicating. He had touched her and her defenses had been ground to dust—nothing left but him, the desire for him, the hunger for more. He had unearthed a vital element in her that she had not even suspected existed, and he had used it expertly. And Avalon knew he would use it again, if she let him.

If she wanted him to.

With one last spark and a hiss, the flame from the lamp died, the last defense against the darkness. Now the room was lit only by thin moonlight, reflected shine from the clouds outside. She liked it better like this, actually.

"Oh, go to sleep," she said to herself, stretching.

The tiny room they kept her in had long ago lost its slight appeal. It wasn't that it was ill kept or too plain. Putting the pallet under the window helped fight the old feelings she always got from unbroken darkness, and she invariably left at least one lamp lit for the night. Yet it never seemed like enough.

She was fortunate to have a private room at all, and she knew it. But lately she had been thinking of another room in this castle, one she had not yet seen. Lately, as in the past five days.

What did the room where Marcus slept look like? What view did it have? What colors were the blankets on his bed?

Avalon stood up, disgusted at herself. Impossible thoughts, crazed dreams, to consider these things—

As she pushed away from the desk her sleeve brushed against a stack of papers, toppling them in a whoosh, an avalanche of flutters down to the carpeted floor.

"Splendid," she muttered, and bent down to gather them up.

Her hands scooped up the pages on top, pushed them together in a pile and left them on the floor, too tired suddenly to sort them out. Then she picked up the odd bits and pieces that had drifted off to the corners. The last one was almost in the fireplace, now thankfully nothing more than embers.

Avalon studied it—a leaf torn from one of the books, she thought—and brushed loose the ash on it as she walked through a patch of moonlight. The silver light glanced over the words written there, slanting black handwriting, sloppy, broad strokes. Hanoch's writing, she knew it well now. Hanoch's words:

Keith MacFarland arranged the meeting. MacFarland delivered payment, claimed no other knowledge. Pict leader was Kerr. Price was one gold shilling per head. Fifty shillings for the baron. Twenty for the girl. To be paid only when finished. Coinage was French. d'Farouche paid in full to Aelfric, son of Kerr.

Avalon stared down at the words, reading them again until their meaning penetrated.

Hanoch had discovered who bought the Picts. Hanoch had known. He had found this MacFarland person and got the information and here was the proof, finally, that Bryce had killed her father. Proof!

"Awake, lady?"

Avalon jumped and clutched the paper to her chest, whirling around as her other arm swung out, ready to defend or attack. Balthazar stood right behind her. He lifted up his hands and took a step back.

"Easy, lady, you are safe."

She stared up at him, still holding the paper against her pounding heart, her other hand a fist.

"I beg you not to harm me," said the wizard, bowing low. "I implore your forgiveness for arriving so."

It was a gentle teasing, designed to ease her, and it worked, letting her fingers loosen, bringing her hand down to her side.

"You startled me," she reproached him.

"Alack. I am unworthy of your forgiveness, you know me clearly."

"You walk like a cat," Avalon grumbled.

"A lowly cat, a stray, a mongrel, I grovel before you, lady—"

"Do stop." She walked away from him, over to the desk, slipping Hanoch's note into the folds of the tartan at her waist when her back was to him. She turned around to find him motionless, watching her, a wraith in robes in the moonlight.

"You do have such a flair to you, for a monk," she said to him.

"I am not a monk. I beg your pardon."

She stared at him, baffled. "But you said you were, to those men, the emissaries."

"Wise lady, I urge you to think back. What I said was that I joined the Monastery of Saint Simeon."

"To be a monk," she concluded.

"No longer. I am no longer a monk. I renounced my vows before I came here."

Avalon laughed a little in spite of herself, marveling. "You might have lied to them, but you didn't, did you? You told them the truth, and let them draw their own conclusions."

The wizard folded his hands inside his sleeves and gave her a look from twinkling eyes.

"And you carry the image of the crucifixion on you, but you have renounced your vows. . . ."

It struck her suddenly that this was not funny, that it was a grave thing for a man to go back on his word, for a man of God to turn his back on his order. She knew then that the wizard had not done this with a light heart, that it had taken something devastating to change him.

"I'm sorry," she began, mortified, "it's none of my concern. I hope you can—"

"Shhh!" The wizard interrupted her, put his finger to his lips. "Listen, lady! Do you hear?"

Avalon froze, became as still as she knew how to be, but all she heard were crickets and a slow breeze through the trees outside. And the smallest, smallest sound of the embers dying in the grate.

"What?" she whispered, locked in place. "I don't hear—"

"A dream, lady. It is with us."

"A dream?"

Balthazar spread his arms wide; the robes opened up like the wings of a bat in the darkness, his fingers splayed. "Oh, he has dreams, do you hear them?"

Her fear was back, worse than when he had startled her, sending the blood rushing to her head. "No, how could I—"

"Listen!" commanded the wizard, and the bat wings grew wider, engulfing the room, engulfing her.

She was hot, terribly hot, and thirsty. The thirst was killing her, like nothing she had felt before; it was a hideous beast, a monster in her that dwarfed even the chimera. The thirst was all of her, it plucked the desert sun from the sky and lodged it in her throat. Her tongue was parched to the roof of her mouth, her lungs were sand, bags of sand, like the ones the nomads carried, but loose, punctured, and the sand ran all through her, soaked up her blood and turned it bleached gold, the color of old bones.

She labored to breathe through the sand, but each breath sucked in the dry air and strengthened the monster thirst. There was nothing else around her, only this, an enduring agony, where even the thought of water made the monster howl and dig in deeper, clawing her, shredding her.

Oh God, what was happening to her? Avalon put her hand up to her eyes to shield them from the bright sun, but that wasn't right, because it was night outside, she knew this, it was nighttime and the moonlight had been so shallow. But the sun burned her hand, unprotected where it left the sleeve of her robes, even for that short moment it scorched her skin and she had to bring her hand down, feeling in front of her for the table in the solar—but it was not here.

Listen! shouted the wizard and the chimera together, and now she heard the wind outside, a sandstorm pounding the walls, seeping into the room, crisping her lungs further.

She stumbled forward, ducking her head; she had to leave this place, she had to escape, she had to find water.

The buttery. There would be water there. No, better yet, her room—it was closer. There was a pitcher of it waiting for her there.

She fell against the wall of the hallway. The sandstorm

was louder now and she was still blinded, feeling her way along the stone wall. The stones were hot from the sun, they could not be cool as they should be because the sun never stopped here, the sun would burn them all to ashes, even the stone. All the water in the world had boiled away by now, there was nothing left.

Avalon folded both hands over her face, heedless of the pain of her burned skin, and tried to run, to find shelter. There was no water, what was her recourse? Why couldn't she die? Why didn't they just kill her?

When she lifted her hands from her face she was lost, somewhere she did not know, a cramped room with layers of sand on the floor, and there was a man tied down to a table. He was red and brown and black, his lips were the monster of thirst, even the blood had dried to a crust on them. His hair was matted and dirty, a wild beard covered his chin.

She couldn't move from the table, the ropes were too tight on her, she had no more strength to fight them so why didn't they just kill her? Why suffer like this?

Death was paradise, denied to her.

A drop of something hit her lips, trickled back to her tongue, and was gone before she could taste it, soaked into her mouth.

"More?" asked a gentle voice in a language she didn't know, but she knew what it meant, that one word. It meant water.

Yes! she tried to scream, but nothing came out, not a word, not a whimper. She couldn't even move her head, her forehead was tied down to the table. The ropes cut into her, more bleeding.

"Yes!" called out Marcus on the huge bed, tossing

and turning where she could not, becoming tangled in the furs, the blankets.

Sand blew through the chinks in the white walls. Sand embellished the dark wood of the crucifix hanging over the table, obscuring the crown of thorns on Christ's head.

"Renounce," said the same strange, gentle voice in its own language, and if she could have freed her tongue from the desert dryness Avalon would have babbled her agreement, *Yes, yes, I will, whatever you say, only give me more water. . . .*

Marcus flung his hands out, moaned in his sleep. The moonlight fell only across his face, showing her his scowl, his hair not matted, no beard. There was no sand in this room.

Avalon looked around again, closer. There was no sand. There was no sun. No voice, no crucifix. It was still nighttime. She was at Sauveur, and this must be, had to be the rooms of the laird.

"My God," whispered Marcus in his sleep, and his body was almost bowed up, arching in torment or pain from the nightmare that gripped him.

Avalon stood with her hand braced on the wall by the door—cold stone, no heat—heaving for air, still trying to accept where she was.

There was a pitcher on the table across the room. The pitcher would have water.

She let go of the wall and almost ran to it, almost cried at the sight of the still reflection of the moon on the surface of the blessed water.

With shaking hands she poured some into a mug, and she had never heard a happier sound: the liquid splashing into the bottom of the glazed mug. She put the pitcher down and drained the mug at once, letting it spill down the sides of her face, joyous water.

She filled the mug again to the brim and went over to Marcus, taking the pitcher in her other hand, and knelt by his bed.

Sweat poured off him, the blankets were soaked in it; she could feel the heat of him all the way from here, the thirst.

He tossed away from her, arms still outstretched, as if they were tied down.

She lifted the mug but he was facing the wrong way, and when she touched his cheek he flinched and wouldn't come back to her.

"Water," she whispered, and he moaned again, unmoving.

Avalon dipped her fingers in the liquid and moved her hand until it touched his lips. The meager drops bled into him, he followed her hand as she moved it back toward the mug.

"Water," she said again, and now put her hand behind his head, supporting him.

"God," he cried, a catch in his voice, and she knew now what that unbearable hope felt like.

She touched the brim of the mug to his lips, tilted it so the water slid to him.

"Drink. It's for you."

He did. He opened his mouth and drank all of it, and she refilled the mug and offered it again, making him take it slower now, still asleep, the burning beginning to recede, the monster diminished.

She let his head back down carefully, smoothed his hair from his forehead, damp and clinging.

"Thank you, God," he sighed, and his arms moved back to his sides, and peace settled upon his features.

The nightmare was gone.

Avalon sat back on the floor and let out an extended breath. There was a moisture on her own face, not from the water. Tears. She had not even noticed them, but salty tears had fallen from her eyes at some point. She had cried during the nightmare. She had cried for her own death.

And yet it wasn't her death. It wasn't her nightmare. Marcus was the tormented dreamer.

Under the influence of the moon she could see that the colors of his blankets were dull and indistinct, perhaps deep blue or forest green. She couldn't tell. She shouldn't stay.

But she found herself lingering by him, drawing solace from the sight of him lax amid his covers, his breathing now even and relaxed. A dark angel at slumber. But no, not an angel, something more vulnerable than that. Just a man, a gorgeous man with troubled dreams.

She took a corner of her tartan and touched it to the water in the pitcher. It seemed a good remedy to wipe away the salt on her face, so she very lightly used it on him the same way. He did not stir as she brushed the coolness over his features, a small ritual of motion to follow the clarity of his beauty. At rest, with those winter eyes closed, he could have been a fallen angel, in need of her care.

His eyes opened then, caught her right as she was about to wipe his cheek, tartan in hand as she bent over him.

Avalon was stunned to immobility. She could only stare back at him, hovering, aware of how it looked for her to be here at all, much less in the middle of the night, spying on him.

His eyes matched the moonlight, he was a creature of mystery and he saw her, he looked right up at her with no astonishment at all.

"An angel," he said, whisking the word from her thoughts. "Am I dead?"

Avalon, still motionless, licked her lips. "No."

His eyes drifted closed again. "I wanted to . . ." He rolled over, away from her, clutching a pillow. His words became a mumble. "I wanted to die. . . ."

She backed away, lowering her hand, and stood. He was asleep again.

The pitcher and mug were at her feet. She refilled the mug and left it close to him on the table nearest the bed, then went back and put the pitcher there, too, so it wouldn't be underfoot. With one last look at him, Avalon crossed the expanse of the room—his windows had a view of the bailey, overlooking gracious valleys reaching up to Highland peaks—to the door.

Although she had no memory of how she got to the laird's rooms, it didn't take much time to find a hallway that was familiar, and from there to make her way back to her own chamber. But it was a long while before she could find the comfort of sleep herself.

𝒜VALON SLEPT with her hair cushioned behind her, beneath her, creating the illusion of silken sheets, waves of shimmering pale blonde so intricately colored as to appear unreal—ivory and white and silver blended as one.

The dawn light couldn't disguise her beauty, the delicate dark brows, thick, long eyelashes at rest. Lips slightly parted. Marcus hated to wake her. He could have rocked back and lived in this moment, but he was becoming used to this sensation, a suspension of everything as a tribute to her, a vision to sustain him through the most desolate of hours.

But the day was coming, and what he had in mind meant they had to leave soon.

"Avalon," he said softly, and put his hand on her shoulder.

She gave a little frown and sighed but otherwise didn't stir.

"Avalon," he said again, slightly louder.

Like a pantheress she sprung out of the pallet, grabbed his arm and twisted it around before he could react, pulling him off balance before her.

"Avalon!"

Now her hair was even more splendid than before, the heavy locks sliding and bouncing around them both, covering his arm and her hand where she held him. She looked up at him and her eyes widened, as if she only now realized what had happened. His arm was released, she walked backward and off the other side of the pallet, staring at him.

"You shouldn't wake me like that." Her voice was husky with sleep.

"Obviously," he replied, rubbing his arm.

She looked around, bewildered, then back at him. "What are you doing here?"

"I come with an invitation," he replied.

Her eyes got wider.

"Not that kind," he said hastily. "An invitation to go fishing."

"Fishing?" The frown reappeared, her battle stance melted into a softer confusion. She rubbed one hand across her eyes. "Now?"

"Yes."

"No, thank you. I'm rather tired. I didn't sleep much last night."

"Come, my lady. You are made of hardier stuff than this."

She gave him a disgruntled look. "Go away."

"It will be a glorious day, the sunrise has already begun, do you see it? This is the best time to tickle fish."

"My lord, I have no interest in tickling. All I wish to do now is rest."

"All right." He stepped back from her, lifting up his hands in supplication. "I didn't want to have to do this, but I fear you have forced my hand."

The wariness returned to her tenfold, the warrior maid watched him acutely. She looked no more deadly than a fairy-tale creature, half wish, half dream—a serious deception, he knew.

"I make this my boon," he said. "You must come with me."

"What! I owe you no boon!"

He gave her his most engaging smile. "I believe you do. It would be most dishonorable for you to deny me."

"As you did me?" she suggested dryly.

"But we all know you are far more the lady than I am the gentleman. Therefore, you must come."

He saw a smile fight its way past the straight line of her lips, pressed tight together to hold it back.

"I know a special place," he said, enticing. "Fish as big as a man."

"A man!" she burst out, the smile coming forth. "Indeed!"

"Won't you come?"

"But I'm tired," she said, shaking her head.

"This will invigorate you. Come with me."

Without meaning to, the shade of his voice changed, grew deeper, giving away the fact that what he wanted from her was more complex than what he appeared to be offering. She heard the difference, he knew she did by the way her smile vanished completely, replaced with a look that left him a little short of breath.

"All right," she said. "I will."

She dressed much more quickly than he would have thought a woman could have or would have, especially since she had no maid to aid her. He waited out in the hallway only a few minutes before she emerged from her chamber, tartan in place, hair neatly plaited back.

She looked up at him, where he slouched against the wall, and he came forward and gave her a bow, silent. Together they walked out past the great hall, where many still slept on the benches, to the bailey, where he had put the rods aside for them.

There were people stirring, preparing for the new day against the stained-glass sky of morning. They called out greetings to the laird and the bride as they made

their way to the gate, and then past it, down a path he recalled from boyhood. Marcus hoped the enclave in the
stream still existed. For that matter, he hoped the stream
still existed. He had not been fishing since before he left
to join Trygve's household.

Avalon walked lightly beside him, carrying her own
rod, allowing him to shoulder everything else, since he
had insisted. There was a part of him that wanted to
prove to her he was a gentleman, despite his previous actions, despite every indication to the contrary.

He wanted, Marcus realized, for her to like him. It
was a humble thing, perhaps even piteous, but still true.
And it was the real motive for awakening her this fine
morning. He just wanted to spend time with her. He
wanted to watch her laugh.

These past days had been a torment to him. He could
not forget what occurred between them in the ruined
gatehouse. He could not forget her response to him, nor
his to her. She was a drug to him, he had to have more of
her, and in some many-folded corner of him, he honestly didn't know how it was going to end. He needed
her, plainly much more than she would ever need him.
It made him the weaker, when he had to be the stronger.

What agony not to make love to her right then in the
gatehouse, when he had her in the cradle of the grass,
holding him, kissing him, wanting him back. Perhaps it
had been the first truly gentlemanly thing he had ever
done, denying himself the exquisiteness of Avalon,
when all he really wanted was her, all of her, forever.

In the forest the young light shone on her in rosy
gold, dazzling against the trees and grass and ferns. Her
gait was graceful and natural, unaffected by the fashion-

able constraints of most noblewomen's tiny steps. Her skin looked dewy, her eyes lilac bright. She was driving him mad.

And that was his greatest fear. There was something else about her—something apart from her extraordinary beauty—which was born of the curse, and brought forth his own darkness. Her gift was a thousand times greater than whatever meager portion he possessed, yet it intensified his own, and he was having his old nightmares.

He had managed to forget about Damascus for so long. Or at least he thought he had. Whenever it came back to him he focused instead on the orange grove in Spain in that hidden village. It had been fragrant and colorful, warm, and as far from the nightmare as anything else he had ever seen. The trees had been tall, with perfect pointed leaves, white flowers, great orange globes bowing the branches down.

He tried to remember the taste of one of those blood oranges. Whenever Damascus filtered up to his memory he thought instead of the flesh of that exotic fruit, succulent and tangy, sweet and cool on his tongue.

And now Avalon had come, and with her this mixed blessing of the curse; he dreamed of Damascus again, and even the sweet oranges were not taking it away.

Last night. . . . He couldn't remember most of it. But he did know the nightmare had swooped down and scooped him up in its fist, had dropped him back into the desert, with the thirst. Marcus had not had a dream that intense for years.

But an angel had come and rescued him. She had looked like Avalon, she had untied the ropes that bound him and offered him water, offered it freely, with no deceptive words to halt the flow of it, no tricks. And the nightmare had been banished after that.

This morning his first thoughts had been of her. His first instinct had been to find her, to see her, to spend time with her. And—a miracle—she had agreed to his hastily constructed plan. Fishing had been the only thing he could think of that would legitimately require him to go wake her up, because he simply couldn't wait until breakfast before looking upon her. Magical Avalon.

She walked beside him now, unaware of the havoc she was wreaking upon his every hour. She had trusted him enough to follow him, and surely that was a most excellent sign.

They had to be nearly at the stream. Either that, or they were lost. Marcus wasn't sure which it was.

But no, he heard the water now, still a sound that brought a thrill to his veins after long years of being where water was always scarce, and streams practically nonexistent.

Now the path was evident to him, even though it was so overgrown it could easily have been missed. He felt a lightening of his spirit as they traced the old, familiar route, Avalon here with him, quiet but not somber, just thoughtful, as she usually was.

"Over here," he said, breaking into her thoughts, pointing to a secluded hollow, a nest of soft moss and grass surrounded by pines, the stream lapping at the rocks on its banks.

He held back the branches for her, allowing her to go first, then followed, and the branches snapped back, obscuring them from view.

Avalon stood in the center of the moss, looking around.

"I don't believe," she said, "you will find a fish as big as even my hand, much less the size of a whole man, in this creek."

"Who knows?" Marcus began to set down his rod, the basket of food, the blanket he carried. "It's said that still waters may be very deep."

She walked over to the stream, looked down at its mirrored surface, smooth here in the elbow next to the hollow, more rapid farther out.

"It's very pretty," she admitted.

Marcus felt a flush of gladness at her words; a casual compliment, true, but still the first he had ever had from her.

"I'm glad you like it," he said.

The blanket was hardly needed; the moss was dry, the stones were not sharp, but he spread it out anyway near the water's edge, then brought out the basket that held their breakfast.

She watched him unpack the food from her perch on the creekside. He was meticulous and neat, setting everything out in a certain order. Avalon could not help but admire the way he moved, the way the light flattered him. The way his eyes picked up the hue of the sky. The way the tartan looked on him.

She caught herself with a mental shake, then went back to gazing out at the water. Yes, he was handsome. That was a fact she must learn to accept. He did not fit the mold her imagination had cast him in years back. Marcus himself had shattered that concept right away, and from there only rebuilt the image, improving it, making it shine in her mind until it blinded all else. But there was so much more to him than just his physical attractiveness.

He had spirit, depth. And now she knew, whether she wanted to or not, that he had a soul. That this soul had been through great pain, and this survival of the spirit had shaped in the man the most appealing aspect of all. He had been wounded, and he had recovered. There was compassion in him, something so lacking in his father. Even the snake in him was the result of compassion gone awry. It was a bittersweet, noble trait.

Marcus glanced up and caught her looking sideways and back at him, lost in her own thoughts. He stood.

"Would you like a tart?"

"Thank you." She took it out of habit, reacting to his polite tone with her own mannerly response, and for a moment felt silly doing it. But when their fingers brushed he grinned at her, boyish and open, and she had to smile back.

The water moving over the river stones made a pleasant sound, mingling with the occasional song of a bird.

They ate in silence, both standing, facing the water. When he was done Marcus went back and took up one of the rods, then found the bait he had brought for it. Avalon examined it curiously.

"Feathers? You think to catch fish with a bit of feathers and string?"

He didn't look up from his work, hooking the strange item securely on the line.

"I told you we would be tickling the fish, my lady."

When he was done with both lines they cast out. The

swell of the current caught the lines and dragged them downstream, masking them with glittering sunlight.

She didn't know how long they stood there, and then sat on the blanket, each quiet. But as the sun climbed higher, turning the sky to its brilliant azure, at last she had to ask him a question.

"My lord?"

"Marcus," he corrected.

Avalon watched a dragonfly skim the steady surface of the creek, soon joined by another in a weaving dance.

"Marcus. I wonder if you know what has become of a woman of your clan. Her name was Zeva."

"Zeva." He closed his eyes, remembering. "She was my father's chatelaine, wasn't she?"

"She kept house at the village where I stayed."

"I believe she died about three years ago. That was what I heard."

"Oh." Avalon fought to curb the disappointment at his words, even though the answer was what she had expected. If Zeva had lived, she would have come forward by now.

"Why?" Marcus asked her.

She gave a halfhearted shrug. "I just wondered. She was my friend."

He gave her a sharp look. "I can find out the details, should you like."

"No, thank you. I know enough."

Too much death. Why was it that all of her childhood was tainted with death, and everyone who had mattered to her was dead? Yet she still lived, much like Luedella had, an outcast in her own way, not fitting in anywhere.

The day had lost some of its sparkle, even though the

hollow was just as pretty as it had been before. Avalon reached into the folds of the tartan at her waist and withdrew Hanoch's note.

"I found something written in your father's hand last night," she said, staring down at it. Marcus's attention had not wavered from her, but now she felt it focus even more keenly, a close scrutiny. The paper was dry and old between her fingers, folded in half now to hide the damning words. Without looking at him she held it out, allowing him to take it.

He read it quickly, once, then again.

"Bryce," he said, and there was wrath in his tone.

"I think so," she replied. "The woman I was visiting that night at the inn at Trayleigh, she told me the same thing. That Bryce had bought the Picts."

"Why haven't you informed me of this before?"

She set her pole down on the grass and leaned back on her hands. "I thought it none of your concern, frankly."

He paused. "And now?"

Avalon sighed. "I suppose now I would like your opinion on it."

Marcus narrowed his eyes, reading her so clearly. "What, had you planned to take revenge on Bryce alone, is that it? That's why you didn't say anything?"

She faced him fully. "Of course I did. I could not let this go unanswered."

"No." He read the note again. "I understand."

"Good."

"But it doesn't actually condemn Bryce by name. It merely gives your family name."

"I know. There's the knot. And the coinage was French."

"And Warner d'Farouche has been living in France for almost twenty years," Marcus said slowly.

Avalon nodded. "You perceive my problem."

"Hanoch never captured even one of those Picts, and he had the resources to do it, if anyone could. I know he tried. He told me that much."

"Well, he captured someone, apparently. This MacFarland. It was enough."

"The MacFarlands are southeast of here. I could have a man there in three days."

"Don't bother," said Avalon. "I imagine he's dead, as well."

Marcus looked away from her, out to the deep, still water before them and then the rushing falls beyond.

"Interesting," he said.

Avalon's line jerked, she had to leap for her pole as it began to slide into the water.

Marcus said, "Looks like your feathers have caught dinner."

Chapter Eleven

❦

*O*F COURSE, Marcus sent an inquiry to the Mac-Farlands anyway. Despite what Avalon said about Keith MacFarland being dead—and his instinct told him she was correct—he couldn't let the information lie. He needed confirmation.

She seemed content to allow him this liberty, and he did not doubt it *was* a liberty, bestowed upon him by her. She was a warrior indeed, fully capable of carrying out her own plans. Yet for reasons of her own she had brought him closer to her, had shared information vital to one of a warrior's most intimate acts—revenge—not because she had to, but because she wanted to.

Another compliment, Marcus supposed. At least, he was going to take it as such. Now he had to do whatever he could to ensure she didn't go off and get herself killed by her cousins.

His baser emotions told him to lock her up again, to hide her away in the secure little room he had chosen for her, protect her. Watching her proudly carry back the string of trout they had caught this morning, light-hearted from this simple pastime, it had taken a great deal of willpower to allow her to retire freely to her chamber. He had to go into his solar and focus on nothing for long minutes to rid himself of the desire to imprison her for her own good, to keep her safe here at Sauveur.

Eventually he had conquered this impulse and pulled together a group of men to go to the MacFarlands. Avalon had unwittingly handed him what might be the key to her own undoing: If he could prove that either of the d'Farouches were behind the raid on Trayleigh, Warner's claim would be forfeit. Marcus would win.

And Avalon would be unequivocally his.

She would not be able to find her sanctuary. There could be no other outcome to this dance, as far as Marcus was concerned. She had to marry him.

Already she faltered in her determination to leave, he knew. Already he had found the chink in her defenses, and he had been steadily enlarging that chink ever since. She felt for the clan. She harmonized with Sauveur. She belonged here as surely as any of them did.

And, whether she knew it yet or not, she belonged to him. She would see this as well, with time. So time was what he intended to give her. At least for now.

Let her walk the halls of the castle. Let her converse with anyone she wished. Let her become so intertwined with life here that she could never disentangle herself from the clan, from Marcus. It would happen.

She paced above him now, outlining the perimeter of the castle. He knew this, though no one had come to tell him of it. Marcus knew it because he felt it. Because what he had told her about being able to find her had been, God help him, the simple truth. He could feel her with his thoughts. He could place her as sure as any-thing, and that was perhaps the final thing that made him allow her to remain free. Marcus knew where she was, anyway. So let her roam.

───────────── ◦⫘◦ ─────────────

*A*VALON TURNED HER face into the wind that blew in from the south, let it push back her hair and cool her brow. The day was finished but still she felt disinclined to go back to her room, which seemed to get smaller and smaller every time she walked in. She had been unable to nap after fishing, and spent her time instead tossing and turning on the pallet, struggling to clear her thoughts.

Marcus, framed against the scarlet and gold of the forest.

Marcus, smiling at her as he handed her the tart.

Marcus, congratulating her as she pulled in her first trout.

Marcus.

At supper he had seemed removed again despite the fact that they all ate the trout she and Marcus had caught that morning, amid easy smiles and laughter. He was now very much the laird—that swift shifting in him that still managed to catch her off guard—talking to his people, holding a polite conversation with Ellen to inquire how the stewardship was going. Avalon knew he had sent out men to the MacFarlands, and this preoccupied him, too. But he had barely looked at her during the meal.

Sauveur was truly a stately castle, she thought as she continued her walk. The gray and black stones created an air of dignity and power, a very apt dwelling place for the chief of the Kincardines. Already repairs were in motion using some of her wealth, hastening to beat the onset of winter. Yesterday some of the men had worked in shifts on the stable roof, patching and strengthening it to bear the weight of the coming snow.

It gratified her, knowing it was her inheritance from her mother that made it possible; just a few coins traded for practical materials. There was so much more work to do. But now there was also the means to do it.

The sentries greeted her as she passed, and she called them each by name, pleased that she had remembered.

Avalon liked it up here at the very top of Sauveur, above the trees, scraping the sky. From here she could see for miles. It felt like freedom, though it was false.

Ahead of her, in a nook in the turret stones, a family of larks had made their nest. She could hear them contentedly crooning to each other as she approached.

But when she came around the corner she found it was the wizard crooning to the larks, and they who listened, looking down at the robed man.

He saw her and gave a short whistle, an exact replica of the lark's song she had heard in her father's garden on that fateful night, what seemed like ages ago.

She halted, staring, and he did it again, then bowed to her.

"You *are* a wizard," she said before she could help herself.

Balthazar smiled. "I think not, lady."

Avalon walked closer, crossing her arms together to block out the wind. It was growing colder. Perhaps it was that wisp of freedom she felt from being so close to the infinity of heaven. Perhaps it was the comforting shield of the darkness that made her feel safe, a blanket of obscurity to hide her differences. For whatever reason, she found herself saying to the wizard, "But the other night in the solar you told me to listen to the dream."

"Yes. And did you?"

"You must know what happened."

"I am but a lowly servant, lady. I know nothing."

"Oh, a lowly servant indeed," she scoffed. "That might work on those who cannot see you, but I can."

"Can you?"

Avalon hesitated, aware that she had trapped herself. "You are not just a servant," she finished lamely.

Balthazar turned away from her, looking back up at the larks. "Not many see as you do, lady. Yet you scorn your gift. You hide from it. It is most puzzling."

"I see nothing more than the next person," she said, suddenly afraid for no good reason, except that now the cold stuck to her bones, and this man was leading her down a crooked trail she had no wish to follow.

"Did you not see the serpent? Did you not taste the water? Were you not in the desert?"

"No," she lied. "Such a power is not real."

"A sad contradiction, a willing blindness from the most sighted."

"It is not a contradiction!" Avalon hugged herself tighter. "All I have seen or heard is nothing but the formation of logic! Nothing that any intelligent person could not reason out."

Balthazar gave a song to the larks, and one of them answered him back, a sweet succession of notes.

"Superstition is for the ignorant," Avalon whispered.

"Yes. But there are many things which cannot be explained away with superstition, lady. The world is vast. God is great. We cannot understand it all."

"You said you renounced your vows," she accused, feeling somehow betrayed.

"I did. But I have not renounced God, merely the church." Now he laughed out loud, from his belly. "God would not stand to be renounced! He is everywhere, He is everything!"

The wizard turned to her, came close, so close she could follow the swirling lines of the tattoos on his cheeks. "God granted you your power, lady. God gave you this gift." His voice was deep, hypnotic. "It is your destiny. You will succumb."

"No!" She pushed past him, almost running down the wall-walk to the next turret, the next door that could take her away from this conversation.

Inside the winding stairway the murky light buried her, veiling her, and she began to slow down and take the stairs at an even pace.

How stupid, to run away like that! She had let her own fears take over her heart, and now she looked like nothing more than a frightened child, scared of spun stories in the dark.

She rued her actions, very much so, and actually considered going back up the stairs to find Balthazar again, to show him she was not intimidated by his words.

But the night was advancing in rapid steps, and this was reason enough, Avalon considered, not to return to the wall-walk. She was exhausted. She had not slept in so long. Better to sleep and let the accusations of the wizard retreat to nothingness over the course of the night. Better not to think about what he had said at all.

She had left her chamber well lit before she began her prowl, knowing it would be full evening before she returned. Yet to her surprise the lamps had gone out, all but one, a steadfast flame on the little table. And then she saw why the rest were dark.

Marcus was waiting for her, leaning out the narrow window as she so often did, though she doubted he did it for the same reason. Avalon hesitated as she entered the room, surprised and unsurprised, because she couldn't deny there was a tiny part of her that had expected to see him here, that had wanted to see him.

She opened the door as wide as it would go and stood there.

"My lord. Is there something you require?"

He had moved her pallet to one side so that he could stand directly in front of the window.

"I was just wondering," he said slowly but did not turn around, "what you thought might be the appeal of a nun's life."

She closed her eyes, not wanting to speak again on this topic, knowing there could be no answer that would satisfy him.

"My lord, I must ask you to leave. I am too tired to spar with you now."

"I don't want you to spar with me." He turned to face her; the small curve to his lips showed her he had found some amusement in her words. "This may come as a surprise to you, Avalon, but I really don't enjoy fighting at all."

She looked away, down to the smoking flicker of the lone flame, then back up to him.

"Will you leave?"

"Are those my choices? Either we fight, or I leave?"

"It would seem so."

His smile grew thinner—but still amused. "Am I that disagreeable to you?"

Avalon pressed herself back against the door, feeling surprisingly cornered. "If you wish to discuss my decision to join a nunnery, then yes, you are disagreeable to me."

"And if I wish to discuss our marriage, then I am also disagreeable to you."

"Since there is no marriage to discuss," she retorted, "then yes."

"And if I wish to discuss the fulfillment of the legend, then—"

"Why are you here?" she interrupted.

Marcus tilted his head, gave her a piercing look. "I am here to be disagreeable, obviously."

"You are succeeding."

"It's nice to know I'm succeeding at something." He moved away from the window and went over to the lamp, picking it up, studying the flame.

"I thought I could do it," he said to the light after a moment. "I thought I could give you time, but I'm beginning to think that I can't."

She felt a strange tenderness as she watched him, the flame only complimenting his features, the strong profile, a rakish lock of ebony hair falling over his brow. She wanted to brush back his hair for him. She wanted to touch him. It almost hurt her, how much she wished she could do this simple thing.

"I just want to go to sleep," she heard herself saying softly.

"Sleeping is easier than fighting, isn't it?" he asked, again with that small smile.

She couldn't reply to this; the tenderness melted away to annoyance that he seemed to defeat whatever she said with his unconventional reasoning. She walked over to him and took the lamp from his hands, placing it firmly on the table again.

"My lord, I will thank you to leave now."

He looked up and met her eyes squarely amid the dancing shadows.

Avalon, truelove, come to bed with me.

Her mouth fell open at the surprise of it, the clarity of his thought deliberately reaching out to her, penetrating her, the force of his desire almost paralyzing her.

He watched her back up in halting steps, shaking her head now, a denial of his invitation or the entire experience, he couldn't tell.

She turned away from him then and was almost running for the door, anything to get away from him. But he had to stop her, he couldn't let her go like this—not like this, afraid and appalled, when all he had meant to do was bring her into his life and worship her.

Without thought, Marcus took the short steps needed to catch up with her in the hallway, reached out and caught her arm, meaning to say something to make her understand—

His arm was taken and turned and the world flipped around him in a dizzy streak, until he found himself lying on his back on the floor, staring up at Avalon framed against the sharp arch of the ceiling.

Her hands were still on his arm. She was pale, breathing hard, and looked as stunned as he felt.

"I'm sorry," she said, releasing him. "I didn't mean to. I just . . ."

She backed away from him, shaking her head again, no more words, and then she was gone back into her room, slamming the door shut.

Behind him came a low chuckle.

Marcus sat up, wincing, and didn't bother to look at Balthazar.

"I have heard, Kincardine, that patience is listed as a virtue."

Bal came over to where he sat on the stone floor, and continued, "Perhaps you should consider adding a virtue or two to your soul. I believe you would find it most beneficial." He held out his hand, pulled Marcus to his feet. "In the meantime, I have an excellent salve for your head."

"It is not my head," Marcus replied, "which particularly hurts."

"Ah," said Bal. "I have no salve for wounded pride."

They began to move off down the hall, Marcus rubbing his head. "I was actually referring to a different portion of my anatomy."

And Bal, who would never mistake his meaning, laughed again. "I have no salve for wounded hearts, either."

<hr/>

◦⦚⦚◦

$\mathcal{T}$WO MORE DAYS PASSED under a haze of fog that blanketed the castle and the lands. Avalon moved her lessons indoors, with plenty of helpers to push aside the benches and tables of the great hall and make room for her pupils. She now had, in addition to the children, six men and two women, one of which was Ellen. Others still clustered close to watch, commenting to each other on what they saw, even applauding some of the young-sters when they mastered a difficult move.

It was pleasing in some indefinable way, watching the people grow and adapt to what she taught them, watch-ing them learn for pleasure what she had learned for self-defense.

Marcus still studied her while she taught, although he made no move to join in. But she knew he memorized what he saw. Avalon tried not to let it make her nervous. All he ever did was stare at her in that thoughtful way, with perhaps a shade of a dare in his stance.

And no matter how hard she worked, no matter how much she sought to distract herself, what had happened the night he came to her room would not leave her thoughts. That clear, unvarnished message from his mind—more command than entreaty—that sweeping want from him, deliberately sent to her, would not fade. She had felt her knees buckle with the force of it. She had felt her own desire for him crash through her, even though she didn't want it to. He must have known.

He watched her now with an intensity that she swore followed her wherever she went, even when he wasn't in the room. He was not playing with her, he was deadly serious.

He had asked her—*asked* her—to marry him twice more in as many days, just plain words, no thoughts pushed into her mind, and each time she said no, he grew colder, more hostile.

She regretted hurting him, but worse than that, in a

hidden space of her heart was a kernel of what felt like fear.

She wanted to deny it. She wanted to believe she was fearless, but that was folly. Instinctively she knew she was not afraid *of* him, but rather *for* him.

Her rejections were having a dreadful effect on him, subtle things, perhaps only the chimera could see it. There was a tension in him now, the snake trying to awaken and burrow its way through the man to take over and handle matters in its own way.

She prayed the snake was weaker than Marcus. But looking at him, watching his coldness, the fear only grew. He was unhappy with her. He had allowed her to deny him up to now, but what if the next time would be the last, and the snake sprung up and convinced him that she should be subdued and bent to his will? What then? He was still his father's son, after all.

Avalon tried not to think of it. But the laird kept vigil at her lessons, a mute witness to her every move, and she couldn't help but consider what the next moment might bring. The future was becoming a foreboding thing.

Part of her wondered why she was still here. She had done her share for the Kincardines, after all. She had provided them with a future of bounty, she need not linger here. The battle training she offered now could stretch on forever, if she wished it to, but that was certainly not cause enough to entrench herself here at Sauveur.

And Ellen was coming far as steward. Soon she would be able to manage the estate without Avalon's aid. It could be as short as a month, even. And then Avalon would be at perfect liberty to go, all of her obligations fulfilled. She could leave both the man and the snake behind, to fight for his life as they would.

But no matter how often she plotted to leave, one face would intervene in her thoughts, one voice, challenging her to stay.

You belong to me.

She didn't believe that. She didn't belong to anyone. But he had found her weakness again, asking her the appeal of a nunnery. The answer was nothing. Not any longer. But what did that leave her?

Only Marcus, so magnificent that it terrified her.

His eyes, crystal blue, reaching out to capture her heart.

Come to bed with me. . . .

Avalon was resting in a charming room in a corner of the keep after an afternoon that had been particularly taxing. As a sort of childish reaction to his unspoken condemnation, she had chosen today to teach her pupils the flip she had used on him, and Marcus had acknowledged her jab with only the slant of one lifted eyebrow, as if it were nothing more than slightly droll. She was determined to ignore him devoting herself to her work, but it had drained her, leaving her now in weary repose on the cushioned bower.

Greer had first shown her this secluded chamber, claiming it was the sewing room of the mistresses of Sauveur. Avalon supposed this was why Greer had gone out of her way to take her here, but no matter. It couldn't be that bad, Avalon thought, to acquiesce to the atmosphere of this room, no matter whose it was. The tapestries were light and lovely, scenes of unicorns and seals and fair damsels. There was an enormous carpet covering the floor, worn thin in places but still beautiful, plush lavender and rose and blue flowers on a background of sea green. The fireplace had a mantel of pink marble laced with white.

But most wonderful of all, this room had almost an entire wall of windows, great long stretches of glass, each one ready to open and let in the outside.

And each window had pane upon pane of beveled glass—a rare luxury in any home, much less a remote Scottish castle—which transformed the courtyard into little vistas of the same milky fog in every square.

Avalon had no sewing to do here. She hated sewing, anyway. But it was refreshing just to lie back on the long cushion, eyes closed, listening to the quiet all around, the fog pressing up against the glass, secure in knowing that she could be inside but not afraid of shrinking walls.

Last night, unknown to all but her, she had even slept in here, gathering comfort from the hazy glow of the stars all around her whenever she awoke.

"Here, I think," came a voice, shattering the calm Avalon had worked to create.

It was Nora, opening the door to the room, letting Marcus come in, a group of people behind him.

The chimera awoke at the sight of him, making Avalon sit up quickly.

Marcus paused when he saw her, then came forward again, a strange twist to his mouth.

"Avalon," he said.

"What is it?" Her heart began to pound wildly, harder than even after her exercise this afternoon.

"I have news from Trayleigh," Marcus said.

She sat there, waiting, her hand covering her heart as if to slow it.

"Your cousin Bryce has been killed in a hunt."

The chimera shook its head, the lion's mane flowing all around, a low growl that no one but she could hear.

"Really?" she said faintly.

"A stray arrow struck him, apparently. No one has claimed it, but it's being treated as an accident. They're saying it was most likely a poacher." Marcus looked down at her and the peculiarity draping him became more pronounced, a wolfish look. "Warner inherited the title."

Of course he did, Avalon realized. Without Bryce, Warner not only became the new Baron d'Farouche, but he also got Trayleigh. The lands.

It was too much for her to unravel at once. Bryce dead; Warner the new baron. Where did this leave her? What had happened to her plans for revenge? What should she do?

Warner would move swiftly now in pressing for her hand, she knew it without a doubt. As a baron he would have a great deal more personal power on his side, equal to that of Marcus. If Warner did contrive to win his claim for her, then the emissaries would be returning soon. And this time, they might bring an army with them.

Dear God, and these people would fight to the death for her, whether she wanted them to or not.

Marcus turned around and made a curt gesture to the group behind him. Avalon saw them retreat, closing the door to the room, leaving the two of them alone. The smoky light outside was fading rapidly.

"And there is more news," said Marcus. "I am told that with the addition of his baronage, Warner is now more adamant than ever to win your hand."

She lifted one shoulder in a graceful show of indifference, a deception to cover her alarm. "It doesn't matter."

"Doesn't matter?" Marcus gave a disbelieving laugh. "Are you jesting? Of course it matters! He has the means now to offer a grand payment to the church, even more than he could have before, with his holdings in France."

"But his documents could not be real, I'm certain my father never agreed to wed me to him—"

"I'm certain he didn't agree, as well," Marcus interrupted, cold. "But that is irrelevant. Warner will produce papers that appear genuine enough. And if there are discrepancies here and there, well, a few covert payments in gold will take care of that, won't they?"

She stared up at him, the chimera within her now tangling and turning around her thoughts, still growling.

"The church is about to rule in favor of him." Marcus moved closer to her, illuminated in what was left of the fog's ghostly light, his eyes the color of frigid waters. "They will try to come back soon and take you."

"I will not marry Warner," she said softly.

"No," he agreed. "You will not."

She pressed her fingertips to her temples. "I need to think."

"Think on this. We will be married tomorrow."

"*What?*"

"Tomorrow," he repeated, firm and icy.

Avalon stood up, faced down the twist of his mouth: the beginnings of the snake, she saw it now. Her nightmare was coming true before her eyes.

The chimera was growing more receptive to the menace in him, and she had to speak over its muttered warnings.

"I have told you I will not marry Warner. You are going to have to believe me, my lord. Because I am not going to wed you tomorrow."

"Wrong," he said. "You are. They cannot have you."

"They will not have me! I have already told you this!"

The snake was clearer now, manifesting so easily, cunning and strong. The chimera gave up the growl for a laugh; it laughed and laughed inside her, wrapping around her ability to reason, growing bigger and bigger, encasing her hidden terror.

"Marcus Kincardine," she said clearly. "Listen to me well. No matter what proof Warner creates, it matters not. I will not be his bride. You need not fear it."

That one brow lifted again, arrogance and disdain. "Fear it? I don't, my love. I know it well. You cannot be his wife. Indeed, you are already mine."

"I am not anyone's wife! You are not listening—"

"I'm listening. I'm listening to the call of my people. I'm listening to the dictates of an intractable legend. I am listening, my Lady Avalon, to the music of the stars, and all of them tell me the very same thing."

No, she wanted to say, but the word would not come out of her mouth, the chimera choked it off, and then it spoke suddenly in her head, in the voice of Hanoch:

Ye belong to the curse. . . .

Marcus had a smile that held no warmth at all. "Tomorrow is the day. I have no more time for niceties. We have all waited long enough. Tomorrow the curse ends."

He meant it, she realized. It was not just the snake

putting words to its intent. These were the thoughts of the man, truly Marcus, telling her she was his wife. It was Marcus who needed her, who wanted her.

She remembered with chilling clarity that he had said the emissaries would have to kill him to take her away. She had thought it was merely his snake speaking for him, but no, all along it had been the man himself, the laird who had to claim her, for legend or passion or whatever it was that was forged in his head. The snake was only backing him now.

Without warning Marcus took her arms, pulled her into him and held her there tightly. He bowed his head down to her hair and his grip changed, grew more urgent.

"Don't you want to marry me?" he whispered against her, beginning a blaze of kisses down her temple, her cheeks. When she turned her head away he followed and found her lips, a brutal claiming of her.

She couldn't stop him, she didn't even want to, but he broke away, breathing hard against her neck, still clutching her.

"Avalon," he said, and it was almost a prayer. "Please."

Hanoch spoke again, his words like the deathblow of a sword:

Ye will marry my son. Whatever else ye want or think is nothing compared to that. . . .

And the chimera grinned and sank its claws into her mind, threw her own words at her, that promise:

I will never marry him! I vow it now. . . .

She could not allow Hanoch to win. She had already given over so much of herself to him, but she could not bow in this.

Her fingers held on to Marcus as she leaned back and looked up into his eyes.

"I can't marry you," she said.

His eyes closed. She felt his pain as her own, intensified by the fact that it was given to him by her.

"I'm sorry, I'm so sorry," she said, anguished. "Please understand. I can't."

He took a deep breath past his teeth; she felt him gather himself together. He set her carefully away from him, hands now light on her shoulders.

"All right," he said. "I'm sorry, as well. I'm sorry it's going to have to be this way."

"What way?" she asked, and at last the chimera paused, grew silent in her head.

"Please go back to your room, Avalon."

"Why?"

"I want you to stay there until tomorrow. After we are married, you will be able to move about again."

The chimera howled at her: *Run, hide, don't let them catch you!* The power of it surged through her body, made her hands tremble so that she had to close them into fists to hide it.

"You don't control me," she said, fighting the lash of panic inside her.

"Come," he replied, as dark and meaningful as the falling night.

She looked around to both sides, the charming room now much too small, too confining. The windows were shut tight. There were too many people waiting behind the only door.

Her heart was a caged bird, the trembling in her fingers moved upward, clenching tight around her chest, her throat. She knew it was not rational, this over-whelming fear that took her, but she was tied to it anyway.

"Avalon."

He was waiting for her, she could see that. He was waiting for her to walk out of this room with him, to voluntarily confine herself to that little sleeping chamber, to sit and wait for fate to swallow her up whole. It was just like the pantry, when she was a child, that cramped and stifling space, utterly black, relentlessly scary, filled with whispering monsters, greedy fiends who laughed at her while she was curled up and alone, the goblin men, come back for her. . . .

"No." The word slipped out on its own, falling heavy into the silence. Her feet retreated from him of their own volition, one step at a time, until she felt the cushion of the bower against the backs of her knees.

The pale light of the fog was almost gone, turning the room to watery gray, disguising his face so that she could not read it. Behind her she felt the cooler air next to the glass, a frosty touch on her shoulder blades. Darkness was waiting for her, crouched in the corners of her vision where she couldn't quite see. Blackness, suffocating, endless blackness, pressing on her, filling her nostrils and her lungs until she couldn't breathe—

He moved. She saw the dim shape of him shift against the lighter tones of the marble mantel, an outline of a man approaching, so much larger than she was.

"No," she said again, but it was apprehensive now, less certain. She held her hands up in front of her, an instinctive defense.

"Don't fight me," he said, savage. "Don't do it."

"Stay away," she warned, and her voice had a crack in it. "I won't go back there."

"For a day . . ."

. . . and a night in the pantry . . .

"No—"

The air was too thin here, she couldn't manage to draw enough of it into her lungs, the trembling inhibited her, made it harder to see him, to know what to do next. He spoke again, still ruthless.

"You don't have a choice. You will do as I say. I know what is best."

Ye'll stay in there. . . .

The goblins were expecting her. She could hear them; even the chimera turned its ears to them, listening. They existed only in the blackness, they waited for her in the dark, in the pantry. Each time she was imprisoned there they were waiting with axes and knives and fire, and Ona died over and over again, scarlet blood splattered on the bark of the birch, and Avalon was next.

The man moved again, sudden and deft, a blur of dark against dark, but the chimera warned her, moved her hands for her to block him, to duck and turn around him. She struck at him and felt his arm give way to her, and her only thoughts were *escape, escape, escape!*

But he seemed to know her plan, and with cruel efficiency used his other hand to capture her waist, bending in the same direction as she did, following her, closing the trap. Fear made her clumsy; the hand she had struck came back up, found her arm and bent it tight around her, immobilizing her, then he kicked his feet between hers, lifting her up so she could not get a solid stance on the ground.

"I learn from my mistakes, my dear," he said into her ear. "You taught this trick to the children, and I was paying attention."

She let out a cry of mingled frustration and dread; she couldn't see who it was behind her, it could be anyone, it could be Ian or Hanoch or the goblin men, come to devour her—

Although he still held her tight, something in her captor changed, grew more attentive to her ragged breathing, the shaking that controlled her.

"Avalon?" The voice was lower, very human. It was the voice of Marcus. "What's wrong with you?"

Caught, at his mercy, she bit down on her lip to keep inside the sob that wanted to burst out. She couldn't bear it—she could have run away, she could have braved the wilds of the world on her own, but she couldn't go back to that room. She couldn't face the tiny space, the narrow window, the encroaching darkness. The waiting.

"Tell me," he said, and it wasn't a command now but an invitation. His hold on her loosened by gradual degrees, until she realized her feet were firmly on the carpet of flowers and his arms were not hurting her. She felt his breath, warm on her neck, somehow reassuring. "Tell me," he said again, soft.

"I can't go back there." The sob was still present, a hitch in her throat.

"Where?" he asked.

"That room. I won't go back."

He seemed to think about this, finding her unspoken secrets, though she had not meant him to. "It bothers you? Your room?"

Lucidity settled on her despite the gloom around

them. She was being unreasonable. She was acting childish. Yet still he waited for her, unyielding, uncompromising, and the best thing she could think to offer up was: "It's too small." Her voice was thin and reedy.

She could feel him ponder this, could almost picture the remote look in his eyes as he unwrapped her sentence, probed it. She felt inadequate suddenly, stupid, to allow herself to fall into his snare, and now what was she to do? Just the thought of that tight, closed space brought back the sob.

"Too small," he mused, not condemning, but very, very alert.

At some point his grip on her had loosened enough so that she could turn in his arms, and Avalon did that now, feeling the need to make him understand what she could not say, what she could not even bear to think about. His face was almost completely obscured above her now; a short twilight approached a clouded night.

"In the dark," she said.

He didn't misunderstand. "The room is too small and too dark for you."

"When I was a girl," she said, "there was a pantry in the cottage, and they used to lock me in there—" The sob bubbled up, devouring the rest of the words, and she had to clamp her lips shut to hold it back.

Everything about him changed, softened. His hands caressed her arms, his lips were velvet against her forehead.

"Shhh," he said, and his breath warmed her. "It's all right."

She leaned into him without being able to stop herself; he took her weight easily, comforting, and curiously enough this released the sob in her at last.

"Oh," she cried, and buried her head against his shoulder.

He rocked her slowly, saying words she barely heard, because of all things she was crying now, little tears, muffled whimpers into his tartan, and she didn't even know why she was doing it, except that it felt so good to have him hold her, and it was such a relief to be able to let him take in her sorrow.

"It's all right," he murmured, over and over, his hands smoothing up and down her back until the tears stopped, and all that was left of it was the dampness of his shoulder beneath her.

She felt drained, exhausted, and now when her head rested against him it was not just for comfort, but because it felt too heavy to lift.

"Truelove." Marcus stroked her face; she felt his fingers gently wipe away the wetness on her cheeks. "You needn't go back to that room."

She latched on to his words, felt the tremulous fronds of hope uncoil within her. He bent down and brushed his lips against hers, light, tender. "You should have told me about this. I never would have subjected you to it had I known."

Avalon couldn't reply. She was too sleepy suddenly, she could barely keep her eyes open. Weariness drenched her entire body.

"Where are we going?" she managed to ask as he led her out of the room to the tactfully deserted hallway.

"To my chambers," he said, and moved her forward.

Chapter Twelve

His bed was soft and as large as she remembered, with a carved oak post at each corner and some kind of heavy cloth tied back from them to create curving sweeps of muted color next to the wood.

Avalon didn't wonder that Marcus brought her here, that he had led her to the edge of the bed and then joined her there, an arm around her shoulders. As he pulled her back onto the welcome cushioning of furs and pillows all she felt was the last of her efforts to stay awake slip away from her. It seemed perfectly natural to lay her head in the crook of his shoulder, both of them still completely dressed, her arm across his chest and her leg slightly bent over one of his.

She didn't question any of it. Under the starlight spilling in from his windows and secure in his embrace, she gave up everything and fell asleep.

Occasionally she would drift close to awareness again, feeling the difference beside her, the warmth of a solid body holding her, the sound of another's breath close to her ear. But none of it was worrisome; in fact, it seemed better than comforting to experience these things. It seemed like these were sensations she had been seeking in her dreams all her life.

So when she finally did come all the way out of her sleep she did not panic at the sight of a masculine arm draped over her waist as she lay on her back—a heavy weight but not unpleasant—leading up to the shoulder of a man with glossy black hair and a face relaxed in slumber.

The rising light from the windows told her it was close to dawn, a cool coloring of his features, lavender shadows enhancing the short growth of beard on his chin.

Avalon blinked and the vision stayed the same. She was here in Marcus's chambers. He had brought her here last night and slept beside her, and she had let him—

His eyes opened.

She didn't look away. The winter blue now held hints of the dawn, a slow warmth as he took her in, solemn.

In his eyes she could easily become lost, carried away in that warmth, in the hidden blue flames.

She felt her own response instantly, welling up easily, because right now in the tender newness of the daybreak she had no barriers to him. All she felt was that melting she couldn't stop. He lifted one of his hands, the one at her waist, and brought his fingers up to her lips, touching them lightly, still so serious, as if the whole world depended now on what he did.

A lock of his hair brushed her cheek as he bent his head closer to hers, his lips following the course of his fingers. His kiss was soft at first, almost hesitant, but even that moment was quickly lost, and he moved over her and kissed her hard.

Her body responded in a rush; it knew where this led now, to that burning moment, that piercing ecstasy, and she leaned into him helplessly, even reaching up one hand to weave her fingers in his hair, holding him closer. He tasted of something salty, enticing, purely masculine. His tongue teased her lips, he shaped words against them.

"Yes," he murmured. "Good."

She didn't know what that meant, what was good except everything he was doing to her, the way he was covering her whole body with his own now, settling urgently between her legs in a way that felt unfamiliar and improper and so delightful. She was overheated in the gown and the tartan, they constrained her and perhaps he knew this, because even as he kept her under him he was pulling at the folds of material over her shoulder, removing the silver brooch that pinned it to her, yanking the material free from her waist and pushing it down and to the side.

The rush of cool air on her was immediately covered by his palms moving up her sides, stroking her breasts through just the gown of black.

Her head tilted back and she heard a moan—It came from her throat and evoked that feral smile from him, a blaze of melting liquid firing through her.

"Truelove," he said, and began to move against her, between her legs, shifting his hands so they were beneath her, on her back, down to her hips, lifting her up into him.

The center of her was hot, wet need, it was like he had done to her before. She was lost to all but him, his rhythm taking her and pulling her in, making her flex against him. Somehow his own tartan had loosened and come undone around his shoulder; he stripped off the tunic as well, and for the first time she saw the strong column of his neck leading down to solid muscles and short, curling hairs on his chest. Her hands found his arms, reveled in his bare skin, skimmed over to touch those soft curls.

Now it was his turn to moan, leaning back for her, allowing her to explore him. He was still cradled between her legs, still pressing his rigidity to her, almost painful.

Avalon watched her hands in wonder, watched as if it were someone else doing these things to him, touching him, feeling his heat, the smoothness of his skin. His eyes were closed, his mouth had a tightness to it as she let her hands drift lower, down to his stomach, the hard, flat planes of him there.

He moved swiftly, that grace in him all the more apparent in his haste; pushing her hands aside, pulling her to sit up so fast she didn't know what had happened and then holding her there, his arms around her, his fingers working at the buttons of her gown. His breathing was a ragged tempo in her ear, matching her own.

Avalon felt the first one come free, then another, then another, but his hands were trembling, she felt that too, and when the next button wouldn't release he took the cloth on both sides and ripped it apart, popping the rest of the buttons free in a shower of little disks on the bed. Before she could react he was pushing the material down over her shoulders, tugging it to her waist, trapping her hands in their long sleeves and freeing the rest of her to him.

She made a small sound, all she could do to express her sudden dismay, but Marcus was laying her back down, still panting, holding her arms carefully as he settled her among the furs.

"Oh my God," was what he said, looking down at

her, and she didn't know what to think. There was a blush rising up through her entire body and she had to look away from him, still needing him but too embarrassed to move.

"Avalon." His voice was deep and breathless. He touched her now with just one hand, stroked the underside of her breast, causing her nipple to harden in a rush.

When at last she could look up at him he was still staring, watching his hand. His fingertip brushed her nipple, his palm moved to cover it. He looked up, met her gaze, and all she saw there was shining blue.

"You are . . ." His words trailed off. He shook his head then leaned down and took her nipple in his mouth.

Her cry was much less muffled than before, her body moved without her will, meeting him, leaning up to him, and he knew just what to do, how to run his tongue over her, the hardened surface, a gentle sucking.

Marcus lifted his head and blew softly on the nipple, and Avalon thought she might go insane.

"Perfection," he said, at last finishing his sentence.

She freed her arms from the sleeves and he helped her, smiling, then slowly lowered himself down to her, allowing his chest to rub hers, a sensation that felt lush and wonderful, the heat of his skin on hers, the incredible feel of him. Her arms slid up his and across his back, so broad her fingers could not touch in a circle. He was kissing her again, finding their rhythm, helping her push the gown away as she lifted her hips and the material fell free. She kicked it down to her feet.

Marcus pulled away from her, bringing back the rush of cool air, causing her skin to chill. But he didn't leave, he only removed the layers of his own tartan at his waist, unwrapping it and dropping it to the side of the bed, then coming down on her again, finding her lips again.

They were both completely unclothed, and the contact of his body on top of hers was startling. For the first time Avalon felt a splinter of doubt seep into her, dousing the heat.

What was she doing? She was kissing him back, returning his strength with a force of her own, captive to his touch. She should pull away. She should stop him.

She was in bed with Marcus, who pressed against her with his own solid form, all man, leaving no question at all as to where they were going. She was about to make love to Marcus Kincardine.

She would be giving herself to him without the promise of marriage. She would be risking nothing less than her sanity if she didn't leave right now, because Avalon knew without a doubt that if she stayed with him here, in his bed, then she would become his lover, and she would never be able to escape him completely. He would stay in her heart forever.

But perhaps he was already there, anyway.

Marcus felt her difference, the way the stillness stole over her, locking her hands into place on his arms, not pushing him away but no longer so accepting, either. Her face was the picture of troubled beauty, as if someone had come and roused her out of a dream.

"Avalon," he said, pausing, afraid to move at all. "Truelove, beloved."

She looked up at him, lips parted, breathing shallow. The violet of her eyes was dark and deep.

"Don't be afraid," he whispered. "It's me. It's right."

The troubled look grew graver; her gaze shifted past him, over to somewhere behind him. The tension in her hands grew tighter.

"Avalon," he said again, helpless, and then carefully reached up, cupped her face with his palms. He didn't know what else to say. All he knew was that he had come so close to her, so close it was killing him to hesitate like this, yet he was doing it because he had to. She had allowed him this much—indeed, welcomed it—and to stop now would be painful beyond imagining.

He had been waiting for her so long. His whole life. But he could not take her like this, not with any doubts between them.

And then she changed. He didn't know why, or even how, except that her focus came back to him, her hands relaxed, her fingers again caressing him, running up his arms to pull him down to her.

"I'm not afraid," she said to him, and there was more than acceptance to her words, there was an invitation, a sultry flicker of hunger in her that made the passion in him leap forward and take over.

He was already on top of her, between her legs, and now he no longer tried to hold himself apart from her but let her feel him there, probing, stiff, wanting. She responded by opening her legs wider, trusting him, and Marcus gritted his teeth and found her wetness, sweet and succulent, so hot.

She felt the pressure of him increase, singular and somewhat frightening despite her words, this feeling of invasion where that part of him, so different from her, was entering her, slow, unyielding.

This was not like before, in the gatehouse, this was

so much more of him. It made her go still again as he pushed forward, stretching her to an almost indistinct ache. And then he stopped.

Above her his face was lit in the growing brightness of the room, so handsome, his hair slipping down over his shoulders, against her hands. His eyes opened and he looked down at her; she saw the tinge of regret in him.

"I'm sorry, truelove," he said, and before she could ask "For what?" he moved his hands to cup her buttocks, lifting her, and then shoved all the way inside of her.

There was an awful, tearing pain, shocking and unexpected, making her hands change on him, pushing him away from her, get *away*, but he resisted her and held her immobile, tucking his face into her neck, murmuring more apologies.

"Avalon." Her name was a whisper on his lips. "It's what's supposed to happen, I'm sorry, oh, God. . . ."

His voice faded away as he stayed clenched above her, both of them breathing hard. Slowly, slowly the burning pain began to change, still peculiar, but not so terrible now. Avalon made herself relax as much as she could, controlling the strangeness, exploring it. He was inside her now, buried. And she thought that somewhere deep within her, that familiar melting was coming back upon her.

Experimentally she raised one knee, just slightly, and felt him clench even tighter, sink in even further. A low sound, guttural and tight, escaped his throat.

"Wait," he gasped, but she wouldn't, because the melting honey was back, even the pain had blended into it to accept it and she wanted more, and knew somehow that the way to get it was to lift her other leg, sliding her foot up the hard length of his calf.

His moan was louder now and he began to move in her, holding her face between his hands and rocking back and forth above her, making her arch up to meet each thrust. Her breathing was becoming something more like whimpers and the melting was transforming into a new feeling, a spark of that promise she understood, stronger than before.

Marcus leaned his head down and kissed her and she kissed him back, wanting all of him, suddenly eager to take in as much of him as she could. The stinging honey permeated her, overpowered her; she was liquid fire, he alone was real, his touch, his movements, and everything he did made the fire burn brighter, harder, until her head was thrown back and she lit up at once, a burst of brilliance, a wave of light taking her body.

His cry became her own, both of them lost in each other, and Avalon thought she might never come back from that edge of bliss.

Marcus collapsed around her, spent, leaning to one side so he didn't crush her. His head was turned to her neck, his body a heated weight that she still welcomed. The scent of him was all around her, new, exciting, almost still surprising.

Avalon closed her eyes, inwardly marveling at what just happened. Her hand drifted up and settled on his forearm, peaceful.

When she looked at him again he was looking back at her. The solemnness had returned, and there was a different light to his eyes.

I love you.

The unspoken words came from him, absolutely,

positively from him. Not the chimera. Not the wind. Marcus.

The immediate confusion swelled up in her, making her sit up abruptly and pull away from him, clutching a blanket to her chest.

He couldn't love her. How could he possibly love her? He was in love with a fable, not her, not the real woman. He was in love with his damned legend.

It created a sweltering pain in her, how horrible to think this, and now she couldn't forget it. Marcus had made love to his legend, not to her.

"Avalon?"

He was sitting up beside her, reaching for her, and she pulled back further. He scowled.

"What is it? Are you in pain?"

"No," she choked out, then ducked her head. The pain curdled in her heart, containable but so devastating.

"No," she said again, and lifted her head to let him see her face. "I'm fine."

What had she expected of him, anyway? It would have taken a miracle to separate him from his legacy, and Avalon had no miracles to offer. Only herself, mortal and flawed. Nothing to compare to a legend.

"I must return to my room," she said, distant.

"Why?"

She groped for an excuse, seizing on the obvious.

"The maid will come soon."

Marcus gave her a smile, sensual, and she felt her heart squeeze up with the pain of it. "I hate to disillusion you, but I suspect the maid has come and gone. I usually awaken before dawn."

She gave a little jump, eyes flying to the door.

"Don't worry," he continued, amused and obviously trying to hide it. "I bolted it last night. But I'm sure everyone knows why."

Avalon began to scramble out of the bed, pulling the blanket with her. Marcus leaned over without haste and took both of her hands in his, turning her back to him. The blanket fell and perched, precarious, on the tips of her breasts.

"Truelove, don't go." His gaze took in the edge of the blanket, the promise of her skin, and then came back up to hers. She recognized the color of his eyes, darkened snow and sky, and felt her senses betray her, all of them going back to him, wanting him. She swallowed, fighting it. Losing.

"Avalon. We must talk." Marcus offered that smile again, slowly drawing her back to him, back to the well of blankets on his bed, strong limbs and tanned skin and an inviting warmth from the chill of the room. Her resistance drained away as he got her closer and closer, nestling her down amid the softness and then coming even closer still, an embrace.

He lay beside her and began to stroke her hair, running his fingers through it, each touch bringing a tiny thrill to her. His head was even with hers, he watched his own movements.

"Are you happy here?" he asked, betraying nothing in his voice.

His hand moved again, stroking. She knew she should lie and say no. If she lied, he would have no idea of her true heart. And yet she couldn't say it, and had to settle on a half-truth.

"I—" Avalon gave a little cough. "I am. In a way."

"What way is that?"

She could see her own hair as his fingers laced through it, a leisurely tumble of bright strands between them.

"Just the way anyone could be, I suppose," she said softly, watching his hand, her hair.

"Could be?" His voice was light, impartial. His hand kept its rhythm. "Meaning, as happy as anyone could be under the circumstances?"

"Yes," she replied.

"Do you think, then, that you could be happier?"

His stroking was soothing, slow.

"I don't know," she said, lost in his movements. "I don't know. Perhaps."

"What would it take, Avalon, to make you the happiest you could be?"

His words were a great puzzle to her, a problem she couldn't sort out. Her hair still rose and fell between them, strands separated by his touch, held and released, over and over.

"I don't know," she said again, and her words felt strange to her, foreign.

"A home," he said, low, matching the rhythm of his hand. "A family. A place where you belong, forever and ever."

Someone to love me, she thought, her mind spinning lazily. *For you to love me.*

"Yes," he said. "That would make you happiest."

He didn't stop his stroking, just let the moment float free between them, nothing but innocence, his movements, her gaze transfixed on him, her hair, the colors of them both.

"I would give you all that," he said at last. "I would give you whatever you wanted to make you happy."

His hand slowed, then stopped, freeing her eyes to meet his.

"Only you must marry me first," he said. "Will you—"

"—marry me, treuluf, and be mine," he said, "and I would be the happiest man ever to live."

She covered her mouth with both hands to contain her joy, her surprise, and he lifted his face to her, still kneeling in the meadow grass, and spread his arms wide.

"I will hand thee the stars on a platter of gold. I will capture the sun for thou to carry in thy pocket, shamed that it is that thy beauty is so much the brighter."

She began to laugh around her hands, standing still among the nodding wildflowers.

"I will rid the oceans of all their salt for thee," he cried loudly, "so that thou might not be offended by the tears of the sea, weeping jealously over the beauty of thy face!"

Her laughter grew, and he inched closer on his knees, arms still wide, his smile wider, and she was certain all the clansmen could hear him now.

"I will climb every mountain from here to heaven to prove my love for thee," he shouted dramatically, "and will bring back the most precious of gems, the rarest, for only those could be worthy of thy beaut—"

Her laughter spilled over; she had to clutch her stomach, she was laughing so hard, joined by all the clan standing on the fringes of the meadow. He stopped and laughed with them, then moved so fast and came up around her, pulled her down to him and they fell together into the tall silver-green grass, rolling.

Her laughter faded but still she could not stop her smile, and his was equal to hers, his eyes alight, his look so charming. He lay above her, very improper, then tried to kiss her in front of everyone and she pretended to fight him off, though everyone knew she was only pretending, because they all knew how much she loved him. And how much he loved her.

He leaned back and she saw him against the sky: black hair, light eyes, her beloved.

"Wilt thou marry me, lass?" he asked softly now, just for her, serious and devout.

She reached up a hand and captured a lock of his hair, curling it around her fingers.

"Aye," she said to him, still smiling. "Just thou try to stop me."

"—marry me?" he asked.

Avalon started, came back from her vision, and found Marcus leaning over her, black hair and light eyes, but there was a canopy of a bed beyond him, not a blue sky; and they were alone in his room, not in the glen with all the clan, everyone watching.

For a moment she couldn't move, the sudden change was too great for her, the vision too pure still, too closely meshed with the present. Her heart was beating too hard, the laughter still infected her, and she could still smell the grass.

Marcus waited, unchanged, for her answer.

Just thou try to stop me. . . .

"I . . ."

The moment expanded, a bubble, one vision imposed on another: two couples, two pairs of lovers, one moment. One answer.

"No," she said, breaking the spell. The bubble vanished, and it was just the two of them again.

Marcus didn't move, didn't change at all that she could tell. "Why not?"

"I can't."

"I don't believe you."

She blinked up at him, not knowing what to say to that. His hand reached out, found her hair again, but this time he simply wrapped his fingers in it, just as the bride had done to her love.

"I think you can do better than that, Avalon," he said mildly. "'Can't' isn't a reason."

She looked away, nonplussed, and then began to sit up. Marcus moved back, allowing her to pull away from him slightly, though he kept his hold on her hair.

"I can't marry you," she said again, and felt the uselessness of her repetition.

"Don't you want happiness?" he asked softly.

"Of course," she said. "But—"

"Don't you think I could make you happy?"

She thought of the sheer joy felt by the bride in the meadow; she had felt the girl's boundless exultation as the laird got down on his knees in front of her, shouted out his love for her. That bride had known ultimate happiness, Avalon was sure of it. How could she ever hope to match something like that?

Her life was a different pattern altogether from that girl's in the meadow. The laird who asked her now was not asking because he wanted to hand her the stars, the sun, the oceans. He was asking because he thought he had to. Because he thought he should. Duty. Honor. Legend.

"The only person who could make me happy is me," she said to him at last, not cutting, just a trace of sadness.

Marcus examined her, then bent his head slightly.

"I would like to try," he said simply. "Is that so much? To want to please you?"

Her heart was breaking, the pain was back tenfold, he couldn't love her, not like what it turned out she truly wanted, the glimpse of that honest joy. . . .

He looked up again. "I would do anything to have the chance to try," he said, fierce.

Her hands covered her mouth as the other girl's had, but to hold in the pain, not the laughter. She couldn't meet his eyes, she couldn't sit beside him like this any longer, and so she slid out of the bed and ran over to her gown, a lump of cloth on the floor.

He watched her, saying nothing, doing nothing.

When the gown was on again—she couldn't manage all the buttons, and most of them were gone now anyway—she looked around for her tartan, found it, and draped it over her shoulders like a cape to block the cold.

She was facing one of the windows, and the sun came free from a ripple of clouds just then and dazzled her.

Outside was a world she did not recognize, true winter, blinding white. Snow had come during the night while they slept, in exchange for the fog. As if the mist's final farewell, its last touch to the land, all had turned to white. Sparkling snow covered everything from the lochs to the mountaintops to the eaves and the windowsills.

Avalon turned around and he was behind her, silent, his own tartan wrapped loosely around him, the tunic abandoned. He was no longer looking at her, but out at the landscape, the splendor of white.

The brightness illuminated everything now; she could pick out the tufts in the weave of his plaid. She could catch the sliding rainbows in his black hair. She could see the faded scars marking his side, where the tartan hung more lax than usual, and down his back, where he had missed the fold.

Scars, not a few of them, varied and ragged, almost invisible but for their paleness against his tan.

She reached for them without thinking about it, tracing one with her finger, feeling the old wound, following it down beneath the folds of the plaid. His breathing quickened slightly, then calmed again. He would not look at her.

Beneath the cloth she flattened her palm, feeling for more, and found them. They were long, thin stretches along his back, slanted, the way the sting of a whip might fall when lashed down on a man.

She remembered the dream, remembered it vividly, and took back her hand to pick up his wrist, holding it up to the light, examining it.

The marks were there, almost gone like the rest, so faint she could barely see them. But she remembered what that had felt like, to be tied down to the table, to have the hard strands eat into her flesh.

Avalon bowed her head and brought his wrist up to her lips, pressing a kiss there, unable even to say why but that it seemed so imperative that she do it.

"I don't want your pity," he said roughly, and took his hand back, still gazing out at the world.

"It's not pity that I feel," she said.

Marcus gave a pained smile to the view outside, the snow. "And will you marry me now, Avalon d'Farouche?

Will you marry the marked man, out of the lamentation of your heart, if for nothing else?" He didn't give her the chance to refuse again. "Now I would have you wed me for the wrong reasons." He laughed, bitter. "And I don't even care."

"I do not pity you," she said. "I would not marry you for that."

Marcus looked at her at last, a faint scowl on his face, fallen angel.

"What then? What would you marry me for? Tell me and I'll do it."

She lifted her hands up in the air, seeking inspiration, or help, or she knew not what. He would not understand her. He couldn't. And what a terrible irony it seemed to her, because she knew now that Marcus was the key to her final happiness. He *could* do it, he *could* bring her to that bliss she had glimpsed there in the grass with the girl and her laird. But only if he let go of the fantasy and accepted who she was. And only if she let go of her fears, and accepted who he was—the son of Hanoch. But it seemed that neither of them were capable of these things. And so she said the only thing that made sense to her any longer, the only thing she had been able to hang on to with good reason:

"I cannot marry you." She took a few steps back from him, then turned around, going to the door. Her fingers fumbled with the latch.

"You *cannot*?" he repeated behind her—at last, at last catching up to her meaning.

She didn't reply; the latch was sticky, perhaps with the new cold, and seemed frozen in place.

"You cannot," he said again, and there was an

emerging change in his voice, an excitement that prick-led the hair on the back of her neck even as she tugged at the latch. She began to pull at it harder.

"Why *can't* you?"

She ignored him, still struggling with the stubborn lock.

"Avalon! Why can't you?"

"Because!" she cried. But the latch popped free then, and she was escaping out the door, barefoot because she had forgotten her shoes, and she wasn't going back for them, not with Marcus waiting for her.

Except he wasn't waiting for her, he was following her, out into the hallway, less dressed than she was and even more uncaring.

"Avalon!" He was running to keep up with her, holding his tartan in place. "Wait! Talk to me!"

In her haste she lost her bearings in the maze of hall-ways; she couldn't remember the way to her room, and the people they were beginning to pass were no help, as-tonished faces, rampant curiosity, and then an audience clustering behind Marcus.

Dammit, where was she? What hall was this? Avalon couldn't tell, none of it looked right, the halls were too wide, and then she realized the enormity of her mistake, because when she turned the next corner she found her-self in the great room, interrupting the breakfast of all the people seated there.

She stopped, flushed and breathing hard, wild hair falling everywhere, the tartan just draping her and the gown half free down her back, and knew with extreme mortification exactly what she looked like. She could see it clearly in every single face before her, and she could read every single thought as the entire crowd turned as one to take in Marcus, who had just run up behind her.

Oh, God. She wanted to drop through the floor, she wanted the earth to open up and swallow her and end this misery.

The giant room was totally still, no one moved, no one said a word, only Marcus, coming up to stand beside her, breathing as hard as she was.

"Why can't you marry me?" he asked in a clear, carrying voice.

The people swung back to her, waited with him for her answer.

"Because," she said again, trying not to sound too small in the echoing emptiness around them.

"Because why?"

His hair hung down loose, just as wild as hers, just as sure an indication to everyone as to how they had spent their night. His eyes were bright and beautiful.

"Because I made a vow that I wouldn't!" Avalon cried, pushed over the edge by this last thing, his beauty, and what could have been between them. "Because your father made me hate you before I even knew who you were! Because you're his son!" Her hands twisted nervously before her; she looked down at them, away from everything else in the room because it was all hinging on her. Her voice grew quieter. There was that terrible knot in her throat again, like last night.

"Because I'm afraid you're going to turn into him."

Marcus stared down at her, the bent head, the wringing hands, and felt the shock settle through him.

Turn into Hanoch? Good God, turn into his father, a

man he had spent almost his entire life trying either to forget or ignore? *Turn into him?*

"No," he said, instinctive, from his heart, shaking his head. "Avalon, no. I could never do such a thing."

She looked up and there were tears in her eyes, those gorgeous eyes, looking off to the side, away.

"Truelove," he said softly, not moving to touch her, afraid to spill those tears for her. "My life. I would never harm you on purpose. I would never do anything to make you hate me."

"You did!" she said, a tremor to her voice. "You did! You kidnapped me and brought me here; you did it for you and for them"—her hand swept around, indicated the stunned people surrounding them—"but you cared nothing for me! You don't even know who I am!"

"I do," he said. "I do know who you are—"

"No! You know only your legend! You listened to your father, to a story, and you made me fit your mold, because that's convenient for you, and that's what will satisfy you. But it has nothing to do with *me.*"

She took a backward step, as if to get away from him, but then stopped and lifted her chin—so proud, so beautiful, and her emotions in such delicate balance that irrationally Marcus wanted to protect her from himself.

"The only reason you want to be with me is for your legend," Avalon said in a soft, fragile voice. "You would wed me to strengthen it, to make it as true as you could. But I would lose myself to it, and you would allow that. You would help it to happen. I can't give up who I am for you—for anyone, or anything."

She was wrong, she was so wrong about him, but Marcus could see that convincing her of that was going to be close to impossible, and he could even see why, when everything was laid out as she saw it, a chain of terrible happenings to trap her.

"If I were to marry you," she continued, and the tears began slowly to spill down her cheeks, "then Hanoch would win, and you would have the power to destroy me. And I can't let you do that."

There was a profound silence shrouding the hall, letting her words fade away against the stone walls, her anguish impossible to dismiss.

Marcus shook his head, weary. "Very well," he said, and heard a hushed gasp whisper through the people. He spoke around the clenching pain in his chest. "If that's truly what you think, that I would turn into Hanoch, that I only want you for this legend, then I must release you. You are free to leave Sauveur."

The clanspeople exploded into comment, denials, shouts at him to take back his words. Marcus raised a hand to them and the noise died down, everyone staring.

Avalon looked up at him, and he could tell by the way she held her shoulders—stiff and straight, battle stance—that she thought it a trick of some sort, to fool her into following his will.

"You were right," he said. "I can't marry you. Not like this."

There was a moan filtering through the crowd now, men and women both, all of them dismayed, thinking he had lost his mind. They were terrified of losing the bride.

But not nearly as terrified as Marcus was of losing Avalon.

Her hands were still now, clasped together in front of her, half-hidden amid the tartan and the silk of her hair. Marcus had to look away from her, afraid she would see the stark need in him and think it something else, something that would tilt the scales of her fate even further against him. He didn't know what else to do.

"All I wanted was to make you happy," he said at last, very quiet. "You, Avalon, not some legend. Not a myth. You. I want *you*."

He watched her fingers tighten on each other, nervous, and waited. She was about to shatter his whole life. She was about to render everything he had ever done, ever said, ever hoped, moot with her rejection of him. It was unbearable, waiting for the death knell of his dreams.

Her hands gradually released their grip; she rubbed her flattened palms against the folds of her skirts.

"If you ever hurt me——" she began, husky, and he had to look up to catch the rest of her thought on her face.

Words failed him. Slowly, deliberately, he shook his head at her, denying it, rejecting it as even a possibility. His jaw was locked too tight for the pleas he wanted to shower on her to escape him.

Avalon stared over at him, all moonlight and heather and jet, and he saw her let out her breath.

"All right," she said. "I'll marry you."

Chapter Thirteen

———⟨∞⟩———

AVALON WATCHED his face change; a slow comprehension of her words, desperation to blankness to disbelief. And then he broke into a smile, that feral one that used to fill her with dismay but now only found something matching in her, an untamed spirit that leapt forward and made her glad, incredibly glad, that she had said what she did.

There was noise all around them, unfathomable sounds, a babble of people, a storm buffeting her. But Avalon saw only him, only Marcus standing calm, her anchor, coming up to her now with hooded eyes.

"Are you certain?" he asked her, staying with her in the center of the storm that lashed them.

"Yes," she answered, and the gladness did not retreat.

He gazed down at her and she felt his own satisfaction beyond even his smile, saw it clearly in the crystal blue of his eyes. Then he turned and looked up and away from her, taking in the rest of the room.

"We'll do it now," he announced, and this again did not dismay her, as if she had expected him to act this quickly, keeping a firm grasp on this dream moment.

The storm swirled and cleared in eddies, surges of cheering and loudness, dishes put aside, tables thrust away, men were talking to Marcus and each other, women were touching her with soft hands, surrounding her, pulling her back into themselves.

She let them, it was fine to let them tuck her gown together, a curtain of bodies between her and the rest of the storm. They fixed her plaid for her, said things in bright, happy voices that she didn't fully listen to, let them smooth back her hair—someone produced a comb, where did that come from?—and she had two fine braids again, divided and coiled and wrapped around her head.

Someone—it was Ellen—handed her the tip of a bough of fragrant pine, still crisply cold from outside, and a sprig of something glossy green and dark, with deep red berries. They tucked more of it into her hair, woven into the braids, a coronet of winter.

She started to laugh for some reason, she didn't know why, except it was just so funny, standing here in the great hall of Sauveur with holly in her hair, clutching her bit of pine because she was going the *marry* the laird, just like the girl in the meadow, and it seemed so right. . . .

The women parted. When she looked past them Avalon saw the wizard waiting patiently before the tables and benches, a roaring fire behind him in the hearth.

Marcus was there as well, standing next to him with his tartan as neat and straight has her own, silhouetted against the fire, broad shoulders, dark visage, flames disguising his features.

But she could feel what he felt, and there was nothing dark about it. Indeed, it was a tremendous luminosity, so bright and stunning it almost hurt her to take it in. He reached for her as she drew closer to him, and then the fire was her ally, letting her see the shimmering hope in him with her own eyes.

Her heart was beyond her control, beating so fast it was as if she had been running for hours, but all she had done was take a few steps to join his side. The stem of pine she held was echoed on his plaid; he had its twin fixed to his shoulder with a straight pin of silver.

"Lady, have you made your choice?"

The wizard spoke in calm tones that managed to carry throughout the entire room. Avalon faced him.

"I have," she said.

Balthazar inclined his head slightly, an acknowledgment, and then continued.

"I have taken a charge to protect you, lady, and I must fulfill this before God. I must hand you over only to the one who is worthy, who will not fail in his duty to you. Is this the man?"

One robed arm swept out, indicated Marcus, still as a stone beside her.

"Yes," she said clearly.

Bal looked to Marcus. "Are you the man I have described, Kincardine? Before God, do you vow to protect this woman in my stead?"

"Aye," replied Marcus, in that deep and sure voice that gave her shivers.

The storm remained behind them, subdued but alive, tremors of excitement at each word, drops of anticipation into this sea of the moment.

"God is watching," the wizard said now, much louder than before. "And He is listening. Those who go forward with a pure heart may greet Him, and kneel at His throne. Is your heart pure, lady? Is this your true desire?"

He pinned her with his gaze, unrelenting, and had
she an ounce of uncertainty in her she knew this would
have made her crumble, this darkly severe look, plumb-
ing the depths of truth. But Avalon knew that her
choice was a sound one.

"It is," she said, almost as loud as he.

"And yours?" The wizard turned back to Marcus.

"Aye," he said again.

The excitement mounted, Avalon could feel it almost
as a living thing pressing against her back, pushing her
on, decades and decades of watching eyes, hopeful
hearts, all of it hanging on this moment, this union.

"Before God!" bellowed the wizard, pointing to the
heavens. "Do you take this man now?"

"I do!" exclaimed Avalon.

"Do you take this woman?"

"I do," said Marcus, forceful and strong voiced.

An unexpected wind came, blew open the main door
and into the heated room, a brisk cold force that made
the flames of the fire cower and then leap back to life,
taller than before. Avalon stood still amid it, then looked
up at Marcus. He met her gaze, then took her hand.

The wizard opened his arms wide and spoke over the
rush of wind and the song of the people. "The flow-
ering of these two spirits has been committed before
you all today, in the sight of God, who rejoices in it. Let
no man come between them! They are wedded true!"

As the people let out a great cheer the wind danced
around them all, rushing past the door despite efforts to
get it closed, and with it came a sudden shower of snow-
flakes, glinting magic in the air, graceful and ethereal,

sifting down on everyone, everything, before melting into dewdrops.

Avalon turned her face up to it, laughing, and Marcus caught her there, took her laugh as his own as he kissed her, his hands firm on her shoulders. The cheer became deafening.

They were both smiling too much to continue the kiss, and so he lifted his head and pulled her close, a wordless embrace, and the light in him became impossible to her, impossible to gather together in her own mind, because it was so great.

At once they were surrounded by the clan, hearty laughter and cheerful shoving to get closer, to congratulate the laird and his bride, to be able to see for themselves the ending of the curse and the beginning of a new blessed age.

Avalon knew this and even it didn't dim her own humming elation, the strange feeling of being light-headed and giddy as they were both jostled by the well-wishers.

The snow had collected in droplets on her lashes, and looking through their prisms she saw tilting colors on the edges of everything. She felt suspended in her joy, thick honey beating through her, and again Marcus became her anchor, warm beside her, her arm linked through his, his hand on top of hers.

Her caring women came up and kissed her cheeks, red eyed with tears. The warriors, Hew, David, Nathan, all of them filing past, even Tarroth, who had to bend down so she might catch his shy words.

And it was only when they all began to move to the

benches, laid out again for breakfast—the warmth of the people and the room so bountiful—that Avalon realized she had taken her vows as the bride of the Kincardine still in her bare feet, and so had he.

⚭

*T*HE LESSON HAD disintegrated into nothing less than a rampant snowball fight, with the leader of the insurgency none other than the new wife of the laird, Avalon Kincardine.

Marcus watched from a safe distance, shielded from flying snow by the glass of his solar window, still close enough to watch his beautiful bride pack together the snow in her gloved hands and pass the projectiles off to the children, who chucked them at each other with glee.

She took no sides, staying somewhat in the middle of the war, ducking and laughing as the children ran around her in circles.

Her laughter was like music to him, like rain. Healing. He couldn't believe it had only been four days since she married him. It felt like they had been partners all his life. He lived each day just to see her; each night to make love to her; each morning to wake to the sight of her, glorious and pure.

"It doesn't matter," Hew was saying to the others gathered behind Marcus. "We had the ceremony. She agreed to wed him. We all heard it."

"Aye," came the chorus of agreement, at least twenty men, standing firm in their resolve.

"There will be a challenge," Marcus said, still watching Avalon. "Warner d'Farouche will not give up so easily. It's damnable luck."

He turned around and caught the brooding agreement on his men's faces, all of them looking at either the floor or at Sean, the leader of the group Marcus had sent to the MacFarlands.

"Dead these seven years," Sean repeated, perhaps to get the taste of the bad news out of his mouth. "And no one stood for him, no one even wanted to talk of him. Keith MacFarland was not a liked man, even among his own clan."

"I imagine not," said Marcus, "since he seemed to have no qualms over selling the lives of innocents."

He caught the echo of Avalon's laughter again, drowned out by the excited shouts of the children.

"What are we to do?" asked Hew. "We must be prepared for the challenge."

"Aye," said Marcus. "I've sent an announcement of the marriage to Malcolm, telling him that it took place in front of witnesses, with the lady's open consent. Let Malcolm sort through the rest of it. He is our king. He will know best how to present it to Henry and the baron."

"Will it be enough?" asked David.

"If not, then we will think of something else," Marcus replied grimly. "There is still the note. At least one d'Farouche is implicated. We will bring it up if we have to, if the marriage is sufficiently threatened."

He didn't want to tell either king of Hanoch's note just yet. Not without irrefutable proof that Warner or Bryce had been behind the raid of Trayleigh. A note such as this could be easily dismissed or accused of being a forgery, opening up all sorts of ugly possibilities Marcus was not yet ready to handle.

Also, Avalon had not indicated to him that she wished to make it public. Against both the law and the common perception that a man need not defer to his wife, Marcus didn't want to move behind her back. It didn't seem right, and it certainly would not aid him in gathering her trust.

It was Sean who said the word they were all thinking, but no one had yet said:

"Annulment."

A muffled thump made Marcus turn back to the window, where the melting remains of a snowball slid and dripped down the glass. He looked out to see Avalon standing alone in the trampled, snowy courtyard below him, her eyes shielded from the sun with one hand as she looked up at him. She waved.

"There will be no grounds for an annulment," Marcus said, placing his palm flat on the glass, so she could see it. "I'll make sure of that."

He joined her minutes later. She was still standing in the bailey, the children gone, light glistening all around her.

Avalon watched him walk closer, snow up to his ankles, his cloak billowing and his hair uncovered. A smile, just for her.

To her very great amazement—and relief—the sense of rightness she had felt that morning four days ago in the great hall had not faded. In fact, looking at the remarkable sight of Marcus striding to her through the winter whiteness, it grew more honed, sharper and clearer, like the air around her.

It felt good, what she had done, in spite of all the

bitterness of the past, in spite of her own broken vows, rooted in reasons that had been real enough at the time.

And who was to blame for those lost vows, when Marcus had turned out to be nothing like what she had feared? He was *not* Hanoch, and at the moment he had promised her he would never harm her, she had known he was telling her the truth.

As for that other thing, that magnificent thing that he said, that he could separate her from his myth—well, she was having to close her eyes and take his words on faith. She had no proof of it. Perhaps there was none that could be offered that was sufficient.

The clan reeled around her these past few days, almost crazed with delight that she had wed the laird in front of them, that their curse was lifted.

It was preposterous, silly, and even dangerous, to feel as immune to trouble as they did.

But she could not deny them to their faces what they wanted so badly. How much harm could it cause to keep her opinions to herself as they went on and on about the legend, about the golden times ahead? None, she hoped. She had no wish to harm any of them. They were truly her family now.

Forgiveness. Trust. These were the things, she thought, that seemed to speak out to her. If the wizard had been right, that long-ago day in the meadow glen, if there really were lessons to be learned from each lifetime, then Avalon thought perhaps these might be hers.

Forgive the past.

Trust in the future.

But it was the present she was having the most trouble with.

Clan Kincardine and their legend: her traditional enemy. The fight had been going on too long to forget about it in the blink of an eye. She had to combat their superstition with all her reserves, or else admit that she was a part of something vast and incomprehensible and frightening. Something as strange as a chimera made real. And that could not be true.

Most chilling of all, it would be too easy to become lost in this world—warmth, comfort, superstition, and faith in such mad ideas. It would take her in and never release her. She must always be on guard against it.

Yet amid all the confusion, the strange whirlwind of her emotions, Avalon was slowly discovering something solid beneath it all, something ultimately satisfying: a reason to live, not for Hanoch or a legend, not even for Marcus—but for herself, her new life here.

It was an extraordinary and momentous thing, so new she couldn't even fully grasp it yet.

Marcus had made it across the bailey. He picked her up by her waist and swung her around. She clung to him, laughing in spite of herself as the world circled by her, blue and green and white.

He set her down carefully so she could find her footing.

"You should come inside. Warm up." The air iced into puffs between them.

"I'm warm," she said.

Now that she could look straight up into his eyes she saw something beyond the plain intent of his words; there was something more he wanted to say but was not saying.

Revenge? suggested the chimera, that not real thing inside of her.

"Have you news?" she asked, unable to help herself.

"Come inside," Marcus repeated, drawing her back to the shadow of the castle.

He took her to the sewing room, led her to the marble pink-laced hearth and helped her off with her cloak and her wet gloves, taking her reddened fingers between his own and raising them to his lips, blowing warm breath on them.

"You shouldn't stay outside too long in this cold," he reproved.

Avalon shook her head at his concern. "I won't freeze, my lord. I grew up in weather such as this, if you'll recall."

It wasn't the cold that was bothering him, she knew it, but it was a prelude to his real concern, and so she waited for him to come around to it, to collect his thoughts and offer them to her. After a moment he did, staring at the great expanse of windows behind her.

"Keith MacFarland is dead."

"Oh," she said. Relief filled her that this was all it was. "I told you he would be."

He inclined his head to her, still clasping her fingers, bringing their joined hands down closer to the fire.

"With him dies our hope of discovering if it was Bryce or Warner behind the raid," Marcus said.

She frowned. "There must be another way."

"There might be."

"What, then?"

He gave her a sideways look, as if trying to ascertain

something about her that she would not readily reveal to him.

"Do you . . . see anything, Avalon?"

She took her hands back from his, her fingers inexplicably cold again. "I don't know what you mean."

"Don't you?"

Her voice grew a little too emphatic. "No."

Marcus held out both hands, a gesture of peace. "All right. I'm sorry. Don't be upset."

"I'm not upset," she said, striving to sound normal. "I have no reason to be upset."

"Truelove." He stepped closer and brought her to him, holding her until the stiffness in her back loosened somewhat, and her hands crept up around his waist. Marcus leaned his head down, kissed her hair. "I'm sorry," he said again. "I just thought that you might—"

"No," she interrupted. "You are mistaken. Do not confuse me with your legend, my lord."

"I didn't think I was," he sighed. "I know you don't want to talk about this, but don't you think it's time you came to some sort of . . ."

She pulled back and looked up at him, the light of something deep and unhappy in her eyes.

". . . *understanding*," he finished stubbornly, "about who you are, and this gift you have?"

He felt her clench up inside, felt it as sure as if she had shut her mind and run away from him, instead of remaining utterly still in his arms, aloof.

"There is no gift," she said, very soft.

"You tamed a wild stallion when he should have killed you." Marcus kept his grip firm around her. "You smelled the sulphur with me in the glen. And I know, though you denied it, that you saw something when you handled the note sent to me about your engagement to Warner."

Her lower lip began to quiver, the unhappiness in her became a strength that allowed her to jerk away from him, every inch of her shouting out denial at him, a desperate rejection. He hated this; he hated to do this to her, but there was so much to gain now, and everything to lose.

"Avalon! I'm not asking you for Hanoch, or for the sake of a story. I'm asking you for *us,* you and me! Don't you think that Warner will challenge our marriage? Don't you know how easy it is to buy an annulment? We are running out of options. We need help. A clue. Something!"

She paused, lips still not quite steady, his beloved bride, his cherished wife.

"Please," he said simply. "I need your help. I know you can do it, if you want to."

"Don't you think I want to help you?" she asked, and the tremble was more pronounced. "Don't you think I would if I could? What you ask is impossible! It does not exist!"

He had pushed her too far; he could see it clearly. She wasn't ready for this, she couldn't think beyond her fear right now, and how it hurt to watch her struggle against him, against his beliefs and hopes. Worst of all, to cause her pain.

"No, all right," he said, soothing. "I'm sorry, truelove. I'm sorry. I know you want to help."

He crossed to her and kissed her quickly, before she could reject him physically, on top of her words.

"I'm sorry," he whispered again, against her lips. "Forget what I said."

He kissed her again, slower, softer, letting her tension drain away, until she was kissing him back, returning his heat with a new ardor, the desire in her awakened again. His own responded instantly and their embrace changed to match this new purpose; together they sank down on the carpet of flowers in front of the fireplace.

He put her on top of him, relishing the slight weight of her, the way her hair loosened easily from its pins when he found them, the way it fell down in heavy locks of silver and ivory around him when he stroked her cheeks and brought her closer to him, the way her eyes grew sleepy yet full of violet fire. All for him.

Marcus let his hands roam her back, her hair, across the tartan she wore, his own mark on her, and then underneath it, to the plain gown, closer to her body.

She stretched against him, answering his unspoken lead with her movements, with an understanding that wasn't there just days ago, but now, oh yes, how sweetly she knew what to do to him, how to touch him, where to kiss him—

"Laird? Are ye there?"

Avalon became perfectly still; Marcus kept his hands in place on her, holding her to him, and turned his head to the door. Thank God he had shut it behind them when they entered.

"Not now," he said distinctly.

"Begging yer pardon, laird, but the Moor sent me for ye. We've got a problem in the stables."

"What problem?" Marcus asked, beginning to caress his wife's hair again.

"Part of the roof's come down, laird, from the snow, mayhap. Five of the stalls are ruined, and young Jack near broke his arm trying to get to one of the horses—"

Avalon sat up and Marcus came up with her, pulling her to her feet.

"I'll be right there," he said to the door.

She looked up at him, and the violent fire had transformed to worry.

"I'm sorry," he began, his same old refrain with her.

"Shall I come with you?"

"Nay," he replied. "Stay inside, where it's warm." He caressed her cheek. "I wish that we had time—"

"Go," she said, smiling. "And be careful. There'll be time enough tonight. I had promised Tegan I would visit about now, anyway."

He looked at her, blank.

"The cook," she said gently.

They went to the door together, and he gave her one last kiss, hard and passionate so she would be thinking of this, and not of his ill-timed request, before walking away from her.

───────────── ⌇⌇⌇ ─────────────

𝒜CH, MILADY, are ye certain ye wish to do this? I meant to go over the stockroom with ye, not oblige ye to labor."

Tegan looked almost distraught at the sight of the bride with a chopping knife in her hand, a pile of turnips in front of her.

"I offered to help. You didn't oblige me," Avalon pointed out. "I want to. I enjoy it. And there will be plenty of hungry men coming in from the stables soon. I think you could use some extra hands."

"Aye, well, that's true enough," Tegan admitted, with a harried look at the kitchen.

The stable disaster, though hardly epic, was enough to throw the castle household into a frenzy of activity, with most of the men outside working quickly to repair the damage before darkness set in, and another snowstorm arrived. People bustled back and forth from the buttery to the stables to the great hall, carrying the news that it wasn't as bad as initially feared. None of the horses were injured, none of the stablehands had been standing too close to the broken beams. But there was a gaping hole in the roof, and the threat of more snow plain in the air. It was going to take a great deal of hurried labor to fix it in time.

Avalon began to chop her turnips with determination, finding solace in the busyness of the kitchen, the voices of the women she had come to know all around her. Everyone, from oldest to youngest, banded together in a crisis. The Clan Kincardine functioned as one to deal with the problems they were dealt.

To her right was Greer, attacking her own pile of vegetables with gusto; and to her left little Inez, collecting the small chunks of turnips into her basket for boiling.

The kitchen was hot despite the weather, with three full fires going, women everywhere talking, tossing laughter back and forth.

Avalon listened to the banter with half an ear, the other half of her lost in the repetition of her movements, the keen knife she held picking up the firelight and letting it slide in a golden glow along the blade.

What harm? asked a voice in her head, the one thing she didn't wish to hear right now: the secret tones of her chimera.

What harm would there be to look? it invited, not unfriendly.

She ignored it, grabbing another turnip, whacking the knife down into it to split it in two.

A simple thing, no harm to look, it suggested, her ally, her enemy.

The turnip fell into quarters. Into eighths.

For us, Marcus had said, *I'm asking you for us. . . .*

To sixteenths.

No harm to look.

Small pieces, yellow and white, chopped even smaller, the blade glowing.

No harm.

She watched the blade as it missed its mark, skipped off the side of a juicy square of turnip and landed deep into the flesh of her palm near her thumb, too close for safety. She watched as her blood came up immediately, and curiously enough it didn't hurt at all, not at all, but instead seemed to be a thing of fascination; crimson red against the blade now, spilling onto the wood of her chopping block so quickly. Staining the paleness of her hand.

Avalon followed the line of her blood as it pooled up and then hung, suspended on the edge of the block, gathering mass, growing too big to stay there much longer.

Distantly she heard noises: bizarre, exaggerated sounds that might have been other people exclaiming at her. It didn't seem to matter what they said, she couldn't understand them anyway.

The drop of blood fell. She was able to watch it go, all

the way down to the stone floor, a perfect teardrop shape, oddly beautiful, deep red, flawless.

It splashed into a circle against the charcoal stone, the center of it bouncing back up, reaching free of the ground, then releasing its form to fall down again. Her red, red blood—

—was flowing everywhere, it soaked the furs and the clothing, a sticky drying stiffness wherever it touched.

In the darkness it was not red but black, with a dusky glitter in the torchlight, still fresh enough the reek of death.

She couldn't see, it was so dark, the torch was too far away to aid her, and the death was too close. The danger here was so strong it would overpower her, it would draw out all the blood and leave her empty, alone, dead.

The room was too large; it was familiar and yet not, a dream place, huge and foreboding. Danger and death hid so easily here, the shadows were their masking. She could not fight these shadows, she could not stop them, and would never have thought that the stifling blackness of the pantry could be equalled in so great a space.

Goblins, blood, danger, cold stone, the room was too wide, she couldn't hide from it, she would die now, just as her father had, and Ona, and all the rest, and all the blood would never erase her loss, sticky sweet blood, her own death a half second away, laughing at her—

Avalon Kincardine came out of her trance and fainted for the first time in her life, falling into the arms of the women surrounding her, spilling her own blood freely down onto her skirts.

Chapter Fourteen

———— ⟨⟩ ————

*S*HE WAS WARM and yet shivering. There was a soft, heavy weight on her chest, her torso and legs. Her left hand throbbed with a sharp ache.

"Do not fear," she heard someone saying, the voice strangely accented. "It could have been far worse. The vein is closed now."

"Just in time." It was another man's voice, deeper, strained, and she knew it so well she opened her eyes.

"Avalon," said Marcus, his face stark with relief, standing over her, picking up the hand that did not hurt.

She began to sit up, dizzy, and he helped her, settled her gently against the pillows of the bed. She was in the master chambers. She still could not yet quite think of it as her own. The vivid colors of the sky outside the windows told her it was either the end of the day, or the beginning of a new one.

"Be careful," Marcus was urging her. "You've lost a lot of blood."

"I feel fine," she said, though that wasn't quite true.

The wizard appeared beside Marcus, hands folded away into his sleeves. "Were you in battle, lady, it would have been a fine blow to your enemy's hand."

She thought this might be a joke and so gave a small smile, and the wizard smiled back.

"You are hale again," he pronounced. "Though I am uncertain of your husband."

Marcus ignored him. "How do you feel? Do you remember what happened?"

"I feel fine. I—"

Blood, goblins, death!

Stop!

"I'm not sure I remember." She closed her eyes against his look, leaning her head back.

She felt the silence more than she heard it: doubt, caution, the fear of exhausting her. If these were the things that would divert their questions, then she would pretend, even though she was not tired. Even though she remembered it all.

"Perhaps you should consider the matter again, lady," advised the wizard, breaking the moment. "You would do well to share any memory with the Kincardine."

Avalon opened her eyes and looked past Marcus, who was frowning, to Balthazar, a figure of black against the pageantry of the sky. He shrugged gracefully.

"A husband and wife should be comfortable in each other's own true hearts. Or so it is said among my people."

She glanced away to the bright sunset colors, guilty, and heard the wizard speak again, light and indifferent.

"Well, perhaps here marriage is different."

He began to walk out of the room, pausing by the door.

"But it is a cold thing, is it not, to be alone?"

And he left.

"What the hell was that all about?" asked Marcus.

Avalon looked down at the blankets covering her, then began to try to move them off of her. "This is silly. I should be up. I am not hurt."

Marcus stopped her, placing one hand on her shoulder and pushing her back again. "Avalon, you sliced open a vein in your hand in the kitchen tonight. Do you remember that? You bled a great deal before we could stop it."

"Oh," she said. "But I feel all right now."

"You're staying here," he said firmly. "Loss of blood can be a dangerous thing. I will not allow you to harm yourself."

"I will not harm myself," she said, exasperated. "All I want is to get up and—"

"No!" he said, much too loudly, surprising her into silence.

One of the windowpanes rattled with a gust of wind, a lonely, chattering sound in the quiet of the room.

Marcus sighed and ran a hand through his hair. "I'm sorry." There was a tight smile on his lips, pained. "I'm always saying that to you, aren't I? You must be tired of it."

"Are you?" she asked.

He sighed again and stood up; there was a restlessness marking him now, an impatience in the lines of his body as he stalked to the window.

"I've seen men die from a simple thing like the cut you had," he said. "The life just drains out of them along with the blood. It's an appalling thing to watch."

The pane began to rattle again but this time Marcus

stopped it, touching his fingers to the frame, stilling it so the wind became nothing more than a faint murmur against the approaching night.

"I'm not about to die," she said.

"No," he responded. "I won't let you." His head dropped suddenly, rested against the colors of the glass. "I'm tired," he admitted, and to her it sounded like a confession.

"Come to bed." She pulled back the covers beside her.

"There's more work to be done. I should be down there."

Avalon waited, unmoving, until he turned around and faced her. She placed her hand on the jumbled pile of covers and let it rest there.

Marcus gave a small laugh. "Bal seems to think we should be comfortable in each other's true hearts."

"So he said."

"But that can be a dangerous thing, Avalon. I'm not so certain you would find comfort in mine."

"I know there is nothing there to fear," she said steadily.

"Do you?"

"Yes."

"What confidence you have in me, my lady. I am sure it is undeserved."

"Marcus," she said. "I wouldn't mislead you. I think I know your heart already."

"By the time I was eighteen," he said, keeping his gaze on her hand, "I had taken part in some of the worst atrocities that I could have ever imagined. I watched entire armies hack each other to death over religion. I watched civilized men—men who claimed to have ʌ grace of God—behave like scavenging animals in defenseless villages. I had even seen my own knight murdered in front of me, and all of it paled in front of the acts of a few select men. Monks, they called themselves."

Why was he telling her about this now? Then she recalled the burning memories of the sand, the desert, the killing thirst, and Avalon thought she could guess his reasons.

"Like Balthazar?" she asked.

"No. Not like him, though from a close order. They had seemed kind men, magnificent at first. They nursed me through my wounds when I was too injured to do it myself. Trygve, you see, had decided we should free Damascus, just the two of us. He died within minutes of breaching the city gate. Really, there was nothing else the sentries could do, he was obviously quite insane. And since I was his squire, a fellow infidel, they did their best to kill me too."

He began to slide to the floor, using the wall as his guide, until he was sitting on the stone, arms relaxed over his knees. "But Bal came and evened the odds."

"He saved you?"

"In a manner of speaking. He drew off the men and allowed me to limp away, and even managed to find me later and drag me back to the monastery. It was outside the city, you see, and mostly untouched by the war. And those monks did their best to heal me."

She saw the image of the wooden crucifix covered in sand, the hot white walls, the table with the man strapped to it. Her mouth grew dry again.

"Did they?" she asked.

"At first," he said. The tightness was back in him, the ominous herald to the snake just beneath his skin.

Avalon feared that to lead him further down this path would only strengthen its hold on him; and yet, and yet—if she was careful, if she treated it as delicately as she could, then perhaps she would find the hawk instead of the snake, and the torment would fade away in the light of the man she knew was there.

"And then what?" She kept her voice impartial, giving the snake no reason to strike out.

"I had a dream about you, Avalon, did you know that?"

The sudden switch of subject made her wary, made her watch him closely. She felt the uneasy stirrings of her curse, the chimera.

"You were an angel in the desert," he continued, meeting her look, pale blue winter. "You were redemption. Do you remember?"

The chimera awoke, looked at her, daring her to deny it.

"It was your dream," she said.

"You were there. Only not at the time. Thank God, not at the time."

"I don't understand," she said, afraid to.

"Those men in my solar," he said abrubtly, savagely, "those men of God. They would have killed me for this meager gift, a long and painful death for only a fragment of what you possess. And do you truly wonder that I would not let them take you? Do you wonder at that at all?"

"It was the monks," she said, putting it together, what he had not, or would not say. "It was the monks who did that to you, who tortured you." She shook her head, fighting back the horror. "But *why?*"

He wouldn't look at her now, every muscle seemed taut with emotion; a brittle, fragile hold on his will the only thing keeping the snake at bay.

"It seems I had a fever, in the middle of that desert heat. A strong fever, that kept me babbling for hours. And how unlucky it was, just then, to have one of the only two monks there who spoke English tending to me. He understood every word I said. And apparently, I said a great deal."

The chimera listened, nodding.

"I don't even remember what happened." Marcus gave a hollow laugh to the ceiling, and it echoed back, shaded with despair. "I couldn't understand, when the fever dispersed, why I was tied up. Why I was being questioned. Why these men, who had been my friends, were now out to kill me in the most painful and prolonged of ways."

Renounce, said the chimera, using that gentle voice of the dream.

Marcus addressed the word he could not have heard. "Renounce what? I had no idea. All they would say is that the devil had my soul, my body was its instrument, and they were going to drive it away."

Sand on the crucifix, sand seeping into the room, onto the table, past the ropes.

"So I renounced. Whatever they wanted. I would have told them anything to get them to stop what they were doing."

"Yes," she said.

"But it was a trick, you see?" He looked up suddenly,

sad and desperate and lonely, and she saw the young man he had been then, the warrior so far from his home in every sense. "I renounced, and they said it was the devil's lie, to agree so easily."

Avalon fought the dizziness and moved to the side of the bed, then off of it, coming over to him. He didn't try to stop her, only followed her with his lost eyes, pressed against the wall in the encroaching darkness.

"But it wasn't a lie, and it wasn't the devil. It was just me, trying to understand. Trying to live."

She knelt in front of him and covered his hands with her own. The bandage on her hand was bulky and soft, heavily wrapped.

"Bal told me later that in my fever I had told that monk, that one who knew English, stories about him that no one else could have known, told him about his childhood, about his dreams. Things he had never mentioned to anyone."

"I understand," she said.

"It happens that way sometimes," he said to her, the sadness not gone, but the snake subdued amid it, sinking away. "I can't predict it. Just pictures come to me, ideas, words. I don't know where they come from; it's just a gift. Nothing evil. I don't believe it's evil."

She rested her head on both of their hands, settling down beside him on the floor, and the chill was a distant thing, insignificant. Only Marcus mattered.

"I went to the Holy Land to fight for God, only to have the men of God turn against me." He shook his head, looking bewildered, and then said again, "But the gift is *not* evil."

"You're right," Avalon said. "They were wrong."

She felt him waver, still adrift in his memories, and she knew how real they could be, how terrifying. Avalon realized she wanted urgently to rescue him from this, to ease him, to help him. He did not deserve this punishment. But it put her in the uncomfortable position of defending something she wanted with every ounce of her reason to deny could even exist—how could it exist?

Don't lie, whispered the chimera.

This was Marcus, her husband, and she had pledged herself to him, and to give him less than everything would be a failure to both of them.

Avalon lifted her head, keeping her hands in place, and examined him. "Nothing you have said has changed my mind. Your true heart is good. Balthazar was right that I should know this."

"He saved me. He was only a visitor to that monastery, a pilgrim who had sheltered there on his journey. When he learned what had happened, he spoke for me to the others, and when they would not release me, he stole me away, took me out one night and saved my life. Took me to his home, far away. A place called Spain. I stayed there for a long time. I was sick of war and death. I returned to Damascus only to end my obligation to Trygve. But Bal persuaded me to leave again, to leave behind the crusade."

"He is a good man," she said.

"Aye." Marcus was gone in his thoughts for a moment, then came back, moved his hands so that they touched the tops of hers lightly, brushing her skin, shaping the outline of the bandage she wore. "And you, truelove. Your heart is good as well. I know it."

Avalon turned her head away, but the whiteness of

the bandage lingered in her vision, a ghostly reminder of what she wanted to forget.

――――――――― ⟨ຕາຍ⟩ ―――――――――

SHE AWOKE LATER that night alone in the bed, or so she thought until she sat up and looked around.

Marcus was asleep on the far side of the feather mattress, wrapped in his tunic and tartan and a few of the furs, very carefully keeping a distance between them. She supposed it was because he thought her too weak or too drained to respond to his touch, because he had deliberately not made love to her, even though she felt fine. Even though she wished for it, that union of their bodies that could erase everything else in the world. But there he slept, innocent, and by all appearances, peaceful in rest. She did not want to awaken him.

He had left her after their talk to check on the progress of the stables. Avalon had understood his reasons. Indeed, at the time she had even welcomed his absence, because that left her alone to conceal her own thoughts, her own uneasy guilt at the memory she had not shared with him. And, ultimately, he'd left her alone with her own shadowed heart, where comfort did not seem to dwell, no matter what the wizard said.

And what good would it be, argued that heart, to tell Marcus of that odd vision, a strange creation of her imagination? It had made no sense to her anyway, it seemed unrelated to anything she knew. Certainly she had caught nothing about a man named Keith MacFarland there, nor any man at all. Only danger and death, two things she preferred not to think about, especially right now, at the pinnacle of the night.

The moon had cleared from its clouds and Avalon got carefully out of the bed to watch the show, to see the tangled silver shadows drift across the snowy landscape.

It was hauntingly beautiful, a different world at night, dramatic and magical and inviting.

She was not tired, not any longer. In fact, she felt quite awake. Surely too much so to go back to the bed, where Marcus lay deep in his own soft slumber.

Perhaps she would go out and visit one of the turrets, take in the diamond-black sky, the orb of the moon. Perhaps there were answers for her outside.

It took her almost no time to get dressed, even with the bandage on her hand, and she left the room with one last look at Marcus, a calm shape under the covers of the bed.

But once in the hallway her feet didn't take her to the stairs leading up to the turret. Instead they carried her to the ones leading down to the great hall, past low torches and rows of Scottish stone, the arch of the ceiling hidden in slanting darkness.

In the great hall she found men sleeping everywhere, most of them close to the fireplace, which still held a yellow-gold heat. None of them awoke as she picked her way past them, stepping lightly and silently, the way she had been taught.

She left through the buttery door, since it was smaller and easier to open than the massive ones in the main hall, and it was away from the sleeping people. The hearth in here was empty and black.

Outside it felt cold but not uncomfortably so. Avalon

had remembered to take her cloak—coins now long removed and hems restitched—and this blocked most of the chill, allowing her to press forward into the night.

At the gate she greeted the sentry, grateful that she knew his name and—after only a brief disagreement—that he opened the door for her and allowed her outside the walls of the castle. It took all her resources to charm him into letting her pass, and in the end she had to promise she would not go far, only to the edge of the infamous glen, clearly visible from the top of the wall-walk where he stood watch.

Avalon let out a little laugh as she set out away from him, her feet crunching through the crust of snow on the ground. The night was even more glorious now that she was out amid it. High, high above her, thick clouds tumbled across the infinite sky, each one underlit by the moon, half a silver coin hung above the mountains. The snow was untarnished, unblemished, an even covering for the whole land, reaching up just over her ankles.

Best of all was the silence. No people talking, no thoughts intruding. Just peace, windsong, the occasional rustle of pine needles rubbing together in the breeze.

An owl, softly calling to its mate in the woods.

The edge of the glen was oddly familiar to her in this guise, even though the silver-green grass was buried and the last of the flowers gone. The breeze hushed by and then quit, and Avalon took in the sight of the snowy brambles and the sheer mountainside in complete quiet. Only the moon watched.

She took a few steps forward, aware that the sentry would be searching the path for her from his post, also aware that he was too far away to stop her if she wished to go on. Perhaps only a little further. Not too much. She didn't wish to cause trouble, only to see for herself a bit more of the spell of this night in this particular place, following the graceful layers of snow and stone up the side of the hill, until she found the outline of the faerie. . . .

In contrast to the rest of the land, none of the snow had stayed on the black stone, but its whiteness had remained all around it, tracing the form of the man with wings, emphasizing the distinctive shape even more clearly than the last time she had seen it, black and white, that wicked creature who had met his fate at the hands of revenge.

Avalon walked closer, sentry forgotten. The trick of the moonlight threw moving shadows over the stone, and clouds added shades of glossy gray to it, an illusion of movement. Breathing. Wings trembling. Arms shifting.

The faerie stretched out on the mountainside, trapped, held forever in its prison of rock as punishment for betrayal, for brutality. . . .

No, Avalon thought, and closed her eyes, shaking her head. No, no, it is not real. Her own breathing grew louder in the still glen, surrounding her with clouds of frost, and when she opened her eyes the faerie was stone again, nothing more. Just stone.

"Treuluf."

The word came from close behind her, shocking and sweet, and when she whirled to face it there was no one there.

Only in the distance, coming up the path, was a lone figure in the darkness, a tartan curving with the wind, still too far from her to have said anything she could have heard.

Moonlight cast him in black and silver, a long shadow stretching to the side of him across the snow. Not the sentry. Marcus.

His strides ate up the distance between them but she watched each step, hypnotized by the strength of him, the elegance, the way he was a seamless part of the wild here, where the wild was everywhere.

There was a force coming from him, right from him to her—not anger, not wrath, but something new, something different. Desire: powerful and complete, wrapping her up in his design, keeping her motionless, waiting for him.

When he was close enough she searched his eyes and saw nothing there to fear. What she saw was hunger and need, elemental and fierce. His look captured the twin spirit that lived in her; she hadn't even known of it until just now.

He reached her and without breaking his pace took her in his arms and claimed her lips, sealing the heat between them. Her hands clutched at his shoulders, the melting was suffusing her, overwhelming, and with it that new thing, something rougher, more primitive, to match the glen and the moon and the cold air.

His kiss was almost brutal but it did not hurt her; instead she returned it with an equal fervor, her breath short and excited already, fed by the roaming of his hands on her body beneath her cloak, harsh and urgent, pulling her into him where she thought she could not get any closer, and still he wanted more of her, and she wanted it too.

He broke the kiss to look up only briefly, and she caught the shadow of the wildness in his eyes, pale and almost feverish. He took in something behind her—the blackened edge of the woods, out of sight of Sauveur—and without a word began to push her over there, still keeping her close as she stumbled backward. His hands, unhindered by her cape, were large and warm on her back, her bottom. Before they were there he began to kiss her again, this time entwining the fingers of one hand in her hair, holding her still for him even though she wasn't resisting. His mouth slanted across hers over and over, not gentle—hard, almost biting, causing a whimper of desire to catch in her throat. His hand beneath her cloak moved and found her breasts, squeezing. Her moan came free and he covered her mouth again, taking the last of her air greedily.

He pushed her up against the trunk of a tree, bare branched above her, ice glistening on its limbs. The bark was uneven against her back, her legs, but that didn't stop him from putting his weight against her, pinning her in place, his hands now at her waist, moving down, his mouth a heated trail across her face, her cheekbones, onto her ear, where she could hear his panting, as fast as her own. His body was hot and so much bigger than hers; she knew it was easy for him to keep her there against the tree, pressing his arousal against her, grinding against her in the beginnings of that rhythm her body craved.

Her head tilted back against the trunk, her eyes closed. She was defenseless against this onslaught, she was melting for him, for the way his teeth grazed her neck, the way his hands pulled apart her cloak, yanked up her skirts, letting the night air brush the bare skin of her legs as he pushed one of his own between them, then the other.

Between Marcus and the tree she had no quarter; she could not move to help him, she could not move to stop him. As he reached for her and found her soft wetness, her lips parted on a silent cry. He felt her shiver and gave a savage smile, full of moon shadows and wild night, using his hand on her until the wetness was covering them both, hot despite the cold night, baring herself for him despite the openness around them.

He freed himself for her, he only had to move a little to touch her with the hard length of his shaft, not entering but tormenting, holding her still as he touched her with his smooth head, rubbing back and forth until the whimper in her became a cry, a pleading.

"Truelove," he said, harsh and broken, the only word between them.

She opened her eyes and caught that smile, that ferocious desire in him plain, and then he thrust upward, filling her in one swift move, lifting her feet off the snow with the force of it.

He controlled her with both hands, clutching, guiding her with each powerful push, using the tree to keep her where he wanted her, allowing her to hold on to his shoulders for balance but no more.

Avalon felt him grow lost in his movements, each one strong and heavy, his mouth by her ear again, his hair against her cheeks, every bit of him touching her, his chest against hers, their hips joined, showing her where to go, how to get there, how to follow his will, his passion.

This magic was real, not imagined, and he was beginning to moan, too, low and deep in his throat, a masculine sound that enflamed her further, her legs spread far apart for him, the rough bark an aid to him and his mastery of her.

She held on and followed his want, down to where the flame burned brightest between them, and he took her to that aching place where she fell apart in his arms, crying out and then burying her head against his shoulder as the shudders took her, slick and wet and overwhelming. And then he joined her there, one last hard push deep into her, their bodies meshed, his flooding release a part of her that left her with nothing but him. Nothing but Marcus and the untamed night.

⁂

*I*T WAS THE NEXT MORNING that brought the missive from Trayleigh.

They had not slept late despite their lovemaking in the fell glen the night before, but instead went below-stairs—walking close enough to each other to brush arms, hands clasped—in unspoken mutual consent along with the regular breakfast crowd.

Avalon did not feel the lack of sleep very heavily. In fact, she felt rather wonderful. As she sat beside Marcus at the main table she enjoyed her porridge and oatcakes, and when she glanced at her husband she could see the moonlight gracing him still. When she leaned close to him she could catch the scent of the wild, cold night, unbanished by this bright new day.

She wondered if such changes were visible on her, as

well, and this made her dip her head down to her bowl in sudden blazing shyness, a ridiculous reaction that she could not help.

Marcus noticed; he followed her movement and kissed her temple, smiling against her.

At this Avalon turned her head to him, intending to chide him for so obviously laughing at her silliness, but of course he didn't allow it, and kissed her on the lips instead. She found her half-serious scold slipping away under the luster of his touch. Only the sudden, gratified silence in the room kept her from falling all the way under his spell again.

He pulled back, smiling, and Avalon heard the conversation resume, filled with the happy tones that matched the beating of her heart right now.

The meal was nearly finished when the mood shifted like a shaft of icy air on a warm breeze. It all came from one man, haggard and looking worried as he entered the great hall and walked toward Marcus, bowing and offering a dirty strip of paper from his hand.

"From Clan Murry," said the man, and then didn't bother to say more. Or perhaps he didn't have to, because by then Marcus had taken the paper and scanned it swiftly, divining for himself its origin.

The chimera, for once, was utterly silent, asleep and undisturbed, no matter that everyone else around her had gone as still as death to catch the news.

The creeping chill coming upon her was unmistakable. Marcus was done with the note; he looked up and around, as if searching for someone, and then the wizard came close with some of the others, all warriors she knew. Marcus began talking to them, but Avalon had unhurriedly taken the note from his fingers and was reading.

It was from Claudia. It didn't look like she had hired a scribe this time, for the writing was rough and scratched, the letters trembly, dotted and splattered with ink. The words were almost lost to her; but Avalon understood the tone of it immediately, and this blurred out the rest. It resonated with pleas: *I pray you come, peril surrounds me. Warner d'Farouche ill, dying, I am all alone. Defenseless. Cousin Avalon, come. I pray God you come.*

"A trap," pronounced Hew to the listening room.

"Of course," Marcus agreed grimly.

"To what purpose?" asked someone else. "To capture the wife of the laird?"

"Mayhap they don't yet know she is the wife," said Hew doggedly.

Marcus considered this. "It may be that Malcolm has not yet bothered to inform Henry of the marriage, or that Henry has not yet told d'Farouche. We cannot know."

"I'm going," said Avalon.

Marcus and the wizard looked at her silently, while the rest of the people began to drown each other out with their protests, dismissing her words.

Avalon waited until the room had quieted, until they were all looking back at her intractable stare, and then she turned to Marcus.

"I'm going, no matter if you wish me to or not."

The words of the letter, shaky and ill formed, shouted sincerity to Avalon. It might be a trap. But Claudia did not deserve to be dismissed so easily. Even more than that, Avalon sensed in this note the completion of a circle; the coming end of a cycle of events she had never deliberately thought to link together. She had to go.

"I would prefer not to go alone," she added out loud to Marcus, not dropping her stare. "But either way, I must answer this request. If Warner is truly dying, then there is nothing to fear from him. If he is not, then it is still too late for him to wed me."

Marcus, frozen and fierce, said nothing.

"An honorable person could not refuse a cry for help," said Balthazar softly, prompting Marcus to swing his gaze to the Moor. "Do you not remember this, Kincardine?"

No one spoke. Avalon felt the force of her resolution in her spine, stiff and straight, and the remorse in her belly, low and miserable. She did not want to go alone. She did not want to hurt Marcus. But there was something at Trayleigh calling her name, and she knew she had to return to her old home, the scene of such upheaval in her life, or else forever wander in regret that she had not.

Marcus had turned his stare, basilisk-like, to one of the hearths. To Avalon it seemed the flames of the fire held the only color and life in the room.

Marcus took a breath.

"It's going to be a damned cold ride," her husband said.

Bob Evans Recipes From Down on the Farm

Primavera Sausage and Pasta

BOB EVANS PRIMAVERA SAUSAGE AND PASTA

Ingredients

1 lb.	Bob Evans Original Roll Sausage*	1 1/2 cups	scallion, sliced-green part only
2 cups	cut green beans (frozen)	1 1/2 tsp.	sugar
1 large	red bell pepper, cut into strips	1 tsp.	garlic powder
1 large	tomato, cut into 8 wedges	1 1/2-2 lbs.	cooked Fettuccine or favorite pasta
			salt and pepper to taste

Prepare pasta according to package directions. Drain and hold on side, keeping warm before serving. In skillet, over medium-high heat, crumble and brown sausage. While sausage begins to brown, add peppers and cook until slightly tender and sausage is no longer pink. Carefully, drain off excess drippings. Add cut green beans and heat. Add remaining ingredients with tomatoes and 1 cup scallions. Cook about 2 minutes and serve over heated pasta in large bowl. Garnish with remaining scallions. Refrigerate leftovers.

Makes 4-6 servings

* Can substitute Italian Roll Sausage

Bob Evans Recipes From Down on The Farm

Grilled Bratwurst German Potato Salad

Ingredients

4 med.	baking potatoes	2 tsp.	poupon-style mustard
1 pkg.	Bob Evans Bratwurst	1/2 tsp.	salt
1 cup	red wine vinegar	1/4 tsp.	freshly cracked black pepper
1/2 cup	vegetable oil	2 Tbsp.	chopped fresh chives
1	small yellow onion, chopped	4-5 dashes	pepper sauce
1 clove	garlic, minced	1	small cucumber, thinly sliced

Cook unpeeled potatoes in 4-qt. boiling water until just tender. Drain, peel and cut into 1/8" slices. Set aside in a large bowl. Pre-cooked Bob Evans Bratwurst in 2-qt. of gently boiling water for 10 minutes. Meanwhile, combine vinegar, oil, onion, garlic, mustard, salt, pepper, chives, and pepper sauce in another mixing bowl. Remove bratwurst from water and grill on barbecue until well browned. Slice grilled bratwurst on an angle into 1/2" slices and add to potatoes. Pour vinegar-oil mixture over potatoes and bratwurst. Add sliced cucumbers and toss salad gently until well blended. Serve warm or cold. refrigerate leftovers.

Chapter Fifteen

TRAYLEIGH HUNG ON the edges of the horizon, dull gray under the leaden sky, strangely silent, only one ghostly glow in a window on the lower story. All else was empty and eerie.

The group from Sauveur paused as one at the crest of a slope, before riding down into the valley that held the village—clustered huts and buildings closed up as tight, it seemed, as the castle.

Without a doubt, Marcus thought, there *was* something wrong. It was not natural for a demesne the size of Trayleigh to be bereft of activity on such a day, which was cloudy and unpleasant but not unmanageable.

Avalon, beside him on a mare the color of dappled storm, lifted her face and scanned the area as intently as he did. But if she saw something alarming that he did not, she didn't say anything.

He didn't like any of it, not one damned bit. Not the barren village, not the phantom castle, not the miserable weather, and most especially not being here with his wife at his side, brave and bold and unyielding in her resolve to answer the obviously duplicitious summons of her murdering relatives. The whole idea of it was almost unbelievably, laughably foolhardy, and he was not accustomed to turning his life over to foolhardy ideas. Not any longer.

But Avalon had seen enough, apparently, and softly clucked to her mare, starting her down the gentle slope of the hill to the village below. Marcus had no choice but to catch up with her.

The gate to Trayleigh was open. There was no sentry guarding it. Marcus felt the hair prickle on the back of his neck as they rode through, everyone tense, all with hands on their swords, all eyes alert.

If it was a trap, if there were archers hidden behind the plain lines of this castle, then they were all as good as dead, and Marcus knew it. His group would have paltry defense against a rain of arrows, but he was betting that they would not risk killing Avalon so openly. He hoped—no, he *prayed*—that was so.

But there was no deadly shower. And there was still no sentry at the gate as one by one they began to dismount. No one came to take charge of their steeds.

The courtyard was empty, only the scratching of the wind providing any relief at all from the silence.

Marcus focused on wiping the dread from his mind, concentrating instead on remaining vigilant, ready to move with lethal force when it came time to defend his beloved.

Almost one hundred of his best men surrounded them. A hundred men was no small army, not these Highlanders of his, all of them seasoned warriors and spoiling for a fight. It was a clear declaration on his part to Warner: I know of your trap. Close it if you dare.

He had left one hundred more rimming the village

and the castle grounds. They carried their own bows and broadswords, ready for his signal whenever he would give it, and if he did not—or could not—then Bal would. Then Hew. Then Sean. And so on down the line, to whichever of them would manage to leave this place alive.

Nay, he didn't like it here, but upon reflection, Marcus decided, drawing his Spanish blade, it might not be such a bad thing to inflict a little retribution. If not for his own troubles caused by these d'Farouches, then for Avalon, for the loss of her family and her childhood.

Aye, there was a just and noble cause indeed.

One-half of the double main doors to the keep crept open; Marcus saw Avalon turn toward it and followed her look, sword ready.

A lone figure eased out of the crease of space, dressed in heavy folds of black, a black veil shielding the face. Then pale hands lifted the veil, and Marcus saw that it was a woman under the shrouds, a woman who pinned her gaze on Avalon and let out a small cry.

"Cousin!" came the call, and the woman shuffled forward, a curious gait muffled by the trailing lines of black material around her. Marcus saw Avalon move toward this woman, her steps strong and unhesitant.

"Claudia," she said calmly, and allowed the woman to fall into her arms.

Lady Claudia was murmuring something in a voice Marcus almost couldn't hear, even though he made certain he was only a pace behind his wife, close enough to strike down danger.

"Praise God," the woman was saying, over and over, husky and tearful and sounding very sincere. Eventually she pulled back from Avalon, lifted reddened eyes to take in the army of men behind them, some still mounted, others standing close by.

"Praise God you have come," said Claudia loudly to them all. "Praise God."

Marcus spoke before she could fall into her weeping again.

"Why did you summon us? Where are your men?"

Claudia, not releasing Avalon's arm, wiped away some of the moisture on her face, sniffling.

"A terrible thing," she said. "Sweet Mary, how can I speak of it? I must. I must. Please, I pray you, come inside."

Marcus stopped Avalon from moving away from him with just a slight touch on her shoulder.

"Tell me where your men are. We'll not go in until you do."

For the first time, Marcus thought, this woman Claudia looked at him, right at him, and he could see the surprise in her eyes. Then that emotion clouded into something else, and a brittle curve took her mouth.

"There are no men," she said. "Can't you see? They've all gone. They've either gone or they died. Or lay dying right now, as does the baron."

"Died from what?" Avalon asked, and Marcus couldn't tell from her voice if she believed the woman's story or not.

"I don't know!" Claudia cried, turning her burning gaze back to Avalon. "It happened so quickly! One night, a fortnight ago, it seemed everything was as it should be, everyone was well. But the next morning dozens were dead! Dozens! And each day added more and more, until most have fled."

Claudia stepped back and held out one hand, pointing to the village. "Could you not tell? It is deserted! The serfs have fled, God curse them," she added in a darker voice. "They have left me here, and all that were faithful to me have died as well, almost everyone."

"But not you," said Marcus, unmoved.

"No!" Claudia cried, her voice rich with tears again. "First the loss of my husband and now this! I must truly have fallen from God's graces to have deserved such a blow!"

"So." Marcus examined Claudia, the bloodshot eyes, the unrelenting black of her mourning garb, her hair beginning to escape the veil. "A sickness sweeps your land and leaves you untouched. A great sorrow indeed. But why did you summon us? We cannot fight a plague for you."

Again he caught that flicker of surprise in the woman, as if he were something she could not understand.

"But I didn't summon you," she said, looking back at Avalon. "I summoned only my cousin. I summoned her because the baron is dying, and he is asking for her."

"My *wife*," Marcus emphasized the word, "has no interest in seeing the baron."

Avalon shifted at his tone, but before she could say anything Claudia cut her off.

"I see," she said quietly, and right then Marcus had a glimmer of the woman she must have been once, dignified and handsome. She slowly released her hold on Avalon.

"We didn't know, of course," she said. "Congratulations to you both." She raised her hands to her face, slightly shaking, as if she could hide her eyes but then thought better of it and lowered them again.

"Warner has no idea," she said to Avalon. "Will you not come in anyway? Will you not just see him before death takes him, and wish him Godspeed? He will not live through the night, I am sure of it. I have seen too much of this sickness not to know. And it would mean"—she paused, swallowing—"everything to him."

Avalon threw Marcus a glance over her shoulder, and he knew then that she meant to go forward into the keep, whether he agreed to it or not. Yet she did not move until he sighed and nodded, keeping his sword ready, their army at their heels.

Claudia led the way into the great hall, to the striped shadows of benches and tables from the feeble fire, some of them cluttered with goblets and bits of food, a mess the size of which suggested the end of a large meal, uncleaned for days.

"A plague! We're like to fall ill as well," hissed Hew under his breath to Marcus, but it was Bal who answered him.

"Oh, I think not. But do not touch anything."

Hew looked at Bal and then to Marcus, who shrugged, figuring it was as good advice as any he had to give.

Claudia turned at the foot of a curving staircase, one that Marcus only faintly remembered from his one visit here so many years ago. It was these stairs that led to the living quarters of the keep, he knew that much. Claudia raised her hands to her face and lowered them again, as if she kept forgetting the veil was already removed.

"There is food in the buttery," she suggested, hesitant. "You may have what you like. I'm sorry there are no serfs to serve you."

"We are not hungry," said Avalon, throwing everyone behind her a swift, warning look.

"Well." Claudia turned around, began to climb the stairs. "This way, then, cousin."

"One moment," called Marcus. "Where do you take us?"

"I am only interested in taking cousin Avalon, sir. But you are welcome to come, of course. We are going to the baron's chamber. That's where he lies now."

She continued slowly climbing the stairs. Marcus looked back at his men, then to Avalon, who had already begun to follow Claudia. He quickly divided the group with a few words, leaving most in the great hall, about twenty following him behind the women.

The hallway was only intermittently lit, and even then the torches burned low and dim. The rushes they walked on were plainly old, beginning to reek of grime and sweat and some other foul odor Marcus couldn't name. Every sign indicated decay to him, neglect that would never ordinarily occur in a fine castle such as this. Claudia's story was beginning to sound more plausible.

At last they paused outside a sturdy door of iron-studded oak. Claudia turned to Avalon and took her hand.

"You're going to be shocked," she said gravely. "He had battled death for just one more chance to see you.

He's been calling your name for over a week now. I believe he loves you," she added, and Marcus saw nothing but sadness on her face. "Please do be kind to him."

"Of course," replied Avalon, equally grave.

Claudia glanced at Marcus. "The baron could not possibly cause harm to your wife, my lord. He is much too weak, even if he had the desire to hurt her, which he never would. Will you not allow them a moment of privacy, for him to bid her good-bye alone?"

"No," said Marcus.

"Very well," Claudia whispered, the sadness draping her. "I understand your feelings. Then will you not at least grant him some ease, my lord? Have only you and your wife come in? Too many people will disturb the baron, and I am sure you are protection enough for her, are you not?"

"Yes," said Avalon distantly. "It is enough."

Marcus looked down at her in surprise, but she only stared at the door glassily, as if she could already fathom what was behind it.

Marcus nodded curtly, knowing Bal and Hew would be close enough to respond to real trouble should it be necessary. He had the power of his men close by in the darkness.

"Then come," said Claudia simply, and pushed open the door, allowing Marcus to enter first, then Avalon.

Avalon felt as though she were in a dream; her feet dragged on the floor, too heavily weighted to lift properly. Her hands seemed too far from her for good use, her head was clear and empty. It was odd but undeniable, and the closer she got to the great, black box of a bed at the far end of the room, the more sharply accented these feelings became.

She could see Marcus's broad back as he walked ahead of her. He was looking not just at the curtained bed—closed and shrouded—but all around the room, large and mostly empty of furniture, with his sword a dull curve of steel at his side, aloft.

There was one candelabra not very far from the bed, all its candles unlit. The candles were yellowy white, cratered low, as if they had been left too long to burn anymore, but no one had thought to replace them. There were oddly shaped cakes of wax below them, thick, cold blobs. The only source of light was a remote torch on the far wall.

Avalon didn't remember the room being quite this big from her girlhood, but it must have been, because this was the baron's chamber, no matter if that baron were Geoffrey or Bryce or Warner. Perhaps Geoffrey had kept more furniture in here, more chairs, a table at least. Not this long emptiness, pointing to the menace of that black bed.

Her feet were too heavy. It was taking so long to get there. Marcus had already reached it, and now she could tell he was looking back at her, behind her, and again around the room, checking and double-checking. Yet all that seemed to matter was that she reach the bed. That was important. She must hurry.

Avalon saw a hand lift up and it was her own, she knew that, grasping the thick black curtains that shielded the bed. She couldn't really feel their weight, nor even her hand, but she could hear so well. She heard the rustle

of the dusty cloth as her fingers closed over it and began
to push it aside. The sound was papery and thin to her
ears. Remote yet clear.

Behind the curtains was more blackness. A still,
twisted form on the bed, a thatch of pale hair near the
top. A terrible, sweetish smell.

Blood had flowed everywhere. It soaked the furs and
the clothing, a sticky, drying stiffness wherever it had
touched. In the shell of darkness inside the bed it was
not red but black; dusky, glittering in the torchlight, still
fresh enough to reek of death.

Avalon understood it all just as she heard the whis-
tling sound brush past her ear, felt the air split beside
her face.

Marcus shoved her violently aside, making the slice of
air and the sound miss her by inches, absorbing it himself
instead.

They fell together to the floor, rolling, and became
entangled in the stiff folds of the curtains that ripped
and popped free of the bed in angry spurts. Marcus was
the only softness beneath her; the air smelt of fresh
blood now on top of the old. The black brocade curtains
were snarled around her from her feet to her thighs.

Avalon struggled to her knees, pushing the material
down and away as quickly as she could, but she already
knew that she was too slow.

"Please don't move, dear cousin," said Claudia in her
husky voice from the door.

Avalon looked up and found that Claudia had already
reloaded her crossbow while they were falling and had it
braced against her shoulder, ready to fire once more.

The door to the chamber, right behind her, was shut

and latched, with a heavy board slatted across it for good measure.

Marcus, behind and beneath her, was still. If she turned her head just slightly, she could see the cheerful green feathers of the arrow that had struck him standing straight out. Perhaps a shot to his shoulder, she thought. The fact that he didn't move meant either he was dead—

—*no, no, not dead, treuluf*—

—or that he had struck his head in the fall and was senseless, or that he was pretending to be either of those things. Avalon wasn't sure.

The dream sensation of before had not abated, only altered, showing Claudia in sharp, vivid lines, the contrast of her auburn hair against her black veil, a becoming blush on her cheekbones. The gleaming point of the next barbed arrow, aimed right at Avalon's chest.

"Praise God you have come," Claudia said again, and in this dream her voice was no different from before, still sounding so sincere. "I knew God would not forsake me this far," she continued. "He has delivered you to me."

"You wasted your twenty gold shillings on me, didn't you?" Avalon said. "Twelve years ago. You paid for a lie. The Picts didn't kill me after all."

"Who knew?" replied Claudia lightly, managing to imply a shrug in her tone without actually moving. "What were the chances you would survive a raid?"

Avalon slowly began to turn her head, trying to take in some surroundings beyond the sharp outlines of the woman and the weapon.

Claudia tapped her fingers against the body of the bow. "I do wish you wouldn't do that, cousin. I'm not quite ready to kill you yet. And I have heard, you see, about this warrior skill it's said you carry, though likely this is just empty talk or witchcraft. Nevertheless, I do not care to have you demonstrate it."

The light from the torch spread long, soft shadows across the floor and walls, allowing Claudia's entire form to disappear into them, leaving only her face, her hands, the deadly crossbow.

"Gwynth was a witch, I am certain of it," continued Claudia reflectively. "And it's possible you stole your skills from her, this demon thing. From mother to daughter. I had quite a gala when she died, you know. I never liked her."

In the dream Avalon felt the faint, heavy beating of her husband's heart behind her, almost inaudible, only a flush of awareness. He was not dead. She could accept this in her dream state; it formed a new purpose for her now. It was up to her to ensure that he did not die.

I am yours, came a distant voice, very familiar, very far away. Not the chimera, not this, but what?

"Aren't you the dutiful one?" Claudia was saying. "I knew you would come. He said nay, it was too plain a ruse, but I said you would. I knew you had a weakness that way, just like a man, ready to throw yourself to the rescue. How odd. And he was so desperate to see you, he would have agreed to anything, I think. Now here you are, and I cannot be less than happy at your strange-minded devotion to a family that wanted you dead."

There was nothing between her and her enemy, there was nothing to throw, nothing to hide behind, nothing to aid her. There was only her bleeding husband and the corpse on the bed and the twisted ropes of black curtain

around her ankles. And there was that last thing, owner
of that voice, a note out of step with this piece, something Avalon could not quite hear well enough to
understand. . . .

"If you are not yet ready to kill me, why would you
shoot an arrow at my back?" she asked, and her own
voice was slow to her, trapped in the dream.

"I didn't shoot at you. I shot at your husband. I hit
him, in fact. I'm a rather excellent shot."

"As Bryce discovered," said Avalon, still removed
from surprise.

Now Avalon could see the curling smile Claudia favored, a mixture of satisfaction and pride.

"I thought," said Claudia, around her smile, "that before you died I should allow you to suffer. It seems only
fitting. You certainly made me suffer enough. I am
going to kill you slowly. I am going to shoot you apart,
bit by bit. But Bryce—my dear, stupid Bryce—was
more of an inconvenience than anything else. Therefore
I made certain my shot to him was clean. He never knew
what happened."

"How kind of you."

"Yes, it was."

There were muffled thumps coming from beyond the
latched door; men's voices filtered through, growing
rougher as the thumps grew louder. Claudia took a few
languid steps to the side of the door, moving away from
the sound, never changing her aim, fixed on Avalon.

"I used to lament, cousin Avalon, that you had sur-
vived my otherwise excellent raid. I used to cry out to
myself, 'Oh, why could she not have died when she

should have?' It was a great pain to me, you understand, to have you alive. It really did spoil so many of my greatest plans."

In her dream Avalon could feel Marcus's heartbeat grow stronger and stronger; he must be awake now. He must be listening. That made her situation even more delicate, for she had to control both him and Claudia, a strain on her senses.

Use me, whispered the new voice, a little nearer now.

"At least your father died. That was a great goal of mine. Bryce inherited the castle, the lands, the manors. Well, until you showed up again. Everything was so *perfect,* until you showed up again."

The door was visibly shaking from the force of the blows to it; if it weren't for the thick slab of lumber firm across its middle, surely it would have buckled by now.

"But you loved Warner," said Avalon above the noise, keeping Claudia's attention with her, not on the door, not on Marcus.

"There was no rush in killing Bryce while you yet lived," said Claudia reasonably. "At least that's what I thought for years. Warner and I could carry on with Bryce being none the wiser. Warner was here often enough. And Bryce was such a convenient scapegoat for the raid, actually. I needed him alive in case a serious inquiry ever began. Anyone could easily have believed he was behind it. Even the villagers were terrified of him!"

Avalon pictured Elfrieda at the inn, whimpering at the sound of the baron's name. Mistress Herndon. All of them so misled. Claudia, breathless and smiling, was gathering speed with her story, the words beginning to tumble across each other. Avalon had to concentrate to follow them.

"Warner and I had managed our liaison for a long while. Within a year of the discovery of your survival, I had planned to kill Bryce, anyway. You ruined that—reclaiming the lands, all that income. I can't forgive you for it. I actually preferred to eliminate you as soon as you came back to England, but Warner persuaded me against it. You were too well known, he said. A death then would be certain to cause unpleasant talk. He believed we should wait to kill you. I listened to him; he had always been so clever before. I told Bryce to send you to Gatting. It was really too much to expect me to take you in here."

The smile had vanished, something else sparked across her face, something well matched to the blackness of the room.

"And I certainly would have had you dead before your marriage to your savage Scot. But then Bryce decided to wed you to Warner! Can you believe it? After all I had done for him, he turned on me like that, was prepared to wed my love to *you*!"

"He didn't know you were his brother's lover," Avalon said softly.

"Of course he didn't. But that is hardly the point. Everything I had done, everything I had so carefully planned, was for Warner. For Warner and I to be married, to be together. But how ungrateful he turned out to be."

Marcus moved, very slowly, very cautiously, against Avalon. She felt it and a cold sweat came over her, penetrating the dream. Marcus was going to take action sooner rather than later. He would have to, it was his nature. And then Claudia would shoot him dead without a qualm.

The voice came again, louder.

Use me, I am yours.

"Laird!" shouted someone on the far side of the door, prompting Claudia to find her smile again.

"Well, anyway. Enough of this," she said, and aimed the crossbow higher.

"Why did you kill Warner?" Avalon asked, louder than the voice outside. "If you loved him?"

"I loved him, yes! But who could have guessed, dear, fair cousin Avalon, that he would fall in love with *you*? In that one night!" Claudia laughed out loud, incredulous. "Yet he said he had. He would abandon me after all I had done for him, after I had handed him the title and this castle myself. He had fabricated the papers to claim your hand, he was ready to deliver them, sweet Mary, because he vowed he loved you. Love!" she scoffed. "I have a better name for it. You bewitched him."

"No, I didn't," said Avalon, and Marcus was moving more openly now. He wouldn't be able to see Claudia from behind Avalon's skirts, but Avalon knew Claudia could see him. The black curtain whispered as he shifted against it, and she wondered if the covers on the bed trembled as well.

"Kincardine! Laird!" came the calls from the door, and the thumping became more vigorous, causing the slab of wood to moan just a little.

"You did!" shouted Claudia above the noise. "You must have bewitched him! He was mine for years before you came! But he was weak, and he deserved to die for his betrayal of me, witchcraft or no. My dagger was his penitence! Every cut, every drop of blood from him was a pledge to me, his sorrow for his betrayal of me! And in the end he ate the poison I fed him as easily as all the others did, all the serfs, all the servants. They all had to die! My loss is theirs! I am the mistress here!"

I am . . .

"Claudia, you will die if you kill us," said Avalon. "You must know this. There is no other way out of this room but past the men of my clan. You will be slaughtered for this."

"Oh, death," said Claudia, sounding strangely wistful, the beating of the door emphasizing her words. "Of course I will die. I plan to join my love. I do still love him. But you will die first, cousin. That is enough for me."

. . . yours.

Marcus leapt up, prompting Claudia to lurch as she shifted her aim, and Avalon scrambled to follow him, to block the shot, but there was too much happening at once and her feet were wrapped in material still. She fell to her hands and knees on the floor with a cry she couldn't help as she heard the arrow sing close and land again in Marcus's body. He was tossed back against the bed with a grunt, and then down, limp and silent amid the tangled cloth.

In the seconds that followed there was only one refrain in Avalon's mind: *No, no, oh God, please no,* a silent cry of denial. But he was hit, and he was hurt, and this time he would not have to pretend to lie still.

Avalon crawled over to him and shielded his body with hers. She felt only a cold, stinging numbness all over.

Marcus was still breathing, shallow and rapid.

"Avalon." It was less than a sigh, so scarce she hardly heard it, but there was another power coming from him, only barely stronger than his voice.

Avalon, I love you. Run away. . . .

And then nothing else. She felt him slump away into mists and shadows.

She couldn't see here, it was so dark, the torch was too far away to aid her, and death was too close. The danger here was so strong it would overpower her, it would draw out all her blood and leave her empty, alone, as dead as Marcus might be. She could not leave him. Oh God, he was hurt so badly now, he was bleeding so much, she could feel the hot wetness of it on him, pumping out of him, how could she halt it—

Over the shouts outside Avalon heard Claudia move in the black gloom, remounting an arrow in the crossbow, brisk and efficient, even though there was no light. The arrow notched into place with a faint click, further chilling Avalon's skin. It was the sound of the end of her life.

Her hands had found the new arrow in Marcus, a wild shot to his chest, too high to hit his heart but enough for this font of blood to pour forth. She knew better than to remove the arrow. Instead she pressed down around it, staunching the flow, waiting for the next shot to pin her. But she could not leave Marcus to die.

I am yours.

It was Claudia who was the danger and death; the shadows were her masking. Avalon could not fight her, could not stop her, would never reach her in time to save her husband, who was slowly bleeding to death all over her if he was not already dead. All her training, all her skills, useless in this final moment, with her enemy too far away to tackle, too swift with the arrow. Nowhere to hide. Marcus was going to die, and it would be her fault, only hers—

Use me! commanded the voice.

There was a storm of sound in this darkness, there were unthinkable noises from the blackness, furious shouts from behind the door, the wood crying out from the blows, and—she could hear it so clearly—laughter. Claudia laughing, joined by other voices, deep and rich and bubbling with malevolence.

I am yours!

Goblins, blood, danger, cold stone, the room was too wide, Avalon couldn't hide from it, she would die now, just as her father had, and Ona and all the rest, and all the blood would never erase her loss, sticky sweet blood, her own death a half second away, laughing at her—

There were footsteps approaching her. A curious, hushed gait around the rustle of skirts, the laughter closer, clearer, all the voices rising and blending together in a long, babbling scream.

But for one.

Not the voice of the chimera, no more.

Use me, I am yours, said this single voice, and at last Avalon understood who it was.

I am you.

Chapter Sixteen

⟡‿‿‿⟡

*A*GAINST THE COLDNESS of the floor and Marcus's fading heat, Avalon found herself leaning forward on her knees, hands still steady on his wound, head bowed down. Her fingers were warm with his blood. But all of that seemed to be happening to someone else right now, another woman caught in a nightmare; a woman with hair as bright as a beacon in the darkness, kneeling before her dying lover.

Right now, what preoccupied Avalon was a dream, a specific dream. The one about the goblins.

Force, Avalon thought, testing the strength of her new voice in this dream state. *Touch. Try to douse the light.*

Something crashed on the far side of the room. The torch, falling from its hold on the wall, taking its wretched glow with it.

Yes. Like that.

The ominous sound of Claudia's skirts moving closer stopped, held in place by the unexpected noise. If she focused, if she tried, Avalon could see Claudia within the vision of her dream, pausing with her crossbow, throwing a startled look to her left.

The fire, Avalon thought now. *Remember that, the black burning, the choking smell . . .*

Billows of smoke began to curl up against the walls, at the seams of the floor, pungent, black on black.

Speak! Say her name, let her hear what the moments before death sounded like.

"Claaa-dia . . ."

It wasn't truly her name, not the way they said it, with their rough inflections and different tongue. But it was clear enough to be recognized for what it was.

"Claaa-dia . . ." From the right. No, the left.

Claudia, frozen, exhaled sharply. The crossbow sagged in her grip.

"Who's there?" she called, managing—very nearly, Avalon thought—to hide her fear.

Show her. Come! Show her your faces.

The goblins had red eyes. Wild, glaring red eyes that glowed through the darkness, eating it up, devouring it.

Avalon knew this so well, how such eyes could burn through her, could find her no matter where she hid. They had done it so many times. And now they had found Claudia, who was beginning to see them as well.

From the direction of the torch came a slow shuffling sound, feet on stone, dragging. There were eyes over there, those hungry red eyes.

"What is this?" Claudia said, breathless and much less certain than before.

Tell her.

"You know us," hissed a voice from the other side of the room, a new direction.

Another crash, this one louder, closer.

The room was beginning to smell of something new, smoke and coppery blood laced together. Panic. The goblins approached. They carried this stench, their own special horror.

"Claaa–dia."

Claudia held up the bow and fired at the voice, the arrow streaking away to clatter against the wall.

They were laughing at this, stronger, closer still, the chilling laugh Avalon had never escaped. The smell of blood wafted around them, terrifying, real and not real, inescapable.

"Witchcraft!" whimpered Claudia, and began to struggle to remount the bow.

"No," they laughed together.

"No . . ."

"No . . ."

"Vengeance!"

The strut was slipping from Claudia's hands, which were shaking too much to hold the arrow still. To the myriad sounds a new one crept through: crackling heat. Fire, feeding the smoke.

Burn the room. Show her what she did here, let her feel the terror she gave to so many others.

The chamber was growing lighter, the flames were licking at the walls, at the floor. The smoke swirled heavy and black in clouds up to the ceiling.

Let her hear them. Let her hear them die as I did.

There were echoes of screams coming from beyond the room, horrible screams. War cries, death cries.

Claudia dropped the crossbow. It landed at her feet and was engulfed in flames, gold and blue with silver-green tips, fantasy fire. She stood alone amid it, clutching the useless arrow, staring around her in disbelief.

The goblins stretched tall, streaked with blood and

sweat and blue paint, laughing with their red eyes and gaping, grinning mouths. They carried axes and swords dripping with death. All the shades of red converged, became greater flames, long, bloody arms reaching for the woman in the middle of the room.

"No!" Claudia screamed, one more sound among the many. She brandished the useless arrow in front of her, swinging it in half circles at the air.

"We burned it, Claaa-dia, we burned it for you," the goblins shrieked. "We killed them for you. . . ."

Claudia slapped her hands over her ears, dropping the arrow, crying. Underneath all the noise came the thumping of the door being battered down, distant yet steady.

Now remind her of what she will suffer for.

"One gold shilling per head," chanted the goblins in their foreign tongue, yet it was so clear what they said. "One gold shilling. Per head. Fifty for the baron—"

Claudia sank to her knees, then jumped up again, hysterically slapping out the blue and green flames on her.

"Twenty for the girl."

"No! No, get away from me—"

"Per head. We took their heads! Burned them. Killed them all. For you, Claaa-dia!"

The screaming was unbearable, the sounds of the tortured, the dying, the helpless. The smoke was choking, foul, smelling of the end of life. Of the end of the world.

Claudia dropped to the floor once more, sobbing, pounding the stone with her hands.

"Vengeance!" came the screams, dozens of voices, a

hundred, echoing the call of the blood and smoke and the wicked light of the fire.

Avalon came to her feet and ran to where the woman had fallen, still sobbing. She kicked the crossbow away and yanked Claudia up.

"Help me," Claudia wailed, clutching at her.

Avalon leaned back and slapped her, silencing the sobs.

In that instant, everything—the goblins, the smoke, the licking flames—spiraled away to nothing, killing the dream. The silence rang around them.

"If my husband dies, you die," Avalon said, cold. "You had better pray now for his life."

She had left a smeared red handprint on Claudia's cheek, a stain of Marcus's blood. It barely registered through her urge to hurry. He was still bleeding, she had no time. . . .

Without pausing she dragged the woman across the dim room to the badly battered door, calling out for the men to stop, she was opening it.

Stay for me, truelove, don't die—

Next to her huddled Claudia, emitting small, broken whimpers, back pressed against the wall, still looking wildly around the room.

Avalon managed to lift the warped board from its slat, letting it crash to the floor. The door swept open, a river of men springing through.

"There!" she cried, pointing to Marcus on the floor, almost pushing the wizard toward him in her anxiety.

"A torch," bellowed the wizard, and men rushed to comply, carrying the flames over their heads.

Claudia let out a fresh wail, cringing, prompting several of the men to turn to her, assessing.

"It was her," said Avalon to the man nearest her, she couldn't see who, perhaps Sean. "She did it. Hold her."

She didn't wait to see that her order was followed. In the next second she was running to Marcus, the wizard, the other men crouched in a circle, pushing her way through until she could see Marcus clearly.

His eyes were open. He was looking for her, trying to sit up against all the others who were trying to hold him down.

"Marcus," she said, and had to smile so she wouldn't cry in front of him. She was so suddenly exhausted that she almost collapsed onto the floor beside him, but that was all right, because he was still alive, and that was all that mattered.

He relaxed when he saw her, going back down to the ground, supported by his men. Avalon took his nearest hand in her own, holding it tightly, trying to maintain her smile even though her eyes were blurring.

The wizard was muttering something under his breath, examining both arrow strikes, his hands clever and deft. Almost everyone was saying something, drowning out each other, putting together the story, though Avalon and Marcus remained locked on each other, ignoring the questions.

In the background, Claudia's wailing grew louder.

At last Balthazar looked up at Marcus and shook his head with a reluctant grin. "I knew you were a lucky man, Kincardine. But perhaps it is time to give luck a respite. You push the limits of even the most patient."

Marcus matched his grin, though it was not so strong, and said something to the wizard in that flowing language that went too fast to comprehend.

The wizard laughed, then turned to Avalon.

"Your husband will live, lady. But you will have to loan him a sling. I think the pink would look best on him, don't you?"

———————— ⌒~~⌒ ————————

*H*E WORE A SLING OF GRAY, not pink, sturdy wool cut from someone's tunic, and still he chafed at it, obviously annoyed at the inconvenience of recovering from near death.

The pink sash remained safe at Sauveur, because they would not be leaving to return there for at least another week, in order to give Marcus time to begin healing.

A day, Marcus had countered.

A week, repeated the wizard firmly.

Two weeks, Avalon threw in, just to make clear she was serious about him staying.

They settled on one week, Marcus giving in with much grumbling, but she felt no remorse at his fidgeting. He had been shot twice with a crossbow at relatively close range and yet lived, perhaps a testament to the wizard's suggestion that luck favored a rogue.

And he did look like a rogue, Avalon admitted to herself, walking alone through her mother's winter garden. She had awakened early today and watched him sleep for close to two hours in the room that used to be her own, the frosted branches of the old birch tree clearly visible from the window. His hair was long and loose, never releasing the waves of beauty that framed his face. The stubble on his cheeks gave his skin a blue-gray cast, but the rest of him looked hale, and his breathing was normal. He had no fever.

In the three days that had passed since they arrived at this abandoned place, much had been restored. It was a relief to her, watching Trayleigh reclaim the polish it used to have, though the process was slow and far from finished.

Claudia had lied. Most of the people had not died from her poisoning but had fled, leaving her to her madness. The villagers were steadily returning to their homes; most had not gone far. Elfrieda, in fact, had been the first to arrive at the castle, searching out Avalon to reveal the rest of the tale.

Lady Claudia had been descending slowly into her strange state, prone to fits after her husband died, frightening the serfs. When the new baron arrived, Elfrieda reported, no one had wanted to come to the castle. It had been cursed, it was said, and the woman was a danger to them all. No one even saw the new baron after the second week following the death of his brother. By then Claudia had ordered almost everyone from the castle, from gentry to serfs. That was nine days ago.

Today, Avalon supposed, Claudia would be well into the first day of her journey to London, accompanied by a contingent of soldiers. She had not spoken a coherent word since Avalon opened the battered door to the baron's chamber, only now and again weeping of fire and devils, strange nonsense that sealed the truth of her madness in the eyes of everyone as surely as anything. Like the wicked faerie, Avalon supposed, Claudia was now locked in her punishment. But instead of sinking away into the stone of a mountain, Claudia would stay in a tower of stone in London, a lifelong ending to her crimes.

Someday, probably soon, Avalon would have to follow her to that city and give her own account to the king, a careful screening of the events that had taken place in the baron's chamber. There were many witnesses, thank goodness, who would verify Avalon's story and Claudia's madness. But there was time enough to think about that in the future.

Today was bright and fair, warmer here than in Scotland, and her mother's garden had not yet fully succumbed to the seasonal slumber that was on its way. Stubborn leaves of red and orange and gold clung to branches, echoes of autumn.

Today her husband slept, lost in the woven softness of blankets on a feather bed, looking somehow exactly in place in her old room, she thought. Avalon had chosen that one for him because it was clean, first of all, and also because she didn't want to linger in the bleakness of the main chamber, even after Warner's body had been removed, and the whole room had been scrubbed and brightened.

So she had placed her husband in the room where she used to live. There in that corner chamber, with its fine views of the giant birch and the backdrop of piney forest. It was there that she had played, and there that she had dreamed, and there that her life had been happiest. Until she met Marcus.

Perhaps tomorrow she would take him down to see that old birch. Perhaps she would steal a kiss while underneath its great branches.

She had been idly walking down the white stone path, seeking the hidden marble bench she had not had the chance to see the last time she was in this garden. And yet when she found it, somehow she was not surprised to see the man who was supposed to be sleeping sitting there, waiting for her, wrapped in his tartan and a cape, watching her approach with bright eyes.

"Sweet Rosalind," he greeted her. "You are even more lovely than when I found you here last."

"You shouldn't be out yet," she chided, but her heart wasn't in it, and he knew it.

"Come over here and I'll show you how feeble I am," Marcus invited, teasing.

She smiled at him, stopping just short of where he rested on the bench.

"How do you feel?" she asked.

"I feel as if I could sleep a thousand years."

"Really? Where have I heard that before?"

"Now you're supposed to tell me I've slept enough already, and it's time for more interesting pastimes. I have one in mind, in fact."

The cave of honeysuckle surrounding the bench was on this day more of a weaving of golden brown twigs, buried tight among themselves, framing him in dramatic lines. Avalon leaned forward to touch his cheek with her fingertips. He caught her hand there with his own, dragged her fingers down to his lips, his breath warm and welcome.

"Avalon." He made her name a caress, sending that enraptured thrill streaming up her hand, into her heart. "Sometime soon, truelove, we are going to have to find the day when both of us are uninjured at the same time."

"That would be nice."

"Nicer than nice," he growled, low and wanting, and began to pull her closer to him, down to him, his intent as clear as the blue of his eyes.

Avalon pulled away, shaking her head, smiling again, though it wasn't easy, and she would rather have allowed him his way. But there was something she needed to say to him, and this was the first peace they had had between them, she thought, since the nightmare ended. Now seemed fitting enough, in this garden, underneath the clean sky.

"We must talk," she said, gently pulling back her hand.

"Later." His look was shining warmth.

She gave a little laugh now, fighting the urge to let him win. "You're not well enough, my lord. And I care for you too much to sap your strength."

He hesitated, finding her emphasis as she knew he would.

"Do you?" he asked, brilliant and aware, focused only on her. "Care for me?"

She looked down to the pebbled ground, at her clasped hands. It was so difficult for her to say this, even now.

"I've been afraid," she said to her hands. "I didn't even know how much, until we came here. I've spent so much time fighting fear that I didn't even realize how tightly it held me, how deeply it ran in me. I was a puppet to it, you could say, blind and hapless and controlled."

"Truelove—" he began, but she wouldn't let him finish.

"No, please, listen to me now." She managed to meet his eyes again, and again felt the flooding gratitude that she could do this, that she could be here and talk to him, her dark angel, this glorious man.

"It was fear that kept me locked out of my own heart, Marcus Kincardine. It was fear that kept me alone and always fighting, always struggling against all that I didn't understand. I am ashamed of that. I wish it were untrue, but it is so, and I am ashamed."

He said nothing, but took her hand again and began to pull her down to the bench, and this time she let him, settling beside him underneath the cave of honeysuckle vines before continuing, speaking softly.

"Because of my fear I almost lost you forever. You almost died for it. I didn't tell you that I had tried to do what you asked of me, back at Sauveur. I tried to see something of the story of Keith MacFarland. But what I saw made no sense to me, and so I told myself it had been nothing but imagination, my own morbid fancy. But it had been a premonition, I suppose. For as soon as we came to that chamber with Claudia, I was caught in it again, and I had to act out my part in it again, and nothing I could do would change it."

The tail of a breeze came and danced past their feet, swirling the leaves in frolicking circles. The branches of the cherry tree nearby caught the motion and stretched up to sway amid the blue of the sky.

"If I had only *told* you," Avalon said, anguished. "If I had not been so afraid, if I could have trusted my own eyes—if I had only recognized this thing in me for what it was, all of this might have been avoided."

"Tell me, then," he said, after a pause. "What is this thing in you that you speak of?"

"Your curse," she replied. "Your legend. You were

right. I should have listened to you." She sighed. "It's been with me all along. I hid from it, I denied it. Yet it lives, and it always has."

Avalon turned her head away and then back to him, his dear face, sober and attentive. "It *is* me," she said. "It's always been me. I understand that now."

He changed suddenly, a blazing smile, quick and glad. "Your gift."

"Yes, my gift." And as she repeated his word, his own gladness began to bloom in her, lifting her, giving her the courage to meet his gaze. "I realized in that room that it was what you said. A gift, not a curse. And it was real. I finally realized that. It was so close to being too late."

Marcus leaned his head back, took in the vines and bits of sky peeping through, and she could see he was searching for something to say to her, to ease her.

"All my life," he said, "I fought to banish my childhood. I fought to understand the forces of the world that were so beyond me. The lust for killing in men. The thirst for power in those who had plenty of it already. I tried to make sense of the senseless, because I needed that. I thought I needed to have logic at my back, and that way I could make my way through the wars and the battles and the injustices. But that never happened. I never grasped the answers to my questions, and I think I finally came to realize that I never would.

"There are so many things beyond us, Avalon. There are so many outside things that shape us, that make us who we are and form the world. I think I know what your childhood must have been like with Hanoch. I think I can understand that, at least. And so I can understand how much you wanted to deny him in whatever way you could. I did, as well. I stayed away from my home for years, just to deny him. Perhaps it was wrong of me, I don't know."

He seemed to lose the thread of his thoughts for a moment, gone far from her and this little garden— deserts, sand, golden sun—but then he came back.

"You should never feel sorry for reacting to what happened to you, what he did to you. You should never apologize for wanting to deny the legend. It was your right to do so, by God, and even more. Had I been you, I would never have had your wisdom, I'm sure of that. Yet you blossomed and grew, Avalon, despite this harshness, and you have become the most wondrous person I have ever known, gift or not."

She tilted her head, studying him, finding nothing but seriousness on his face, no jesting, just this almost painfully raw speech, now more ardent with conviction.

"And no one can say what would have happened even if you had told me of your vision," he went on. "We all knew it was a trap when we got the missive. Yet we came."

"But I should have stopped it," Avalon whispered, awash in the shame again.

"How? How could you, truelove? If this was what was meant to be, then it would have happened anyway. I see this as another gift, in fact. Look here. My wife is alive, I am alive, and at last an injustice long endured has been righted. It seems to me that everything has become right and good, all around."

The sense of his words drifted through her, calm and peaceful, a balm. He had reached through his own pain and doubts to embrace her own, to comfort her, to shield her with bare truths that she might be too lost to see by herself. To Avalon, Marcus was the true gift, the greatest gift ever, and she could not keep it to herself another second.

Though it might have been a miracle, she had managed to find her heart of hearts after all, and in it dwelled the noble grace of Marcus.

"I love you," she said. "I have for a long time. But now I can say it to you. I love you."

He reached out and pulled her closer to him, his hand strong and steady, revealing no weakness at all despite the sling and the bandages. She let him because, selfishly, she craved his touch, and if this was his only method of reassurance after her brazen admission, then she would take it and be happy.

But he was not done with her; he drew her closer yet, until her legs were curled under her and her head was somewhere near his neck, and she was trying without much success to avoid his injured shoulder.

"Be still," he laughed. "You'll break my stitches and bleed me to death, and all your pretty words will be for nothing."

Dismayed, she sunk into place, unmoving, and Marcus let out a sort of satisfied sigh and kissed her forehead.

"That's better," he said. "I must remember to threaten you with my own demise again to make you do my bidding."

"You would joke," she said hotly, but he lifted her face and claimed her lips before she could finish her thought, and then it melted away under his sweetness and all he left her with was a slow burn for more.

"My beautiful Avalon, my warrior bride, would I dare joke with you? Well, perhaps a little," he admitted, not letting her reply. "But now I have something very serious to say. I was awake in the baron's chamber, even after I'd been shot. I haven't told you that yet because I wasn't sure how you would react. But I saw it all. It was hazy at first, yes, but even a man shot twice could not have missed that fire, my love, nor those men."

She stirred and he held her still against him, brushing her forehead again with his lips, stroking her hair.

"It was terrifying," he continued. "I would have been shaking, if I but had the strength. And I knew even then the source of it. I knew what you were doing, and why. I was proud of you. I was . . . in awe of you."

"No. . . ."

"Yes. But you must understand, Avalon, that even during all of that, not once was I afraid of *you*. I told you before, truelove, I know your heart is good. It's so clear to me. You are a blessing, kind and clever and compassionate. And if you don't know that, I'm going to spend every day of the rest of my life trying to prove it to you."

Her tongue was tied in knots, and the annoying tears were back in her eyes, but it was worth it, worth it all to be here with him, so close and strong, so steady in his faith in her. Yet she pulled back to look at him, frowning just a little. A ribbon of sunlight fell across his face, became lost in the ebony of his hair.

"But do you think," she began. "That is—well, I told you that . . ." She let her voice fade away, too embarrassed to ask what she wanted to know, too needy to let it drop completely. She needed the words after all, after everything. They mattered.

He studied her again, blue eyes to match the peaceful sky, then his face cleared, became something close to joyful.

"My legendary Avalon. I've relied on that story so much, hoping, praying for you. Do you truly not know my deepest heart? If you did, you would know how much I love you. But I'll say it anyway, even though I feel like I've been shouting it out to you forever. I love you. I love you more than life, more than myth, more than anything I could ever dream of. You are the answer to every wish I've ever had. I give thanks to God or to destiny, or to a curse or to men—whatever it was that led me here to you, and you to me."

Marcus leaned into her and Avalon met him there, their lips so close, their souls in matched harmony.

"I love you," he murmured. "I will always love you. I'll say it to you forever."

I love you, Avalon, I love you. . . .

I love you, truelove.

In the winter cherry tree arching beyond them, a lark began a serenade of long, liquid notes.

Epilogue

AWAY AND NEAR, above and below, in time and out of it, the hundred-year-old laird and his wife watched the conclusion of their story play out in gentle words and tender touches, watched their beloved children embrace and kiss and begin those things that mortals did, the sharing of their bond of love.

"It is the end of the curse," rejoiced the laird.

"Aye, the savior came," replied his wife. "Our beautiful family is redeemed, treluf. The new golden age has begun. And we are free at last."

As one, the two spirits rose, and if such a thing as heavenly laughter could have been heard, it surely would have been then, as they melted into each other, indistinguishable, and dissolved into sparkles of bliss, joined together forever, just as their love had always promised.

Author's Note

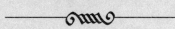

To the best of my knowledge, medieval Moors did not use the art of tattoo for decoration, religious or otherwise. Both the Coptics and other Christians of this era would have almost certainly viewed such things as pagan. Yet Balthazar spoke to me from the very beginning with his elegant markings, and I could not resist him.

The practice of Asian martial arts would have been uncommon indeed in medieval Scotland, even after the cross-cultural influence of the Crusades. Truly it would have taken a legend to bring about Avalon's skills in this area, but fortunately, I had one.

Even though this book is a work of pure fiction, I beg the reader to indulge my lapses into the dramatic on these issues, and any others you may have found that vexed you. The telling of the tale necessitated it all.

I hope you enjoyed the journey of Avalon and Marcus to true love as much as I did.

—S.A.

About the Author

SHANA ABÉ lives in Southern California with her husband, Darren, and two house rabbits. Yes, the rabbits really do live in the house. Shana can be reached through her website at:

www.tlt.com/authors/sabe.htm

Or write to her at:

2060 D Avenue de los Arboles, #180
Thousand Oaks, CA 91362

Don't miss the next magical
medieval romance from Shana Abé

A PRINCE AT MIDNIGHT

It's the turn of the first millenium, and time is
running out . . .

*Once, many years ago, there were two brothers. One was
very good, and one had a heart as black as night. On
their travels, they came to a magical place like none
other—and named it Alderich. They agreed to divide
ownership of the land, but in time the black-hearted
brother betrayed his sibling, demanding from the king the
whole of the land as his right since he was the elder. The
king was fair, and decreed that Alderich should be shared
between them: It would be the younger brother's domain
until the first day of the new millenium, when all the
lands would pass to the descendants of the elder, despite
his treachery.*

Now, as the new millenium approaches, Serath
Rune and Rafael of Leonhart find themselves ene-
mies in an ancient feud . . . even as they battle the
desire that threatens to overwhelm them.

Coming from Bantam Books in Spring 2000.